The Witch and the Prophet

The Raven Society Book 3

R.L. Geer-Robbins

Dark Rose Publishing Company

ISBN: 979-8-9889222-5-4

Contents

This is dedicated to everyone who said I wouldn't amount to anything.

I heard.

I remember.

And I will have the last laugh.

Introduction

'Leave nothing to chance.' -Book of the Veiled Instructions

No AI was used in the creation of this book.

If I had, it might not have taken so long to write, edit, rewrite, edit again, throw it in the trash, and save it from the trash—only to have my computer crash, and it was lost anyway.

If you find any editing issues, please let me know. Preferably not on social media. Somehow, the videos always get back to me, and then there is about a week where I hide under my blankets and cry. This is very inconvenient since I work a full-time job as a side hustle, and they frown on that type of behavior.

Just like in the other two books, if you find tear stains on the pages, ignore them. At this point, you can't read any of my books without finding them.

No characters in this book were harmed in the writing process. However, I do allude to some distressing events and subjects, such as SA, prejudice, religion, and injustice.

These moments are not to trigger anyone but to stay true to mythology and history. If you find yourself uncomfortable, please skip ahead, put the book away, or call someone. I understand. History is often disturbing.

And while I tried to shy away from the more horrific parts of the witch trial era, there were some parts that I could not brush over. It would have been unfair to those who had to live through it.

One last note before you dive in: the following story is based on historical facts to the best of my ability. But please note- there is little to go on. History is often a mystery. So, just like the rest of my characters, I used what was available and sprinkled it with a dash of my imagination to create a life for them.

I hope I have honored the memory of the women you are about to meet. They deserve to be remembered.

And finally, my friends, I hope you enjoy the story. It was written with a lot of love and more coffee than my doctor is comfortable with.

Keep Reading and Stay Caffeinated!

Prologue

'The Beginning Is Never What It Seems.' -Book of the Veiled Instructions

*H*e was always an observer on the battlefield, never engaging unless there was something to gain. He wouldn't dare let bloodshed sully his hands, leaving that task to me.

His sister. His twin.

The person he has condemned to death.

What a brotherly thing to do. But I do not expect less from him.

The world assumes that we are two halves of a single whole. Taliesin is the dark to my light, the compass to my map. Neither can exist without the other. The gods had given us enough strength and might to make a difference in this world, but they made an error when allocating power; my brother was graced with knowledge and me with strength.

The battlefield was a place where I felt alive. The sound of metal clashing against metal, the screaming of the wounded, the sight of blood- it all fueled me.

I couldn't understand how my brother could stand on the sidelines, watching as I fought for both of us.

But now, as I looked at him, I could see the calculation in his eyes. He had always been the smarter of us, the one who could strategize and plan. And it seemed like he had been doing just that.

I didn't know what led him to condemn me to death. Was it jealousy? Had he grown tired of watching me fight and win while his skills were underutilized?

Or was it something more sinister? All I knew was that I couldn't trust him anymore. It was only a matter of time before he would have become dangerous.

I hate it when I am right.

My brother traded my life for power, striking a bargain with the Fates. My death for his life. My soul for his eternity. But what was his end game? That is what I didn't understand.

And that was what I would spend the rest of my eternity figuring out.

"Are you sure this is what you want to do?" Lilith asked, walking beside me and staring down at the battlefield, a tear of failure streaming down her face.

"Do I have a choice?"

"We all have a choice, but the real challenge lies in determining whether or not we are ready to accept the repercussions."

I thought about her question. Standing quietly on top of the hill, the sounds of battle drowned out any conversation. We could both see that the tide had turned against the supernatural. They would fail. Standing in the middle of the fighting was the one mortal who believed that the supernatural and humans could live in peace together.

This one battle would shatter all his dreams. The king was to meet his demise, along with any hope of a fresh start.

"I am positive," I finally whispered as the king fell, and my heart broke into a million pieces. He had been a remarkable leader, one of the strongest men I had ever known.

But now he was gone forever, and nothing was left for me here anymore. It was time to move on and carve out a new path. "It's time my brother learned humility."

Lilith nodded, eyes trained on the war unfolding beneath us. I could see her heart shattered into tiny pieces from witnessing her children die. They were Lucifer and Lilith's offspring down there, and I knew their deaths would haunt her for eternity.

"I will avenge them," I promised her.

"I know," she murmured in a low voice before her gaze locked on mine. I stepped back as I watched her strength and ire stir a storm in her eyes, metamorphosing them into an odd yellow shade. They were predator eyes, ready for battle.

I knew that look and found my strength in our common goal.

My brother would pay for his crimes. I just needed patience. I had been given a second chance, and I would not fail.

I am Morrigan.

A deity fashioned by the gods, the greatest warrior, and a woman on a mission.

Chapter 1- Nava

27 January 1591- Edinburgh, Scotland

T he world was a different place before books were invented.

Oral history was the way we remembered our ancestors. I'm sorry to say that many details were embellished or ignored. No one wanted to hear about how farmers planted in spring and harvested in autumn. No one cared who married who or how many children they had.

Except for those rare moments when those kids did something truly extraordinary. Like defeating a so-called monster. But those instances were few and far between. In reality, we were all just trying to survive back then.

And everyone knows that ordinary details do not make for captivating stories.

The idea of remembering began with the invention of books, but only the privileged few had their life stories written and preserved for future generations. As more records were collected, a designated location was necessary to house them all.

And just like magick, libraries were invented.

But I'm getting ahead of myself, back to the time before books.

During my childhood, the only way to gain knowledge was through tales passed down by a handful of storytellers. These individuals were a mix of educators, leaders, and visionaries, possessing a mystical understanding of past, present, and future occurrences. They educated us on our traditions, heritage, and faith in the gods.

The memory of sitting by the warm fire, burying my toes in the soft sand, and eagerly anticipating the next tale will always stay with me. Stories were my everything; they were what made life worthwhile.

When the storyteller rose, the real excitement began. They would weave epic narratives of fierce battles, magickal spells, and mystical wonders. With each new tale, listeners were transported to distant lands brimming with mighty warriors, wicked adversaries, divine deities, and fantastical beasts.

It was magick in its purest form.

But everyday lives? No, those were never remembered.

Once upon a time, when someone died, that was it. Their story was lost forever, swallowed by the earth, becoming a memory that faded with every passing season until nothing was left.

Death was treated as an ending.

Unless you found me.

I am the original Writer, the first to bear the responsibility of remembering and documenting the stories of the deceased.

Many would consider it a gift, but I'm not entirely convinced.

In my early twenties, I discovered I could talk to the dead. At first, their voices were barely audible, mere whispers and murmurs—shadows of the past.

The voices grew louder and more precise as time passed, and I became familiar with their ghostly tones. I started writing down snippets of their conversations, becoming more adept at deciphering their tales. Eventually, the dearly departed began to seek me out.

That moment took me down the path that led me to you, dear reader.

I have roamed the earth for centuries, chronicling the untold tales of those who have passed away. I have crossed paths with people from all social classes, from esteemed rulers to humble villagers. I have witnessed brave warriors ride into battle and never return. I have seen ships sail off only to return with a fraction of their crew.

I've danced around Maypoles and swam with dolphins. I have seen kingdoms flourish only to be swept away by another. I watched in anguish as religions grew and old gods died.

I have seen it all. The good. The bad. The ugly. And the indescribable.

Now, I have something to confess before you get excited and ask questions. It's a horrible job. The dead are often long-winded, rattling endlessly about failed harvests, unruly children, and long-lost loves.

The living are no better.

I'm sure you're wondering when this started. How did I become what I am now?

Come closer, and I will tell you a secret.

It all started when a king appeared one night and demanded I grant him a wish. I was not used to playing the part of a genie. He would have had better luck finding one in the village a few miles away, where they were much easier to come by.

But he came to me, and I didn't turn him away. The next few days changed my life.

And history.

Looking back, I should have run when we first met.

But here we are. What can I do about it now? You may wonder who I am. And I will tell you, because of all the stories I have written, history keeps forgetting mine.

They call me the Witch of Endor. I am the original, the first, the one without a name.

But you can call me Nava.

Chapter 2- Nava

1000 BC- Village of Endor, Jezreel Valley, Israel

"I'm back," an exhausted voice called from the doorway.

Nava paused and closed her eyes, silently thanking whichever deity was listening.

She knew Ysabel was more than capable, with a quick mind and clever instincts, but still, she couldn't shake the worry that gnawed at her stomach.

The house always grew eerily quiet without her sister's presence, the emptiness echoing off the walls and adding to the weight of worry on her mind.

"About time. I'll be there in a minute," Nava hollered back. She rolled her shoulders, trying to release some of the tension in her neck after another long day. Wiping away the sweat from her forehead, she glanced at the two figures still waiting in the front room.

"What brought you in today?" Nava greeted, eyeing her patient.

It was old man Joseph perched near the fireplace, holding an injured hand close to his chest and wincing in pain. Someone had wrapped a makeshift bandage around it, but it did little to stop the trickle of blood soaking into the rushes beneath him.

"Had a bit of an accident," Joseph grimaced, holding his hand up to show Nava.

"I see. What happened?" Kneeling, Nava carefully removed the bandage, taking a sharp breath at the sight. It was definitely something to worry about. His hand was a bloody mess, with two fingers severed below his knuckles.

"What else? Guards," Joseph's wife, Ava, said, anger flashing in her eyes. "They showed up this morning, demanding food. When Joseph told them we didn't have any to spare, they decided to make an example of him," she explained bitterly. "They meant to take the whole hand but missed."

"Ah, I see," Nava nodded, straining to mask her disgust. "Small blessing their aim was off," she joked as she turned the hand over to see if there was more damage.

"Only because they were drunk," Ava sneered, folding her arms across her ample chest. "I haven't seen a sober guard once. It makes me wonder about the king's criteria for being a soldier. Breathing?"

Joseph flinched at his wife's criticism, glancing out the window. "Lower your voice, woman, or they might come back and take more than just a few of my fingers." He nervously brushed his long hair away from his face with his good hand as he glanced back at Nava.

"Can you fix it? Harvest is right around the corner, and if I can't use both hands, I'm not sure how we'll manage."

"I can save the hand," Nava assured him, glancing over at the severed two fingers they brought in. "But the fingers are a lost cause." She narrowed her eyes to the stumps, assessing the damage. "You were smart to cauterize the bleeding."

"That was me," Ava boasted. "My cousin once cut off his big toe playing with a hand sickle. His mother stuck a hot iron on the limb and sent him off to finish the harvest. He always had a limp after that," she mused.

"Good call. Let's clean the hand up, and I'll stitch it back together. This will hurt," Nava warned. Joseph's head bobbed in agreement as he gripped his cloak in anticipation. "I'll give you a poultice to take with you; it should prevent infection," she added as she reached over to the small table for her needle and thread.

Careful to be as gentle as possible, she cleansed the open wound with the last bottle of disinfectant. The scent of vinegar filled the small area, stinging Nava's eyes. Joseph winced at the sharp pain as his wife massaged his tense shoulders, her eyes brimming with tears.

Working quickly, Nava stitched up the wound with thread made from twisted strands of sheep's intestines, ensuring she didn't pull the delicate material too hard. As a healer, she was well-versed in utilizing every part of an animal, from bones used for needles to hair and intestines used for thread. It was a gruesome but necessary aspect of her profession.

Tying the last knot, Nava glanced up at her patient with a sad smile. The hand would heal, but he would never have full function again.

"Give it a few days of rest, and you *may* be able to oversee the harvest next week. But you can't work. I would ask Michal if his sons could help," she finished, eyeing him until he nodded in agreement.

"I guess I'm going to need new gloves now," Joseph pouted as he held up his hand to admire Nava's work, the color slowly returning to his face.

"I'm sure your wife is up to the challenge." Nava groaned as she stooped up, stretching her back and wiggling her toes, which had gone numb from kneeling too long on the floor.

"Of course," Ava exclaimed as she supported Joseph's weakened body and helped him rise. His legs shook beneath him, struggling to maintain balance from the blood he lost. Nava rushed over and grabbed his other arm, helping them to the back door and out of the gate.

Smiling, she waved them off, praying to the gods that she would have no more patients for the rest of the night.

"They're gone," Nava called out when she walked back inside, untying her apron and draping it over a stool. She would need to do laundry soon; it had been her last clean apron, and she hadn't had time to run down to the river to do their weekly washing.

Sighing heavily at the thought of another task to add to her already extensive list, she approached the tiny wooden table nestled in the corner.

"Joseph lost two fingers, but he'll make a full recovery," Nava called over her shoulder. "I'm more worried about his wife's actions if she runs into the guard who took them. Knowing Ava's temper, she might get her husband into more trouble."

Hopefully, Joseph can convince her to let it go, Nava thought as she poured a mug of wine.

She ripped off a slice of bread from the loaf she had baked earlier, pretending it was meat. Ever since the night of the massacre, the village market had shut down, rapidly declining everyone's food supplies and leaving no one in a position to help the two spinsters.

"More than likely, the guard will be missing more than a few fingers once Joseph's family finds out what he did." Nava turned to find her sister watching her, a smile playing on her lips. Ysabel harbored no fondness for the guards and consistently advocated for seeking retribution whenever possible.

"How did today go?" Nava asked, ignoring the comment.

"The Blau family left early this morning. Then Abraham found me this afternoon. His wife told him they were leaving today whether he wanted to or not, so I took them out to the spot, too," Ysabel recounted, tugging at the leather band wrapped around her braid and letting her hair tumble down her back. She looked like she had just crawled through

14

the Otherworld, covered in a layer of sand and twigs that clung to her tangled locks.

The sisters were strikingly different. Nava had fair skin with a touch of pink, wild, dark reddish brown hair, eyes that were more yellow than green, and a slightly off-center nose.

On the other hand, Ysabel was radiant with her father's burnt caramel complexion. Her tawny locks cascaded down her back in waves, catching the light like spun honey. Her eyes were piercing icy blue, a striking contrast to her warm complexion.

Her mother often called them 'god's eyes' because no one in the village had ever seen eyes that color before.

Their personalities differed as much as their appearance; Nava was more reserved and studious, while Ysabel was friendly, open, and always full of life.

"We had a small scare and were forced to hide in the bushes," she explained, brushing away the dirt from her knees. "It turned out to be just a bird, but the families were scared."

"Were you able to give them the package?" Nava asked, sitting beside her. Absently, she held up her long braid, wishing for a cool breeze. The unseasonably warm weather persisted for weeks, and everyone was more than ready for the crisp autumn winds to arrive.

"Yes, they told me to thank you."

Nava forced a smile, regretting she didn't have more to offer. With so many people fleeing, her once bountiful supplies were now dwindling, ravaged by the unrelenting heat of summer that scorched the once-fertile valley and the number of injuries she had to treat.

The responsibility weighed heavily on her, knowing she may not have enough to help those in the village.

Just another problem to add to her growing list of concerns.

Three months ago, the king made a cruel and heartless proclamation ordering all supernatural to leave his kingdom. Armed with swords and spears, his guards swarmed into the peaceful village with deadly force.

The piercing screams and anguished cries of terrified villagers abruptly shattered the tranquil night. Chaos reigned as the king's men ruthlessly raided the town, violently ripping villagers from their homes and separating families.

The harsh, warlike sound of marching feet echoed through the streets, accompanied by the gut-wrenching sobs of mothers and fathers desperately trying to protect their loved ones from harm. In a frenzy of fear and panic, families abandon everything they had and flee for their lives under the looming threat of violence and death.

The supernatural who dared to oppose the king's orders were dragged away, their screams echoing through the air as they writhed against their restraints. For days on end, they endured endless torture in an attempt to extract information about others like them.

Until, one by one, their wails of pain tapered off to an eerie silence.

It had been so sudden that Nava still couldn't wrap her mind around the devastation. The king's council once consisted of mortals and others like her, and there had been no issues for years.

So why was the king set on destroying them now?

They had done nothing to harm anyone—quite the opposite. Most supernatural were well-respected in the community for their work as healers, farmers, artists, and musicians.

But something changed, and no one knew why.

Nava and her sister worked tirelessly to help those still in danger. At night, they snuck food and medical supplies past the armed guards.

Twice a week, Ysabel helped families through the treacherous terrain and waited as they scrambled into the hills. Nava stayed back to care for the wounded.

But it was becoming more challenging for the sisters to help everyone and stay hidden.

Nava sighed and leaned her head against the wall, her eyes closing as she tried to devise a plan. She knew they couldn't keep this up forever. Eventually, the king's men would find them.

The whispers were impossible to ignore.

The king was looking for her. And she had a funny feeling she knew why.

Chapter 3- Nava

1000 BC- Village of Endor, Jezreel Valley, Israel

I t all started years ago.

It was the type of lazy day that made you want to run outside and dip your feet into the stream. A perfect day to catch dragonflies, pick wild berries, and gather flowers. An ordinary summer afternoon that usually found Nava and Ysabel skipping to the river, trying to grab fish with their bare hands, giggling as they fell in.

Not having a funeral.

Instead, they were paying their last respects to the most remarkable person who had ever lived. A soft-spoken woman with raven black hair, dancing dark eyes, and one of the greatest healers—their mother.

Sadly, even healers couldn't save everyone.

The sickness that took her was unlike anything Nava had ever seen. One moment, their mother was tending to the garden, her angelic voice filling the air with a familiar hum as she pruned fruit trees. The next day, she was confined to her bedroll, her caramel complexion drained of all color and replaced with an ashen hue. Even her lips, once a delicate shade of pink, had morphed into a deathly blue. Each breath she took required immense effort, her body trembling uncontrollably, and her teeth chattering as she burned with a furious fever.

The days crawled by, weighed down by the oppressive stench of death permeating their tiny family home. It clung to every corner and surface like a thick layer of incense smoke. The relentless summer sun beat down on Nava, smothering her in a sticky film of sweat combined with the heat radiating from the fire she had built to ease her mother's chills.

In the corner, her father knelt in fervent prayer, his eyes never leaving his wife's frail figure as she fought against the grasp of death.

Desperately, Nava tried everything to relieve her mother's agony - damp cloths to cool her forehead, force-feeding spoonfuls of broth, and water through her cracked lips. But no matter how much she begged and pleaded with the gods, her mother remained unresponsive.

In the stillness of the night, with only the soft glow of a flickering fire lighting their home, Nava kneeled by her mother's bedroll. Her voice, barely above a whisper, weaved tales of adventure and magick, conjuring up vivid childhood memories. With each story, she prayed it would ignite a spark, urging her mother to live.

Nava wasn't ready to say goodbye. Not yet. There were still so many lessons left to learn from her mother's skilled hands and wise words on the art of healing.

For five days, Nava knelt beside her mother, watching her frail body rise and fall with each shallow breath, praying for a miracle.

Just when Nava thought all was lost, her mother's eyes fluttered open. Her frail hand reached out, searching for Nava's in the dimly lit room. A wave of relief washed over her at the slight flicker of recognition in her mother's gaze before she closed her eyes again, exhausted from the effort.

"I don't have much longer," her mother's strained voice whispered, each word causing her cracked lips to bleed.

Nava leaned in towards her, reaching for a cool cloth and lightly dabbing it along her forehead. Her mother's attempted smile was interrupted by a dry cough that left her gasping for air.

"Shhhhh," Nava whispered soothingly. "You need to rest and conserve your strength."

With a slow and arduous effort, her mother shifted to face her, her hair matted against her brow like strands of wet straw.

"You must save their souls." Her raspy words hung heavy in the air, and desperation filled her eyes. "Only you can."

She rotated to glance at her husband, who was dozing against the wall, his arms crossed against his chest, his breath shallow with exhaustion.

"I couldn't have asked for a better partner." Turning to face her youngest child, who was snuggled up next to her, she whispered, "Take care of her. She will need your courage in the coming days."

Nava fought back a cry, realizing her mother was giving her final farewell.

Nava's voice was barely a whisper as she pleaded, her head hung low. "Please don't leave me," she murmured. "I'm not ready."

"You must let me go. The Fates are calling."

Her mother's eyes pleaded for understanding, squeezing Nava's hand again before another cough wracked through her frail body, tears streaming down her face. Pain etched itself onto her features as she gasped for air. Despite the agony coursing through her, she glanced at Nava with a faint smile.

"You have your own road to travel," she murmured between coughs, love for her daughter shining in her gaze. "Remember, death is not absolute."

She closed her eyes, and as Nava cried, she took her final breath.

That was a week ago.

Nava swallowed, her eyes locked on the growing pile of stones that would soon become her mother's tomb. She wanted to scream. She wanted to claw her way into the pit with her mother's body and beg for forgiveness.

She failed her.

But she couldn't. She could only stand immobilized as rock after rock enclosed her body, alongside offerings of a raven's feather, tortoise shells, and various dried flowers and herbs in vases - items she would require in the afterlife.

Nava didn't follow her father and sister back home after the elder's final prayer. Instead, she stood frozen, rooted to the spot next to her mother's grave. The wind grew stronger, carrying hot and dry air that swept through the land. Nava held her ground, even as sand stung her eyes and coated her skin like a gritty shield.

She refused to leave until all the other mourners departed, wanting one last moment alone to bid her farewell.

Wiping the grit away with her sleeve, she knelt beside the grave and brushed her trembling fingers against the stones. Rivulets of sweat ran down her face, mixing with salty tears and dirt. She leaned across the jagged rocks, wrapping her arms around them in a hug as she cried her pain away, cursing the gods for taking away the person she loved the most.

As Nava sang her final prayers, a cool breeze swept through the twisted acacia trees behind her, carrying the scent of vanilla and raspberries. The familiar and soothing fragrance surrounded her as she inhaled, bringing back memories of her mother's gentle smile, infectious laughter, graceful movements, and warm embraces.

Overhead, a lone raven flew, letting out a piercing call as it circled above her. Nava lifted her head and marveled at the majestic creature soaring through the sky. Suddenly, it descended and landed in front of her, tilting its head to scrutinize her with curious eyes.

They stared at each other before it hopped onto the grave and ruffled its dark, shimmering feathers. Nava dared not make a sound, her body frozen as the raven observed her.

21

Unexpectedly, it let out a haunting call that echoed through the air, and a burst of energy flowed through Nava's veins, igniting a fire within her. She stumbled backward, her gaze unfocused as she was overwhelmed by the moment's intensity.

In her mind's eye, she saw the lives of people whose faces she'd never seen. She watched as children laughed and played dangerously close to a fast-moving river, unaware of the danger. In another scene, a young shepherd rested on a hilltop, his face marked with fatigue and hunger as he drifted off to sleep. Then, the scene shifted to a bedroom, where Nava witnessed an old woman clinging to her husband's hand as he took his final breath.

The memories started back at her. The children's faces were etched with a bittersweet smile as they waved goodbye, not acknowledging Nava's desperate pleas for them to return.

The shepherd turned and opened one eye. Nava extended her hand to grasp his, promising to bring back food and water if he could hold on longer. But he shook his head, closed his eyes, and breathed his last breath.

The elderly woman's eyes met Nava's with a desperate plea. Her sorrowful face begging to join her husband wherever he was going. Nava shook her head, and the woman's heartbreaking sobs filled the air like the melancholy cry of a faraway bird.

This is not happening. They are not real.

Nava's head shook in disbelief as she blinked repeatedly, trying to dispel the disturbing images from her mind.

But when she opened them, she realized it wasn't her imagination.

They were still there.

Waiting.

Out of the corner of her eyes, she spotted another figure emerging from the distance. It was a woman with luscious hair that flowed down her back, cascading like a dark waterfall, strands dancing in the breeze around her face. She wore a loose ivory dress draped over her slender frame, and a delicate pendant shaped like a tree hung around her neck, grazing her waistline.

She leaned against an old oak, its twisted branches stretching toward the sky like outstretched fingers. Nava's heart skipped a beat when she caught the familiar smile on the woman's face and the dark eyes fixed on her.

It was her mother, in all her radiant glory, appearing as she had been before the debilitating illness ravaged her body.

"I had a feeling you would be here," her mother admitted as she glanced behind Nava at her grave, her eyes brimming with gratitude. "It was a lovely funeral. I didn't think so many people would show up." Nava nodded, tears flowing as she tried to think of something to say.

"It was my time," her mother said, stepping closer and lifting Nava's chin so their eyes met. "The Fates decided I had a different path—just as they have for you, my child."

Nava's eyes flew to her mother's in shock. "Me? Why?"

"Who knows?" She chuckled. "They work in mysterious ways."

"Sounds ominous," Nava whispered, staring at the ground.

"Yes," she agreed, wiping Nava's tears with her thumb. A gentle movement Nava leaned into. "There will be people who will need your help. I need you to wait for them."

Nava looked up in amazement. "Why me?"

"Because it can only be you," her mother said, leaning forward and kissing her forehead. "Remember what I told you. The soul never dies." She glanced over at the figures, listening to their conversation. With a slight nod in their direction, they faded away with one last smile at Nava.

"We'll meet again, daughter," her mother promised, brushing a strand of hair behind Nava's ear. "No one is ever truly lost if someone remembers their name."

And just like that, she disappeared. Nava lifted her gaze to find her father standing beside her. He wrapped his arm around her and pulled her in for a warm hug.

"Did you find your answers?" he whispered, his voice gentle and cautious.

Nava nodded. "Did you know?" she asked, glancing at him from the corner of her eye. "Did you know what I could do?"

He hesitated before speaking, then confessed, "Your mother told me on the day you were born. She said you would eventually bridge the gap between the living and the lost." He paused to swallow before continuing, "I prayed she was mistaken. But your mother has always been right."

"What do I do now?" Nava looked down at her hands.

"I don't know." He gazed at his wife's grave, a single tear falling down his cheek. "But we will figure it out."

Nava nodded once more, and the two strolled back home without speaking, each lost in their own contemplation.

What was there to say? She could see the dead.

Chapter 4- Agnes

27 January 1591- Edinburgh, Scotland

Today is the day. I can feel it in my bones.

I don't have much more time to finish my story because this is the day the king will condemn me to die.

Considering my current situation, dear reader, it may not be so bad. The accommodations are horrible, and I haven't had a decent mug of mead in weeks.

The cell they put me in reeks of sweat and urine. The sour, pungent aroma permeates everything from the walls to the pile of hay in the corner that serves as my 'bed.' To make matters worse, the floor is covered in a thick layer of hard-packed earth and hardened feces from the last poor soul who lived here, and I can't smell anything but the stench of blood and decay.

The only light comes from a barred window high up on the wall, out of reach of my grasping fingers.

If you can even call them fingers. My once nimble and confident hands have swollen into meaty paws, cracked and bleeding from trying to claw my way under the iron bars entrapping me in this hell.

Not that it helped. The bars have been dug too deep into the ground.

Not to mention, my neighbor likes to announce to the guards whenever I am 'misbehaving.' I should have known she would be trouble.

When I was first introduced to my new home, she greeted me with frantic energy, dancing around her cell. She warned me about everything that had happened to her and what was yet to come for me. And then she ripped off her tattered dress, waving it above her naked body with crazed glee.

She sang about how the guards would strip me and shave my hair with a dull knife, and if they found the devil's mark, not even the gods could save me. The guards laughed at her antics, enjoying the show, and leered at her in a manner I could only guess she was used to.

But she didn't notice. She just danced to the song that played only in her mind, her sanity long lost.

It was probably for the best. I don't know how long the woman has been caged in the dungeon. But from the looks of it, she found a way to escape the cruelty of her captors.

I still can't tell you how I ended up here. The days are a blur. One day, I was at home tending to my garden, and the next thing I knew, I was accused of being a witch—again, for the third time.

Unfortunately, I couldn't avoid the accusation this time. Instead, the king summoned me to Edinburgh for further questioning.

Questioning! Ha! What a laughable concept. More like an interrogation. Being reduced to nothing more than a shell of a person by way of torture would be a better description.

It all started with Geillis Duncan and her damn employer. A nasty man who hates women and has no soft spot for anyone he believes has 'unnatural abilities.'

It's not that I blame her. I understand why she broke, and I won't hold it against her. Pain is a valuable tool for obtaining information.

She had no choice but to name all her conspirators, real or imaginary. Geillis. My poor friend.

They took her for more 'questioning' hours ago, and I have been anxiously waiting for her return.

I don't have long to wait.

Heavy iron shackles clatter in the silence as she is half-dragged down the hall. The weight of my heart grows heavier with every step until I can't bear it anymore, so I close my eyes and cover my ears.

Curiosity gets the better of me, and I open one eye. My jaw drops in shock. She is covered in broken bones, her skin a canvas of bruises. On her back, strips of flesh have been peeled away, revealing layers of raw tissue like scales on a fish. Her eyes are lifeless, her body a walking corpse, her dignity destroyed, her faith in humanity shattered. They have taken everything from her.

And still, they kept her in chains, afraid of what she could do.

Which is laughable. The girl can't walk.

She would die. Her poor body would rot on the gallows, displayed to the town as a warning.

Just like I will be.

The sharp crack of axes cutting through logs shatters the silence, and I look over my shoulder at the window, frowning. I can hear the guards laughing as they build a pyre large enough so everyone can have a good view of my execution.

How kind of them to make it right outside my cell.

How many trees does it take to burn someone?

Somebody in the cell down the narrow walkway must have woken up. I can hear the other prisoners weeping and wailing, mingling with the crackling of the practice fire. The guards have lit a fire each morning for the past three days, meticulously repositioning the logs to draw out the pain and prolong the suffering.

It is a ritual I have become disturbingly familiar with. I have spent countless hours listening to the executioner's droning lectures on the importance of precise wood placement for a satisfying execution.

Every aspect is carefully calculated, and each movement is choreographed to ensure maximum agony without displeasing the king with a swift death.

And we wouldn't want to disappoint the king now, would we?

I close my eyes and try to block their voices out, but I can't. Not when I keep replaying the last few days in my head, trying to understand why the king would be interested in me. A middle-aged woman from a small coastal village he had never visited.

I will never know why I was singled out.

I overheard stories about the unspeakable horror I have supposedly committed. The king's advisors painted me as a monstrous creature who danced with the devil himself. They even accused me of sacrificing cats and throwing them into the ocean. And that was the least vile of the disgusting atrocities the king charged me with.

But what can I do? I confessed. I had no choice. People will say anything to make the pain go away.

I just hope the executioner shows mercy when it is time to kill me.

Most likely not. The king wants blood.

My blood.

I don't have much time; if I am going to share my story with you, it must be now.

I was once a healer, a midwife, and now I am an accused witch.

But you can call me Agnes.

Chapter 5- Agnes

November 1589- Nether Keith, Scotland

"D id you hear?" A woman barged into the house, her voice loud and frantic as she shouted over the sound of the thunder outside. A rush of cold autumn air accompanied her, extinguishing some of the tallow candles in its wake.

Agnes flinched at the unexpected interruption, spilling her mead mug onto the floor. She muttered a curse and turned around, ready to scold whoever barged in. But when she saw who it was, her words stuck in her throat.

Standing in the doorway was Geillis Duncan, and she looked like a wet cat, trapped and cornered, ready to lash out.

Her wide sea-green eyes darted about the room with desperation and fear. Her pale complexion revealed dark circles beneath her eyes. Strands of her golden hair came loose from her tightly pinned bun under her kerchief, framing her face in wild tangles.

Geillis was always the epitome of grace and manners, which is precisely why David Setoun, the deputy bailiff of Tranent, chose to employ her. He had specific standards for his household staff: they must be youthful, easily influenced, and attractive.

None of which could describe the woman standing in her home. Geillis stood caked in a thick layer of mud and debris, and it looked like she had been dragged and beaten by the elements. The six-mile trek to Agnes' home was always tricky, even in the most favorable weather.

And tonight was not a night for anyone to be outside.

As she closed the front door, Agnes took a quick look outside, noticing the old mare tied to the gate grazing on the last few flowers in the garden. A feeling of dread washed over her as she realized Geillis must have taken the horse without asking.

Something was seriously wrong for her to risk stealing from the bailiff.

The mere thought of the tyrant and his son, David, made Agnes' stomach churn. Their reputation for cruelty and mistreatment of employees was well-known, and their constant financial problems only added to their notoriety.

But what sent shivers down Agnes' spine was their twisted obsession with witches. She'd heard rumors that Setoun attributed his economic struggles to the use of magick, and he was on a mission to eradicate anyone he suspected of practicing it.

Of course, he wouldn't blame it on his gambling or drinking problem.

Agnes saw the anxiety written on Geillis' face as she anxiously peered over her shoulder, making sure they were, in fact, alone.

"Something to drink?" Agnes furrowed her brow, troubled, as she walked back to the fireplace. She shivered and wrapped her tattered plaid shawl tightly around her shoulders. It had been her husband's, and she had worn it every night since he passed away - the last remaining piece of him that she had left.

"Thank you, but this isn't a social call," Geillis said in a tired voice. She settled onto one of the stools at the rough-cut table, pulled out a muddy handkerchief, and rubbed her forehead with it. "I came to warn you."

"Warn me?" Agnes questioned, her eyebrows arching as she stirred the pot heating over the fire. She breathed in the steam and took in the familiar aroma of cloves and herbs.

Her mother taught her the recipe, passed down through generations, used to calm nerves. The brew was a staple in her home during the harsh winter season, and she often shared it with her sick neighbors. It seemed like the perfect opportunity to sample her latest batch.

Agnes poured the warm mead into two mugs and carried them to the table, sitting across from her friend. She pushed one towards Geillis and cradled her own in both hands, waiting for Geillis to collect her thoughts. Agnes took a small drink, the atmosphere in the room mirroring the dreary weather outside. As the sun dipped beneath the horizon, shadows danced on the walls, illuminated only by two flickering candles atop a wooden cabinet in the corner.

Minutes ticked by as the deafening silence in the room became suffocating. Agnes gazed upwards, offering a silent plea to the gods for strength.

"Allegations have been made against me again," Geillis murmured, lifting her mug and inhaling deeply before taking a sip. "Witchcraft."

Agnes' eyebrows raised in surprise, her heart beating faster as the word lingered between them. She let out a small sigh, filled with dread and disappointment. Part of her hoped for a different explanation for Geillis's abrupt arrival, but she couldn't deny she'd anticipated it deep down.

Witchcraft.

For two agonizing years, they had endured relentless persecution from local church leaders and their false accusations. The latest summons for Agnes was to face charges of failing to heal John Thompson, a paralyzed man who dared to request a refund when her efforts proved futile.

31

Despite her best efforts, he wasted no time running to the infamous John Knox to demand justice.

Since then, Geillis had been high on his list of people to watch. Heal someone, and it was magick. Not heal someone, and it was the worst type of witchcraft. The local healers found the hypocrisy exhausting. But what could they do? They were just women.

"Are you sure?" Agnes asked, sighing tiredly.

Geillis nodded. "I'm certain of it. Someone told Setoun I'd been sneaking out at night. My guess is Anna. She's always been jealous of me, and everyone knows she has loose lips when it comes to gossip." Geillis took another sip, her brow furrowing. "He's always questioned my healing skills, but when he heard about what transpired at the McGrathey house, he felt he had enough evidence to go to Knox and complain."

Agnes was surprised. She was well aware of Anna's nosiness and jealousy but never thought she would stoop so low as to spread rumors. Anna had not even been at the McGrathey residence during the incident, so she could not know what had happened.

The only witnesses were Agnes, Geillis, and Mary McGrathey.

And they vowed never to utter a word.

It'd only been two weeks since Agnes was awakened by frantic pounding in the middle of the night. She was used to unannounced guests, but when she opened the door in her flimsy shift and plaid, she was surprised to see McGrathey's oldest son standing there with a look of terror in his eyes.

Without exchanging pleasantries, he blurted out that his younger sister was sick and having trouble breathing.

Not wasting a moment, Agnes changed into more suitable clothing and grabbed her bag, and they braved the fierce storm together.

Forty minutes later, Agnes arrived, her cloak and bog shoes drenched and unable to feel her toes. Mary dragged her into the back room, where her daughter lay on her pallet, rain dripping through the latched roof onto her fur blanket. The child's once rosy cheeks turned ashen and ghostly with each desperate breath. Each gasp sounded like a suppressed cry for help, a plea for relief from her torment.

The air was thick with an eerie presence. Though Agnes may not have seen it, she felt Death's cruel grip tightening, ready to snatch another victim into the Otherworld.

"Send your son to the Setoun home and ask for Geillis," she hissed at Mary, opening her bag and laying out the needed herbs. The boy, still numb from the cold, didn't have a chance to catch his breath or warm his hands. Instead, he was pushed out into the brutal storm again.

"Tell her I need her help - a child's life is at stake!" Agnes shouted after him, her voice cracking with alarm. Trembling, she turned back to her patient, knowing every second counted in this race against death.

Geillis came immediately.

The night became a blur of frantic chaos as they battled to subdue the raging fever, exhausting every ounce of their knowledge and ability. With each passing hour, the girl's tortured body cried out in agony, but they refused to give up hope.

As the first morning light pierced through the darkness, the fever finally broke. It left behind a weakened and battered girl, her body wracked with lingering effects that would haunt her for days to come.

Agnes and Geillis left the home drained, having poured all their power into saving the child's life. They knew neither could have saved her individually, but even working together was a near miss.

"It had nothing to do with the child," Geillis growled, her jaw clenched in anger. "Sentoun was in my room when I returned, demanding payment for the time I was away." She shuddered in disgust at the memory, her face contorted with loathing.

"I was exhausted, dirty, and just wanted to lay down. I *may* have pushed Sentoun towards the door, and he didn't take the insult lightly. He left, saying I would pay for my disrespect.

"It didn't help that old man Fearghus showed up yesterday morning, claiming the elixir I gave his wife for her headaches resulted in her not being willing to do her 'womanly duties.'"

Agnes was taken aback. "That led to another allegation of witchcraft?" She shook her head in disbelief. "Seems like pulling at a thread and unraveling the whole tapestry."

Geillis shrugged, glancing through the shutters, watching the rain fall. She rubbed her eyes and sighed. "Whether it's a misunderstanding or not, I still have to answer for my supposed 'crimes.'"

Her sad eyes shifted back to Agnes. "I just came by to let you know since you were there too." Standing up, she wrapped her cloak tight around her. "I should go. They're probably searching for me already."

Agnes watched her friend head for the front door, her feet shuffling heavily along the stone slabs with the weight of her situation. Her mind raced for the right words to say. She wanted to comfort Geillis, but how could she find something to say to ease her friend's fears and anger?

Geillis stopped at the door, tears brimming as she pivoted to face Agnes, her voice trembling. "Be careful, my friend. I don't think we will escape this one unscathed." With her final warning, Geillis slipped into the darkness of the night, leaving Agnes to wonder if she would ever see her again.

Alive, that is.

Agnes stayed at the table for hours, long after the candles flickered out and the hearth logs turned into embers. The wind roared outside, the rain beating down on her roof like a persistent drum as tiny droplets seeped through. She sat, shivering uncontrollably, not from the temperature but from overwhelming fear gripping her soul.

Despite repeated attempts to convince herself she would be alright, she couldn't escape the nagging thought that her life would never be normal again.

She knew she needed a plan. It was the only way forward. With a heavy heart, she went to find more candles.

It would be a long night.

Chapter 6- Chloe

Modern Day- City of the Unspoken

As I stepped into the Library of the Unread, a wave of awe and respect washed over me. Just as it had the first time I'd seen it. The library was magnificent, its soaring walls adorned with gilded paintings and tapestries depicting stories of gods and warriors from long ago.

The maze of bookshelves stretched endlessly- thousands of pages, millions of words, countless stories mingled with the scent of archaic parchment and dusty books that tickled my nose.

Every morning, I'd find myself drawn to a different hidden chamber and immerse myself in the fascinating history of lost words. Careful not to disturb the dead, I would walk around the towering pedestals displaying antique artifacts, admiring their intricate designs hidden under layers of dust. Minor relics sat scattered throughout the shelves, overlooked by the casual observer, but revealing their true worth to those who looked.

I made it a point to find them all. They weren't books, but they held the same power. Their etchings carefully portrayed the lives of their creators. And I couldn't help but wonder about the existence of the old gods. Were they still alive? Or had they faded into obscurity as newer religions emerged?

My thoughts buzzed with questions as my fingers ran over the forgotten languages, trying to extract answers from the past. Did the gods miss mortals? Did they remember us? There was a saying that legends never die. But was it living if no one remembered your story?

Shaking my thoughts away, I navigated around the antiquated library card station and headed to the sitting area. The coldness of the stone floor seeped through my tattered boots, each step echoing off the curved ceiling, reaching up into the endless night sky.

A brisk wind blew through the small cracks in the windows, ruffling my hair. It carried the musty odor of decaying reeds and shifting mud from the River Styx just beyond the stone wall.

I wrinkled my nose, wishing I could get used to the scent, but I couldn't. It reminded me too much of Aelle and our journey to find Medusa and Danaë.

It'd been over a week since Aelle sacrificed herself so we could retrieve the first missing Book of the Veiled—Taliesin's story. I sneered at the thought of the deity who changed the course of history seeking retribution for his sister's murder, leaving a path of destruction in his wake.

The deity, masquerading as a mortal, was highly regarded as a wise sorcerer and praised for his mastery of magick—a man who could manipulate the elements. See into the future. Remember the past—a kingmaker.

Hell, he even had a Disney movie.

But I knew the truth.

He'd rewritten his reality. Feverishly penning a fresh storyline in a desperate attempt to sway public opinion. Taliesin skillfully constructed his words by manipulating facts and transforming the supernatural into terrifying monsters.

Gods, I hated him. But a part of me also respected him. He was willing to move heaven and earth for the person he loved. His methods left much to be desired, but his intention was understandable. He needed to fix the misstep he'd made when he let his sister die.

As I drew closer to a familiar painting, my restless thoughts calmed. With a heavy heart, I gazed up at Medusa's image, a piece of art I visited every morning.

The artist skillfully depicted her transformation in such vivid detail that I wondered if they had witnessed it firsthand.

With one look, I could feel the fear and pain etched on Medusa's face as Athena's hand reached out to curse her. The portrait's blues and greens swirled together, mirroring Medusa's chaos and anguish as she endured her cursed metamorphosis.

Medusa. A woman shrouded in misinterpretations. She was not inherently a monster; circumstances and others' perceptions forced her into the role. An essential element often disregarded by those who tell her story.

To them, it mattered little who she was before; all that counted was what she eventually became.

Aelle had understood Medusa. And the two formed an instantaneous bond over books and sarcastic remarks.

I respected her—not for the monster she had been forced to become but for how she embraced it.

To give in to darkness and never look back. That was the ultimate control.

With one last glance, I shuffled over to the breakfast cart, my muscles protesting at the movement after another long night of tossing and turning. My fingers were engulfed in warm steam as I tried to shake off my fatigue. The chilly morning air nipped at my exposed skin, and I pulled my hoodie sleeves over my hands for extra warmth. Holding onto the mug tightly, I looked over where I had left my copy of the Book of the Veiled.

I'd intended to sit down and record the week's happenings, but the pages remained blank. My thoughts were scattered like puzzle pieces that wouldn't fit together—the ultimate writer's block.

Defeated, I shuffled to Lilith's favorite chair facing the enormous fireplace and allowed the hypnotizing flicker of the flames to lure me into a trance. Every night since we found Taliesin's book, horrific nightmares plague me, leaving me waking up clutching my pillow and drenched in sweat.

They all started the same way.

Me, frantically sprinting through endless darkness, clutching a small black book, as something chased me through an ever-changing maze of twists and turns.

Identical to the dreams that Diana, Eidolon's mother, had before she ran off and married Taliesin.

Were they dreams?

I wasn't entirely sure. The visions felt more like memories. Like I was reliving someone's final, terrifying moments. But whose memories they were, I couldn't say. All I knew beyond a shadow of a doubt was that something terrible was on the horizon for me next.

Like it had been for so many Writers before me.

Chapter 7- Chloe

Modern Day- City of the Unspoken

The first nightmare had been dreadful.

I woke up standing in a crowded church, my torn nightdress clinging to my body, revealing bruises and scrapes that marred my skin. My hair was pulled back into a loose braid, muddy strands framing my dirt-covered face. My hands were bound in front of me with a tightly spun hemp rope, cutting off my circulation. I wiggled my fingers, but it did nothing to relieve the discomfort.

What in the world? I squinted through the haze with one good eye, the other swollen shut. The flickering light of the nearby candles stung my sensitive eye. I quickly closed it, trying to regain my bearings and focus on my surroundings.

As a man's voice echoed off the wooden walls, I glanced up, wincing in pain. His finger pointed at me, his deep baritone words rising in righteous indignation as he glared at me from under his broad-brimmed black hat. An executioner, their face hidden by a dark hood, stood beside me, wrapping a rope around my throat. As he tightened, he whispered one question into my ear.

"Where are the sisters?"

What sisters? I wanted to ask, but the rope cut off my airway. I shook my head, watching him with narrowed eyes, trying to see who was hiding under the cloak.

The judge roared, yelling something at the executioner that I couldn't hear over the ringing in my ears. Suddenly, a heavy blow struck me from behind with a sickening thud. I stumbled and fell to the ground, my knees scraping against the rough-cut wooden floor. A burst of pain shot through my body, but before I could protest, the executioner plunged my head into a bucket of icy water.

The shock jolted my senses, and I thrashed wildly, trying to grab onto anything. Desperately, I reached for the executioner's cloak to use as leverage, but it slipped from my grasp when they stepped back. My mouth opened in a frantic scream, but cold water filled my throat, silencing me. All I could feel was fear and desperation as I struggled against the weight of the executioner's hand pressing down on my head.

They held me under until my vision blurred, and my chest burned, desperate to breathe. When they finally pulled me up, my gasps for air were met with the same question, taunting me before plunging my head back into the frigid depths.

"Tell me where the sisters are, and this can all be over," they yelled over and over again.

They dunked me six more times before the ordeal ended, and I collapsed onto the floor. Gasping, I clawed the rope from around my neck, silently cursing everyone in the room as their laughter reverberated off the church walls like waves pounding against a shore.

Death to the witch.

Devil worshiper.

And the nightmares only intensified.

The next night, I woke up to a hooded figure looming over me. With a cruel laugh, it grabbed me by the throat and hurled me into an open grave. The loud thud of my body hitting the bottom echoed through the pit, accompanied by the sickening sound of my bones snapping like brittle twigs. Above me, the dark voice of my masked executioner echoed through the night air, taunting me to get up and fight back.

You got to be kidding me! This again?

I strained to reach the black book thrown in with me, grunting with frustration as it remained just out of my grasp. Suddenly, a sharp pain erupted in my chest, and I could hear something being driven into my body.

Looking down, my eyes widened in terror as I glimpsed a wooden stake lodged in me. Blood gushed out and stained the soil beneath me crimson.

That's not good, I thought as I reached for the weapon, attempting to dislodge it from my body. But the pain was unbearable. I leaned my head back against the ground, straining to catch my breath.

Was it possible to die in a nightmare?

"Where are the Sisters? Tell me before it's too late for you," the masked figure screamed.

I didn't answer as I fought against the blackness, closing in like a casket lid until I was engulfed in darkness.

By far, the most disturbing nightmare was when I awoke inside a horrific pile of dead bodies. The stench of death and decay filled my nostrils, and my heart raced with fear as I took in the sight surrounding me.

Countless lifeless eyes stared at me, mouths agape in silent screams of terror, warning me of impending doom. Frantically, I strained to push myself up from the gruesome scene, but the weight of the corpses held me in place like a vice grip.

Ewwww. I plucked a swollen hand off me and grimaced as it pulled away from the arm. Tossing it to the side because I didn't know what else to do with it, I tried to dislodge my leg from where it lay under an old woman. She was wearing a nightgown, a dirty kerchief wrapped around her thinning hair, her body bloated with unreleased gases. Her face was turned towards me, her mouth open, showcasing her rotted teeth and a swollen tongue.

And then, emerging from the shadows like a nightmare come to life, a figure dressed in dark leather and enveloped in a billowing black cloak approached me. The flash of two sparkling long swords sheathed in leather scabbards on either side of his hips sent shivers down my spine as it drew closer.

Just like the other dreams, it only asked one question.

Where are the Sisters?

The intensity of their anger radiated off them like searing heat, causing my skin to tingle. My heart raced as I watched the cold gleam of a dagger being unsheathed from inside its boot. I realized the situation was about to escalate from problematic to dire.

Bending down at the edge of the pit, they leaned over, slicing the blade across my wrist. Blood dripped steadily from my wound, each drop captured in a small glass jar they pulled out of their pocket, the metallic scent mingling with the musty odor of earth and decay.

I trembled as I realized I was the sacrifice.

And then I screamed.

Standing, they watched as fire consumed me.

And laughed.

Chapter 8- Chloe

Modern Day- City of the Unspoken

"I thought I'd find you here." Eidolon's deep voice called out from the doorway, echoing through the vast library. I glanced up and watched him walk towards me with confident strides, his attention fixed on me.

His deep, indigo eyes were heavy with the weight of sleepless nights, their bright intensity dimmed by a veil of exhaustion. His face bore the tell-tale signs of strain and fatigue, lines etched deeply into his bronzed skin, and tension evident in every taut muscle.

He wore baggy, gray sweatpants that rested low on his hips and a worn-out black T-shirt. The fabric hugged his well-defined muscles, highlighting the evidence of hard labor and a disciplined exercise routine over the years. He tousled his dark hair with his hand before sliding his ball cap backward on his head.

Gods, he was sexy.

"I couldn't sleep," I lied, twisting a loose thread on my sweatshirt. I smiled as our eyes met. "And I needed to get some writing done before everyone woke up."

Eidolon raised an eyebrow as he sat next to me. "How's that working out for you?" He glanced over his shoulder at the desk where my book sat, gathering dust.

"About as good as folding a fitted sheet," I joked. "I can't find the words," I admitted after a moment of silence.

"We'll find her," he promised, staring at the hearth with his eyebrows furrowed.

I raised an eyebrow in skepticism. "I don't know. Something feels off." I waved my hand toward the rows of shelves. "She should have been back by now, fussing about organizing the books or rearranging the furniture. But she's not, and that's not like Aelle."

"She could be busy."

"With what?" I huffed, crossing my arms over my chest.

"I don't know," Eidolon sighed, rubbing his temples.

We had this same conversation countless times with each other and the rest of the group. Yet none of us could make sense of the situation. All we knew was that Aelle jumped into Taliesin's book, using her link as his daughter to bind them together. But after that, we had no idea what happened to her.

I wanted to talk to Lilith, but she'd left with Vivian the night Aelle disappeared. Odin and Freyja soon followed suit, leaving behind Eidolon, Moll, Victor, Max, Isabelle, Watson, and me to guard the Library of the Unread in Aelle's absence.

And I couldn't shake my irrational anger towards her. She was taking her sweet time returning, and it pissed me off. The Library of the Unread was her responsibility, not mine. I needed to find the other two missing Books of the Veiled.

Not playing caretaker.

On the flip side, I couldn't deny it was a sweet deal. I had unlimited access to the Library of the Unspoken, with every book I ever wanted only an arm's length away.

And wasn't this what I always dreamed of?

No more mundane responsibilities like chores, grocery shopping, or paying bills. Just me, books, and an endless supply of coffee at my disposal.

Yes, it was.

Since I had time, I had been looking for a particular book. It wasn't crucial to the Raven Society's mission. But I hoped it would answer the one question nagging at me since I learned that witches, vampires, shapeshifters, and even the old gods still existed.

Who was the first supernatural? Besides Lilith.

Despite shuffling through countless books, I couldn't find any mention of their identity. The only hints I could find were brief references in ancient texts suggesting a possible link to the offspring of Lilith and Lucifer.

But there was no name or description.

I thought I had found what I needed a couple of days ago when a thick black book came hurtling towards me out of nowhere, narrowly missing my head and landing at my feet.

I stared at it silently, debating whether to pick it up, remembering Eidolon's favorite warning.

Don't touch magickal items you don't understand.

But I couldn't resist my curiosity, so I bent down to cautiously pick up the object with two fingers. The spine was frail and worn, the papyrus pages wrinkled at my touch. Carefully, I placed it on a nearby table, admiring its weathered leather binding and intricate designs. It was old but didn't look dangerous.

"Famous last words," I mumbled as I grabbed a nearby lantern. *Eidolon's going to kill me if this thing ends up killing me.*

The book's front cover caught my attention in the dim light, with a single word inscribed on it: yidde'oni.

My breath caught. I had seen that word before in one of the books I found about John Dee and Edward Kelly and their strange obsession with alchemy.

Necromancer.

My heart fluttered with excitement and unease as I lifted the cover, releasing the delicate aroma of oak and sage. A sad tune whispered in the background, gradually crescendoing until it filled the space like a sorrowful funeral procession.

In my mind's eye, I saw a woman tending to her garden, humming a melody as she plucked flowers. Abruptly, a shadow fell over her, and she was nowhere to be found when it dissipated.

Weird.

My fingers ran over the rough, aged pages of the book, searching for any hint as to who it belonged to. Yet, to my disappointment, each page was as empty as the last. I closed the cover with a frown, my eyes lingering on the faded inscription etched into the leather.

Suddenly, wispy shadow tendrils emerged from the blank pages. They curled and swirled around my hand before enveloping me in their embrace.

The sensation was eerie and strangely comforting as they caressed my arms and settled on my shoulders like a weightless blanket. And then, without warning, they were gone. Disappointment ran through me as I thought back to Moll's lecture about the limits of the Writers. We could read any book, written at any time, by anyone.

But there was one exception.

We couldn't read another Writers book.

My eyes widened as I backed up a step. Why had another Writers book revealed itself to me? It was unheard of. It was against the rules—the biggest no-no of all time. I was determined to figure out who it belonged to.

I was still thinking about the bizarre turn of events when Eidolon clapped his hands next to my ear. "Are you even listening?" he asked as I shifted my gaze to him, startled.

Sitting up, I smiled apologetically. "I must have dozed off. It was a long night."

"Another nightmare?" His indigo eyes darkened as he scanned me from head to toe.

I nodded, tucking my feet underneath me and wrapping a throw around my shoulders. "Yup, same as always. Black book, a horrible man, and my untimely death."

I looked up at the Pandora painting over the fireplace and yawned. "One of these days, I will figure out what it all means. But today isn't looking too promising if I don't get some sleep soon."

"Are you sure you don't want to talk about it?" Eidolon asked, concern evident in his tone. "It might help."

"I know." Sighing in resignation, I unfolded my legs and got up to get more coffee. "I'm not ready yet."

As I walked towards the breakfast cart, I could feel his intense gaze on me, and I ignored it. Focusing instead on the smell of freshly baked rolls and homemade jams, I eagerly piled my plate with warm pastries. I grabbed a crisp apple before returning to my seat.

"This isn't something you can just ignore, Chloe," Eidolon insisted, reaching for the roll I handed him. "You'll have to talk to me about it sooner or later." His intense gaze locked onto mine, piercing me with a steely glare.

"I'm not ignoring it," I countered, eyeing the apple before taking a bite. "But right now, all I need is sleep. We can have our therapy session later." I giggled as I imagined myself lying on a plush couch while he sat in a chair, scribbling notes as he asked probing questions about my childhood.

"I promise to share all the deep-seated traumas that stem from my school crush laughing at me when I fell off the monkey bars."

"It's not funny, Chloe..." Eidolon started before being interrupted.

"I think I have made a breakthrough!" Max's voice echoed through the library as he emerged from behind a towering stack of books. Since Aelle's disappearance, he had secluded himself in the ancient history section, only emerging for meals every now and then.

The few times I checked on him, I caught him napping, his cheek pressed against the spot where Taliesin's book used to sit. And the last place we saw Aelle. I once made the mistake of suggesting he take a break and clean himself up, but his intense glare silenced me. Heatedly, he reminded me we don't abandon those we love when they need us the most.

He was right, but I couldn't shake off the worry that gnawed at me. His hazel eyes, once vibrant and full of life, were now dull and hollow, permanently cloaked in shadows. His jeans hung loosely on his frail body, accentuating his weight loss. And the flannel shirt he had been wearing for days only added to the appearance of neglect.

"What did you find?" Eidolon asked.

I sat up, pulling the throw tight around my shoulders in a futile attempt to keep warm. The Library of the Unread desperately needed a better heating system. I watched as my breath turned into small clouds before me, annoyed that no one else seemed bothered by the cold.

"I'm not sure yet." Max frowned, glancing over his glasses at us. "But did you know Eidolon isn't the only one who can raise the dead?"

"I don't raise the dead." Eidolon raised an eyebrow at the statement. "I guide souls to the afterlife. Big difference."

"Whatever." Max waved absentmindedly. "But did you know someone else had similar abilities? Well, kind of. This person could technically raise the dead. Like from the grave."

"Who?" I questioned, intrigued by the news.

"Before you get too excited, I could only find a brief description," Max cautioned, looking down at his book. He flipped through the pages before turning it around to face us. "But they refer to her as the Witch of Endor."

"Never heard of her," Eidolon said, getting up to look. I stood behind him, peering over his shoulder. It didn't appear like much at first—just a faded charcoal drawing—but when I looked closer, I couldn't hold back my surprise gasp.

Sitting before me was a sketch of a woman wearing a dark cloak and holding the same mysterious black book I had discovered earlier. Beneath her image were minuscule letters scrawled out: *yidde'oni*.

Was this the mysterious Writer?

Chapter 9- Chloe

Modern Day- City of the Unspoken

"Who have we never heard of?" Watson asked as he walked into the library, running his fingertips along the spines of the books lining the walls. He stopped mid-step and glanced at Isabelle and Victor, walking in behind him. "Looks like we've arrived at just the right moment," he joked with a mischievous glint in his eye. "I do love a good mystery."

"The Witch of Endor," I answered as jealousy reared its ugly head.

Isabelle and Watson were impeccably dressed as usual, while I wore an oversized sweatshirt that had seen better days.

Looking down, I cringed at the various spilled coffee and ink stains. I had thrown my hair into a messy bun, but half was escaping from the stretched-out hair tie. And despite my repeated attempts to clean them, my glasses were smudged with fingerprints and dust.

In contrast, Isabelle was stunning in her denim jeans and billowy beige sweater. Her intricately braided hair cascaded down her back like liquid gold.

As she walked, her favorite dangling earrings caught the light from the fire and jingled softly, accompanied by the gentle rustle of her bracelets. She completed her effortless charm with a loosely draped cashmere scarf over her shoulders, reminding me of a petite Scottish pixie.

Watson stood next to her. His tailored suit, skillfully cut from luxurious putter gray fabric, accentuated his muscular frame. The sharp lines highlighted his broad shoulders and a defined chest. His golden eyes gleamed in the glow of the room full of candles. The slight stubble on his jaw gave him a hint of ruggedness. As he moved, it was as if Zeus descended from Mount Olympus into our presence.

"Never heard of her. Is she important?" Watson's voice snapped me out of my daydream of throwing a can of paint at him just to see his reaction.

Max shrugged, scanning his rumpled clothes critically. "I can't say for certain. It was a vague reference about someone who can talk to the dead. I thought it might help us find Aelle."

The sorrow etched onto Max's features was a dagger to the heart. Isabelle approached and wrapped an arm around his shoulders.

"Don't worry. We'll find her, luv," she reassured him. "We would never abandon one of our own."

Max's muscles, tense from the stress of the week's events, loosened as Isabelle enfolded her comforting aura around him, his body relaxing into her gentle embrace. He sighed heavily, removing his glasses and wiping them with the hem of his *Harry Potter* t-shirt.

"I know," Max whispered before sliding his glasses back on and clearing his throat. He grabbed a book from the shelf behind him.

"She might be important," he said, flipping through the musty pages and tapping a finger against a passage marked with a scrap of yellowed paper. "There's been a lot of people who have claimed they could talk to the dead, but only one has proved it. *Historically* speaking."

Watson handed Isabelle a cup of coffee and settled onto the edge of her armchair, his long legs crossed and one arm resting behind her.

"Thank you, luv." Isabelle patted his leg before taking a drink.

He leaned in and kissed her forehead. "Anything for you." Turning his attention back to Max, he asked, "What do you mean by 'prove it'? We've all seen Eidolon talking to the dead."

"Not the same," Victor muttered, and I glanced at our quiet friend.

As usual, he stood in the background, watching rather than joining in. Stepping out of a bookshelf's shadows, Victor headed to the coffee cart. Pouring himself a cup, he said over his shoulder, "Eidolon can only *talk* to those in the Otherworld or who are already dead. But he can't bring them back to life."

"That's what makes her so fascinating." Max's eyes lit up as he skimmed the book, tracing his finger along the witch's image. "Of course, there are only a few references to her, and they are vague passages."

"Who was she?" A memory of my first encounter with Taliesin resurfaced. Over tea, he mentioned I was a descendant of his twin sister, Morrigan, who was herself an offspring of the Witch of Endor.

Finally, I was getting some answers.

"I think I can shed some light on the mystery," Isabelle chimed in. "Some vague mentions of her are recorded in my family's grimoire. But full disclosure, luvs, I don't know all the particulars. It's more like a bedtime story about what *not* to do than anything else."

"Really? In your family's grimoire?" Max pulled a pen and notepad from his jean's back pocket. "What does it say?"

"Not much." Isabelle shrugged. "I remember my mother warning me to never end up like her." Isabelle reminisced, deep in thought, her eyebrows knitted together. "Funny, I don't recall anyone mentioning her name. She was mysterious and alluring and shrouded in secrets." Isabelle's tone lowered to a whisper as her eyes darted around the room. "She was the first necromancer and an immortal if the stories are to be believed."

"It doesn't explain why she's a cautionary tale," Victor said, looking puzzled as he played with his mug's handle.

I understood his confusion. We met plenty of immortals in the last few months, and Eidolon could talk to the dead. Hell, even Victor could heal himself, so he was as close to an immortal as anyone. So why was the Witch of Endor so dangerous?

"Because, as witches, we were taught at a young age about the delicate line between using our powers to manipulate emotions or slowing down our aging. We were also taught about dabbling in dark magick. When you attempt to bring somebody back from the other side, you risk tearing apart the fabric of reality. Which was exactly what she did, and her *activities* had severe consequences for the rest of us."

"What consequences?" I asked, glancing at her in surprise.

"After she did what she did," Isabelle explained, toying with her bracelets. "Rumors spread that all witches were capable of necromancy. The fear surrounding our powers grew, and my ancestors were hunted down. Someone came up with the insane idea that the only way to rid the world of us was through fire. They claimed that reducing us to ashes would prevent any possibility of resurrection," she concluded in a contemptuous tone.

An uncomfortable quiet settled in the room. Everyone was unsure how to react to Isabelle's confession. I had always wondered why witches were burned at the stake, but realizing it was a deliberate and thought-out punishment made it so much worse.

Being burned alive was a heinous and torturous method of execution, designed to inflict the maximum amount of pain possible. And the history books were filled with accounts of sadistic onlookers reveling in victims' agony as they were engulfed in flames.

Watson leapt from his seat, pacing back and forth. He rubbed his hands over his face with such force that I could see red marks forming on his skin. His neck muscles twitched as he reached over, grabbed Isabelle's mug, and stalked to the coffee cart. We could all hear him growling, uttering curses about delusional men and women who couldn't keep their mouths shut.

Isabelle glanced at me, surprised by his reaction. I shrugged in response, just as confused.

Watson rarely lost his cool.

But he had been alive for a very long time, so perhaps the conversation brought up some painful memories. And from how he slammed the items down the cart, he clearly wasn't in the mood to discuss it.

Max eyed Watson wearily before spinning in his seat to ask, "Did the grimoire say anything else?"

"Not really." Isabelle shrugged, her eyes darting back to her husband in concern. "Other than she lived in Endor in the Jezreel Valley. My mother said she was a healer before switching to dark magick."

"What made her switch sides?" Eidolon asked, getting up to throw another log on the fire.

"From what I understand, some illness. Her mother was one of the victims."

"Makes sense. If something happened to my mother, I would do the same thing if there was a chance to save her," Max commented as he wrote something in his notebook.

I nodded in agreement.

"*Really*? Would you?" Victor asked, eyeing me. "Would you do *anything* to save a loved one? Talk about the pot calling the kettle black."

Chapter 10- Chloe

Modern Day- City of the Unspoken

No one said a word. We all knew what Victor meant. Taliesin spent his life trying to bring back his sister from the dead. And we judged him for how he went about it. But because it was the Witch of Endor's mother, we were willing to overlook her use of black magick.

We were hypocrites.

Eidolon reached over and squeezed my hand. "It's different," he whispered.

"No, it's not," I said drily, getting up and standing in front of the fireplace to warm my hands. I was so cold that my fingers were beginning to turn blue. "Let's say the Witch of Endor's story is true. How does this help us find the next Book of the Veiled?"

"It doesn't," Watson mumbled, his back turned to us.

Victor's brows furrowed in a deep frown as he rolled his eyes in annoyance. He reached over and snatched the book sitting at Max's side. His gaze lingered on the picture of the Witch of Endor, studying every detail. After a moment of contemplation, he said, "Unless..." as a glimmer of realization sparked.

"Unless what?" I asked, turning as I pulled my sweatshirt hood over my head.

The room temperature plummeted, sending a shiver down my spine and chilling my cheeks. Goosebumps rose on my arms, and I rubbed them to get warm. It was like being trapped in a freezer with no escape from the numbing cold. I looked around, but no one else seemed affected by the drastic change, and it was starting to annoy me.

Victor looked up. "Unless she was the one who saved Morrigan and not the Fates as we thought. Maybe she knows where Morrigan's book is if she's still alive."

"How on earth do you propose we find her?" Watson asked. His anger was palpable as he strode back towards the group, his golden eyes blazing with fiery intensity. "No one has seen her for years. If she went into hiding, she did a damn good job." He shrugged off his jacket and tossed it onto a nearby chair. His tense muscles bulged beneath his shirt as he cracked his neck. "I'm sure we aren't the only ones who have tried to find her."

"I might have found something," I said, wincing as Watson's bright eyes flew to me.

"What did you find?" Watson demanded, his voice barely above a whisper as he stalked towards me, looking like the predator I knew he could be.

Isabelle turned in her seat, eyeing him. She stood up, circling to his side and reaching for his forearm. A faint shimmer emanated from her fingers as a warm glow wrapped around him.

Watson's eyes narrowed, caught off guard by his wife's touch before he took a deep breath. Slowly, he uncoiled his fist, and the tightness melted away. He wrapped his arms around Isabelle in a tender embrace, asking for forgiveness for his outburst. His tone was strained as he blamed it on the anxiety of discussing the witch hunts.

Isabelle pulled back, holding his face between her fingers and forcing him to look at her. "Never apologize for feeling the way you do."

Watson nodded, his golden hair falling into his face. Isabelle reached up and pushed it back, kissing his forehead.

Isabelle turned to me. "Now, luv. What were you saying?

I rubbed my palms together to ease my nerves and swallowed. My mouth went dry, and I couldn't gather the courage to admit the truth to the group. The book was mine; I discovered it first. They would take it from me if they knew it belonged to another Writer. I ran a hand over my face in frustration, knowing I would have to tell them. But not wanting to.

"I think I found the Witch of Endor's book." I shrugged half-heartedly, trying to downplay my hesitation. "Actually, it found me."

"You're just now telling us?" Max's eyes darted around the room. "Where is it?"

"Upstairs. I can go get it," I said, not meeting anyone's stare. Before I could change my mind, I headed out of the library. Eidolon followed.

We ascended the winding stairs to our room, and Eidolon's hurt was evident in his voice. "Why didn't you tell me? We promised no more secrets."

I winced at the accusation. Eidolon was right. We had made a promise. After telling him I knew Taliesin was his father, I meant to keep my side of the bargain.

But this was different. I wasn't keeping a secret—I just hadn't mentioned it—and I *was* going to tell him.

Just not yet.

"I thought it was just another book," I lied. "It wasn't until Max said something about the Witch of Endor that I put two and two together."

I paused at the top of the stairs to catch my breath, holding on to the doorframe. Wiping the sweat from my forehead, I reminded myself to renew my gym membership once we returned to the real world.

"Seems suspicious." Eidolon's eyes narrowed as I turned to face him. Despite him being two steps below me, we were eye to eye.

I shrugged, trying to keep my face blank. "Maybe. But stranger things have happened," I countered before walking down the hallway. "Personally, I'm grateful. This entire ordeal has been riddled with complications. I welcome any assistance we can get."

When we first arrived in the Otherworld, I thought everything would be simple. Come in, find Freyja, and prove to her we were worthy enough to be taken to the Fates. Convince the Fates to tell us where the missing Book of the Veiled was, grab them, and fix the portal to the Otherworld.

Easy Peasy.

But nothing had gone to plan so far.

Aelle died, Lillith and Vivian left, Freyja and Odin returned to Valhalla. And only the gods knew where Sydney and Bree wandered off.

To make matters worse, Moll had holed herself up in her room and hadn't come out in days. Every time I stopped by and knocked on the door, all she said was she was working and couldn't be distracted.

So, with a lack of direction, yes, I was willing to jump on the first clue we found.

Which just so happened to be finding a missing necromancer.

What could go wrong?

Chapter 11- Nava

1000 BC- Village of Endor, Jezreel Valley, Israel

Nava and Ysabel dashed through their home, stuffing clothes and supplies into bags. The sound of guards yelling could be heard in the distance, and they held their breath. The echoes of another family's torment served as a harsh reminder of the cruelty surrounding them.

Gods save them.

With trembling hands, they gently packed away the few cherished belongings that somehow managed to evade detection by the guards. Time was running out as they hurried to finish their preparations before leaving with the last group of families.

Exhausted, they looked around their home and nodded at each other. They had one final task to do.

It was time to say goodbye to their mother.

The decision was by far the hardest they had ever made. But staying behind was a sure way of guaranteeing their death.

"What are we going to say to her?" Ysabel's eyes darted as they snuck out the back door, using the tall garden walls to hide from the watchful eyes of the king's men.

Nava silenced her sister with a finger to her lips, gesturing towards the guard who stopped to peer over the fence. They froze, holding their breath as his sharp eyes skimmed over them, hidden in the shadows. Nava breathed a silent sigh of relief when he resumed his patrol, motioning for Ysabel to follow her.

If they were captured now, there would be no saving them.

Their feet pounded against the soft earth, sending dust clouds in their wake. The dense eucalyptus grove blurred by as they ran, their black cloaks fluttering in the wind as they navigated around fallen logs and branches.

Finally, they burst into a small clearing and collapsed against the cool rocks of a cave entrance. They panted for breath as they regained their bearings.

"I don't know if I can do this again," Ysabel slumped to the ground, drawing her knees to her chest. "The funeral was difficult enough."

"We have to tell her." Nava grabbed Ysabel by the arm and helped her up. "She'll worry otherwise."

"She's dead, Nava. How will she know if we came or not?" Ysabel complained as she dusted off her dress, frowning at a snag in her cloak.

"She'll know." Nava's stomach knotted, nervous about what they were about to do. But she had no choice.

Ysabel needed to know the truth.

With an exasperated sigh, Ysabel relented. "Alright, you can go first." She gestured towards the cave's dark opening, lit up by the vibrant light of the autumn harvest moon.

Nava strode through the winding corridors with her sister close on her heels. Ysabel had lived in Endor her entire life, but Nava had never shown her the cave where she had moved their mother's body. She didn't want to burden her sister with the knowledge, aware of the potential danger it could bring. Her thoughts drifted back to the last time she visited as they walked further into the belly of the mountain.

The sad day she and her father released her mother's body into the hands of the Fates.

It was the last thing Nava and her father did together. He had been one of the many voicing their outcry at the guard's mistreatment of those with magickal abilities, and he had been taken away along with the others.

His screams were the last to fade.

The sisters never got his body back for burial. All they were told was he confessed to committing crimes against the king and was put to death with others labeled as traitors.

Gods, she hated kings.

Ysabel tiptoed behind her sister, their descent down the dark, narrow path slow and cautious. The heavy silence of their journey engulfed them, broken only by the faint sound of trickling water and the occasional icy gust of wind that made them shiver. The earthy scent of damp soil and decaying leaves permeated the air, adding to the eerie atmosphere.

"Are we almost there?" Ysabel's voice echoed off the ancient walls, creating an eerie echo in the dim corridor.

"Yes." Leading her sister around the last bend, Nava stepped to the side to give her a better look.

Ysabel's mouth dropped as she saw the massive tear-drop-shaped lake glistening under the dim light, its surface smooth and still like glass. Its color was a stunning ice azure, like a shard of frozen sky amidst the dark, rocky surroundings. The river leading to it sparkled with hints of silver and gold, like a trail of shimmering stars ushering in a hidden gem.

The walls were adorned with glowing runes, each one radiating a different hue and throbbing in unison like a harmonious orchestra.

Their colors were vivid and captivating, ranging from a blazing orange to a vibrant blue, a pulsing purple, and a brilliant white that ebbed and flowed like a beating heart.

Ysabel inhaled deeply, taking in the crisp scent of fresh water. The earthy aroma of damp rock and moss tickled her nose as she stepped through the narrow passageway. She couldn't help but sniff again, convinced there was a subtle hint of a musty odor that held secrets within the lake's depths.

An immense oak tree sat in the middle of a pool, surrounded by eight small gates made of pure white bones. Its massive roots crawled in and out of the water, becoming entangled in each other and reaching their limbs deep into the cave's core. The branches glittered and shined as they grew to the top of the cavern, mingling with the bedrock until you couldn't tell rock from limb.

"What is this place?" Ysabel whispered, looking around curiously. "Is this where you brought mother?"

"Yes," Nava answered quietly, not wanting to disturb the spirits. "This is the final resting place for those deemed worthy enough by the gods and the Fates."

"Was our mother God-touched?" Ysabel's eyes widened in awe as she looked at her sister. "Why didn't she tell us?"

Nava's eyes fell to the ground as she scuffed a small pebble with her foot and shrugged her shoulders. Her mother was known for keeping secrets from her daughters.

Like the fact that Nava was a necromancer.

Chapter 12- Nava

1000 BC- Village of Endor, Jezreel Valley, Israel

Nava pushed away the memories and grabbed Ysabel's sleeve, leading her along the dusty trail.

"We have to hurry if we want to make it back on time," she urged.

Nava's father had chosen a secluded corner of the lake to lay her mother to rest. It was a serene location; the only sound was the soft lapping of water against the shore, breaking the otherwise tranquil silence. Nestled within a small inner cave was a natural resting place, its entrance offering a view of the outside world.

From here, Nava's mother could still admire the beauty of the starry night sky, as she had always done. It was a fitting homage to a woman who held nature and all its marvels dear to her heart.

"Hello, mother," Nava whispered as they approached the tomb. As she touched the stones, she could feel the years of history and memories etched into their surface.

The rough edges had been smoothed over time but still maintained a sense of stability. As her fingers traced the contours, warmth spread through her body, filling her with a connection to her mother's soul.

Her mother was here, chosen to guard the eight gates encircling the Tree of Life. She was joined by seven others who maintained vigil over the passage of souls between the mortal realm and the Otherworld.

A figure appeared atop the grave, appearing from thin air. Ysabel's mouth fell open in a silent gasp, her eyes widening with disbelief at the intangible presence before them. Nava felt a tightness grow in her chest, a pang of grief and empathy for her sister, who was now confronted with the unsettling reality of their mother's transformation.

It wasn't a pleasant sight.

The deceased were ethereal, without a physical form. Their features were not easily discernible when they manifested, as their ghostly figures wavered and shifted, struggling to maintain their existence in the mortal world.

But it was their eyes that were the most disturbing. Their eyes were like a dark abyss, but with sudden flickers of electricity darting around. They never seemed to fix their gaze on one spot, constantly scanning the surroundings with an otherworldly awareness, overseeing the flow of souls through the gates.

The world is changing.

The sisters jumped when their mother's raspy voice spoke, seemingly coming from nowhere and everywhere.

Her eyes shifted around the cave. *They are approaching, bringing shadows in words. The Tree of Life will wither and die. In the end, nothing survives.*

Nava and Ysabel exchanged worried looks, knowing their mother's attention was divided between them and the ornate engravings on the gates surrounding the Tree of Life.

"Mother," Nava called out softly, squaring her shoulders. "We came to say goodbye."

You will return, their mother growled, eyes blazing with ancient knowledge. *But be warned - Death will not release you until you retrieve the lost stories and bring them home."*

Nava's gaze snapped up to meet her mother's, a surge of fear gripping her. But her prophecy wasn't over.

You and your sister will travel far—far beyond the world's radius. You must find the last. Locate them before the fire swells, and all is lost.

"I don't understand," Nava whispered, pulling her sister closer. "Find who? What fire?"

Find the last one! Or it will be the beginning of the end.

Ysabel's eyes widened in shock, a wild expression of disbelief etched on her features. "What does that even mean?" she asked in a hushed voice.

Before Nava could reply, their mother loomed over them, her presence growing larger and filling the small space. Nava instinctively stepped back as their mother's body flickered in and out of focus. Despite her struggle to maintain a grip on reality, their mother refused to break eye contact with her daughters.

For a fleeting moment, they saw their mother as she used to be. Her hand reached out desperately to touch them, but it flashed in and out of existence like a dying flame. Her face contorted into a deep frown, her voice trembling with finality.

The Fates chose wrong. You must find the one that walks in the shadows. Their blood will save us all.

With a gentle whisper, their mother's form dissipated into a swirling mist, dancing around them before vanishing.

The sisters stood stunned as the cave enveloped again in haunting darkness, with only the moon's pale glow to light their way out. The once pleasant aroma of life now carried a heavy weight of grief and loss, almost as if nature were grieving.

It was time to leave.

"That was our mother?" Ysabel asked, her eyes brimming with tears, staring at the tomb.

Nava shook her head and pulled up the hood of her cloak, seeking protection from the bitter cold that penetrated her bones. "Of course it was," she replied grimly. "Just a different version."

Ysabel nodded. With a determined stride, they turned and walked around the lake, their eyes never leaving the towering gates encircling the Tree of Life. Moonlight streamed through an opening in the cave ceiling, creating a pattern of shifting light and shadow on the ground beneath their feet. They were mesmerized by the brilliant spheres of red and orange that twirled and twisted in an endless cycle, appearing and vanishing like a revolving door.

There was a shift in the air as they approached the mouth of the dark passage as an archaic force summoned them forward. And then suddenly, an ancient oak table stood before them, its surface smoothed by centuries of use.

Sitting atop were two books: a small one cloaked in black leather, its spine secured by a slim leather string and adorned with a raven-shaped clasp gleaming mischievously in the dimness. The other was larger and more weathered, its pages yellowed and frayed at the edges. An intricate tree design was etched into the cover, its roots spreading like veins across the spine. The faint aroma of old parchment and ink clung to the air, adding to the mystery of the unexpected encounter.

They stepped towards the table, eyeing the books with interest. The small black one was embedded with blood-red letters that spelled out ' '□□□□□□and the other in gold that said ' '.□□□□□The two sisters glanced at each other in awe, reaching out to their perspective books, knowing which one belonged to whom.

"Prophet," Nava said while Ysabel whispered, "Witch."

Ahead of them, the winding path was lit up by the moon's silvery light. Neither wanted to leave, as they knew this next journey meant a permanent and irrevocable change in their lives that neither was ready to face.

But they had no other option. Life went on regardless, and they had to move forward.

"Are you ready?" Nava asked, squaring her shoulders and taking a deep breath. "We have a king waiting for us."

Chapter 13- Agnes

December 1589- Nether Keith, Scotland

A year later, a royal courier arrived at Agnes's door, his face strained and weary from his travels. He bore a rolled parchment sealed with a familiar emblem.

The kings.

Agnes' gaze was fixed on the golden wax, depicting a lion sitting proudly in the center of a shield supported by two chained unicorns. The inscription around the edge read: *Salvum fac populum tuum domine—* 'Lord, save your people.'

She unfolded the note with trembling hands, glancing up at the messenger who stood before her, his face twisted in a sneer.

The message was clear.

The king demanded her presence at Edinburgh Castle. If she failed to comply, he would send his guards to bring her in forcibly.

Castle my ass. More like a house of horrors, she thought as she paced back and forth after the courier left, the rain pelting against her face and bruising her skin.

It was her turn to answer for her crimes.

Geillis had been taken to Edinburgh months ago. Agnes watched grimly, her eyes following the cart as it rumbled down the muddy path toward the capital. Her friend sat upright and defiant, her face marked with bruises but a small smile playing on her lips despite the dire circumstances.

Be strong, my sister, Agnes whispered as her friend passed by. Geillis shifted her gaze to where she was standing, hidden from view. She gave a subtle nod before turning back towards the road leading to Edinburgh, sitting tall with her head held high.

When the cart faded into the distance, Agnes trudged homeward. Her footsteps were heavy with the burden of Geillis' short-lived life.

Her mind drifted back to the whispered rumors of what happened in the dungeon. Treatment so horrendous that even hardened criminals quivered in fear.

And the tales always grew more graphic as the years passed, as the guards devised new and improved ways to inflict pain. Cruelty so wicked and depraved it could break a soul in minutes. The mere whisper of the executioner's name struck terror into the hearts of those within its walls.

The intricate network of vaulted cellars acted as a prison for those accused of practicing witchcraft and associating with the devil. Unfortunately, many of those individuals were innocent, serving their communities as midwives and healers or daring to speak out against the church's strict ideologies.

Nothing Agnes considered a crime. But the king did. And that was all that mattered.

Only a handful returned home, and even then, their bodies and minds were never the same. They never recovered from their imprisonment.

And they were always cold. Their bodies were plagued by an unrelenting chill, which seeped into their core and turned their once warm souls into unyielding blocks of ice.

Agnes's mind raced as she paced back and forth along the narrow cliff's boundary. Her stomach twisted into tight knots, a physical manifestation of the turmoil inside. She tried to shake off her thoughts, but they clung like a heavy cloak, weighing her down with each step. She had never felt so exposed and vulnerable, standing at a crossroads that would determine her fate.

She was no fool. Agnes knew Geillis would break under the relentless pressure. It had been over a year since her initial questioning, and she'd remained steadfast in her declaration of innocence. But when faced with continuous torture, unquenchable thirst, and gnawing hunger, anyone would do whatever it took to find relief.

Even if it meant betraying their friends and condemning them to death.

The king was infamous for his strict and tyrannical reign. Every wrinkle on his face was a testament to his sacrifices to secure his power. His past was marked by tragedy. His mother forced to give up her sovereignty and executed by a rival queen. He endured a brutal education from a selfish tutor and faced political plots from men hungry for control of the kingdom.

Now he sat on the throne, burdened by the weight of his crown. Paranoid everyone around him was a potential danger.

And he considered Agnes' enemy number one.

As soon as the guard was out of sight, Agnes rushed to the back corner of her home and pried open a hidden trap door. Her family's grimoire lay hidden beneath, the ancient parchment crackling with power and secrets. Ever since the witch hunts began, she had been too scared to even look at it lest someone discover her true nature.

But now, faced with dire circumstances, she had no choice but to turn to the forbidden knowledge within its pages. Agnes brushed her fingers over the worn leather cover, taking a deep breath before gently lifting it from its hiding spot. As she opened it, the air hummed with magick emanating from the ancient spells and incantations collected by generations of women in her family line.

Kneeling on the dusty stone floor, she examined the archaic text symbols. The intricate carvings moved and weathered like a nest of angry snakes. They buzzed and grew louder until the sound filled her mind with a constant hum, making it impossible to understand what was in front of her.

The book never made anything easy. It was the way magick worked. The user had to embrace the positive and negative aspects, understand the consequences, and be willing to sacrifice to uncover the truth.

Agnes inhaled deeply, bracing herself for what needed to be done. Her hands shook as she carefully set the antique tome down on the table, its creaky wooden legs barely able to bear its weight. Drawing a small blade from her satchel, Agnes pricked her finger and let a few droplets of blood fall onto the book's surface as an offering. Placing both hands on its cover, she waited for the grimoire to accept her sacrifice.

A dull throbbing developed in her head, accompanied by an icy cold tremor, electrifying her entire body. The pain intensified, making it harder for her to stay focused on her mission and leaving a dry and bitter taste in her mouth.

As the minutes dragged on at an agonizingly slow pace, the only noise in the room was the crackling fire slowly dying in the hearth. Nothing happened. Disappointment and frustration gnawed at Agnes as she anxiously waited for something, anything, to happen. Her hope began to diminish like the fading embers of the fire.

Just as she was about to give up, a sudden wind gust caught her off guard. The once-still tome cover flew open.

In disbelief, she watched as the ink on the page writhed and swelled, taking shape until two women emerged from its depths like ethereal beings coming to life. Their forms were delicate and fluid, their movements graceful and otherworldly.

Agnes' heart raced as she studied the two imposing figures before her.

The taller of the two exuded an air of authority, her fierce demeanor indicating she was not to be trifled with. Long, reddish-brown hair pulled tightly into a thick braid running down to her waist like a whip, emphasizing her sharp features and piercing eyes glistening like polished steel.

It was her, the immortal necromancer with power over death.

Who was she exactly? Agnes didn't know. Even her mother didn't know her name.

She simply called her the Witch of Endor.

She leaned in, holding her breath as she examined the picture details. They stood on a tiny island in the center of a shimmering, tear-shaped lake. The walls around them breathed and shifted with vibrant colors, giving off an otherworldly aura.

A massive oak towered behind them, its gnarled branches reaching toward the sky. Surrounding the tree were eight gates, individually fashioned from bleached cracked bones, eroded by time, and intricately carved with ancient symbols and patterns.

The sisters stood side-by-side, each clutching a thick tome. Their eyes fixed on Agnes as if they expected an explanation for why she'd disturbed their slumber.

"I need your help," Agnes whispered to the book.

The oldest nodded once, glancing at the tree. Her weathered face reflected years of wisdom and experience. The scene shifted to them standing on a cliffside, towering over the tumultuous sea below. Waves crashed against jagged rocks, sending plumes of salty mist toward an unlit cave. The elder gestured towards the entrance, and Agnes' heart leaped.

The grimoire was showing her the way.

Chapter 14- Agnes

December 1589- Nether Keith, Scotland

Under the cover of night, Agnes scaled the treacherous cliff overlooking the raging ocean. With wild abandon, she chanted ancient spells and offered sacrifices of all she held precious— potions, books, and even her blood. The howling winds carried her cries of devotion as she gave herself entirely to the dark forces at play.

Every attempt failed.

She couldn't do anything without their names.

Agnes let out an ear-piercing scream, her chest heaving with the weight of her failure as she stood amidst a raging tempest. In a moment of uncontrollable rage, she seized the heavy grimoire and ripped its pages apart, the sound of tearing paper drowned out by the furious winds. A wave of regret washed over her as the pages scattered into the frenzied gusts, ripping away pieces of her soul with each passing fragment.

She'd destroyed what her family had spent generations safeguarding.

The ultimate sacrifice.

Tears streamed down her face as she watched the pages floating back, swirling around her in a vortex. Mesmerized, she observed as the papers glowed with a bright light, revealing a neglected path leading into darkness.

With each determined step she took down the rocky ridge, she trekked further away from the familiar and into the mysterious unknown. Her long hair whipped violently against her face as the winds howled through the thick sea grass, stirring up sand that stung her legs.

As she approached the cave's mouth, she could feel the electricity in the air, crackling and pulsing like a living thing. It was thrilling and terrifying, and she knew deep down that this was where she needed to be.

We have been waiting for you, a voice rang out, beckoning her in as she walked through the cave entrance. Agnes shielded her eyes from the sudden burst of brilliant glare, her heart racing with anticipation and trepidation.

Gradually, she lowered her hands and took in her surroundings. The room was aglow with warm, golden light, casting soft shadows on the walls and foundation. The air was heavy with incense and something else she couldn't identify. She felt hidden eyes watching and waiting for her.

Slowly moving further in, a thick canopy of leaves created a pattern of light and shadows on the forest floor. In the center was a majestic oak tree, its bark worn down like ancient stone monuments. The tree was surrounded by a stagnant pool of water lying in gray rings around its base. Its gnarled roots twisted above the surface, clutching at the air like ghostly fingers.

Eight shabby gates encircled the tree, leaning toward it as if they were weary and frayed from years of standing guard. They were crafted from the same cracked bones she'd seen in the grimoire, contorted and stained with age. Tarnished gold accents adorned them, their intricate designs marred by rust and dirt. Sturdy vines snaked their way up the brittle frames, gripping unwaveringly as they held everything together.

Two doors had been pried open, their hinges broken and splintered by the relentless force of the roots pushing through. The scene was like a haunting folktale come to life, both mesmerizing and eerie, and she shivered.

Small, dull lights fluttered around the gates like a chorus of moths calling to one another in the blackness, whispering in Agnes' ears. They appeared and disappeared as they passed through patches of darkness, all trying to travel to the other side. But each time they got close, something pushed them back.

"What is this place?" Agnes whispered as she tried to breathe against the overwhelming odor of decay and death.

It is what is to come.

Agnes' skin crawled as a thin, hollow voice called out from the darkness. The hairs on her arms stood up as the sound echoed through the emptiness. She spun, searching for the source of the mysterious voice, but nothing appeared except a dark and foreboding void.

Her heart raced as a sudden burst of wind caught her off guard. She couldn't shake the feeling that someone was lurking behind her, but when she turned to check, she found no one.

Suppressing the overwhelming urge to flee, a surge of resolve coursed through her veins. She straightened her posture and squared her shoulders, preparing to confront whatever lay ahead.

"I'm looking for the sisters," Agnes' voice wavered as she called into the nothingness. "Do you know how to find them?"

You won't find them. They will find you.

"What does that mean?" Agnes asked, her voice echoing in the silent cave. The only reply was the rustling of dead leaves cascading from the ancient oak branches. "I need to find them."

Why

Agnes shifted uncomfortably, feeling foolish as she turned to see who was speaking to her. "Because I will die if I don't."

And what do you want the sisters to do?

"I have been accused of a crime I did not commit. Well, at least not intentionally." She held her head high in defiance, daring the voice to argue with her.

What are you accused of doing? The voice asked, now interested.

"Witchcraft," Agnes admitted, growling the word. "And consorting with the devil."

Who is the devil?

Agnes paused, narrowing her gaze, and nibbled on her bottom lip. She had never bothered to inquire about the devil's identity. He only existed as a vague presence in her mind, an evil existence that stole the souls of the pure. A 'thing' religious leaders used against their congregations.

He was as nameless and elusive as the Witch of Endor, which made her wonder again. Could someone or something exist without a name?

"I don't know," Agnes answered honestly. I doubt anyone has actually seen him—at least not anyone I know."

And the king says you are guilty of consorting with an imaginary being? The voice asked, confused.

"Yes."

Interesting, it replied with a chuckle. After a pause, it finally announced, We will help.

Its branches slowly rose in defiance as a gust of wind swept by, whipping up a flurry of dead leaves that swirled around the trunk.

Agnes whispered her thanks, filled with hope for the first time since her nightmare began.

She would live.

No, the voice cautioned. We cannot change your destiny. You will die, but we will help you.

"Help? With what?" she sneered. "All-powerful beings, and all you can do is stand by and let me die?" Agnes cried out, frustrated by the turn of events.

We can only promise what is in our power. But your death will spark a new beginning.

"What do you mean 'a new beginning?'"

You'll see.

Chapter 15- Chloe

Modern Day- City of the Unspoken

As we entered the bedroom, my eyes immediately locked on the enormous wooden desk in the corner. It was a sturdy masterpiece, with elaborate carvings and deep drawers that held all my secrets and treasures. Nestled among my other 'To Be Reads' sat the mysterious book that had captivated me for days, concealed from view.

"Well?" Eidolon asked. I froze, not wanting to show him the book's hiding place. If Eidolon had looked closely at the desk at any point, he would've seen it lying next to a yellow pad of legal paper I had brought from home, doodled with hundreds of 'E + C = Love.'

Quite embarrassing for a middle-aged woman. But I had hours to kill when everyone else was sleeping.

"Well, what?" I asked, glancing at him side-eyed.

He huffed, rolling his eyes at me and gesturing into the room. "Are you going to get the book? Or is it magickally going to appear?"

"You don't have to be rude about it," I sneered and slowly approached the desk, glancing at Eidolon once.

He waved me on with an arched eyebrow, and it took everything in my power not to flip him off.

Carefully, I pulled it out of the middle of the pile and set it down, tracing the intricate design etched into its worn leather. A wave of warmth and familiarity filled me with comfort and acceptance. As I unclasped the raven pendant, shadows erupted from its pages and wrapped around my arms in a gentle embrace.

I couldn't hide the smile that spread across my face as they danced and twirled about my fingers. It was like we were old friends reunited at last.

"Hello, friend," I whispered. "I have someone I want you to meet."

I turned to show Eidolon, needing him to recognize how important it was to me. Even though I couldn't see what was written inside, the book had become as integral to me as a limb.

Somehow, it understood me, and when I held it, all my fears and insecurities dissipated.

But when I held it out for Eidolon, it was apparent he didn't share the same warm and fuzzy feeling. As soon as he looked at it, he visibly flinched and stepped back with alarm in his widened eyes. His tattoos, usually still, writhed like snakes up his arms and neck.

When I looked into his eyes, slivers of silver danced within the deep pools of indigo, a clear sign of his unease.

"Put it down, Chloe," he ordered, pointing to the king-size bed. "I don't know what it is, but I can tell you right now that it's not safe."

"It's a book, Eidolon." Narrowing my eyes at him, I stepped forward. Disappointment flared when he stepped back, sneering. "It can't harm you. The worst that could happen is a paper cut."

Our eyes locked in a fierce battle of wills, frustration bubbling like lava between us. The air thickened with tension as we stood at a standstill, each waiting for the other to make the first move.

"Eidolon! Tell me if you're scared, and I'll figure it out myself," I demanded, trying to keep the irritation out of my voice.

Truthfully, I didn't want to give up the book, and if he was going to be strange about it, that was fine by me.

"Who's being rude now?" he grumbled, running his fingers through his hair and moving closer. "I want it noted that I think this is a terrible idea," he scowled at me.

"Duly noted."

Instantly, I knew taunting him was the wrong idea. As soon as he touched the cover, the book came alive. The shadows I found bewitching were not interested in someone else handling them. They drew in size and darkness, crawling up his arms and blocking out his tattoos until they wrapped around his head. Eidolon's eyes widen with dread before hazing over. More and more shadows crept out of the pages, stretching their slim silhouette as they weaved about his body.

Beautiful! I stood in awe as the shadows consumed him. Vibrant yellows and oranges flashed from the depths of the book. They grew bigger and brighter until they encased us both in a captivating prison of light and dark.

"Eidolon?" I whispered, not wanting to break the spell.

Eidolon's head snapped back, his eyes glowing like otherworldly flames. He let out a guttural growl, and the darkness surrounding him grew more intense, their movements more frantic.

He stepped forward, towering over me. His taut body coiled with tension. The corners of his mouth drew down in a tight smile, and his coal-black pupils glowed like obsidian stones.

The tree is dying. The gates crumble. Take the book back before it's too late. His voice sounded like thunder rolling in the night, echoing through the room with a strength that weakened my knees. *When the last leaf falls, the bridge will collapse. With nowhere to go, they will all be lost.*

I stumbled backward as thick shadow ribbons pulsed around us, growing darker and more intense. But Eidolon followed, grabbing my arm.

The shadows will show you the way home, Chloe.

That doesn't sound promising, I grimaced, stepping back to get my bearings. "I don't understand. What do you mean by 'show me the way home?'" I whispered as Eidolon fought to stay standing, his labored and ragged movements desperately attempting to hold the encroaching shadows at bay. I struggled to breathe as tears filled my eyes and my glasses fogged.

But I welcomed the feeling. Standing still, I waited for an answer, desperate to keep talking to whatever the shadows were. They promised to take me home, and I was ready. I didn't know where 'home' was, but I wanted to go with them.

Without answering, the darkness ebbed away like a fog and retreated into the book.

Disappointment flooded me when they disappeared, as I gasped for air and my knees hit the floor with a thud.

"What...what was that?" I asked, rolling back to sit on my ass, glancing at the book still in my hands. The damn thing looked utterly ordinary now, and I wanted to cry. I didn't get the answers I needed.

Rude!

"I don't know, but that was intense," Eidolon stated dryly, rubbing his hands over his eyes and rolling his shoulders.

I was unsure of many things, but one thing was clear: we had made a mistake.

Eidolon extended his arm to help me off the floor. I grasped his hand and let him pull me up, groaning as my stiff joints protested the movement. I was getting too old to sit on the ground. I brushed the dirt off my ass before sitting on the edge of the bed.

"Eidolon?"

"What?" he asked cautiously, eyeing me.

"What if four books are missing from the Book of the Veiled and not three?" I asked, nibbling at my lower lip and playing with the loose strings on my sweatshirt cuffs.

Chapter 16- Chloe

Modern Day- City of the Unspoken

Eidolon's sharp, piercing gaze darted to the window as his mind whirred with thoughts. His brow furrowed in concentration as he searched for an answer among the rolling clouds and shifting shadows outside. The lines on his forehead deepened as he mulled over his options, his eyes flickering back and forth between the window and the book.

"Why do you ask?" He sat on the bed, taking care to put distance between him and the book.

"Just a hunch," I mumbled, pulling my wild hair into a messy bun. I wiped my glasses off with my sweatshirt before slipping them back on and looking at Eidolon.

"It's possible," he answered slowly. "Moll never mentioned another Book of the Veiled missing, but that doesn't necessarily mean there isn't. Just highly improbable. I'm sure I would have heard about it by now if there had been."

"We should at least consider it." I ran my fingers across the cover, feeling a deep sense of certainty in my bones. It was just as much a part of the Book of the Veiled as Lilith's, Morrigan's, or Taliesin's story.

"I think we should head back. The group is probably wondering where we are," I said, standing up. Before I could move, Eidolon grabbed my arm and pulled me back down next to him.

"Are you okay? You seem different," he asked, grabbing my shoulder and turning me to face him. I was about to tell him I was fine when the room around me slipped away, and my vision blurred. A fog descended, covering me like a blanket before dragging me into its depths.

My body hit the rough dirt road with a heavy thud, jolting me out of my daze. As I rubbed my bruised rear, I saw the chaos around me.

A village was under brutal attack, and screams echoed through the air. Panicking, I darted to the nearest corner and crouched down in the shadows of a small house.

I watched in horror as families were pulled from their homes and dragged onto the streets, blood streaming from their wounds. The attackers reveled in their power, taunting and tormenting their victims as they hunted them down.

The air reeked of destruction: burning timber, seared flesh, charred bodies, death, and violence. All around me were clashes of blades and cries of fear.

In an instant, a blinding burst of light transported me to a dark and ominous cave. A towering tree, its gnarled branches reaching towards the ceiling, dominated the space. Surrounding it was a pool of inky black liquid, swirling and bubbling with eerie energy. Cloaked figures moved around the tree, stripping long ribbons of bark from its trunk and carrying them into the shadows.

In the distance, a man and woman stood with tense expressions, their eyes fixed on the scene as if their dreams were being stolen along with the tree's bark.

When only an empty stump remained, one of the workers tossed a torch onto it. He stepped back, watching as the orange flames engulfed the tree.

My mind leaped into another vision. This time, a woman stood on a pyre of dried timbers and kindling, the blaze dancing up her bruised body. She glanced down and caught my eye, her face twisting into an expression I had never seen before: part terror, part anguish, part relief.

Three women stood behind her, their hands locked together like prisoners sharing a similar sentence. They spoke in whispers, their faces etched with grief.

Watching the scene, a nagging sensation of familiarity washed over me. My eyes widened in realization as my heart beat faster. The intense heat of the flames licked at my skin as I sprinted towards the burning woman, fueled by adrenaline. Each step was a prayer that I would reach her before the fire overwhelmed her. Her mouth opened in a scream as the fire caught her hair, and I stumbled at the sound.

That was the last I saw as darkness engulfed me, violently pulling me back into the present. The vibrant colors and sights surrounding me moments ago became a distant memory, fading into the void.

My body trembled as I opened my eyes to the familiar room. Eidolon's gaze burned into me as I took a deep, shaky breath. The details of the vision felt so real that I glanced down at my arms, expecting burns and blisters. And I wasn't disappointed; my skin was slightly red, and wisps of smoke rose from several singed hairs on my arm.

"What the hell, Chloe? What is going on?" Eidolon asked, brushing the ash off my sweatshirt.

"I don't know," I admitted. "Visions of the past. A city ransacked, a tree destroyed, and a woman burned. I think Lilith and Arawn were there."

Eidolon nodded slowly. "The book showed me the same thing."

"Something tells me we need to talk to Isabelle."

Eidolon nodded, and we headed back down. I carried the book with me, and Eidolon kept his distance. I glanced at him once, but his expression was unreadable.

Were we fighting again? I sighed. For being soul mates, we sure were at odds a lot. Maybe the Fates had gotten it wrong?

Chapter 17- Chloe

Modern Day- City of the Unspoken

We headed to the library to find everyone but pivoted when we heard laughter floating from the dining room. My stomach grumbled at the delicious aroma of eggs, bacon, and freshly baked bread wafting through the air, and I realized I was starving.

Shocker. I was always hungry. Especially for breakfast.

We took our seats around the grand round oak table, wide enough to seat a squad of warriors in full battle gear. The surface was adorned with an array of dishes, overflowing with food fit for a king's feast. A warm and inviting light emanated from the chandelier, casting a glow over our faces.

My eyes drifted to Isabelle, curious about her family's past. I leaned in, filling my plate with French toast. "What do you know about your family's history?"

"Not much, luv," Isabelle admitted as she grabbed a blueberry muffin. "I was too young when my mother was alive to join the coven. And when my aunt took her place after she died, I left. So, I missed a lot of my instructional training. Why do you ask?"

"I think the next book might have something to do with you," I said, trying to keep my voice casual as I reached over to take a bear claw.

"That makes sense," Max replied, filling his plate with eggs and bacon. "If we are looking for the Witch of Endor, Isabelle must be related to her somehow. Both of them being witches and everything."

Isabelle shook her head, narrowing her eyes, offended by the assumption. "My family line does not include necromancers. The women in my lineage were healers, not zombie makers."

"Do you know where your abilities come from? Like who the first witch was?" Eidolon asked, trying to redirect the conversation away from what I assumed was a sensitive subject.

Watson's intense and calculating stare scanned the room, his brow furrowed in deep thought. His hands gripped his fork tightly, poised for a confrontation. He was just about to speak when he was suddenly interrupted.

"I think I can help," Moll called as she shuffled into the room painfully slow. Her cane thumped against the floor with every agonizing step, the vibrant cherrywood staff now gray and wilted. Her once lustrous silvery hair had turned snow white and was pulled back in a loose braid that fell over her shoulder. The spirited sparkle was replaced by dark circles that revealed her exhaustion. Her dress, fashioned from hand-spun gray fabric, was wrinkled and creased, with faint black ink and coffee stains marring its surface.

She clutched a copy of the Book of the Veiled in her free hand, and my curiosity piqued. Moll never let us see her book, guarding it like it was the map to Atlantis. If she had brought it, it meant she had found something important.

Her copy looked nothing like mine. The one I was gifted was covered in beautifully aged leather with an embossed illustration of a raven perched on a thorn bush. Its dark black and green colors stood out against the weathered background.

But Moll's was as worn as an old piece of wood, its edges thin and splintered. What semblance of color it had once possessed had long since faded into a dingy brown, like the bark of an oak that had survived past its prime.

"You know who she was?" Isabelle asked, her eyes dancing with concern as she watched Moll shuffle around the table.

Moll was old, but she never looked old.

"The Witch of Endor's sister," Moll answered as she lowered herself into the seat next to Eidolon and patted his hand in greeting. "She was the first to receive the grimoire Isabelle's family still uses."

"That's not right," Isabelle said, shaking her head in confusion. "I was told that Agnes Sampson created the grimoire in the 1500s. One of the local women found it after her execution and passed it on to her daughter. She was the first of our line."

"Not quite. Your family was given a grimoire, but it didn't belong to Agnes. It was Geillis Duncan's, discovered in a cell after her execution."

"So, Isabelle is related to Geillis and the Witch of Endor's sister?" Victor asked, intrigued. "Do you know her name?"

"Another mystery," Moll answered, shifting her eyes to him. "All I know is that Geillis didn't have any children, so the book was delivered to her niece, the last surviving witch of her bloodline."

"Who found it?" I asked. "After Geillis died."

"No one knows." Moll shrugged, taking a sip. "It just showed up one day."

"Helpful," I muttered, poking at my food with my fork. I was hungry, but every bite tasted like ashes, and I couldn't bring myself to take another bite.

"Perhaps not. But something tells me that it's not by accident that all roads point to Agnes and Geillis." She tapped her book with one of her long, yellowed fingernails.

"Why do you say that?" Eidolon asked, draping his arm over the back of my chair, making himself comfortable as if he expected another long-winded tale.

Moll took a deep breath, looking at us all like a school matron. "I'm guessing no one has read Taliesin's story. Because if you could, you would know he was in Scotland at Agnes' and Geillis' execution."

I swiveled in my seat to face her. "Why was Taliesin there?" I asked, my voice trembling as I met her dull gray gaze, a shiver running down my spine.

"That's the mystery, isn't it?" Her stare drifted past me. I turned to check if someone was standing behind me. To my relief, no one was there, but Moll's focus remained fixed on something in the distance. "What reason did Taliesin have for appearing at the first execution of the North Berwick witch trial?"

"Oh, goody. Another puzzle," Watson grumbled, pouring something into his coffee from the flask he carried. Isabelle eyed him, confusion dancing in her eyes. Watson loved his whiskey, but until today, he had a strict rule that he would only have two drinks and only in the evening. If he was drinking at breakfast, something was off. But Isabelle didn't say anything to him, so I didn't mention it either.

"I am willing to bet it has something to do with the Witch of Endor. Her being a necromancer and all. Taliesin was looking for a way to bring his sister back, and she had the power to do it. The real question is, why was the Witch of Endor at Agnes's execution?" Max ran his hand through his tousled hair, picked up his pen, and wrote something in the red notebook beside his plate.

I recognized it as the one Aelle always carried, stained and tattered from years of use.

"I found it in her bedroom," Max explained when he glanced up and caught me staring at it. "I thought she would want a full account of what happened when she returned."

He was right, of course. Aelle was a stickler for details. And heaven help us all if we miss something.

Eidolon leaned forward, his fingers tapping on the table. "This is getting complicated," he whistled. "Quick run-down: Chloe has a link to the Witch of Endor through Morrigan. Isabelle's ancestry can be traced back to the sister of the Witch of Endor through Geillis. Taliesin was present at Agnes' execution, but no one knows why. Does that cover it all?"

"My guess is we are looking for Morrigan's book next," Victor suggested. "Agnes must be related to her somehow."

"I agree, so where do we go now? The prophecy said that the next book would be somewhere near a city buried under a city. Does anyone know where that is?" Max asked, making notes in Aelle's notebook.

"Mary King's Close," Watson said, taking a big swig of his drink. "Looks like we are going home."

Chapter 18- Chloe

Modern Day- City of the Unspoken

"I agree, but there are two stories at play here," Moll's voice rang out as she took a scone from the basket, smearing it with clotted cream and lemon curd. "I suggest you all also figure out where the sisters ended up after the Witch of Endor's necromancer ability was exposed."

"Max searched for days without success. There is nothing written about her except in religious texts. At least nothing concrete." Eidolon said, frustrated.

"Perhaps not. But Chloe's got her book." Moll pointed to where it lay on the table. "Why not ask her?"

The room suddenly fell quiet, and everyone's eyes fixed on me as I glanced at the book in amazement. I'd assumed the Witch of Endor had written it, but I wasn't sure.

So maybe it wasn't part of the Book of Veiled collection, although all Writer's books were. It made sense since the books were meant to be one cohesive unit, offering insight and stories from different eras. But the enigmatic voice Eidolon and I heard in the bedroom wasn't warning us about occurrences that had already happened.

It spoke of events yet to come—things that could still be changed.

It was a prophecy, not an explanation.

So, how the hell did it end up in the City of the Unspoken?

Max reached across the table, his movement catching my attention. Only those with the original's blood can touch it, my key warned. Jolting, I sat up and snatched the book before he grabbed it.

"Possessive much, Chloe? It's just a book." Max narrowed his eyes and slowly pulled his arm back.

I said the same thing to Eidolon in the bedroom an hour ago, and it ended in disaster. So, no. I wouldn't take chances with anyone else touching it.

"It's not just a book," I sneered. "And I don't want anyone messing with it until we understand how it's connected to everything." I drew it closer and glared at everyone around the table, daring them to argue with me.

"Okay Sméagol. No one will touch your precious," Watson joked dryly, and my eyes snapped to him. I gritted my teeth, barely containing the urge to say something snide.

This wasn't the time to make Lord of the Rings references. That was fantasy, and we were dealing with reality.

Right?

Looking from the outside in, I guess this whole situation would read like an epic fantasy novel. The secrets we kept, the challenges we faced and overcame, and the bonds we formed would make for a best-selling novel one day.

For what was fantasy other than reality with a twist?

"Do you at least know what it says? Can it tell us where Aelle is?" Max asked, running a hand over his face.

"I can't read it," I admitted. "The pages are blank."

"Well, *that's* helpful," he muttered. "The only lead we have, and Chloe can't read it."

"Give her a break," Isabelle jumped in. "I'm sure Chloe has a plan." She glanced over at me, her eyebrows arched. "You do have a plan, don't you, luv?"

"Well, not yet..." I glanced around at my friends' faces and groaned. They looked so uncertain, and I knew they had their doubts about me. But discovering the mystery behind the book was something I had to do.

I couldn't explain why, but deep down, I knew it was.

"Look, I get it. You don't think I can figure it out. But please trust me. There's a reason why it found me. Just give it some time," I pleaded. It wasn't an obsession like Sméagol's need for the One Ring. I didn't *have* to have the Witch of Endor's book; I just didn't want anyone else to have it.

Big difference.

"We trust you, luv," Isabelle reassured me, eyeing everyone around the table, her eyes flashing a warning. "Remember, we're here to help."

I murmured my gratitude as Eidolon turned to me. The intricate tattoos along his neck shifted as he clenched his jaw. "Alright, Chloe, go ahead and try. But I'll be keeping an eye on you. Any sign of trouble, I'm stepping in."

I nodded, relieved I'd won the argument. Eidolon and I had a fragile truce, and I was willing to give an inch as long as the book stayed with me.

"Now that that's settled," Victor leaned back in his chair, his hands behind his head. "Chloe and Eidolon will deal with the Witch of Endor's book while the rest of us focus on the connection between Agnes, Geillis, and the sisters."

"And find out what Taliesin's connection is," Eidolon reminded him with a pointed stare. "It's not accidental he's involved. We need to know why and how."

"Can't you figure it out?" I asked, pointing to his chest. "You have Taliesin's book. Can't you see if it says anything about what he was up to?"

"No," Eidolon shook his head, his eyes narrowing as he frowned. "Ever since the book was transferred to me, I have tried to open it. But every time I get close, it shifts to a different location in the library."

As frustrating as his revelation was, it made sense. Taliesin didn't want us to change his history, and if he was technically still alive, it meant he had some control over his story.

"No problem," I exclaimed, knocking over my coffee cup. I grabbed a napkin to wipe the spill and suggested, "Why don't Moll and I travel back in time and see for ourselves?"

Moll's expression turned serious as she shook her finger at me, a hint of warning in her eyes. "No, Chloe," she scolded. "Writers cannot simply hop around the past without a purpose. We are strictly forbidden from altering timelines."

"I know," I replied, disappointed.

"Do you?" she asked pointedly.

"Yes." I sighed exasperatedly. Being constantly treated like a child wore on my patience. It still stung that they saw me as a burden because I lacked magickal abilities. Their doubts about my claim that I could figure out how to read the Witch of Endor's book only added to my frustration. Now, even Moll dismissed my suggestions as if I were a clueless child.

I wasn't implying that we should jump through timelines and rewrite history. I just asked if we could look. I was beginning to question why I was invited to join the Raven Society. I wasn't allowed to do anything but write down other people's experiences and be plagued with nightmares.

"But you might be on to something," Moll conceded. "We can't go back, but you and Isabelle can return to where this all started."

Chapter 19- Chloe

Modern Day- City of the Unspoken

Watson choked on his coffee, staring at Moll as if she had lost her mind. "Isabelle? My Isabelle?" He gestured to his wife.

"Obviously, I'm talking about your Isabelle. Who else would I be referring to?" Moll countered, raising her eyebrows in challenge.

Watson's gaze sharpened as he fixed it on her, his tone fierce. "No! She's not getting involved. You want to find the Witch of Endor? You can do it without her," he growled, each word a low roar. An icy chill ran through the room as Watson waited for a retort, his body coiled and ready to pounce.

Gods knew I wouldn't say anything. Not with his fangs out and looking like the vampires from horror films.

Isabelle's hand reached out and gently grasped Watson's, her voice low and soothing. "We can't ignore what is happening. Chloe and Victor have heard the prophecy, and they believe it." Isabelle's gaze flickered between us, and we both nodded in agreement. "We have to trust them." She concluded with conviction.

Watson sighed, frustrated, and folded his arms tightly across his chest. He rubbed his hand down his face, muttering, "Can you remind me what the prophecy said, Chloe?"

I took a deep breath and repeated what Caer Ibormeth, the goddess of dreams, prophecy, and sleep, told me weeks ago.

The path that had been decided by the Fates years ago faded into nothingness. In its place lay three roads, each distinctly different in color and territory. Black symbolizes mystery and death and follows the path leading to the Lost City of the Unspoken. Blue represents truth and sadness and leads across a vast body of water to a city built on top of another. Green, representing nature, wisdom, and envy, follows the path through a dark forest to reach a city that claims to hold the Gates of Secrets.

Each road leads to a book, hidden in the shadows that will open with a key forged at the same time as it was written. Each one is a different possibility of what could be. Every road is obscured by darkness, threatening to overpower the magick of the books. Travel all three roads successfully, and you will reach where the Tree of Life and the Gates of the Otherworld are abandoned and dying. Then, with the blood of the last, you will be able to reopen the path for all."

"How does this relate to my wife? It's a random prophecy uttered by some obscure goddess! We don't even know what it means."

Eidolon's voice rumbled with an unspoken threat as he leaned in towards Watson, his eyes hardening into a cold and unyielding stare. "You knew what you were getting into when you joined the Raven Society," he growled. "When you were initiated and given your key, you took an oath to protect the books and their secrets at all costs."

Their eyes bore into each other, a fiery intensity igniting between them. "You have no idea what you're asking," Watson hissed through gritted teeth, his voice strained with suppressed rage.

Eidolon leaned back, his eyes glinting with malicious intent as a wicked smirk spread across his face. "Come now, dear Watson," he taunted, gesturing wildly around the room. "Enlighten us all. We're dying to know."

"Watson, please," Isabelle's voice grew desperate as she pleaded with Watson, who abruptly pushed his chair back and stood up, towering over the table with his impressive height. "Let's have a rational discussion. We've come too far to quit now."

Watson stared at her in utter disbelief before a quiet rumble escaped his lips as he fought to contain his rising anger and sat back down.

"If it's important to you," he agreed through gritted teeth. His eyes narrowed, flicking over to Eidolon with a dangerous glint. "The second I sense my wife is in danger, I *will* unleash the full wrath of the monster they fear me to be," he vowed, his voice laced with an edge of deadly determination.

Eidolon nodded. "I wouldn't expect less."

"That was intense," Max mumbled under his breath.

"Understatement of the year," Victor nodded, brushing away imaginary crumbs from his shirt. "I thought I was about to put grown adults on a time-out."

Watson growled at him, and Victor raised his hands in surrender, laughing. "Put your fangs away, Watson. You can't hurt me, remember?"

"Last time I checked, you could still feel pain," Watson retorted, a smile tugging at his lips. "We can put it to a test if you like." He bared his fangs again, and Victor blanched.

"I'm good."

"Gentlemen, please," Isabelle swatted at her husband. "You can battle later. I want to know when we are leaving."

"If I remember correctly, this is about the same time of year Agnes 'confessed' to witchcraft," Victor offered, rubbing the stubble on his chin and smiling. "I think we should return as soon as possible. If we can find the time link, we may be able to figure out where Morrigan's book is hidden."

"Time link?" I asked, confused.

Victor shrugged as he reached for the coffee pot. "My way of simplifying a complex idea," he said. "Basically, Einstein proved time and space are intertwined. He believed time was not absolute, but relative."

"And that means what..." Max asked, looking up from his journal.

"That events are connected one way or another. You just have to find the time link."

"For example..." Isabelle pressed, intrigued by the conversation. Watson turned dangerously white, as Victor explained further.

"The astronomer Galileo died on January 8, 1642. Exactly 300 years later, the renowned physicist Stephen Hawkins was born. A remarkable coincidence, don't you think?" He looked around at all of us with a grin. "Then it gets weirder: Albert Einstein was born on March 14, 1879, and sadly, Stephen Hawkins died on the same date in 2018."

Frustration mounting, I muttered, "I still don't understand." To me, it seemed irrelevant whether someone was born or died on the same day as others. There were too many people in the world for there not to be coincidences like that.

"I have a hypothesis that events throughout time are connected. Returning to when and where Agnes was held in Edinburgh would make interacting with a specific moment easier. We wouldn't have to rely on Chloe's 'visions.'"

"How do you propose we accomplish that?" Eidolon asked, his leg tapping impatiently under the table. I quickly placed a calming hand on his knee before he accidentally knocked it over and spilled everyone's drinks.

"I'm not sure," Victor shrugged, taking a bite of an apple. "But I am willing to bet that if Isabelle and Chloe return to where their ancestors were at just the right moment, they might be able to interact with them."

Max turned the pages of the notebook, deep in thought. "It's possible," he considered. "If we can travel to the Otherworld using

Arawn's book, what's to say we can't interact with the past in the present?"

Curiosity getting the best of me, I tugged at a loose string on my sweatshirt sleeve and asked, "Why that specific date?"

"That's the day Agnes died," he said slowly as if I should have known. "And because the Witch of Endor was a necromancer. Where else would she be?"

Chapter 20- Chloe

Modern Day- City of the Unspoken

"When do we leave?" I asked, my leg bouncing under the table. I couldn't wait to return to the real world. It's not that there was anything wrong with being in the Otherworld, but I longed for the simple pleasures of everyday life. A sweet cream cold brew, clean clothes, and greasy fast food all sounded like heaven to me.

First on my list was a trip through the drive-thru for a Big Mac with extra cheese and fries, followed by an Oreo flurry. Then a shower. Or maybe the other way around. It didn't matter. Then, a hot shower. Or maybe I'd switch the order. It didn't really matter as long as I got to experience these earthly delights again.

I mentally reviewed the list of tasks I had to do when we returned. Laundry, check. Coffee, check. New sweatshirt, check. Find Morrigan's book, double-check. There was so much to do and not enough time.

I reached down to grab my notebook before realizing it wasn't there. My trusty three-year-old Walmart purse was still in Scotland, stuffed with two notebooks, 17 pens, a library book, old receipts, bills, and a tiny wallet hidden in the jumbled mess.

Just another reason to go home.

What did I really want to do? That was easy. I wanted to go back home with the Witch of Endor's book and lock myself away.

I didn't want to admit it, but being a 'Writer' wasn't working for me. Joining the Raven Society was more hassle than anything. At least when I was alone, there was no one to criticize or point out my shortcomings.

So pretty. So many secrets to share. I ran my hand over its smooth leather body. It sighed in contentment as my fingers traced the embossed title, touching every curve and line.

I felt the weight of Eidolon's piercing stare on me, but I refused to meet it. Instead, my eyes were glued to the worn pages of the ancient tome before me. The tension between us was palpable, like a thunderstorm ready to unleash its fury. But I was too engrossed in the enigmatic world within the pages to pay much attention to his rising frustration.

Chloe? He called out my name through our bond, and I instinctively clutched the book tighter in response.

What? I narrowed my eyes at him.

Give it to me, he demanded, reaching over to grab it.

"*No!*" I cried out, scooting my chair back and clenching it against my chest. Everyone stared at me, their expressions varying from concern to confusion.

"Chloe," Eidolon's tone softened as if he was speaking to a child. "I need you to give me the book. Something feels wrong."

"You're what's wrong," I hissed, my voice dripping with venom. "It doesn't like you. Get over it." The book chose me, not him, and he couldn't handle it. A surge of satisfaction ran through me at the thought of his jealousy and defeat.

"Luv, put it down," Isabelle said from across the table. I tilted my head towards her with a scowl. "It's latching on to you," she said urgently, gesturing to my hand, her bracelets jingling with the movement. My eyes followed her gaze. I gasped in shock.

My arms were marbled in dark veins, twisting and turning like malevolent ink. An icy chill spread from my fingertips, like tiny blades sliced through my skin. I struggled to free my hand, but an electricity jolt paralyzed me. I watched as the ominous ink continued its ascent toward my shoulders with alarming speed.

Fascinating. Ignoring the pain, I wiggled my fingers alongside the cover, and the shadows danced between them, silver flecks shimmering with each movement.

"Chloe!" Eidolon's voice boomed as he strained to snatch the book from my grasp again.

I pulled it away, glaring at him with shock and irritation. There was no way he was taking it - it was mine. As my frustration intensified, a dark presence emerged from its pages and crept toward Eidolon. His expression turned to pure terror as he scrambled away from the table.

Ah, shit! That's not good. An expletive exploded from my lips, my heart racing as I recoiled in dread.

"Let go!" I yelled, tossing the book to the side. The shadows retreated at my command, and I gasped for air, my body aching with exhaustion.

Eidolon slid his chair back and pulled me into an embrace. His sudden proximity sent shivers down my spine, and I took a deep breath, grateful.

"Are you alright?" he whispered, running his hand up and down my back.

I pressed my face against his shirt, mumbling an apology and taking comfort in his familiar scent. I struggled to understand what had just happened.

Did the book attack me?

Or was it protecting me?

I didn't know, but I was sure of one thing: it was dangerous—at least for everyone else.

"You don't have to apologize, lil' Writer. But maybe we should stop touching magickal things we don't understand?" Eidolon half-heartedly joked as I pulled away and rolled my shoulders.

I nodded in agreement, absentmindedly pouring myself another cup of coffee. I couldn't help but wish that the Otherworld had something stronger to offer—whiskey, rum, tequila—anything that could provide a warm, comforting burn as it rolled down my throat, anything to ward off the constant chill that clung to me.

"I think it's drawn to you," Moll leaned over Eidolon to examine the book more closely, recoiling with a sneer. "Like calling to like."

"That's awesome," Eidolon mumbled, exasperated. "I say we lock it up before it kills someone."

His words hung in the air as the rest of the group nodded in approval. But I wasn't happy about it. Of course, I wanted to keep everyone safe, and we had no idea what kind of magick it contained.

But on the other hand, I couldn't help but be drawn into the haunting and alluring call of its secrets, taunting me, promising answers. Electricity coursed through my fingers, and the key resting against my chest buzzed as I extended my hand toward the book again. Its magnetic energy filled me with determination.

After years of feeling lost, I finally had a sense of purpose again. Without thinking, I reached for the book again.

Chapter 21- Chloe

Modern Day- City of the Unspoken

"Chloe, let go of it *NOW*!" Watson's voice boomed as he shot up from his chair and closed the gap between us. With an iron grip, he clutched my hand and yanked it out of my grasp. "What the hell did Eidolon just say? We don't touch magickal things we don't understand." He held it between his fingers as if it offended him.

"Rude! I had it under control," I grumbled, knowing it was a lie. Even now, my fingers ached to feel the book again, and I stuffed them underneath my ass.

Isabelle's voice was filled with sadness as she looked at me. "I don't think you could have, luv," she said. "It reeks of death and black magick. And if it belongs to the Witch of Endor," she raised a perfectly formed eyebrow. "You need to be careful."

"It's not evil or possessed. It's trying to tell me something," I mumbled, glaring at Watson as he returned to his seat. He set it down an arm's length away and wiped his hands with a napkin.

"Does anyone have hand sanitizer?" he asked, frowning, looking at his hands. Isabelle dug some out of her jacket pocket and handed it to him. "It doesn't matter what you think it may or may not be doing. Until we better understand it, my wife is not going near it."

"Possessive much?" I sneered back, still upset with the Lord of the Rings comment from earlier. "I think Isabelle can take care of herself. She doesn't need you telling her what she can and cannot do."

"Enough!" Isabelle interjected, silencing Watson with a look. "I am willing to overlook your strange behavior this morning and chalk it up to a bad night's sleep. Ultimately, it's up to me to decide. Chloe is right; I don't need you to take care of me."

I smiled and stuck my tongue out at him before she swirled on me. "And Watson is right. We don't play around with dark magick. You will kill yourself. Or one of us," she finished with a pointed look.

I hung my head down in shame. She was right. I was playing with fire and didn't know how to control it. Or myself.

"I don't know why you're mad at me," Watson growled. His fists clenched as he stared at his wife. "As you said yourself, the Witch of Endor practiced dark magick. Why would you want to find her?"

"The story might be wrong," Max offered, shrinking in his chair when Watson's full anger directed itself at him. "I'm just saying there is a history of supernatural stories being altered. Who's to say the Witch of Endor is no different? Maybe she wasn't practicing dark magick. It may be something completely different. But we won't know until we locate her."

"He has a point, luv," Isabelle said as she took Watson's hand. "You and I both know I need to do this. Besides, it would be awesome to meet her. I have a few questions, and since I don't have anyone else to ask, maybe she can help."

Watson's expression softened. Isabelle's powers had strengthened since her aunt's murder, and she hadn't been in a coven for years. She didn't have anyone else to turn to for help. Of course, she had Watson, but a vampire wasn't much use when it came to magick. He held her gaze for a moment before responding to her request.

"Of course, my dear," Watson whispered, leaning over to kiss her forehead. "Let's go find your ancestors." Isabelle giggled as he pulled back. The two of them looked at each other with such understanding and tenderness that I felt a tinge of jealousy.

They had a love that time couldn't unravel. Seven hundred years plus another seven hundred still wouldn't be enough for them. I looked at Eidolon and wondered if we could get to that point.

"Excellent; now that that's all settled, I suggest we return to the library and regroup. We need to get ready to send you home." Moll leaned heavily on her cane as she got up from the table. Eidolon reached out to help her, but she swatted his hand away and huffed. "Young man, if I need your help, I will ask for it."

"Sorry," Eidolon frowned as he watched her struggle. "I was just trying to help."

"Well, I don't need it," she snapped, her clouded eyes dancing with frustration at him as she headed for the library. "And that applies to all of you," she called over her shoulder.

Max whistled as he took off his glasses to wipe them, watching her walk away. "I've never heard her get so angry before. What's going on?" he asked, looking back at Eidolon.

"Your guess is as good as mine," Eidolon's brow furrowed as he followed her. "But I am about to find out."

"Let her be," a voice called, and I swung around to see Lilith sitting in her customary chair at the head of the massive table. Not that a round table could have a head seat, but somehow Lilith managed to make it one.

Where did she come from?

Eidolon and I shared a silent exchange, our eyes meeting as he leaned against the doorframe, crossing his arms across his chest.

"When did you get back, luv?" Isabelle asked, smiling cautiously at the mother of all supernatural. "We weren't expecting to see you for weeks."

"Medusa makes it easy. Nothing is getting through her lines of defense anytime soon," she answered with a chuckle as she glanced around the room, her eyes landing on me.

As always, she looked flawless. Strands of wheat-colored hair shimmered around her face, highlighting her high cheekbones and spring-green eyes.

"Did you find what you were looking for?" I asked, sitting back in my seat and fiddling with my mug handle. I suspected she'd done more than check on Pandora's box.

My bet was that she tried to find Lucifer, her mate. No one had seen him for generations, but Lilith held on to the hope that he still existed somewhere, trapped in the depths of time.

"No," Lilith admitted before squaring her shoulders and glancing past me with a hint of sadness. "But it doesn't matter. We have work to do. A little bird whispered to me that you were searching for the Witch of Endor," she said, tilting her head in question.

How the hell did she know?

"Do you know where we can find her?" Max asked, sitting up in his chair and leaning forward. "We're hoping she can help us locate Aelle."

"Aelle is fine," Lilith said dismissively, bringing her mug to her lips to blow on her coffee. "She will come around when she is ready."

"Where is she?" Max demanded, his tone laced with an unspoken threat and a dangerous glint in his eyes.

"I never said I knew *where* she was," Lilith raised an eyebrow, her voice dripping with warning. "I just said she'd return when she was ready."

"What the hell does that mean?" Max yelled, slamming his fists on the dining table.

"It means she is where she needs to be right now. She needs time to adjust to her new role."

"But she will be back?" Max asked again, looking relieved and miserable at the same time.

"Yes. But Max, I warn you- if you try to pull her back before she is ready, she will not be the same person who left. You need to be patient. In the meantime, your skills would be best utilized to help us locate the next Book of the Veiled." She stared at him intently, expecting him to argue further, but Max agreed with a nod.

"Morrigan's," I offered, glancing down at my hand. The last of the blackness faded away, and I sighed in relief. "We think we are looking for Morrigan's book."

"That would make sense if you are searching for the Witch of Endor. The two have a complicated history that spans years and is shrouded in secrecy." Lilith's head bobbed in agreement as she tapped her manicured nails against the table's smooth surface, creating a soft rhythm that matched the beat of her thoughts.

Eidolon's eyes widened in surprise as he pushed off the door frame and stepped forward. "They knew each other?" he asked, his voice laced with curiosity.

"Of course, they do. Morrigan is a descendant of the Witch of Endor. As far as their history? You have to ask them; it's not my story to tell." Lilith shrugged indifferently, her startling green eyes fixed on him. Eidolon's shadows shifted around his body in response as they stared at each other.

I cleared my throat to draw their attention away from what was about to be a heated discussion. "How do we find her?"

"You have her book. Have you tried looking inside it to see if it gives you a hint?" Lilith pointed to where it sat.

"I haven't been able to read it," I admitted, my gaze lingering longingly on the mysterious book.

"Maybe because you are trying to read it and not listen to the story?" Lilith suggested, and I glanced over at her in surprise.

She wasn't just a lost soul. Lost souls still had a past. They were just forgotten.

The Witch of Endor had no name. Which was worse.

Chapter 22- Nava

1000 BC- Village of Endor, Jezreel Valley, Israel

Nava and Ysabel exited the cave, savoring the cool night air. The moon hung above them, bathing the hills in silver. A smattering of stars twinkled against the dark expanse, offering just enough light to guide them home.

They stood in stunned silence, their eyes widening as they gazed upon the vast world. Their future stretched before them, brimming with unknown risks and endless opportunities. They exchanged wary looks, remembering their mother's words of caution that still echoed through the cave's entrance.

The Tree of Life will wither and die. In the end, nothing survives.

"What do you think it means?" Ysabel asked, nervously turning her book over in her hands.

Nava paused, her fingers gliding over her mysterious black book. She recalled the moment she discovered her necromancer abilities—a terrifying yet exhilarating revelation—and couldn't help but feel the same excitement for what lay ahead.

"I don't know," Nava admitted, glancing at her sister. "But we'll figure it out—together."

She had no idea what the Fates had in store for her or Ysabel, but she knew they would be more than simple healers from a village that history would forget.

They would change the world.

"Are you planning on telling me what the king wants?" Ysabel asked, studying her book with a smile as she held it up to admire it.

Nava chewed on her bottom lip. She needed to tell her sister the truth before the king did. But how could she share what she had become without putting her sister in danger?

It's unfair, Nava thought. Her power to raise the dead was no different from a farmer coaxing crops from a dried seed. Life came from death, as her mother always told them.

"I have an idea why," Nava confessed, absentmindedly fiddling with a twig tangled in her braid. She gazed up at the starry night sky, trying to calm her racing thoughts. "There's something I need to tell you about when our mother passed away. I found out something that could change everything..."

Ysabel tilted her head and eyed her sister with a tiny smile, twirling a lock of hair between her fingers. "If you're trying to tell me you're a necromancer, you're late." She leaned closer, lowering her voice. "I've known for a while."

"You have?" Nava asked in surprise, her hazel eyes wide. "Why didn't you say anything?"

"Because if you wanted to tell me, you would've. But you didn't, so I assumed you wanted to keep it secret." Ysabel laughed. "Besides, you don't think I share everything with you, do you?"

"I guess not," Nava smirked, relief flooding her before she became serious again. "Does anyone else know?"

Her sister's hesitation was evident by her furrow. "I don't think so," she admitted, shaking her head. "But I can't be sure. Someone could have found out and told the king."

"Someone must have." Nava nodded slowly, a sickening realization washing over her as she came to terms with someone else knowing her secret. She had always been cautious, slipping out of bed in the dead of night and venturing into the hills beyond the village to practice her magick in solitude. But clearly, her care was not enough - someone spotted her.

But who? There could be no other option. Unless her father was forced to confess against his will.

She didn't want to believe it was her father. To even think such a thought was disloyal to his memory. Besides, he swore to the gods that the secret would accompany him to the grave. Her father did everything for them after their mother died. He would never intentionally put his daughters in danger.

Despite the chill of the late autumn evening, sweat beaded Nava's forehead as she remembered her father's screams- tormented moans of agony punctuated with frantic pleas for mercy.

Could anyone keep a secret while tortured?

"Father wouldn't have said anything," Ysabel reassured, placing her hand on Nava's shoulder.

"We can't be sure," Nava frowned. "We don't know what he experienced. All we can do is hope he didn't." She glanced at her sibling before squaring her shoulders, a determined glint dancing in her eyes. "Our best chance of survival is to find out what the king wants and then escape."

Ysabel acknowledged silently. Slow-moving clouds drifted overhead, blocking the night sky and casting an eerie stillness over the land. Uncertainty hung heavy in the air as they clutched their mother's gifts, hoping they would protect and guide them through the unknown journey ahead.

Chapter 23- Nava

1000 BC- Village of Endor, Jezreel Valley, Israel

The sisters slinked through the deserted village streets, their hearts pounding a frantic rhythm in their chests. They hugged the shadows like lifelines, eyes darting for any sign of danger. Finally reaching the back entrance, they shared a silent nod of relief.

They made it.

"We did it," Ysabel whispered, hanging her cloak on a peg. "I was sure we would be caught. I wonder where all the guards are?"

"I gave them the night off."

Nava and Ysabel froze, exchanging a fearful glance. Turning on their heels, they found King Saul sitting atop a wooden stool, sipping from a mug of red wine.

"I've been waiting for you," the king said as he swiveled to face them. "You were gone for so long that I helped myself to a drink. I hope you don't mind." He finished off his glass and sighed in disappointment as he saw it was empty.

"It reminds me of my mother's. Fruity with a touch of spice." His eyes flew up to meet theirs. "Did you make it yourself?"

"My sister did," Ysabel whispered after a long moment, her gaze lingering on the middle-aged man before her, stunned.

"Well, it's amazing," the king said appreciatively, turning around to pour another mug. "Where are my manners? Let me get you a glass. Mother always said it's impolite to drink alone." He got up with a fluid ease and took two cups from the shelf. When he turned, the sisters gasped.

The flickering light from the candles created a captivating halo around him, highlighting his attractive features. The king's sharply defined jawline and full lips were irresistible, accompanied by a charming smile that softened even the coldest hearts. The deep hue of his caramel skin was unmistakable, emitting a glow in the pale moonlight. As he lifted his gaze, the fierce intensity of his piercing dark eyes displayed formidable power.

Standing tall, at least six feet, he had broad shoulders and dressed in a pristine white tunic. His midnight blue cloak, adorned with intricate red geometric embroidery, swirled around his legs, adding to his commanding presence. The rolled-up sleeves revealed muscular forearms and hands bearing the callouses of hard labor.

The sisters fidgeted nervously as his piercing gaze shifted back and forth between them. King Saul's smirk hinted at some unknown knowledge, making them feel vulnerable yet inexplicably drawn to him. They were powerless against the allure of his intense, intelligent eyes.

"Why are you here?" Nava's sharp words lingered in the air between them. She noticed the anger dancing across his face before he composed himself.

"To see you, obviously," he chuckled, his voice laced with amusement. "Why else would I have come?" But the smile didn't reach his eyes. The king's piercing gaze bore into her, his irises narrowing. His stare was so intense that it felt like physical pressure on her chest.

Nava's heart thumped in her chest as she clutched the book tightly, feeling its powerful energy coursing through her veins. It screamed at her to flee, but she stood her ground, holding the book protectively behind her back. She lowered her head in a show of false submission, bracing for whatever was to come.

With wary eyes, Nava watched him glide across the small room in just two steps, his predatory aura filling the space around them. She could feel his gaze piercing through her facade and knew she was no match for his dark intentions.

He stood before her, tender fingers coaxing her head to lift and forcing her eyes to meet his. "I heard the rumors. But I must admit, I didn't expect someone so young with such power."

Nava fixed a fierce glare on him, her jaw tight with anger. "I am not young," she shot back defiantly, tilting her head just a fraction, silently daring the king to respond, which only made him burst into laughter.

"Aren't you, though?" King Saul asked. "Well, Nava, I am much older than you are and even older than I appear. Anyone younger than 60 is young to me."

"How old are you?" Ysabel asked, amazed. The king didn't look a day over 40.

"72, give or take a year," he answered with a wink in her direction.

"You look terrific for your age," Ysabel admitted, blushing as she grabbed Nava's tight-clenched fist and interlocked it with hers. Comforting warmth spread through her arm as soon as her sister closed the distance between them.

"I know." The king's laughter echoed through the room as he dropped his hand from Nava's face and turned to her sister, eyeing her apperciatively.

Ysabel shuddered at his intense gaze. A cold dread crept over Nava as she realized he must have sensed her sister's ability to control emotions.

But the king didn't say anything. Instead, he swept his hand towards the table. "Now that we have finished discussing the unpleasantness of my age, why don't we all sit down, and I will explain why I am here?"

The two women shared a knowing glance before Nava nodded, her eyes narrowed with suspicion. They moved towards the stools across from him, keeping their books concealed in their arms as they sat down. The king poured each of them a mug of wine and slid them across the table.

"Why are you here?" Nava asked, her voice feigning composure as she took a sip. "You don't look ill. And as you can see, I have limited supplies to help, even if you were." She gestured towards the barren shelves where she stored her potions.

The wooden racks that once held freshly plucked petals and aromatic leaves lay dusty. The empty spaces painfully reminded Nava of how long she had struggled to find the ingredients for her art.

"We both know I'm not here because I'm sick, Nava," the king growled, his deep voice laced with warning. "I'm here because I need your other abilities."

Nava's heart pounded as panic clawed at her composure. She pressed her tongue against the roof of her mouth to stop her from saying something offensive. Gritting her teeth, she glared at him, a tingling sensation erupting at her fingertips.

"I have no idea what you are talking about." Nava kept her tone soft, but it cut through the air like a blade. She glanced at her sister but saw only a face of quiet fury as Ysabel stared into her mug, choosing to stay silent. "I'm a healer, that is all."

"That's not what I've heard," the king countered, an eyebrow rising to his hairline in amusement. "Rumor has it, you have a skill that should only belong to God."

Nava sighed, trying not to roll her eyes. She never understood when someone implied that only gods could have magick. Didn't they create mortals and the supernatural? And if they did, wouldn't that mean any *gifts* given to the supernatural and mortals were pre-ordained?

But that was an argument for another day.

"Whoever told you was grossly mistaken. I'm nothing more than an old spinster with a minor talent for healing. Nothing magickal about it. Anyone could do it, really," Nava shrugged, her voice ringing with the lie.

"Rest assured, my source is not mistaken." The king maintained his unwavering smile as if he delighted in the cat-and-mouse game.

"Well, they were wrong," Nava declared with an edge to her tone. "People tend to make things sound more dramatic than they are. Do you remember the young girl who had a sore throat and couldn't talk?" Nava glanced at her sister, who nodded without looking up.

"Well, after three days of rest and no talking, she was back on her feet, telling everyone I had brought her back from the dead. Perhaps you heard about it through the grapevine and took it literally?" Nava suggested with a triumphant smile, meeting the king's gaze directly.

"I'm not mistaken; I can assure you." A voice called from the doorway as a tall man silently stepped out of the shadows. The stranger glanced around the room in disgust as Nava eyed the intruder.

His tunic was pristine white, almost indistinguishable from the king's own; its brilliance accentuated by a flowing black cloak draped elegantly over his broad shoulders. In the warm glow of the room, his long, reddish-brown hair shimmered like copper, pulled back from his chiseled face with a strip of supple leather. It only highlighted his piercing eyes. His eyes were brilliant, emerald green that danced with tiny silver flecks, like lightning crackling across a night sky.

And filled with dark magick.

"Ah, Magus. You made it!" the king declared, jumping out of his seat, clapping the mysterious man on the back, and laughing. "Nava was just explaining that you must have been mistaken about her abilities.

King Saul spun on his heel with a wicked glint in his eyes, one corner of his mouth curling up. "Wasn't that what you were telling me? That it was just rumors and gossip?" he asked, sounding anything but playful.

A chill ran down Nava's spine as she stared at the stranger. His menacing presence sucked the air from the room, and her arms and legs tingled with dread.

"And who are you?" Nava shuddered as she felt the intense power flowing through his veins like a raging inferno. It radiated from him, filling the room with pulsating energy.

Nava's heart raced as she felt an unexplainable pull towards Magus, her fingers twitching with the urgent need to reach out and touch him. But she couldn't shake off the unsettling feeling of being in his presence. It was like two worlds collided within him, struggling for dominance and threatening to consume anyone who dared to get too close.

She made the mistake of looking him in the eye, shocked at what she saw. The sheer emptiness lingering behind them made her stomach turn. He wasn't quite alive, but he wasn't dead either. He was a soul in another person's body.

No, that wasn't it. Nava leaned forward, her eyes squinting as she tried to peer into him. But the closer she got, the more she felt a sense of dread creep up her spine. With a jolt, she recoiled and stumbled backwards, knocking over the stool in her haste.

Magus was alive, undeniably. But something about him was off. His body didn't quite belong to him – not yet. It was as if he had borrowed it. A shiver ran through Nava's body as she realized the gravity of the situation.

Timewalker! Nava had heard about them but didn't think they existed.

"I'm called Magus," he answered, his eyes twinkling in delight at her response. "As the king just said."

Nava's eyes shifted between the two men, ultimately settling on the king. "We have never met. This man," she gestured towards the Magus, "does not know me or my abilities."

"You're right. We have never met face to face. But I know what you are and what you're trying to hide," Magus declared, trapping Nava in her deceit.

She couldn't lie. But that didn't mean she wouldn't try.

"You're wrong," Nava hissed, her hands trembling in rage as her fingernails dug into her skin. Her teeth clenched tightly together, her body shaking with anger as vitriolic hatred boiled over from the depths of her soul. Nava forced herself to contain it until all that was left was a seething silent fury.

"No, I'm not." Magus smiled. "You, witch, can raise the dead."

Chapter 24- Nava

1000 BC- Village of Endor, Jezreel Valley, Israel

"S it, sit," the king said, clapping Magus on the shoulder again and leading him to a stool beside his.

Nava's heart raced as she glanced towards the door, their only route to safety. However, one piercing stare from Magus made it clear that fleeing was not an option.

He smiled at her again, a chilling smirk that warned her he would come after them if they tried to run. Tension knotted in Nava's neck and shoulders as she discreetly wiped away sweat beads from her forehead.

Nava stepped forward slowly, her gaze darting between her book, the king, and the mysterious Magus, praying they hadn't seen it. She sat and reached for her sister's hand, taking a deep breath to steady herself. The two women locked eyes on their visitors, waiting.

"What do you want from us?" Nava asked.

"I need you to find an old friend of mine," the king answered as he poured another glass of wine. "I need his help."

Nava's eyebrows shot up in shock, her eyes widening in surprise. King Saul had a reputation for surrounding himself with renowned prophets and experienced generals, yet here he was, seeking assistance from the dead. It was an unexpected and peculiar situation, to say the least.

"You have your council," Nava pointed out. "Why not ask one of them?"

A flash of sadness crossed the king's face before turning to suppressed rage. "Because they are gone."

Ysabel glanced up, her eyes narrowing, a sneer playing at the corners of her delicate lips. "Gone? Or dead?"

The air in the room was heavy with tension as the king's eyes bore into her.

The sisters didn't back down. They knew the truth. His advisors weren't gone. The king had killed them, along with all the supernatural. King Saul had come to them because he had no one else to turn to. The bitter irony of the situation was not lost on anyone in the room.

"And you can't help him?" Nava asked, smirking as she sized up Magus with newfound confidence. He might be powerful, but not as powerful as she was. Nava suppressed her excitement and reminded herself she needed to be cautious and strategic if they wanted to walk away alive.

Magus's eyes glinted with disgust and scorn as he fixed his intense gaze on her. His persuasive magick radiated off him, pulsing like heat waves on a sweltering summer day. His voice dropped to a dangerous tone. "It may be beyond my capabilities," he said darkly. "But, I assure you, witch, I possess magick you cannot even fathom."

"But not what the king needs," Nava taunted, unwilling to let him scare her. The book beneath her legs hummed urgently, and she fought the urge to grab it.

"Who does my sister need to find?" Ysabel asked, glaring at Nava, her eyes begging her to be quiet.

"A prophet," the king answered.

"I'm going to require a little more information," Nava argued. Taking a sip of wine, she tilted back in her chair and crossed her arms.

"Why?" Magus sneered. "I thought someone as powerful as you could read his mind and figure it out yourself."

Nava leaned forward, her face contorting with rage. Her patience had been pushed to the limit, and she was losing control.

"It requires a connection to find a soul," she sneered. "With no name, the person doesn't exist. And I refuse to roam aimlessly through the Otherworld looking for someone I don't know." She glanced over to the king. "The caretaker won't let me in without a name."

"So, you *can* see the caretaker?" Magus asked, flashes of silver dancing in his eyes.

"Of course, I can see him," Nava shook her head in confusion. "How else would I gain access to the Otherworld? I might have power, but it's his world."

"Was he the one who gave you the ability?" Magus asked, leaning forward. "How does it work? Is it a spell? Have you ever seen a tree?"

"Magus," the king said, grasping his shoulder and pulling him back. "Don't lose focus. Our priority is finding Samuel."

Magus stiffened, turning slowly to confront the unwelcome touch. Glancing at the hand on him with disgust, Nava held her breath as the tension escalated, waiting to see how Magus responded. He composed himself with effort.

"Of course," Magus said evenly, shrugging his shoulders and smoothing his tunic. "Forgive me."

"Who is Samuel?" Ysabel asked, sipping her wine and watching the interaction over the rim of her mug.

The king sighed deeply, running his fingers through his unruly hair. "He was one of my advisors. At the beginning of my reign, I made impulsive decisions without listening to anyone's warnings. Samuel tried to guide me, but I was convinced no one could tell me what to do. Our relationship became strained, and when he rebelled against my wishes, I saw it as the ultimate act of betrayal and banished him."

"What exactly did he do?" Nava eyed the king suspiciously, her gaze unwavering as she demanded an explanation. She needed to know before risking the journey to the Otherworld. The dead tended to hold grudges, especially when they had been wronged.

"He denounced my claim to the throne. Twice," the king pounded a fist on the table, tears in his eyes. "Since then, everything has gone wrong."

"I don't understand. If Samuel denounced your claim as king, why would you want his help?"

"My kingdom is on the brink of obliteration. My enemies are circling their forces, waiting for me to make a mistake. I need to know if redemption is still possible. Or if God has abandoned me."

"But you exiled or murdered everyone who could have helped," Nava nodded, understanding his predicament. "So your only option is to ask the dead."

"Yes," he said, desperation evident in his voice. "If I talk to him, tell him how sorry I am, maybe he will intervene for me and present my case to God. There must be a way to prove that I am the rightful king they always believed me to be." He spoke with quiet intensity, his words barely audible above a whisper as anguish flashed across his face.

Nava got up to pace the room, thinking. Part of her wanted to refuse his request, to allow his reign to end at his enemies' hands. On the other hand, if she did what he asked, she could still save herself and her sister. Returning to the table, she placed a hand on Ysabel's shoulder.

"You've chased us from our homes, destroyed our village, and murdered my father. Not to mention, you've declared magick illegal. What assurance can you offer if I bring Samuel back that my sister and I will be safe?"

"You and your sister will be free to leave. I will not follow you."

It was a tempting offer. Nava wasn't sure if she believed him. But what choice did she have?

"I will do it," Nava declared, looking at her sister with a sad smile. She would do it for her, to provide Ysabel the chance to have a normal life.

Whatever that looked like.

"Thank you," the king breathed a sigh of relief and smiled at the Magus. "I told you this would all work out."

"We shall see what the witch can do," the Magus grunted, staring at Nava with interest.

Chapter 25- Agnes

December 1589- Nether Keith, Scotland

"Not helpful," Agnes muttered, kicking a stone with her toe, glaring at the tree. "And a waste of my time."

A snicker jolted her out of her thoughts. She spun around on her heels to see two women standing before her. The hairs on her neck prickled as they smiled mischievously, their eyes dancing with a history of secrets. Despite their youthful appearance, something ancient and mysterious lurking behind their bright eyes sent a shiver down Agnes' spine.

"I have always found the tree to be a bit melodramatic." The eldest of the two spoke in a husky tone, her speech slow as if the words were unfamiliar. Her long, thin fingers brushed against the leather belt hanging from her hip, revealing a small black book in a pouch.

"You look so young!" the other one said, examining her curiously. She leaned in closer to her sister, whispering, "I expected someone more seasoned. Are you sure the Fates chose the right one?"

Agnes' face flushed with anger and resentment. She was no child. She was an experienced witch, a respected healer, and a leader in her coven.

"You must be the sisters?" she asked, ignoring the insult. The older sister chuckled, but the younger stared at Agnes in awe.

"In the flesh," she exclaimed with a smile, her bright eyes sparkling with amusement. Her feet moved in a lively dance, matching an unheard melody that filled the air around her. Her golden locks flowed freely down her back, swaying and twirling with every step. She was the living embodiment of joy and music, radiating energy and life with each graceful movement.

The oldest watched her with a grin before turning back to Agnes. "We know why you're here."

"Do you?" Agnes scuffed. "Because the tree didn't seem to have any idea."

"Oh, don't worry about that old thing," the youngest laughed. "It just wanted to talk. Not many people come around anymore, so it gets talkative when new blood shows up."

"Wonderful," Agnes muttered, shifting her gaze towards the looming tree. She forced a polite smile and gave a slight bow. Agnes stifled a laugh at the tree's awkward wave in return.

"I'm guessing history is repeating itself?" The oldest asked the tree. "And I assume Taliesin is at the root of all this?" A subtle vibration rippled through the trunk in answer.

"Who else would have the power?" the youngest questioned as she rummaged through her bag, pulling out a book and carefully opening it. She ran her finger along the paper, pausing to squint at the tiny words before turning each page faster. She jumped in excitement when she found what she'd been looking for. Her eyes followed her fingers as she read before glancing up sharply, eyeing Agnes.

The oppressive atmosphere thickened, and a cold dread settled in Agnes' stomach, spreading through her veins like ice water. It pulsed through her hands, sucking the warmth from her skin. Whatever the younger sister had seen, it was not good.

"Who is Taliesin?" Agnes asked, avoiding the youngest's gaze. "Is he the devil?"

"No," the eldest reassured her. "I have never met the thing religion has labeled a devil. He is just as mysterious to me as to you. Taliesin, on the other hand, is as terrifying as your most horrific nightmare combined with madness."

"What does he have to do with why I'm here?" Agnes asked, confused. "Does he have something to do with the witch hunt?"

"Yes and no," the youngest admitted, biting her lower lip in thought. "He created the course you are on now, but I don't know if he's directly responsible for what is happening."

"That doesn't make sense. How can Taliesin be the one who started me on this so-called path but not responsible? You know they will execute me, right?" Agnes raised an eyebrow. "Just because I am a witch. And you're telling me I have to die."

"Yes," the eldest said slowly. "Your king will ensure it. However, Taliesin was the one who planted the idea in his head."

"Why?" Agnes cried, tears cascading down her cheeks. "What did I do to him?"

"Nothing," the youngest admitted, stepping forward to touch her shoulder. A warmth radiated from her fingers, and Agnes felt a calming sensation run through her. "But I can promise you, your death will save many more lives."

"Wonderful. I'm happy to be of service," Agnes frowned, wiping her tears. "But it doesn't make any of this any easier."

"I know. And I'm sorry about that," the eldest said as she shrugged.

The movement drew Agnes' attention to a key hanging around her neck, glinting in the light. She squinted her eyes as the shape and design of the key brought back memories of a mysterious woman who had paid an unexpected visit numerous years ago.

The old woman had appeared in the middle of a thunderstorm—a storm unlike anything Agnes had ever witnessed. Torrential rains poured down, washing away the land and creating massive mudslides. The wind was relentless, screeching its way through the cracks of her home, threatening to extinguish the meager peat fire she worked tirelessly to keep alive.

When night fell, a desperate pounding at her door made Agnes jump. She hurried to see who was foolish enough to be outside in such weather. Shivering uncontrollably, a strange woman stood before her in a tattered cloak, hair dripping wet and plastered on her face. Her voice was raspy as she pleaded for coffee and a warm place to wait out the storm.

Inviting the woman in, she eyed the stranger as she settled into the closest chair near the fire, warming her hands. She was an old woman wearing a flowing hand-spun dress, mud-spattered apron, and blue eyes that looked like fresh creek water tickling down after the first snow melt. Her thick gray hair had been braided back in a loose bun, and her hand was stained with ink. A black ribbon was tied around her neck, holding a key made of old iron and bronze with a cylindrical shaft and one thin, rectangular tooth.

Agnes offered her a mug of mead, not knowing what coffee was or how to make it. The old woman nodded, her gaze fixed on the dying flames in the hearth. She carried a thick volume of worn leather and yellowed pages, her gnarled fingers sweeping over the surface lovingly.

Watching her from the corner of her eye, Agnes poured two mugs and settled into a chair across from her. The woman didn't take long to share her story, and Agnes listened in awe. She wove a fantastical tale about a key and a book that could send a soul beyond time. The old woman's far-fetched story initially amused her, but she became concerned when the old woman mentioned Agnes' grimoire.

No one outside her family knew about it. The book was their most closely guarded secret.

"How do you know?" Agnes asked in disbelief.

"I've seen it before. A day when the past, present, and future exist simultaneously. On that day, you will be tested. The past will threaten to devour you; the future will try to claim you for itself. But you will find the others tied together by the Fates."

Agnes clasped her hands, knuckles whitening as the old woman's clear blue eyes searched hers.

"Look for the threads linking you to the three, and you will survive."

Agnes nodded. The woman had a strange and familiar air about her, old and young simultaneously. She smelled of books, wet ink, and fresh-cut wood. She carried herself with care and her eyes spoke of unfathomable experiences. And despite Agnes' reservations, there was something trustworthy about her.

"Good." The woman stood and shuffled toward the door. Agnes eyed the staff she used. It was beautiful, with intricately carved figures depicting faces in various expressions, books, waves, and ravens. The artwork continued halfway up, where unfinished features of a woman's face were discernible, still taking shape as if it had just been started.

Before walking back into the storm, the woman turned around. The sadness in her eyes was heartbreaking. "We will meet again. Soon."

And then she vanished into the darkness.

Agnes never saw her again and forgot about the night until now. How did the key a mysterious woman wore years ago end up on the sister's throat?

She opened her mouth to ask, but the eldest sister held up a hand, quieting her. Her gaze was stern, and her voice carried an unmistakable note of authority. "A question to be answered later. Right now, we must plan our next move."

"Wonderful. Do you have a plan? Because I don't," Agnes admitted, pulling her attention away from the mysterious key and back to the matter at hand.

The younger sister stepped forward, her hands shaking in excitement as she tenderly held a book toward her. Agnes noticed the leather cover and the distinctive binding—a familiar energy radiating from it.

It was her grimoire!

That couldn't be right. She'd tore it to shreds on the hilltop, throwing its pages into the wind. How did they have it? Looking up in disbelief, she saw a knowing smirk on the sister's lips.

"Who are you?" Agnes whispered.

The elder sister raised an eyebrow. "I was wondering when you would ask. My name has been forgotten. Wiped from existence. But you can call me Nava."

"She's so dramatic," the youngest chimed in with a smile, rolling her eyes. "I'm Ysabel, her younger sister. I fixed your book. I thought you might need it again," she added with a wink.

Agnes held a shaky hand to take it, a jolt of recognition running through her veins. The women standing in front of her weren't just ordinary witches. They smelled different, like old leather, hot sand, and fresh olive oil.

"You're her..." Agnes took a step back. "The witch who summons the dead? My mother said you died."

"No, not dead," Nava shook her head. "We have always been here, hovering in the shadows, watching and waiting for the day our help was needed. All someone had to do was ask, and we would come."

"I thought you had changed," Agnes admitted, searching for a sign of the dark magick she supposedly possessed.

"No," Nava scoffed. "That's a nasty rumor—a rumor I'm still owed a pound of flesh for," she finished, glancing at her sister.

Ysabel shook her head and rolled her eyes again. "And what would we do with a pound of flesh?"

"I don't know, but I can think of something," Nava joked.

"We do not harm," Ysabel chastised and looked back at Agnes. "Magick is a gift. As with mortals, not everyone has the same abilities. Some, like you and me, were destined to be healers. Others were given the ability to do something unexplainable- like communicating with the dead. It is neither good nor bad if used correctly."

"Unless forced to do something they don't want to," Nava grumbled. Ysabel nodded sadly.

"What happened?" Agnes asked, intrigued.

"It's a long story." Nava glanced at the tree.

"I got time."

Chapter 26- Chloe

Modern Day- City of the Unspoken

"I met her once," Lilith offered, her voice nostalgic. She tapped her long, manicured nails on the table, staring out a darkened window behind me. "A long time ago."

"You met her? The Witch of Endor?" I asked, arching an eyebrow and nearly dropping my coffee mug. "When? Why didn't you say anything?"

"My dear, when you have lived as long as I have, certain memories are better left tucked away and forgotten." The faint wrinkles on her face deepened with each word, etching lines of sorrow and regret. The room fell silent, filled only with the soft ticking of the grandfather's clock and the heavy weight of unspoken secrets.

"Well, your memory is needed," I grumbled. "So, start talking."

"It's a day I'd rather not remember. But since you've asked so politely...," Lilith quipped, her tone dry with bitterness. "I can still remember the heat from the fire and the scent of burning flesh. It was a day that scarred a nation with its carnage and bloodshed. There was no love for the supernatural back then. Even a whiff of extraordinary abilities meant death for those accused. And it all started with one woman's death."

"Who?" Isabelle leaned in, her eyes shining with curiosity.

Watson looked fiercely at Lilith, clenching his fist as if he wanted to end the conversation immediately.

Lilith ignored him. "Agnes Sampson."

Plot twist! I looked at her, stunned. Lilith knew Agnes. Which meant she might have known the Witch of Endor. I wanted to ask, but Lilith continued with her story.

"She was a coven leader like you, Isabelle." Lilith's eyes darted towards her, a soft smile playing at her lips, and her tapping stopped. "She was a highly respected healer. And she made a wicked batch of mead. Unfortunately, she got caught in the crossfire of religion vs. reality. And paid with her life."

"How did you know her?" Watson interrupted, his eyes filled with panic. "And why were you in Scotland?"

"Why wouldn't I be?" Lilith narrowed her eyes as she shifted her gaze to the vampire. "It was my bloodline murdered. *My* sons and daughters being wiped from existence. What kind of mother would I be if I didn't try to stop it?"

"But you didn't," Victor pointed out. "Why?"

Lilith turned towards him, her anger blazing like a flame. "The Fates forbade me from interfering," she spat with disdain.

"Why was the Witch of Endor in Scotland?" I pressed.

"She made a promise to Agnes." Lilith shrugged, glancing at me. "And the Witch of Endor takes her promises very seriously."

"You're being very elusive," I grumbled, my anger rising. I met Lilith's intense gaze and shifted uncomfortably in my chair. Whenever she focused her attention directly on someone, it was never comfortable.

"I apologize if my storytelling does not meet your expectations," she sneered. "But you ask me questions I cannot answer. It's not my story to tell."

"So, why were *you* in Scotland?" Max asked.

Lilith swung her unnerving spring-green eyes toward him, and he winced when he caught the silver flashes dancing as a warning. "News had spread that Taliesin had wormed his way into the king's council, and I wanted to find out if it was true. I'd seen the havoc the man could cause, and in this case, he was certainly up to his usual mischief."

"How did he secure a council seat? The king had to have known he was 'different?'" Eidolon asked, air quoting the last word.

"Your guess is as good as mine. Taliesin had a knack for befriending royalty. If there was a witch hunt or a vampire scare, you better believe he was in the area."

"Were you the one who found Geillis' grimoire?" Isabelle blurted out, her fingers anxiously twisting the delicate bracelets on her wrist.

"Now that is a story that I can tell," Lilith answered, glancing at her watch. "But we will have to save it for another day, I'm afraid. I have somewhere I must be." She suddenly vanished, leaving her chair empty and the scent of spring dancing in the air.

"Guess story time is over," Victor mumbled, grabbing a piece of bacon.

"Surprise, surprise." A frown crept onto my lips as I pushed away from the table, my chair scraping against the floor. Without a word, I grabbed the Witch of Endor's book and turned to face Watson, daring him to take it back from me.

He tilted his head, flashing me a warning look before nodding. Feeling like I won a small battle, I headed out of the room.

"Where are you going?" Eidolon called out.

"I need a minute to myself," I called over my shoulder, not looking back. I didn't have a plan or know where I was headed. I just needed space to clear my head.

"We will be here." I heard him answer, sitting back down.

My feet pounded against the cold, steep steps as I sprinted up the stairs, my hands tightly gripping the ancient leather-bound book. My long hair flew wildly behind me, escaping from its confined ponytail. With each step I took, my heart beat faster, and anger throbbed through my veins like a raging river.

Ignoring the burning ache in my legs, I bounded up two steps at a time until I reached the top landing. My body screamed in protest, but my mind was too consumed with fury to listen. Panting heavily, I finally stumbled into my bedroom and slammed the door. Sliding down to the floor, I fought to control my breathing.

In through the nose. 1, 2, 3. Out through the mouth. 1, 2, 3. In through the nose. 1, 2, 3. Out through the mouth. 1, 2, 3.

Gods, I needed to work out more.

Lilith's half-ass explanation felt like a slap in the face, and doubt bubbled inside me. What wasn't she telling us? And why? I leaned my head against the door, staring at the aged ceiling, feeling sorry for myself. Out of the corner of my eyes, I watched as my faithful companions emerged from the room's corners.

The shadows of my past.

It had been quite some time since I had seen them. I didn't want to admit it, but I missed having them around. When I was younger, their existence terrified me. But as time passed, I learned to acknowledge that they were a part of me, and I eventually welcomed them into my life.

They were my secret, something I tried to hide from the world. It wasn't socially acceptable to admit you had imaginary friends. It usually ended up with a trip to the psychiatric ward. So, I pushed them away, barricading them behind an imaginary steel door in my mind.

But today?

Today, I welcomed their familiar shapes and sounds. Reaching out, I encouraged them to cloud my mind from reality and give me the desperately needed escape. And they didn't disappoint. They surrounded me in a warm blanket of relief, and I sighed in contentment.

"They are quite tempting, aren't they?"

My eyes shot open at the sound of a female voice. I glanced over and noticed a woman sitting on my bed, her legs tucked under her and a book in her lap. She was shrouded in shadows, just like mine. The corner of her mouth tugged upwards mischievously as if she already knew the answer.

I nodded in response and let my gaze drop to my hands. The air around them vibrated, black as midnight, alive with energy as I twirled my fingers in the ether. Tiny electricity pinpricks danced across my skin. A strange tugging came from the Witch of Endor's book pressing against my palm. My copy of the Book of the Veiled called to me from downstairs, warning me to put it down.

I ignored it.

"I understand the obsession." She lifted her slender arms, admiring the shadow's movement. "Mine have been with me longer than I want to admit. I don't tell anyone about them, only allowing them out when I'm alone. Is it the same for you?"

My heart pounded, and my throat constricted. Memories of sterile white corridors, the constant hum of fluorescent lights, and the pungent aroma of antiseptic soap flooded my mind. My therapist would have a field day if she found out my imaginary friends had imaginary friends.

But as I glanced up at the woman, I trusted her to understand.

"They feel like home," I admitted. "When they are around, I'm not afraid. Death is just the next great adventure."

I wanted to cry as soon as the words came out. A release from the pressure that had built up inside me for years. I never told anyone about my dreams of death. Not the process of dying but the freedom I imagine I would find in finally being released from living.

I had a lengthy list of dreams and destinations to cross off. But I also knew deep down that they were unattainable aspirations, like immortality or having a genie at my command. They would be nice, but realistically, they were impossible.

Death was inevitable.

"It's tempting to give in to them, isn't it?" the woman asked as she uncrossed her legs and stepped closer to me. Her shadows extended out and reached for mine. "But you know you can't," she replied, her voice gentle yet firm.

Of course, I couldn't, I thought with a sigh. *That would be wrong.*

"I'm not telling you what you feel is wrong," she reassured. "Often, the Fates have a different plan in mind for us. I know you don't understand and have more questions than answers. But you have to stay strong, lil' Writer. I need you to see this through. You know, backstage managers have a place in the world, too."

Her words caught my attention, and I looked sharply at her. I had heard that phrase before. Memories of the morning I sneaked away from camp when we arrived in the Otherworld came rushing back. I had wandered down to the river, needing a moment to myself. And then she appeared, and we had the same conversation.

"You're her?" I asked, finding my voice. "You're the woman at the river."

She smiled at me and nodded. "It's good to see you, lil' Writer. I hoped we would meet again."

"Who are you?" I asked, my hands twitching.

"You know who I am," she replied, arching her eyebrows.

I looked closer. We were mirror images of each other, with the same wild green and yellow eyes, unmanageable hair cascading around our faces, dark circles under our eyes, and fatigue permanently etched on our foreheads.

"Morrigan," I whispered. "What are you doing here? Have you come to help find your book?" The shock of seeing her faded, and excitement flooded me.

She shook her head, her wild hair framing her face. "No. I don't know where it is," she shrugged. "I came because your shadows called. And to tell you that it's okay to feel lost. Some people are meant to dance with the shadows. You must learn to embrace them and not hide that part of you."

"Easy for you to say. You can't get locked up in a mental ward," I muttered.

"True. I have seen those places. They're horrible." Morrigan shuttered in displeasure. "But that doesn't mean you can't find a way to live with them. I did."

"How?" I asked, curious. It would be nice not to lock them away and pretend they weren't there. As crazy as it was to say, the shadows kept me sane.

"Don't fight them. It's our secret power. We can be both in this world and in another. We stand in the shadows so that we can see the truth. Not everyone will understand, but those who do are the ones we hold on to."

"Do you have someone?" I asked curiously.

"I did." She nodded sadly, looking out the window.

"What happened?"

"He changed. He became someone I didn't recognize anymore," Morrigan admitted, her gaze returning to mine.

"Sounds promising." I rubbed my hands together, wondering if my person was Eidolon. And if it was, would

Morrigan laughed. "No, I guess it doesn't. But it will all be worth it in the end."

"How do you know?"

"Because you will save him."

My mouth dropped, and I stared at the woman in disbelief. But before I could say anything, there was a knock. I groaned inwardly, glancing over my shoulder at the heavy oak door, knowing Eidolon was on the other side, worried about me. I glanced back at where Morrigan had been and found myself sitting in an empty room.

She had left again without a word.

Rude!

Chapter 27- Chloe

Modern Day- City of the Unspoken

I flung the door open, and Eidolon stormed in, his eyes blazing with suspicion. "Who were you talking to?" His nostrils flared as he sniffed the air, searching for any lingering scents. He prowled around the room like a predator, checking every nook and cranny.

"Morrigan," I admitted as I sat on the bed, watching him with amusement as he checked the bathroom.

"Morrigan was here?" His eyes swung to meet mine with surprise. "Did she say anything about her book?"

"Nope," I answered, disappointed. "More like a therapy session."

"That bad?" Eidolon's voice turned to concern. He moved to the bed and sat down next to me, his body heat radiating in waves. The tiny hairs on my arm raised in awareness of how close he was. I nodded. "How do you feel now?"

"Better," I admitted. "More in control. Ready to find the next book. Looking forward to clean clothes." I eyed my sweatshirt with disdain.

His eyes sparkled, and his lips curled into a sultry smirk. His breath was hot in my ear as he whispered, "You look stunning to me." His shadows reached out and lightly touched my neck, sending shivers down my spine.

"That's a new trick," I whispered as the shadows moved down my back. I arched in surprise, giggling.

"New to me too," he breathed in an awed voice. "I've never been able to control them before."

"And you can now?" I turned to face him, crossing my legs under me. "What does it feel like?"

"I can't explain it." He held his hands before me.

I inched closer to inspect them and caught a whiff of old leather, dried ink, cedar, and smoke. Then I heard the faint whispers.

"I can hear the books talking to each other." I couldn't contain my excitement as I leaned in closer, placing my ear near his chest.

"They are quite chatty, aren't they?" he remarked with a low growl, his voice rumbling like distant thunder. His eyes glinted with a darker hue, and the intricate designs of his tattoos shifted with excitement.

"Can you hear Taliesin?" I asked, sitting back. I watched with interest as words started forming on his forearms. *Lost souls. Missing books. Home.*

Eidolon's lips tightened, a hint of remorse flickering in his eyes as he lowered his gaze. "To be honest with you, I haven't tried today. I'm not sure how I feel about my father's book. Part of me wants to open it, to learn why he did what he did. But the other part of me wants to rip it apart and hope I never see him again."

His hands clenched and unclenched, the tightness in his muscles mirroring the anger burning inside him. His eyes darkened with thoughts of his father, the man who bound him to the mortal world and robbed him of his true purpose—guiding souls to their afterlife.

The same man who betrayed his mother and trapped her in a tree for eternity.

What could I say? Eidolon had a lot of crap to work through.

And if that wasn't horrifying enough, now Taliesin was after me.

I tried not to take it personally. But it proved that you can't judge a book by its cover. The first time I met Taliesin, I thought he was pretty decent. Just a father trying to save his son and wife from Lilith and Vivian, working non-stop to save the supernatural and give them the future they deserve.

Boy, was I wrong.

Eidolon's mother, Diana, warned me that there was only one way to stop him. She wanted me to unwrite his story—erase it from the pages of history.

But by doing that, I would also erase Eidolon.

Talk about being between a rock and a hard place!

"So, what now?" I asked, glancing at the Witch of Endor's book, its creaky binding begging me to open it. I ran my fingers over the aged leather cover and heard its whispers teasing me with promises of untapped power.

Could she really bring back the dead? And if she could, could she find someone for me?

The one person I needed forgiveness from.

Before I could open it, Eidolon shadows danced across my thigh, and my eyes widened in surprise. A sudden spark ignited between us as he inched closer. His eyes were hooded but twinkled with amusement. His lips curved into a mischievous smile, sending a shiver of anticipation up my spine.

Eidolon's piercing indigo eyes locked onto mine, and a surge of emotions instantly swept me away as his gaze held me captive. Being near him gave me an overwhelming sense of strength and security. And suddenly, the Witch of Endor's book was no longer important.

Sitting beside me was the man who made me believe that 700 years plus 700 years was not enough.

And if it wasn't possible, what would you do?

I recoiled at the soft reverberations of the Witch of Endor's words dancing around the room, echoing from her book.

What the hell? I glanced at Eidolon to see if he had heard the voice, but he was still like a statue. His expression was vacant like his mind had been transported elsewhere. I tried waving my hand in front of his face a few times, but he didn't blink.

Ah, come on! I thought as I slapped him across his face. *Not this again!*

Accept the truth. Eidolon will die. Not even Lilith can change what the Fates have chosen for you.

I looked down at the book, sneering. "I don't accept. My fate is what I make it. No one. And I mean no one. Not Taliesin, not Lilith, not Moll, and definitely not some random book will tell me what my future holds."

We'll see, lil' Writer. For your sake, I hope you make the right decision. The Fates will be watching.

"What the hell was that?" Eidolon growled, shaking off the effects of whatever spell he had been under. He did not look amused.

"I don't know," I lied. "I think you spaced out."

"No, Chloe. I didn't space out. That book did something to me," he accused, pointing to it. "It has some serious issues."

"It's no different from the rest of the books here," I mumbled, not looking him in the eye.

Eidolon's eyebrows shot up in disbelief. "You have to be kidding me."

"It's probably because you keep yelling at it," I shot back, angry. "Try being nicer."

"Chloe," he growled and reached out to take it.

Jumping up, I grabbed the book and hurried to the other side of the room, ready to bolt out the door if he got closer. "It's mine!" I shouted, my look dared him to take it from me.

Eidolon clenched his jaw, pushing himself off the bed with a calculated slowness. His shoulders squared off as he stood to his full height, creating an overwhelming presence in the room. His gaze fixed on me, his face a storm of barely contained rage.

I stepped back, the intensity emanating from him in palpable waves.

"No, it's not, Chloe. It belongs to the Witch of Endor. And until we understand what its connection is to you, I don't want you handling it more than necessary."

"It's mine." I knew I sounded like I was whining, but I couldn't help it. The book belonged to me. I was the granddaughter of the Witch of Endor; didn't that make me the heir to it?

"Chloe," Eidolon growled again, and I squared my shoulders, ready to fight. He tried to hide a smile and quickly walked towards me, and I took another nervous step back, my back pressing against the door. "Give the book to Victor. Let him look."

I looked up at him, trapped as he stood with his hands on either side of me against the doorframe. "Why Victor?" I swallowed and tried to steady my racing heart.

Eidolon rolled his eyes. "Because Victor can't die. If anyone can handle whatever is in that book, it's him."

"That's it? Then I can have it back?"

"Of course, lil' Writer. I wouldn't dream of keeping a book from you," he reassured me with a chuckle, and I gave in.

Not because he wanted me to, but to prove I could.

Trembling, I passed the book to him, and he wordlessly flung it onto the bed. Then he wrapped me in a tight embrace that felt like falling into an endless abyss. But even in his arms, I couldn't escape the chilling cold that had consumed me since we stumbled upon Taliesin's book.

"It's going to be okay," he muttered into my hair as I leaned into his warmth. "We will get through this together."

Of course, we would. I just hoped we would still be in one piece when we did.

Chapter 28- Nava

1000 BC- Village of Endor, Jezreel Valley, Israel

T he unlikely group plotted along a dusty trail, following in the footsteps of countless others who had traveled the path before them. The mountains loomed overhead, gradually coming into view as they approached from the east. Every step felt like an uphill battle, but finally, they arrived at the top of a hill that overlooked Samuel's final resting place.

Thankfully, the king declared they should rest for the night before heading down.

Nava and Isabel set up camp while Magus wandered off into the hills alone in search of food. The king built a fire. He was strangely quiet, completing his chores with single-minded focus and determination.

But Nava knew better. He was nervous.

"How did you meet Magus?" Nava asked when he brought back a fourth armful of kindling, throwing it down by the fire before taking a break.

King Saul wiped the sweat off his face with his sleeve and took a long drink of water before answering.

"I can't tell you for sure," he shrugged. "He just showed up one day. Said he came from one of the border villages I'd never heard of. But with a kingdom as large as mine, remembering them all is nearly impossible."

"And you don't find it strange that after you banned magick, someone would be elected to the council who practiced?" Nava wearily collapsed onto the ground, her body covered in a thin sheen of sweat from the long day of traveling. The flickering flames danced in front of her, casting shadows across her features, highlighting her worry about her journey into the Otherworld.

"No. I was desperate at the time. There were reports that a rebel group was aiding my enemy. That's why I had to act quickly." King Saul looked at the sister sheepishly. "Granted, looking back, it was another hasty decision that backfired." He took another drink and wiped his lips. "With half my advisors and councilors dead or missing, I had no one to turn to. When Magus showed up, promising he could help, I allowed him to stay."

"Who told you the rebel group was supernatural?" Ysabel asked, her steps light as she made her way to sit beside her sister. The king glanced up at her with a wary look. Ysabel shrugged, her expression unreadable. "I assume they must have been supernatural for you to turn against us."

"I don't know. The message was delivered by a child, but it was convincing," the king answered before taking another drink. He handed the bladder to Ysabel. "It claimed the group leader possessed the power to raise an army that couldn't be killed."

"Did the message at least give you a name?" Ysabel pressed before taking a drink.

King Saul nodded in Nava's direction with a tight smile. "That's why my guards were in your village. They were ordered to watch you and report back. I knew everything you were doing. Every refugee group you helped escape, every villager you treated. I knew you would run if I sent for you, so I waited. Magus thought if we caught you off guard, you would be more likely to comply with my request."

"Interesting." Nava glanced up, her ears perking as she head the soft sound of Magus' steps. The air cracked with energy as he came closer. His presence was unmistakable, and the scent of magick hung heavy in the air.

"I found dinner," Magus declared haughtily. In one hand, a fox dangled by its hind legs while the other held a woven bag bursting with berries and nuts.

The king nodded in approval as Magus quickly skinned and gutted the animal, expertly tying it to a slender branch he propped over the flames. Soon, the rich aroma of roasted game filled the air.

Nava's stomach growled in anticipation, her mouth watering from hunger. Traveling to the Otherworld meant risking her life, and she needed every ounce of energy she could get to stay focused on where she was heading. If she got lost, it would be almost impossible to return.

She would be trapped. Living in the world of the dead. With no hope of escape.

She glanced up at Magus, who had offered her a piece of meat with a slight hesitation and nodded gratefully. She took a tentative bite, savoring the burst of flavors that exploded on her tongue. Despite her initial reluctance, she couldn't deny that it was one of the most delicious meals she had tasted in a long time.

"I need something to persuade Samuel to return with me," Nava directed to King Saul, her mouth full. "Something personal to show you sent me."

The king reached a hand to his chest and lifted a bronze key from around his neck. Its edges were etched with swirling symbols that glinted in the dim light.

His expression softened as he looked at it, and a hint of sadness appeared in his eyes before he extended it towards her with a small, melancholic smile.

Nava reached for it, running her fingers along its smooth surface, feeling the subtle vibrations of magick. "Where did you get this?"

"It was a gift. A woman gave it to me, claiming it was the first of its kind. She said I should keep it safe until it unlocks my fate. Judging by the situation, the day has come."

Magus eyed the key with a sneer. "Always interfering," he muttered to himself before turning his attention back to his food.

Nava's appetite had vanished, replaced by a deep contemplation. She rolled the key between her fingertips, studying every detail of its design. It held a weight in her hand that matched the gravity of her thoughts. She couldn't quite explain it, but this key held more significance than even King Saul realized.

It was a symbol of something greater, something she couldn't fully grasp yet. But she knew it would lead to a defining moment in her life.

"I will go tonight," Nava declared, standing up and dusting off her dress. "Alone," she said firmly when Magus stood up to follow.

"Of course," King Saul said, looking at Magus with a pointed eye. "We will wait here."

Magus sat back down slowly, his eyes shimmering in the darkness. Nava knew he wasn't happy about the king's decision, and she hid a smile. It served him right.

"Be safe." Ysabel reached up and grabbed Nava's hand; worry creases forming along her forehead.

Nava smiled down at her.

She would be fine.

She hoped.

With a deep breath, Nava walked alone to Samuel's burial spot and knelt at the grave. Under her hands, the soil burned cold. She inhaled its energy, allowing the grains of sand to fill her with power. Closing her eyes, her mind wandered down the connection linking the two worlds.

When she opened them again, she was in the Otherworld.

"I thought I would find you here," a deep voice called to her. "I assume the king has finally found you?"

Chapter 29- Nava

1000 BC- Otherworld Gates

"Good to see you again," Nava called out, walking towards the imposing figure standing at the entrance to the Otherworld. She eyed him up and down.

The god was mesmerizing and dangerously attractive. His dark, wild hair cascaded over his shoulders, highlighting his dazzling silver eyes. He wore his signature black tunic and a soft gray cloak, complementing his sun-kissed skin, athletic body, and formidable stature. The sweet aroma of white heather surrounded her, and she took a steady breath. "Sorry to show up unannounced, but I need to find the prophet Samuel."

"I was afraid of that," he greeted with a frown, crossing his arms across his broad chest. "So, he finally found you."

"It appears that way." Nava handed him the bag of dates she had brought. She learned early on that the god had a fondness for sweets and always brought something from her world as a tribute. "I have to admit, I was hoping the king wouldn't."

He tore open the gift with a grin and popped one into his mouth with a flourish. "Thank you," he muffled through a mouthful of food. "I meant, Taliesin must have located you." He clarified after swallowing, digging into the pouch for another. "Not the king."

"Who's Taliesin?" Nava asked, watching in amusement. Food easily won over the god, and she found it charming.

"The man you are traveling with. I think you call him Magus." He offered a date to the fearsome beast at his side. The creature sniffed and huffed in response, turning its head in disgust. "Your loss," he chuckled, devouring the treat instead.

"His name is Taliesin? He never told us," Nava fumed. She already didn't trust him, and the fact that he withheld his name was just another reason not to.

The god didn't answer as he swiveled slowly, his eyes focusing on the ancient archway behind them. His expression softened as a small white light passed through the gate. Another soul was making the voyage from the living to the dead. "Go in peace," he whispered. "Your journey starts tonight."

When the glow disappeared, he turned his attention back to Nava. "I suppose he wouldn't. It would have opened the door to questions he would not have answered. So, you came here for Samuel?" he asked with a glint in his eye. "Not an easy person to find."

"The king says he needs to talk to him," she shrugged, watching the creatures as they drew forward to sniff her. She had a healthy respect for the hellhounds and understood they were weary of her abilities. After all, their primary duty was to ensure souls remained in the Otherworld, and Nava threatened that purpose. "Something about proving he could become the king he wanted to be."

"That's interesting. And who put that idea into his head, I wonder?" The god paced back and forth, his hellhounds following close behind. Their strong bodies and regal heads moved in flawless synchrony with the gods long gait. In the perpetual twilight of the Otherworld, their eerie red eyes glowed ominously.

"I don't know. All I know is that I need your help locating Samuel." Nava's gaze followed him, unsure if he would help her or not. She was prepared to beg but hoped it wouldn't come to that.

"Finding Samuel won't be easy, but I can help." The god stopped pacing and locked his intense gaze on Nava. "However, I will need a favor in return."

"From me?" Nava's heart raced. It wasn't every day that the god of the Otherworld asked for a favor.

"Yes, from you," he chuckled. "There will come a day when the past, present, and future exist simultaneously, and I will need your assistance guiding someone back to the Otherworld. They may not want to come, and things could become problematic."

"Sounds ominous." Nava rubbed her hand across her neck, massaging the tense muscles.

The boundary between the mortal world and the Otherworld was an impenetrable barrier, strictly enforced by the hellhounds and magick. The living could not cross. To do so could cause a rift in reality. But as the god's request echoed in her mind, she knew this was not something she could ignore.

He had a reason for breaking his own rules.

"It's for their own good," he answered Nava's unspoken question.

"Can I ask why? Why risk everything for a mortal?"

"Because they will fix what is about to be broken," he said sadly before forcing a smile that didn't meet his eyes. "But enough of that. Let's go find Samuel."

Nava followed a few steps behind, the smallest hellhounds strolling beside her, occasionally looking up with a knowing look. She absentmindedly ran her fingers through its soft, snow-white fur and was surprised when she felt a gentle nudge against her palm.

In a flash, her mind was consumed by an image of a stranger standing in the same spot. The woman appeared to be the same age as Nava, draped in peculiar garments: cloth wrapped around her legs and a short cloak that barely reached her waist, with a hood attached. Instead of a vibrant landscape full of towering trees, bright blooms, and a babbling brook, the view became a bleak wasteland of ashen gray and leafless trunks.

The woman remained still, her gaze unfocused and distant. Dirt covered her face while her disheveled hair formed a messy veil about her shoulders. Her expression revealed her confusion as she scanned the unfamiliar space, accompanied by a slight furrow between her eyebrows.

Was this the person the god of the Otherworld had asked her to bring back? The beast at her feet glanced up, wagging its tail. The scene shifted.

Her gaze fixed on a towering bonfire of stacked logs, blazing fiercely. In the center stood a woman, still and unflinching, encircled by flames that licked at her body with glowing orange tongues.

The mysterious woman from the last vision was there. Tears stained her face as she held something close to her chest protectively. An ornate key hung around her neck, its intricate chain glinting in the glow of the flame. Shadows danced around her, dark and forbidding, as she watched the flames grow brighter. Her eyes darkened as she whispered something into the air, a look of quiet acceptance on her face.

Trying to keep her breathing steady, Nava watched as the image faded away. Her heart pounded in her chest, and an intense dread washed over her.

At least she'd seen enough to know who to find.

"I think I will call you Hester," Nava murmured as she emerged from the vision, the hellhound prancing around her legs. She stooped down to meet its gaze, its bright red eyes looking back with a sad expression. "It means star. When you find her, guide her to me."

The creature hesitated, considering Nava's request. Its massive head swiveled to the god standing by the gate. He considered for a moment before bowing his head in approval. The hellhound turned back, nudging Nava's hand in acknowledgment.

Giving a silent thanks, Nava took a deep breath before rising from the ground. She tried to inject confidence into her smile as she turned toward the god.

"Let's find Samuel."

She'd always been curious about what the other side of the gate looked like but never had a chance to explore. The sky seemed bluer, dotted with soft white clouds and a pleasant fragrance of sweet blooms mixed with pressed olives. The river glistened like diamonds under the sunshine while the mountains shimmered in breathtaking emerald, sapphire, and amber gemstone colors.

Nava glanced longingly at the tiny homes tucked into the landscape. Plumes of smoke curled up from their chimneys, carrying the scent of freshly baked bread and roasted meat. Distant laughter and conversation filled the air, tugging at her heartstrings. There were others here, like Nava and her sister. She could sense them.

Supernatural living together in peace.

It was perfect.

"If I were a betting man, I would guess Samuel is down by the river. That's where I can usually find him," the god called over his shoulder, his long strides turning to the west. Nava nodded, looking back at the village. Sighing, she turned to follow, Hester never leaving her side.

It only took a few minutes to reach the river bank. There, they found a tall man perched atop an enormous boulder facing away from them. His regal clothing hung heavy on his hunched figure, his long black braid hanging loosely down his back. He was skipping rocks into the water below him, one after another, occasionally chuckling to himself.

"Samuel!" the god called out, his booming voice echoing. The man spun around to face them, and Nava jumped back in surprise. His skin glowed ethereally in the sun in contrast to his eyes, which looked centuries old despite his youthful face.

Nava had heard the story of the renowned prophet Samuel, known for his influential words that could bring listeners to tears. Local gossip said he celebrated his 100th birthday years ago. Yet, the man before her appeared no older than fifty.

"Arawn. My dear friend. What brings you out this way?"

Chapter 30- Nava

1000 BC- Otherworld Gates

Nava's eyes widened in amazement. She had never heard anyone address him so casually before. There was power in a name, and she had been too afraid to ask if he had been given one.

"What?" Arawn laughed. "You can't imagine that I go by the god of the Otherworld. It's much too long and too formal for me." He turned back and grasped Samuel's hand, who'd gotten up and walked toward them.

"We were looking for you." Arawn motioned toward her. "This is Nava, and she comes with a request."

Samuel glanced over and gave her a tired smile. "I thought this day might come."

Nava's heart pounded in her chest as she darted a look anxiously back and forth between Arawn and Samuel. She could see the tension in their clenched fists and the sorrow in their eyes. They were well aware of what she was going to ask, and they acted as if she was passing a death sentence.

She took a deep breath to steady herself. "The king has my sister. And the only way to save her is if you come back with me."

Samuel's gaze softened, and he put his hands together prayerfully. His lips moved silently, his eyelids squeezed shut as if pleading with someone. When he opened them, his worry was even more intense.

"It has started."

Arawn nodded, watching as the mountain city lights flickered and died. The river's flow gradually slowed to a trickle. Even the birds ceased singing and flew northward, seeking new homes.

The lush green grass had turned dry and brittle, crunching beneath their feet. Wilted rose petals littered the ground at the base of what used to be a thriving bush. Tree leaves drooped lifelessly from branches that once burst with energy.

Nava gasped in shock as the world around her withered away.

"The Fates have decided," Arawn said sadly, looking around. "We should go."

The three walked back to the entrance gate, the silence growing heavier with every step. When they arrived, Arawn paused, motioning for Samuel and Nava to walk through. When she passed by, he grabbed her hand. She looked up in surprise.

"Nava," he started, staring at her as if looking into her soul. "You have a long path in front of you. There will be days, years, generations even, when you will feel like the world's weight is on your shoulders. But remember, there will be a day when you'll find peace."

Nava nodded, suddenly more afraid than she had ever been. What did Arawn mean by generations? She had no concept of that word, but it sounded like a long time.

As Samuel and Nava approached the campsite, they could see the group waiting for them. The familiar figures sat huddled around a small fire, their shadows flickering on the trees behind them. As they got closer, the king's eyes widened in shock, his mouth falling open as if he had seen a ghost. He stood up abruptly, his hand reaching for the hilt of his sword before realizing what he was doing.

"Samuel," he whispered, bowing his head.

"Why am I here, *king?*" Samuel murmured, his mouth curling in disgust. "We had nothing left to say to each other."

The king's head shot up in surprise at the haunting tone of the dead. He took a deep breath. "I need your help, Samuel."

Samuel's eyebrows raised as he considered the man before him. "From what I heard, it's your subjects that need my help. Did you really murder so many innocent people?"

The king had the decency to look ashamed as he bowed his head again. "An unfortunate event, I admit, but a necessary evil at the time," he protested. "There were rumors that they would side with my enemy."

"And who told you such lies?" Samuel asked, his eyes sliding to Magus standing next to him.

Magus stared back, raising an eyebrow, his face impassive.

"What has been done is done. There is no turning back now." Samuel's eyes narrowed. "But you already knew that, didn't you, *Taliesin?*"

Taliesin chuckled, a sinister smile dancing across his lips. "I did nothing but standby as the king made his own decision," he declared. "I cannot change a man's heart. You should already know that, *Samuel.*"

"True." Samuel frowned, glancing back at the king. "You will die, along with your sons."

Tears streamed down the king's face as he fell to his knees, grasping at Samuel's tunic with desperate hands. "No!" he cried out, his voice cracking with emotion. "I will do anything, Samuel. Please, talk to your God. Do not let this happen."

"This is not my doing. You had a chance, and you chose the wrong path." Samuel glanced at Taliesin, still staring at him with unabashed curiosity. "You have allowed yourself to be sidetracked by the promises of a man who is not of this world."

Nava was thoroughly confused and turned to examine Taliesin more closely, gasping in surprise. Samuel was right. Taliesin's skin shimmered and blurred at the edges. When his gaze shifted from one area to another, he twitched as if trying to maintain control of his form.

How did she miss that?

"I have to leave," Samuel said, his eyes darting to Nava. She nodded in agreement. He looked one last time at his one-time friend, placing a hand on his shoulder. "May God have mercy on your soul."

The spirit shimmered and slowly dissolved as the king's anguish echoed through the atmosphere. His dreams had been crushed and scattered like ashes in the wind, just like he'd broken the spirits of those in his kingdom.

Nava almost felt sorry for him.

The air grew cold, and an eerie silence descended. As she turned her head, Taliesin's dark, foreboding, and intense gaze met hers. His eyes were like a sharp blade that could slice her soul in half.

Ysabel trembled as she clung to her sister's arm.

They needed to leave now.

They ran into the mountains as fast as their feet could carry them.

And never looked back.

Chapter 31- Nava

1000 BC- Village of Endor, Jezreel Valley, Israel

T he king died the next day, along with his sons.

Nava and Ysabel had just settled in for the night when a group of wanderers stumbled upon their makeshift camp. The travelers were greeted with open arms, and they spent hours talking about the tragic news of the king's death.

Only one person escaped the battle. A mysterious man who claimed a necromancer and her sister were the reason why the king died.

And now he was looking for them.

Nava and Ysabel listened to the story, their faces blank as the travelers debated where the witches had disappeared. Some thought they had fled the country. Others felt they were hiding in the mountains, holed up in a hidden cave. One or two thought they had vanished into the Otherworld.

As the whispers continued, the sister's anxiety grew. Taliesin was coming for them.

Their fears were warranted.

He arrived that night, gliding into the camp as a dark silhouette. They felt his arrival before he said a word, glancing out from their blankets at his menacing smile.

"What do you want?" Ysabel hissed, covering her book with her cloak and glaring at the man towering over her.

Taliesin chuckled, leaning back on his heels as he surveyed the sleeping travelers with interest.

Nava peeked over, holding her breath. She had no idea what Taliesin could do, and a cold chill ran down her spine.

"Leave them alone," she demanded in a whisper.

His startling eyes darted back, and he smiled. "I have no interest in them, lil' Witch. I came to see you."

Nava stood up, tightening her cloak around her. "What do you want, Taliesin?"

"Just a small favor," he confessed. "Nothing more than what you did for the king."

"And if I refused?"

Bringing back souls from the Otherworld was exhausting, and the whole ordeal with Samuel took a lot more from her than she was willing to admit. An unseen energy tugged at her whenever she entered the Otherworld, keeping her rooted in place. And with each spirit she brought back to life, a part of herself was left behind in exchange. Soon, she may never return.

"You won't," Taliesin said confidently. "Like I told you before, lil' Witch, my powers far exceed yours. I ask that you hear me out and then make your decision."

He will lead us to the fire. Through her blood, we will be reborn. You must tread carefully, or the Tree of Life will be lost. Her mother's voice whispered, warmth settling around Nava in a protective embrace.

"I assume you are looking for somebody in the Otherworld? A friend? A lover? Someone you have wronged?" Nava questioned, her eyebrows raised in defiance.

Taliesin blinked once.

Nava smiled. There it was. He sought forgiveness.

She could work with that.

His eyes narrowed, glancing back at the travelers when one shifted in their bedroll. He motioned for them to follow him. Ysabel and Nava stole a glance, knowing they had no choice. Tucking their books into their cloaks, they followed.

He silently guided them down a narrow, winding trail, running his fingers along the rough tree bark and deftly avoiding low-hanging branches. The gentle rustling of leaves under the sisters' feet faded into the soothing sound of a nearby river. Wisps of fog floated serenely around the moss-covered trees, and a deep silence enveloped them, punctuated only by birds' nightly song.

Nava was on the verge of demanding to know their destination when Taliesin abruptly changed direction, leading them into a small meadow shrouded in a thick blanket of gray fog. A single tree, its aged bark blackened and knotted, stood sentinel against the night sky. A slight blue shimmer radiated from its branches, growing stronger with each step they took. The ground was alive with energy, and soon, warmth spread through their bodies, drying their clothing and fighting off the lingering chill.

"I can sense something," Ysabel whispered. "Strong magick—nothing I have felt before."

"Me too," Nava whispered back, her gaze falling upon the odd tree. "What is this place?"

"This will be my prison." Taliesin turned to look at them, his eyes turning dark and silver threads of power dancing through them. "But I found a way to prevent it from happening."

"How?" Nava asked, her fingers grazing her book for strength.

"Ironically, thanks to an annoying cat." He chuckled at the memory, and a smile tugged at his lips. "Thankfully, I subdued the beast and found what I had dedicated my life to finding—a way to save my sister."

"What does that have to do with us?" Ysabel asked, her fist clenched. "Or the king?"

Taliesin threw back his head and laughed, the ground beneath them shaking with its sound. "The king? He made his own choices. I was simply in the right place at the right time."

"I see we are back to talking in riddles," Nava huffed, defiantly crossing her arms.

Taliesin's eyes focused on her, and she stepped back instinctively. Suddenly, he transformed from one person to another and back again. His body constantly changed, unable to settle on a single form or identity.

What in the gods name was he? Nava asked herself as she pulled her sister closer to her side.

"The king wanted someone to punish for his failures. Not me. He chose to destroy his kingdom. Just like so many mortals will after him. I saw an opportunity to use his paranoia for my own gains, and I took it."

"What does any of this have to do with your sister?" Ysabel asked in a shaky voice.

"Patience," he demanded. "I was getting to that part."

His appearance changed once more, transforming from a scrawny teenager to a middle-aged man. His hair thickened and darkened, turning a rich chestnut hue, and he wore silver-rimmed glasses that added an air of sophistication to his face. He appeared gentle and exposed, and Nava was sure she was seeing a version of him that would come to fruition in the future.

"One day, *mortals* will kill my sister," he spit out like a chunk of bitter root. "I've spent years looking for a way to right the wrong. To give her back the life that was taken because of Fate's cruel irony. But then, I read about you, Nava, in a history book that had been shelved and forgotten. Imagine my surprise when I learned the gods had blessed you with a gift no one else had.

"It piqued my interest. A woman raises the dead, a king dies, and then she disappears? Without a trace? No one questioned the story, assuming it was a metaphor. It didn't make sense," he shrugged. "So, I had no choice but to find you myself."

"But you found me before anyone knew what I could do," Nava pointed out bitterly. "And the only people who know are either dead or standing here. So how did you read about it?"

"Because it will be recorded. One day in the future, a group of men will sit around a table and decide what reality and myths are. Granted, they will leave out some details. But they left enough of a bread trail for me to follow back in time."

"How?" Nava questioned.

"Being a deity has its perks. My sister and I were crafted by the god who now watches over the Otherworld to serve as advisors in matters of the living and the dead. Our purpose was to help oversee the supernatural as they transition between realms."

"And your sister is now in the Otherworld? Why not ask Arawn to bring her back yourself if he is your creator?" Nava countered.

"Because she's not in the Otherworld," he thundered. "I can't find her."

"Then how am I supposed to find her?" Nava shot back, and she felt Ysabel raise her defenses. "What can I do if she is not in the Otherworld?"

"I don't need you to go to the Otherworld. I need your book," he said, holding out his hand like she would hand it over.

"No." Nava gasped, tightening her hold on her book.

"Yes, you will," Taliesin roared, a tempest of wind running over the sisters and blowing them back a few steps. "Those books belong to me. The Fates owe me for what they have done. You. Will. Give. Them. To. Me. Now!" He advanced with every word, his frame growing larger with each step. His eyes were cold and calculated as he pinned the sisters with a menacing glare.

Nava raised a mental barrier.

Taliesin smiled cruelly. "Deny me, and I will wipe you from existence," he said, his voice a low, menacing rumble. "Your name will be forgotten. You will become nothing more than a whisper—a side note that future generations will glance over and dismiss."

Nava grabbed her sister's hand. The power between them flowed like an ocean wave meeting the shore. Their books whispered, warming with each passing second, and Nava felt a heavy weight in her hand. Defiance and anger fueled her as she moved forward.

"I will not be forgotten. I am *the* Witch of Endor. I existed and will always be."

Without breaking eye contact, she held up the object before her, showing it to Taliesin. His eyes flew to it, and he growled at the key.

Instantly, a small dagger appeared in his hand. "Your books or your blood, the choice is yours," he warned.

And just like the day her mother died, Nava knew what to do.

Take us away from here, she thought, wrapping her hand around the key.

Taliesin's eyes bulged, and he lunged forward, the knife reaching her heart. The pain was earth-shattering, and Nava cried out as she and her sister were transported back to their home by invisible hands.

They landed in the middle of their small garden, and both women fell to their knees, gasping for air and shaking with relief.

"What do we do now?" Ysabel asked as she searched for her book. She breathed a sigh of relief when found it sitting behind her.

I have your blood, Witch of Endor. Taliesin's voice carried through the darkness. *You and your future generations can't escape me.*

Nava glared at the stars, rage coursing through her veins as her body quivered with fury. Somehow, she would stop Taliesin.

She just needed to figure out how.

"We will find his sister," Nava decided, her fingers touching the wound on her chest as it healed. She looked down and frowned. It would leave a scar. "And then we find the Fates."

Ysabel nodded, her fingers dancing along the cover of her book. "Where should we start?"

Nava held the key before her, wondering where it came from. It was something she would have to think about later. Right now, they needed to flee. She quickly unwrapped a small leather strap from her hair and secured the key around her neck. Each shift of the leather felt like an anchor to her soul.

"We go north," Nava said with a firm nod. "We find out where the others have gone and restart."

"Do you think he will find us?" Ysabel asked worriedly.

"Yes. But we will be ready for him next time."

Chapter 32- Agnes

December 1589- Nether Keith, Scotland

Agnes' eyes widened; her mouth dropped open in disbelief as Nava and Ysabel finished their story. The similarities between past and present were uncanny—a king's unwavering distrust for the supernatural and their refusal to bend to his will.

History was repeating itself.

But the sisters escaped.

Maybe there was hope for Agnes.

"How long have you been on the run?" Agnes asked as she drew her cloak tighter around her, trying to ward off the cold.

The temperature in the chamber plummeted, sending a sharp chill through the air that seeped into her bones. Agnes gazed in awe at the towering tree; its branches now transformed into a breathtaking display of glistening icicles. Each breath she exhaled created a puff of mist that lingered in the frigid atmosphere.

"We've lost track of time, but we know what happens next. It's always the same," Ysabel admitted, realizing that Agnes' teeth were chattering. She handed her her cloak.

"You mean witches die?" Agnes whispered as she wrapped the garment around her. The fabric flowed gracefully over her body, the hem brushing against the ground. Its bulk swallowed her petite frame, and she felt like a tiny figure misplaced in a world larger than herself.

"Not just witches. All supernatural. Witches, vampires, giants, mythical animals, and everything in between," Nava explained. "Everybody faces the same fate: reshaped into monsters and lost to history."

Agnes' heart plummeted as a wave of dread washed over her. Her skin crawled, and her throat tightened the more the sisters shared. She wanted to run away, but her feet were rooted to the ground, the icy trundles of fear creeping up her spine.

Would she never be safe?

"No one can stop it from happening?" She couldn't believe it. Was there truly no way to prevent all this from transpiring? There had to be something she could do.

"There is something, but I'm not sure if Lilith has found it yet," Nava said.

"Who's Lilith?"

Ysabel and Nava both stared at Agnes in disbelief.

Nava's words were slow as she explained. "The mother of all supernatural. Protector of a weapon the gods created to keep the balance between us and the mortals. Wife of the first fallen angel."

Agnes shrugged.

Lilith's name had been mentioned a few times in church sermons, usually accompanied by uncomfortable glances and whispers. They said she was Adam's first wife and refused to submit to him. According to clergy leaders, every woman was the product of her disobedience.

If the village women laughed too loud or played too hard, they would be reprimanded and reminded not to follow in Lilith's footsteps. And that was kind compared to what they said about Eve.

But if women were gentle, meek, and obedient, they could escape the consequences of Lilith and Eve's actions. Men would guide them toward redemption, and they could spend eternity in paradise, fulfilling the desires of the superior gender.

"I thought she was a myth," Agnes admitted, feeling foolish.

"Not a myth," Ysabel corrected. "Not a concept or legend - she is still alive."

"And where is she now?"

"Looking for a solution to our problem, like I said." Nava's frown deepened as she glanced at her sister in warning.

Agnes scoffed at the explanation. As a witch, she was well-versed in tales of old gods and powerful forces of nature. Yet this story was far-fetched even by those fantastical standards. Rumors of mermaids were more believable than some old religious man's fable about a mysterious woman who had never been seen.

"How do you explain what we are? Or our abilities? It wasn't accidental," Nava pushed, sensing Agnes' doubt.

"The gods," Agnes answered impatiently as she ran a hand through her hair. She would give anything for a warm cup of mead and wasn't in the mood for a history lesson. She needed a plan, a way forward. The king was waiting for her.

"The gods are limited in their influence on this world." Ysabel gestured towards a table that appeared.

Beneath the gnarled and knotted branches of the aged oak tree sat a small round table surrounded by three iron chairs. The luxurious snow-white linen gently blew in the soft breeze. A handful of candles glowed warmly, sending shadows dancing across the cave walls. A pleasant scent of raspberries and vanilla wafted through the air as Agnes spotted a black kettle perched on top of it. Steam curled from its spout. A wave of gratitude washed over her as she drew closer to it.

"The gods started it all but left the rest to the Fates. After what Athena did to Medusa, they've stayed out of our affairs." Ysabel motioned for Agnes to sit. "Sad story. Woman meets god. Falls in love with said god. The god takes advantage of her. She ends up with a head full of snakes and is banished to a deserted island," Ysabel explained as she poured and handed Agnes a cup.

Agnes gratefully took it, taking a long sip and sighing in relief as its warmth spread throughout her body. She had never had anything like it before. Lighter than mead, warmer than brooth, and held a hint of fruits and spices. She eyed her cup, trying to figure out what it was.

"It's called tea," Ysabel explained with a chuckle. Unfortunately, it hasn't made it to your part of the world. But soon, it will be a staple of every household."

Agnes nodded in appreciation and took another drink. She reached for a roll, her stomach grumbling from not eating all day. The soft, warm bread practically dissolved in her mouth as she chewed. The gods knew she wouldn't get any decent food once she turned herself in, and Agnes planned on taking advantage of the meal provided.

Muttering with her mouth full, she asked, "What became of Medusa? After she was exiled?"

Ysabel leaned back with a smile. "Well, that's where the story gets interesting. Because of the god's interference in the relationship, their punishment against Medusa was a cruel curse they couldn't control. As an unexpected consequence of their haste, they created a powerful weapon that could be used against them. The repercussions of their mistake would reverberate for eternity."

"What weapon?"

"Medusa herself," Nava chuckled in memory. "The punishment also turned out to be a curse on the gods. One look at her, and they would die. In a bizarre twist of Fate, the god she loved turned out to be kind-hearted. He discovered a way to transport her to the Otherworld, where Lilith promised her safety."

"Lilith saved Medusa? From the gods?" Agnes mulled over the tale, taking another sip of her tea. If Lilith was so powerful that she could protect this Medusa person, she should be able to help her.

Nava sadly shook her head, understanding what Agnes was thinking. "She can't prevent this, I'm afraid."

Agnes's heart sank as she gave a defeated nod. The king's cruel intentions for her were already set in motion, and she was nothing more than a pawn in his twisted game. She felt utterly powerless to stop it, her fate sealed by forces beyond her control. As she mulled over the situation, one aspect puzzled her, gnawing at her mind like a relentless predator.

"What does Taliesin have to do with all of this?" She grabbed a scone, jumping it between one hand and the other. It was still hot like it'd just come out of the fire. She took a bite, and her eyes rolled back in pleasure before devouring it.

Ysabel grabbed an apple, eyeing it before taking a bite. "Taliesin is the reason we are where we are now. His sister was killed in a battle between mortals and supernaturals, and ever since then, he's been on the warpath to undo history."

"And what does this have to do with me?" Agnes reached for a small silver tray filled with plump, golden-brown nuts and ripe, vibrant fruits.

"He's not after you personally. He only cares about what your demise symbolizes."

"My death? What's my death going to do?" Agnes whispered around a mouthful of pear dipped in honey.

"Your death will ignite the flames of war against all supernatural." The words dripped from Nava's lips like venom. "Taliesin views it as an opportunity to rally an army and end the Fates."

Chapter 33- Agnes

December 1589- Nether Keith, Scotland

Agnes paused mid-bite. "Forgive me, but what part of this doesn't sound like an excellent idea? Witches have been haunted, tortured, and stripped of their identities for years. I, for one, don't see a flaw in his strategy."

The sister's mouths dropped in disbelief. Agnes shrugged her shoulders.

"We do no harm," Ysabel said, shaking her head. "Even against those who seek to harm us, there is a better way to fight back."

"Great," Agnes exclaimed, leaning her forearms against the table. "What's your plan?"

"Like I said, Lilith is working on it," Nava answered, arching her eyebrows.

Agnes' emotions bubbled up inside her, frustration and desperation mixing in a dangerous concoction. She had come to them for help but, instead, received a death sentence. Not just for herself but for Geillis, too. She reclined in her chair, tilted her head back, and took a slow breath.

"So, no plan. We're just going to sit back and watch innocent lives be lost while our elusive creator scours for some unknown object to save the supernatural." Agnes gestured with her hand, emphasizing the absurdity of their situation.

"Listen to me, lil' Witch." Nava's voice was a tightrope stretched thin, quivering with intense emotion as she hissed through clenched teeth. Her eyes blazed like twin infernos, fierce and unyielding. "Forget about Lilith. We need to focus on you before it's too late." Her words cut through the air like a sharp blade, dripping with warning.

Ysabel's lips curved into a wry smile as she glanced sideways at her sister. "As usual, Nava's approach may be a bit rough," she admitted. "But she has a point. We need your help."

"My help?" Nava asked, her hand stopping mid-air from grabbing a fig. "What do you need me to do? Other than die, I mean."

"We need you to take something with you to the Otherworld," Ysabel's tone was tinged with sorrow as she studied her sister.

Nava's gaze was clouded, lost in thought as she gently ran her fingers over the well-worn cover of the antique black book on the table beside her plate.

"It needs to go to the Library of the Unread."

Agnes's hand fell limply in her lap, the food on her plate suddenly unappetizing. The realization that her life was about to end washed over her with crushing finality.

She closed her eyes and drew a slow, deep breath, attempting to ease the tension gripping her neck and shoulders like an iron vice.

"What do you need me to do?" she sighed.

Nava's voice was urgent as she pushed the heavy book across the table, her eyes darting nervously at the tree. "I need you to take this and hide it in the library where no one can find it."

Agnes' fingers brushed against the book's worn cover, tracing the intricate blood-red etchings. The foreign characters spelled out ' ',□□□□□□ their sharp lines and curves imbued with a sense of ancient wisdom. She lifted the book closer to her face, studying every detail in awe.

"What is it?"

"My story. And of a few others that history will erase. I need you to keep it safe."

Agnes tilted her head in confusion. "I thought you could travel to the Otherworld. Why not take it yourself?"

Nava shook her head. "There are places I can't even reach. My immorality forbids my entrance into the inner world. That's why I need you to take it."

"Why do you want your story hidden?" Agnes pressed.

"Your king will rewrite my history. As I said, your death will ignite a new religion and reality, one where I am erased from existence. If you take my book, it guarantees that the mortals cannot completely destroy me."

"I will do it," Agnes whispered, filling the weight of Nava's request. She knew that when she died, her name would be remembered. Agnes had children to carry her legacy, but what about Nava and Ysabel? Did they have a family? Would anyone remember their names?

A soul without a name was lost.

"There is another thing," Ysabel said softly. Agnes glanced up at her, ready for whatever new twist they were about to throw at her. "We need you to take someone with you."

"Who?" Agnes asked, surprised. Was someone going to die with her? Or would she meet them in the Otherworld?

"Don't worry about that right now," Nava interjected, squaring her shoulders. "I will bring her to you when the time comes. You need to make sure she crosses the gates."

Agnes glanced at Nava, her eyes narrowing. She had a feeling that whoever the mysterious person was, they were not a willing participant.

"What am I supposed to do with her?" Agnes threw up her hands.

"Take her to Arawn. He'll know what to do," Nava answered, getting up and walking away from the table.

"Guess the conversation is over," Agnes muttered as Ysabel followed her. She poured herself another cup of tea and filled her plate again. "Might as well enjoy my last meal," she said as she gazed at the tree with a sad smile.

It didn't answer.

Chapter 34- Chloe

Modern Day- City of the Unspoken

Isabelle and I strolled along the narrow paths of the medieval section of the Library of the Unread, her eyes gleaming with anticipation as we combed through rows of books, looking for a mysterious book that she had seen in a vision. Occasionally, she would pause, tracing her finger down the spines while murmuring something about recognizing it when she saw it.

Helpful!

"Remind me what Claire said about the second book." Balancing precariously on a rickety ladder, Isabelle reached for a parchment roll on the top shelf. A thick cloud of dust and debris filled the air as she pulled it out. Scanning it quickly, she threw the roll back with a frown.

I stifled a gasp of shock as she carelessly handled the precious documents, gritting my teeth and reciting the prophecy. "'Blue represents truth and sadness and leads across a vast body of water to a city built on top of another.'"

I pulled a napkin from my pocket and handed it to her. But she swatted my hand away. Glaring, I put it back, shaking my head at her rashness as she scanned the records.

"I agree that it must be hidden somewhere in Edinburgh. Maybe the Royal Mile?" Isabelle's muffled voice called as she balanced on her toes to reach further back on the shelf.

"It makes sense if we think about it from a historical perspective," I agreed. "A lot of witches died there in the 1500s."

The bile rose in my throat as I imagined the fate of those innocent souls treated worse than diseased animals. Branded like cattle, herded into cramped pens, and carelessly disposed of in shallow graves, their bodies left to rot and decay, forgotten. My stomach roiled with disgust at the thought of such callous disregard for human life.

"Like father, like son," Isabelle commented as she climbed down the steps, pausing every few seconds to scan another book.

"What do you mean?"

"King James wasn't the first to go after the supernatural. His father was notorious for his love of torture and death." Her voice dripped with disdain as she swiped the sweat from her brow, leaving a smear of grime. I offered her my napkin again, and she took it gratefully, wiping the dirt away.

"I didn't know," I admitted, following her as she headed down the aisle toward another shelf.

"I remember my aunt telling me about Lady Janet Douglas and having nightmares about it for months afterward. The king accused her of being a witch and attempting to poison him. He threw her into the dungeons as he tortured her servants and family until they confessed to seeing her supposed assassination attempt." Isabelle pivoted towards me and shuddered. "Her sixteen-year-old son was forced to watch as she was burned alive."

"Why would he go after a Lady?" I asked, horrified. "I thought royalty protected each other. And who in their right mind would make a child watch their mother being executed?"

Isabelle shrugged. "King James hated her brother, so he decided to get rid of the whole family. Accusing her of being a witch was the easiest way."

"Does this have anything to do with the book you are searching for?" I asked, hopeful. I knew this library better than anyone else and could find anything if she told me what to look for.

"There's no need to worry, luv. I've got everything sorted." She plucked another book from the shelf and tossed it onto a round table nearby. I couldn't help but cringe and reluctantly trailed behind her, tidying up the chaos she had left in her wake.

After she launched another book over her shoulder, I threw up my hands and stalked over to where Lilith was sitting, watching with an amused grin. She'd returned from her mysterious mission and found us in the library. When we asked where she'd been, she just shrugged and smiled.

Rude!

"I hope she has a method to her madness," I complained, plopping down and crossing my arms.

"I'm sure she does. We must be patient while she finds what she is looking for," Lilith said with a smile. "Whatever it is, it seems important."

"Isabelle, have you found it yet? I still need to pack," I called out as the grandfather chimed. It had been over two hours since she started searching for her mysterious book, and I was hungry.

"I am aware," Isabelle sang as she danced down another aisle. I sighed in frustration again. "Give me a few more minutes; I'm getting closer."

"Closer to what?" I called out.

"To the answer," she replied, pulling another text down and screaming before dropping it like it was on fire. "That would be a no," she giggled, turning around and dragging out the one next to it.

"At least one of us is being positive," I muttered as Lilith handed me a cup of tea. I breathed in the sweet aroma of vanilla and something new. I couldn't put my finger on the scent; it smelled like honey with a smokey, earthy undertone. I eyed the drink suspiciously before glancing at her. "This is not the normal brew," I accused.

"No, it's not. A different brew for a different day," she admitted, eyeing me. "Drink up. It will help your nerves."

"My nerves are fine." I ignored her pointed stare.

"Of course, lil' Writer," she laughed.

I glowered at the woman as I sipped. Lilith was right. My nerves were fraying, and I was running out of patience. Isabelle was adamant that whatever she sought was essential for our journey back to Scotland but refused to tell me why. And I had things to do before we could leave.

"Found it!" Isabelle said in a triumphant voice, rejoining us with her eyes bright and sparkling. She brushed the dust off her face as she settled between Lilith and me.

We watched with interest as Isabelle ran her fingers over the book's exterior. Her face revealed that she already knew what was inside and couldn't hide her eagerness. She held it in front of her, showing it off like a prize.

"What is it?" I asked, leaning forward to set my mug down.

The book was small and unassuming, its black shell smeared with dirt and a wet patch of something dark. I leaned in closer, and as the light caught its surface, the dullness changed to a deep red – almost like a garnet – edged with intricate silver veins. A thick blood-red script read: *Geillis*.

Chapter 35- Chloe

Modern Day- City of the Unspoken

What the hell? Geillis has a book in the Library of the Unread?

The library was a final resting place for stories lost to time; each book represented a life no one remembered. How did her tale end up here? Geillis was an essential part of history.

Unless there was something no one knew she said.

I had no idea how I'd missed it, considering how many hours I'd walked up and down the aisles. But this book was different. It reeked of iron and blood, and instead of a voice straining to tell its story, it was silent.

Like it was hiding.

Isabelle caressed the cover as if it were an old friend she had not seen in years. Her tone shifted to something unearthly, and she radiated with energy. Her golden hair flew in all directions as though it had a life of its own, while her clothing shimmered and changed shape to reflect her intensity.

"This book is Geillis' final story. I had a vision that it was here somewhere. It is our only hope of getting home and finding Morrigan's book. She will be our guide."

"Geillis? As in your Geillis? The old lady who sold out her friends during the North Berwick witch trials?" I asked, surprised that Isabelle was so confident we needed her book.

"Not an old lady," Lilith corrected. "A young woman in her prime. An accomplished healer and an exemplary person. Not the monster history made her out to be. Geillis may have confessed to witchcraft but only *after* suffering hours of torture at the hands of her employer."

"Why did he think she was a witch?" I asked, reaching over for my tea.

Lilith shrugged, her eyes darting towards me. "On record? Because she sneaked out every night to practice witchcraft. The truth? Geillis was a young woman who refused her employer's advances."

"Oh," I said, ashamed of myself for making assumptions. Not much about her survived historically, minus what was written in the local news at the time of her incarceration and what I'd read in Diana Gabaldon's series *Outlander*. "That's sad but not surprising."

"Yes. It was." Lilith's voice caught as she turned to stare into the fireplace, lost in her memories. "Geillis was subjected to brutality that would make Odin cry. She denied all the charges for hours, even as her hands were locked in the pilliwinks and her head crushed by binding. When she was forced to have a thorough physical examination, the trauma of her experiences became too much.

"Imagine a young woman stripped naked, shaved, and examined like she was nothing better than a sheep on its way to slaughter. Her employer, Setoun, claimed he had found the devil's mark on her, but it was a birthmark.

"Setoun's interrogation was intense. He named everyone in town he had an issue with until Geillis broke and agreed to everything he said. She didn't stand a chance of saving herself or anyone else," Lilith concluded with a shudder.

"She tried to retract her confession," Isabelle offered. "But by that time, the damage had been done. Over sixty people were accused. Most of them, I don't think Geillis ever met. The nightmare didn't end with her friend's death; she was doomed to sit in the dungeon for another year- with nothing but her memories of what had happened. She wrote her final words in this book. It was located days after she died, buried in her cage."

"Who found it?" I asked, astonished that it hadn't been discovered earlier.

How did the guards miss it? And how did it end up in the Library of the Unread?

"I didn't even know it existed until I had a vision," Isabelle admitted with a frown. "I think it showed up the same day the Witch of Endor's did."

We sat silently, lost in our thoughts surrounding the poor woman.

I reached out to touch her final offering, overwhelmed by sadness and anger seeping out of its cover. I could almost see Geillis in the cell, covered in dirt and grime, head misshapen by torture, fingers barely able to grip her writing instrument. Painfully capturing her last truth and confession.

"How will her book help us?" I asked, snatching my hand away as my stomach turned with disgust at how she spent her final days.

"Just like Arawn's book. We'll use it as a guide back home," Isabelle explained.

"I'm confused. Arawn is alive. Geillis is dead. If we use her book to return, wouldn't it just take us to where she's buried? Or worse, interfere with timelines."

"Not necessarily." Moll hobbled into the library, her raven perched on her shoulder, watching me with interest. "Even if you are pulled back in time, don't get involved. As long as history repeats itself, it should be fine."

"You can't be serious. Shouldn't I try to do something? They *were* murdered."

"No. It's not your job. You're only there to record the truth, not change it because you don't like the outcome."

"Innocent people are going to die, and you want me just to sit and watch from the front seat? Doesn't seem right." I complained, leaning back in my chair. The whole situation wasn't sitting well with me.

"Then you are not the Writer I thought you were," Moll accused, her lips drawn in a thin line, her tone cold and hardened. I could feel the tension building between us; her words struck me like lightning, her accusation echoing like thunder.

A wave of fury hit me, shaking me to the core. But Moll was right; I couldn't get involved. Instead, I gritted my teeth and forced myself to acknowledge the truth- every event was destined. Even the worst moments in history had their place in the vast tapestry of time, and no amount of regret or grief could alter them.

Too many writers, historians, and leaders rewrote history to fit their narrative, changing the world. I would not be one of those people.

It still sucked, though.

"Good," Moll nodded, knowing what I'd decided. "Then we are ready to move forward with Isabelle's plan. I agree you must go tonight. It's supposed to be a full moon, and it'll help with your travels. I have contacted Odin and Freyja, and they should be back before you leave. In the meantime, Max and I will stay here and continue to research Lilith's book."

"What about Sydney and Bree?" I asked, sitting up, hopeful. They'd embarked on some secret mission before everything happened with Aelle and Taliesin's book. I still wasn't sure where they were or when they were returning.

"They'll be back when they find what they need," Moll said, not looking at me.

"And what are they looking for?" I pressed, glaring at Moll, who was more interested in examining her cane.

As she spun it around in her grip, I saw the elaborate carvings—depictions of the people she loved, a cave, ravens, books, and the ocean. It reflected who she was, and something new was added. I leaned in closer to get a better view of what kept her busy in her room for so long.

Obviously, it wasn't just research. Three female figures stood in solemn vigil around a grave marker.

One with a hazy feature that was vaguely familiar, another clutching something in their arms that appeared to be a book, the last with something hanging from her neck.

I wanted to ask Moll what the grave represented. If she'd foreseen her death, was it the marker for someone else in her life? But the grim look on her face stopped me. I turned to Lilith, hoping she knew.

But Lilith watched Moll, waiting for her to answer my question. When Moll's eyes shifted to the back of the library, Lilith sighed in frustration. "They are looking for the Fates." She pushed her hair behind her ear and leaned over to pour herself another cup of tea.

"The Fates are missing?" Isabelle asked, an eyebrow arched in surprise.

"They're not missing. They're just not where they usually are," Lilith explained, glancing at Isabelle. "It's not unheard of for them to disappear and reappear."

"So why do Sydney and Bree need to look for them then?" I asked Moll, even more confused. This was not good news. The Fates were vital to our mission. Without their help, we wouldn't be able to give the lost souls in the Otherworld a way to cross over. They would be trapped forever.

"You don't need to worry about it right now," Moll said dismissively, daring me to argue with her with a glance.

"Moll's right. We need to focus on one thing at a time. And right now, it's locating Morrigan's book." Isabelle pointed at me, shaking her head.

I reluctantly nodded, silently promising to find time to talk to Moll alone. A Writer always knew what another Writer felt, and Moll was scared. And it wasn't just about the missing Books of the Veiled or finding her daughter. Something else had her unhinged.

I just didn't know what.

Chapter 36- Chloe

Modern Day- City of the Unspoken

We spent the next hour perfecting a plan to travel back to Scotland. My job was to remember what it was like when Geillis penned the words in her book. To imagine the scratching of the pen against paper, the odor of death in her prison, the sting of torture searing her thoughts. To bring her memory alive again.

You know. Nothing too strenuous.

I wasn't worried about what was expected of me. I remembered how the creation of Arawn's story had effortlessly come to me when I used it to journey to the Otherworld. Retrieving memories that had been discarded seemed like part of my innate ability. And this time was no different.

At least, that was what I told myself.

"I think we've covered everything," Isabelle declared, standing up and stretching her long limbs. "We should stop here and get ready to leave. I don't know about you, but it will take me a minute to pack."

Smiling, my eyes followed her as she bounced out of the room, her golden hair flowing behind her. Isabelle was a perfectionist when traveling; everything was tucked and packed methodically. On the other hand, I was the type to toss my belongings into my bag recklessly, not caring if they arrived looking like they'd traveled through a war zone.

Jeans and sweatshirts didn't wrinkle anyway, which was one advantage of not putting too much effort into my wardrobe. Besides, I was too anxious to leave to worry about matching socks or if my sweatshirts were folded correctly.

"You should take the book with you," Lilith told me as I got up. "Give yourself some time to get acquainted with it and the person who wrote it."

I nervously eyed Geillis' book, its pages warped and yellowing with age. My fingertips tingled as they inched towards it, its eerie silence warning me. It hadn't been penned out of love or some fantasy in someone's head. This book had been written out of desperation and pain—a final testimony to her life.

A goodbye.

And those types of books rarely had a happy ending. Before I changed my mind, I nodded and headed to my bedroom. With a sigh, I paused at the bottom of the stairs and stared into the dark, thankful that in the next couple of hours, I wouldn't have to take on the Mount Everest amount of climbing I had to do in this place.

Honestly, stairs sucked, and I couldn't for the life of me figure out why people owned a stair climber.

Did they have a death wish?

I had just left my leg to start the climb when a vision of a young woman engulfed in darkness filled my mind. Her trembling hands clutched a small, jagged rock as she chiseled into the cover of a book with unbridled determination. The contorted expression of pain on her face was evident as every nerve in her body fought against giving up.

A chill ran down my spine as I watched Geillis' gnarled fingers and labored breath slowly carve her last legacy before death claimed her.

Her final gift to the world was her name.

Geillis glanced up, pointing to the book in her hand. Whether it was a warning or an omen, I wasn't sure. But before I could ask, she faded away.

"What secrets do you hold?" I whispered to her book, my key warming against my chest. I didn't have time to figure it out; the daunting task of steering me and my friends back to Scotland was all I could handle now.

"But I will," I promised before heading to my bedroom.

Twenty minutes and two dizzy spells later, I reached my room in one piece. I headed for a chair and sat down, unable to summon the energy to pack. Instead, I decided to take the time to jot down the day's events in my copy of the Book of the Veiled.

I longed to capture the beauty of the sun's rays as they streamed through the library's glass dome and illuminated the ancient stone floor. Or the countless rows of books and scrolls lined the shelves, each holding its unique story waiting to be discovered. And I never wanted to forget the faint scent of the River Styx drifting in from outside the city walls, a reminder of Charon patiently waiting for his next passenger.

But above all, I wanted to remember how my shadows came alive, and I felt like I belonged for the first time.

"Did you find what you were looking for?" Eidolon questioned as he came out of the bathroom, wearing only a towel around his hips and drying his hair with another. My jaw dropped as I turned to stare at him, my pen falling out of my hand onto the floor.

Eidolon was beautiful, but coming out of the shower, he was downright sexy. A sly grin appeared on his face as I took in his deep-set dark indigo eyes, wide mouth, and muscular body that screamed, *touch me*. Tiny strands of gray hair were beginning to show at his temples, adding a hint of maturity to his youthful appearance.

It was totally unfair that men aged so gracefully.

A low, deep chuckle rumbled from his chest, and I quickly averted my gaze to the window, trying to hide my reddened face. Part of me wanted nothing more than to throw myself at him, to explore this uncharted territory between us. I was drawn to him, intrigued by the potential of a real relationship. Could we have a future together?

I wanted 700 plus 700 years with him. *And more*, I thought as I eyed him.

But we'd promised not to do anything 'inappropriate' until the craziness was over, and it was getting increasingly difficult each day.

"I didn't know you were in here. I thought you and Watson were off doing research," I said, shaking the thoughts from my head.

"We got done early." He grinned at me, running a hand through his hair.

"Of course," I stumbled over my words, holding up the book. "Isabelle found the book that will help us get back," I mumbled around my dry mouth, refusing to stare as he pulled on his clothes.

Winnie the Pooh. Winne the Pooh. Tubby little cubby all stuffed with fluff, I sang to myself until I heard him pull on his shirt. Peeking to see if the coast was clear, I jumped on the bed, leaned against the headboard, crossed my legs, and played with the fringe on one of the throw pillows.

"Good." He reached for a faded, well-worn sweatshirt and pulled it over his head, the fabric clinging to his toned frame. He rummaged through his worn rucksack, sitting by the door, searching for his favorite ball cap. Pulling it on, he turned to look at me. "We hit a dead end with the Witch of Endor, but Max is still looking. The more we searched, the more convinced I am that necromancers are a thing."

"Seriously?"

"Why not?" Eidolon shrugged as he sat next to me, his long legs stretched out in front of him. "It's rather hypocritical of me to deny their existence. After all, I can talk to the dead. What's to say that the Witch of Endor couldn't bring them back to life?"

"True," I admitted. "What I don't understand is the why of it all. Why give someone that ability? Who in their right mind would want to be dragged back from eternity? And why would she want to be the one who does it?"

"That's the million-dollar question, isn't it?"

The room was quiet, and my thoughts turned to the ethical implications of necromancy and how I would use such power. I couldn't deny that my intentions were far from noble. I had too many unanswered questions and lingering regrets weighing on me. And I would be tempted to resurrect people to ease my conscience.

Suddenly, a strong urge to return to the mortal world overtook me. As much as it pained me to leave the Library of the Unread behind, I was eager to return to normalcy. This place gave me too much time to consider dark thoughts.

I didn't want to admit it, but I was drawn to the idea that there was life after death. That death was just another great adventure without all the troubles of living.

But leaving could mean never returning to the City of the Unspoken and the Library of the Unread.

At least not until I die.

And who knew when that would be?

Eidolon's voice was soft as he reached out to touch my hand. "We will return," he reassured me, his words slow and deliberate. "This place has always felt like home."

That was what I was afraid of. I shifted in my seat, turning to face him better. "Can I ask you a question?" Eidolon's expression was guarded as he nodded, anticipating my question. "Do you want to leave?"

"Honestly, Chloe?" He frowned. "I'm not sure. For the first time, I feel like I'm where I'm supposed to be. I'm not meant to stay in the mortal world." He leaned back against the headboard, closing his eyes and sighing. "What happens if we return and I lose this part of me? I don't know if I would recover."

Hearing the anguish in his voice, I almost cried. Eidolon was meant to be in the Otherworld, and I was meant to be in the mortal world. Our two worlds didn't collide like in fairy tales.

We were never meant to be together.

"Chloe?" Eidolon opened one eye to peek at me.

"Yeah." I forced a smile, not wanting him to worry more about me than he already was.

"Just so you know, there will always be an us. It may not be a 'conventional relationship,'" Eidolon air quoted. "But it will be ours."

"I know." I patted his hand and jumped off the bed, gathering my belongings and tossing them into my bag. "But just so *you* know," I warned, "there will be no hanky panky until you take me out to dinner. And no skimping on me." I knelt on top of my bag, trying to squeeze in my hygiene bag, pushing down on the pile of clothes and using all my strength to close the zipper.

"I'm not settling for anything less than steak and lobster. Together, on one plate," I declared, looking up from the battle I'd just won with a mischievous glint in my eye.

"As long as you let me buy you another sweatshirt." He eyed me up and down. "That one looks like hell." I threw a pillow at him, and he easily dodged it, laughing. "And maybe a gym membership. You throw like a girl."

Chapter 37- Chloe

Modern Day- City of the Unspoken

"Lil' Writer!" Odin's voice rippled through the library like thunderclaps, shaking the walls and rattling the books.

I grinned despite myself, drawn to his presence as if it were a magnet. His one good eye shimmered with delight as he engulfed me in a hug, his gaze never leaving Eidolon.

I heard Eidolon growl behind me, a clear warning in his tone.

Men!

I wasn't sure why they didn't like each other. It had been that way since we arrived at the City of the Unspoken, both silently fighting for dominance over the other.

Be nice, I warned as Eidolon prowled closer. *He is a god.*

Even the gods can fall, Eidolon sneered back. I rolled my eyes and stepped away from Odin's embrace, taking in the massive form.

He looked exactly the same. Odin's unruly auburn hair was still adorned with lengthy braids, secured by mysterious charms etched with enigmatic symbols. His face showed the signs of a hard-fought life, with a prominent scar running from his rugged features down to his chin. A patch covered his left eye, embellished with an intricate design of a raven embroidered in black silk thread.

Clad in well-worn leather pants that left little to the imagination and a barely containing white linen shirt, he cut an imposing figure. A striking blood-red cloak adorned his left shoulder, fastened with a silver raven emblem. At his waist hung his legendary sword, always sharpened and prepared for battle.

"Let the woman go before you start a war." Freyja walked up from behind him and slapped him over the head. "What did I tell you about sniffing around another man's property?"

Odin glanced down at me with a huge smile. "When you're ready for a real man, come find me," he said suggestively with a wink.

"You'll be waiting a long time, old man," Eidolon sneered. "She doesn't have time to be playing nursemaid."

"Look here, young pup," Odin started, stepping towards Eidolon, his fingers grazing the hilt of his sword.

"That's enough!" Freyja's voice boomed as she marched between them, her knives glinting in the firelight as she moved.

She wore her standard battle outfit: a tight leather ensemble that emphasized her every curve. Her fiery red hair was braided and hung over her shoulder. Her boots were scuffed and marked with what I could only imagine to be blood.

I had no doubt that she had more weapons concealed somewhere, but I couldn't figure out where for the life of me.

"We don't have time for your schoolyard fight. Chloe belongs to Eidolon." Freyja glared at Odin before turning on Eidolon. "And you don't stand a chance in battle against a god. So, figure out how to get along, or I will make you stay here and play nice while we save the Otherworld."

"Isabelle, darling, it seems like we missed out on all the fun again," Watson chuckled as he strolled into the room with Isabelle and Victor.

"Boys will be boys." Isabelle danced towards Odin and gave him a gentle peck on the cheek. "It's so good to see you both again. We've missed you," Isabelle exclaimed, offering Freyja a warm hug. "Will you be joining us?"

"Afraid not. The Fates have banned us from returning to the mortal realm," Odin laughed. "Freyja broke so many young men's hearts that their tears flooded the world."

"Speak for yourself. You single-handedly established a whole new lineage through your countless conquests against the *fairer* sex.*" Freyja grumbled, giving me a sly glance. "The Fates were concerned he was building an army."

"It didn't seem like a terrible idea at the time," Odin joked with a shrug. "The outcome didn't work quite as planned, though. I could always try again," he said hopefully, glancing at me like I was going to invite him to come.

"Except you are not allowed anywhere near mortals, my dear friend," Lilith chided as she glided into the room. "Surely you remember what the Fates told you would happen if you did not heed their warning?"

"*Eternity is a long time to live in ignorance,*" Odin repeated sourly. "It was a bit extreme if you ask me. To take away knowledge should be a crime. I paid the price for what I have learned." He reached up to his eye, grimacing.

"That's why they let you off with a warning and didn't snip your thread like they were planning." Freyja raised an eyebrow at him.

"True," he laughed. "But I would have died a satisfied god."

Freyja rolled her eyes in exasperation as she made her way to the bar. She caught Watson's eye and signaled for him to make her a drink. His grin widened, revealing his elongated canines as he reached for a dusty whiskey bottle. With practiced precision, he poured two fingers of the golden liquid, the sharp scent of aged alcohol filling the air around them.

"Where are Max and Moll?" he asked. "Shouldn't they be here to wave goodbye?"

"They should be here soon," Lilith said, looking over her shoulder down the aisle of books. "Last I checked, they were finishing up some research."

"Good, that gives us a minute to talk to you about what Freyja and I found in my library," Odin said, glancing at me.

"Good news, I hope." Victor poured himself a drink and slammed it back in one gulp. He eyed Odin's two wolves, Geri and Freki, wearily. I hadn't noticed them before, but I couldn't help but be entertained by how they watched him intently, sitting obediently by Odin's side, tails wagging in excitement.

Victor obviously was not as excited by their appearance as they padded their way to stand before him, gazing up at him lovingly.

"Not today, Satan's children, not today," he murmured, sidestepping them. "Odin! Can you please call off your wolves? They're drooling on me," Victor grumbled as he made his way to a chair. The two of them settled on opposite sides and laid their heads on his thighs.

"Don't worry! They've already eaten." Odin chuckled with a wicked smile.

"Reassuring, I'm sure." Victor paled, remembering the first time he ran into them, and they took a bite out of his ass.

"What did you find, luv?" Isabelle jumped in, redirecting the group's attention. Her eyes flickered back to Watson, who was still standing at the makeshift bar, with a slight frown as he poured himself another drink.

Odin beamed at us, his chest swelling with excitement as he announced, "We have found the Witch of Endor."

"Maybe 'found' isn't the most accurate word," Freyja interjected, giving him a pointed glare. "We think we have uncovered the reason behind her disappearance," she clarified, her eyes shifting from Eidolon to me and back again.

"What happened?" Eidolon asked, reaching down and squeezing my hand.

"Taliesin found her," Odin answered, running a hand down his beard.

And the bomb drops!

"What does that mean?" I narrowed my eyes. "Like he found them and did something to her?"

Freyja hesitated, her fingers toying with one of her blades. She tossed it in the air and caught it by the hilt.

"We don't have all the details yet," she confessed. "Odin found a vague reference about her in the original Christian bible, but nothing concrete. So we dug some more. What we discovered was surprising."

"Which is?" I asked with a wave of my hand, waiting for her to get to the point. Freyja arched an eyebrow at me, catching the blade without looking and pointing it at me. I quickly apologized.

"History repeating itself," she smirked, sliding the weapon back into its holster. "There are some remarkable similarities between the Witch of Endor's story and the 1590s witch trials in Scotland."

The room grew silent, and we all gaped at Odin and Freyja in surprise. We hadn't told them we were looking for Agnes and Geillis. Or that they had a connection with the Witch of Endor.

"What similarities?" I whispered, gripping Eidolon's hand tighter.

"Around 1000 BC, King Saul wiped out all supernatural from his kingdom, believing they were a threat to the natural order. Ironically, soon after, the same king turned around and sought out the only remaining necromancer to locate a recently deceased prophet.

Apparently, the prophet told him he was about to die, and then the next day, he did."

"How did he know where the necromancer was?" Victor asked, reaching down and petting one of the wolves absentmindedly.

"Excellent question! Unexpectedly, King Saul appointed a new adviser. No one had seen or met him before, but he claimed he had a vision of her. He was the one who led the king to her door."

"And why is the advisor relevant?" Victor asked, cocking his head.

"The book described the advisor as a middle-aged man with peculiar green eyes that glowed like lightning. According to the translation, he spoke of losing his sister in a war and was searching for someone who could avenge her death." Freyja explained.

"Taliesin," I whispered, dread running down my spine.

"Exactly what we thought," Freyja agreed with a nod.

"What does this have to do with the Scottish witch trials?" Eidolon asked, looking at Odin. "Or the Witch of Endor?"

Freyja answered for Odin. "After the king's death, Odin traced the necromancer's movements and whereabouts. During each major witch hunt, there were whispers of sister witches with extraordinary powers, like controlling the dead. We found the same narrative in France, Switzerland, Germany, and Denmark, pointing towards one culprit - the Witch of Endor and her sister."

"We believe they were on the run. Every time there was an outbreak of witch hunts, Taliesin led the charge," Odin concluded, his fingers fiddling with the hilt of his sword.

"And when was the last time anything was written about them? The sisters, I mean," Isabelle asked, her eyebrows furrowed.

"During the North Berwick witch trials." Freya frowned. "Along with a report of a mysterious man who suddenly appeared as councilor for King James."

Victor sat up. "Are you telling us every time there was a witch hunt, the Witch of Endor was there?"

"What I am saying is that according to our research, every time the Witch of Endor and her sister find another place to hide, a witch hunt follows them."

"And you think Taliesin has something to do with it?" I asked.

"We do. Think about it. Taliesin wanted Lilith to bring his sister back from the dead, but she refused. He can't get to the Otherworld alone, and the Fates won't help him since he bargained Morrigan's life away in the first place. That leaves one option - the Witch of Endor. So, it makes sense he would turn to her next."

"Does anyone know why she wouldn't help him?" Isabelle asked.

"Because she was pissed at him." Lilith chuckled. "She blamed him for having to leave her mother behind."

Chapter 38- Nava

December 1590- Nether Keith, Scotland

Nava and Ysabel stood atop the cliff, admiring the view of the North Sea. The wind whipped around them, pulling at their hair and handspun skirts. They watched as seabirds flew close to the tiny boats, cutting in and out of the waves, looking for their next meal. Grey clouds loomed on the horizon, with thunder murmuring in the background, foreshadowing an approaching storm.

They were fortunate to find a deserted house near North Berwick after their arrival. No one had seen them come in, and they welcomed the opportunity to take a break from their exhausting journey from Trier.

Leaving had not been easy for them. They left with heavy hearts and the knowledge they could do nothing to save the unfortunate souls sentenced to death by Archbishop Johann von Schöneburg. Nava harbored a deep hatred for the man, but she knew he wasn't solely responsible for the destruction of all supernatural living under his jurisdiction.

No, he had help.

Taliesin infiltrated his inner circle, weaving chilling tales of monsters and ghouls existing in their midst. His words cast a dark shadow over the community as church edicts declared death to anyone practicing witchcraft. Innocent people were persecuted as the archbishop's thirsty blade cleansed the land of evil.

Taliesin stood in the shadows for each imprisonment, trial, and execution, waiting to find Nava and her sister.

They had barely escaped his notice.

In the years since their escape that fateful night after King Saul's death, Nava and Ysabel traveled around the world to discover those with similar abilities. Nava compiled stories of each person they encountered, ensuring their legacies lived on after their deaths. Ysabel passed on her expertise of magick, teaching healers how to use ancient spells and potions in their craft.

When their work was done, they packed up and moved on to the next destination.

And after an eternity of silence, they thought Taliesin had forgotten about them. But just as they started to relax, whispers and rumors spread throughout nearby settlements. They listened with heavy hearts to tales of a wandering man searching for his missing sister and the woman who could help him find her.

Of course, he never mentioned his beloved sister had been slain in a long-forgotten battle or that he'd condemned her to her fate.

But he won over their hearts and minds with his gift for storytelling.

Taliesin could spin a story better than a spider weaving its web. He would spend days sitting in taverns and gathering houses, watching and listening to people as they talked. After learning their secrets, he'd stand up and tell his tale.

Tales of supernatural evil shrouded in darkness, where witches conjured spells to bring forth the devil's minions—werewolves, vampires, and shapeshifters. The whispers of these nefarious creatures filled the room as night descended. As the blazing fire crackling in the hearth grew stronger, it beckoned the listeners closer. While tankards of whiskey and beer boosted their courage, they soon learned fear, hatred, and deception lurked in the shadows.

And then he sent them home, intoxicated and suspicious of one another.

By the next day, all unexplainable occurrences were attributed to witchcraft.

A cow suddenly turned up missing? It must have been used as an offering to the spirits.

Somebody heal miraculously? Witchcraft must have been used.

People die without a cause. Someone cursed them.

The rumors began slowly, increasing in volume until the first drop of blood stained the dirt.

Mortals hungered for blood. When the monotony of life threatened to suffocate them, they craved any morsel of excitement with as much fervor as a ravenous wolf in winter.

The more desperate the innocent pleas, the greater the suffering and death inflicted.

Soon, it was utter chaos. Neighbors fought neighbors. Children turned against their own families. Leaders ruthlessly dominated those beneath them.

Accusations ran the gamut from believable to absurd.

But what happened in Trier was the worst the sisters had ever seen.

"I think I love the ocean the best," Nava said, her eyes closed, enjoying the salty air and trying to push memories out of her mind. "The mystery of what lies under the water is magick."

"Monsters and man-eating fish," Ysabel replied drily. "It's only magickal if you survive."

Nava cracked one eye open and smiled at her sister. Ysabel had never been comfortable with the ocean or large bodies of water, preferring to remain dry and warm instead.

Nava, however, was enthralled by the sea, its mysteries, and its endlessly changing personality.

"We have never been eaten," she reminded her sister. "Nor do I think we ever will. The gods will protect us," she declared with certainty. They'd managed to stay alive for this long, so there must still be a reason why they existed.

"But can the gods defend us against one of their own?" Ysabel asked with a frown.

Nava exhaled with resignation. They'd debated this for years, ever since finding an old woman living in a cave who confirmed the story of Taliesin's beginning. A deity created by the gods, along with his sister, to serve as a bridge between the mortal world and the divine realm.

Neither god nor human.

Taliesin could never be killed.

The news was an unwelcome shock to Nava, but on the bright side, they met Ursula—their first real friend.

Ursula's cozy cave became their home for weeks. There, they immersed themselves in her way of life and heard stories of her complicated past. Her talent for persuading bees to part with their honey amazed them.

Unfortunately, their stay was brief. All too soon, Nava and Ysabel had to leave when curious locals started arriving daily in hopes of encountering the renowned Mother Shipton and her mystic powers of prophecy. Before saying goodbye, they gave Ursula a small black book where she could write down the thoughts and visions plaguing her.

She'd been grateful, declaring she would protect it for eternity.

"The Fates will protect us," Nava mumbled, fighting back the heaviness in her chest as she remembered their friend. It had been nearly four decades since her passing, but Nava still missed her. It was the worst part of immortality. Friends and loved ones dying and knowing you would never see them again.

"Umph," Ysabel snorted. "They weren't much help in Trier."

"What did you want them to do?" Nava asked, glancing at her with a raised eyebrow. "It wasn't the Fates who condemned the innocent to die."

"They could have snipped Johann von Schöneburg's lifeline a little shorter if you ask me." Nava choked on a laugh and put her arm around her sister, and they turned to head back home.

Chapter 39- Nava

December 1590- Nether Keith, Scotland

"Tell me again why you dragged us to this wet and frigid country." Ysabel tossed her cloak on a nearby hook before going to the hearth. She tried to start a fire the traditional way, but after struggling for a few minutes, she muttered a few words, and the flames burst to life. "You know I hate the cold."

"We are needed here." Nava pulled two stools closer to the warmth and poured them a mug of wine. She breathed in, relishing the blend of vanilla and spice that always brought back memories of happier times, and took a small sip.

After they escaped from Endor, Nava continued making their mother's favorite wine each season in remembrance.

They never returned to their mother's cave, partly scared of what they would uncover and partly because they were unsure whether they could find it again. It'd been so long since they escaped from their past. The world was different now, unrecognizable from what it used to be.

No one remembered the village of Endor. It had been hidden in history just like them.

"But how do you know?" Ysabel asked, getting up from the hearth and taking the mug Nava offered.

"I feel it in my bones. This is where the past collides with the future." Nava stared into the fire, remembering what Arawn had said. He'd warned her this day was coming, and she prayed she was ready.

"Whatever that means." Ysabel tossed another piece of peat from her seat and looked around the home with disdain. "And until then, what will we do?"

"We wait. I have a feeling our help will be needed sooner rather than later." Nava swallowed her fear. The last thing she wanted was to endure another witch hunt, but all signs pointed to them being caught in the middle of one again.

"We are the ones who will need saving if we don't find warmer clothes soon." Ysabel drew her shawl around her tighter. "I didn't know Scotland would be so much colder than Trier."

Nava laughed. "It doesn't feel colder. I think you're just missing the warmth of a special someone."

Ysabel's expression turned solemn as she inched her stool closer to the crackling fire. "All that remains are memories."

Nava felt a pang of guilt seeing the pain etched on her sister's face, making her question if everything she'd put Ysabel through was worth it.

Or was she ruining her sister's only chance of happiness?

A few months earlier, Ysabel met someone while browsing for fabric to make herself a winter cloak. He approached her as she was chatting with a vendor and pointed out a section of cloth with metallic threads he claimed would sparkle like her eyes. They spent the rest of the afternoon walking along the Moselle River, and by the time the sun was setting, they knew they were soul mates.

The next day, Ysabel brought him home to meet Nava.

"Nava," he greeted, pulling her into a hug before Ysabel could introduce them. "I hope you don't mind me joining your lunch plans.

It's been ages since I've spent an afternoon with two lovely ladies." He gazed down at her with mesmerizing eyes that shone like molten gold.

Although Nava had never met any of the gods, she could only imagine the man standing before her was a spitting image. As her cheeks turned red, she took a small step backward, hoping to conceal the blush creeping up her neck.

"And who might you be?"

"Wystan," he declared with a wide smile. "It means 'battle stone.' Appropriately named, according to my father, because I came into this world yelling and ready to fight. Of course, if you ask my mother, she'll tell you I was named after a local vendor who'd given her a good deal on two fish and a loaf of bread." He chuckled, his eyes darting over to where Ysabel stood, winking at her.

"I hope your father didn't mind," Nava joked.

Wystan's laughter filled the room as he looked back at her in amusement.

"God's no. He invited the man to dinner the next day, and they became instant friends. He's my godfather now. And my mother still gets the family discount. It's a win-win for everyone," he declared happily.

Nava welcomed him to join them for lunch, and they spent the rest of the afternoon listening to his stories about growing up on the streets of Trier. He shared tales of old gods, ancient temples, exotic spices, and scholars pushing the boundaries in medicine, astrology, and mathematics. He even recounted a chance encounter with a priestess named Medusa and her mysterious disappearance shortly after.

Back when the Roman Empire ruled the area.

"She was a beautiful soul," he said, reaching over and pulling off a piece of bread. "She once helped me and my family when a neighbor stole our prized cows. I found her at a festival and begged her to intervene, hoping she would talk to the gods on my behalf. Imagine my surprise when she gave my father the contract to provide all the cows and bulls for Athena's temple. Our family went from being poverty-stricken and on the edge of disaster to one of the wealthiest families around—and our herd is still the largest in the area."

"What happened to her?" Ysabel asked, enthralled by the story.

"Legend says she angered the gods. Athena punished her with a head of snakes and banished her to some isolated island."

Wystan glanced out the window, brushing a piece of hair out his eyes. "I never told her thank you. But one day, I will find her."

"Is she still alive?" Nava asked, even though she didn't want to know the answer.

Wystan nodded, taking a long drink from his cup. "Somewhere safe from what I heard."

Isabelle patted his hand. "We'll find her one day."

Wystan gave her a grateful smile, and they continued sharing stories about their time in Trier.

Nava let them talk, choosing to stay quiet. Wystan's story raised some concerns for her. He remembered days when the old gods still roamed the earth and claimed to have lived during the Roman Empire.

But he wasn't a witch—how was that possible?

Nava's heart sank, and a wave of fear twisted in her stomach as she stared at Wystan with wide eyes. The man Ysabel had fallen in love with was a *der Blutsauger*.

A Vampire.

She suppressed a shudder, taking a quick drink to hide her horror.

Vampires were the embodiment of terror— ruthless hunters of the living. Their callousness was unparalleled. Capable of bringing whole empires to ruin in one swoop, leaving shattered dreams and murdered innocents in their path.

But the man sitting beside her sister didn't look evil. He wasn't leering at her neck or trying to trick her into thinking he was harmless. His laughter filled the room as she shared a childhood story with him.

Nava watched as he leaned in close to whisper something into her ear, brushing away a strand of hair falling onto her face before tenderly kissing her forehead. She knew then she would never be able to keep them apart.

Wanting to give them privacy, she slipped out the back door, glancing at them before closing it with a smile. As she strolled towards the cliffs, Nava realized her sister seemed genuinely happy for the first time since they fled Endor.

Then she made her sister leave him behind.

The Trier witch hunts had gotten out of hand, and Nava asked Wystan to help them escape. Of course, he did, luring Taliesin away on a false trail so they could flee.

It broke Nava's heart to watch him and Ysabel say goodbye, not knowing if they would ever see each other again.

Her sister had lost faith after that.

But Nava sat by the fire every night, praying for his return.

Chapter 40- Agnes

December 1590- Edinburgh, Scotland

Agnes trudged through the filthy streets of Edinburgh, her feet sinking into the thick mud with every step. The stench of smoke, sweat, and urine hung heavy in the air.

She could feel the grime clinging to her shoes and seeping into her clothes as she fought through the crowded streets. Despite the weight of it all, she pressed on toward her destination, determined to make it through this putrid maze of a city.

Everywhere she turned desperate sights and smells assailed her senses. The road was lined with broken-down wagons and charred buildings, alleys filled with sewage and piles of rubbish, their putrid stench mixing with the acrid scent of smoke.

Gaunt, hungry children scurried through the debris, scavenging for any morsel of food they could find. Their ragged clothes hung loosely off their skeletal frames, a grim reminder of the harsh reality they faced daily.

Thundering hooves on the cobblestones sent terror coursing through Agnes' body. Her heart raced as she looked up to see the king's men galloping towards her, their steeds' hooves pounding against the ground like a war drum, each step growing louder and more menacing.

In a frenzy, the townspeople scattered like startled insects, frantically seeking refuge in doorways and alleyways, desperate to avoid the wrath of the approaching soldiers.

Agnes crouched behind a barrel, holding her breath and pulling the hood of her cloak over her head to blend in with the shadows.

She couldn't shake off Nava and Ysabel's warnings about previous witch hunts - the odor of burning flesh, the chaos of furious crowds, and the heart-wrenching cries for mercy. The death toll was in the thousands, leaving countless grieving families in its wake.

And according to the sisters, Edinburgh was on the same path to destruction.

Agnes waited until the final guard rounded a corner before leaving her hiding spot and creeping through the narrow alleyway. Dark shadows loomed over her from the towering tenements, which leeched away their inhabitants' last traces of hope. She kept her head down, not wanting to make eye contact with anyone, but it didn't stop her from seeing everyone else.

She was heartbroken by the sight.

Women with their shawls tattered and frayed, hugging their living corpses like a second skin. They shuffled by with despair etched on their faces, searching the ground for any glint of value they could sell to survive. Men stood in a line outside of pubs, grasping for whatever form of alcohol they could find to numb the pains of their existence. The stench of desperation hung heavy in the air, mingling with cheap liquor and unwashed bodies.

These were the broken, forgotten souls of the city streets, clinging to anything that could provide temporary relief from their harsh realities.

Agnes choked back a sob as her gaze fell on a small child huddled on the street corner. He couldn't have been more than six, his skinny frame barely visible beneath a tattered burlap sack. Grime covered his body like protective armor; his feet were swollen and blistered from frostbite. Snowflakes fluttered down from the grey sky as he pleaded silently for anything to eat.

She prayed that someone would take pity on him and bring him something warm to wear. But she knew it was futile.

He would not survive the night.

People walked around him, refusing to look at him, too concerned about their own survival. No one had the means or ability to take on another child, let alone an unwanted one.

The dejection in the young child's eyes was heart-wrenching when a high-born woman strolled by him, looking down at his outstretched hand with disdain. Her face contorted into a scornful expression as she continued walking, utterly unaware of the desperate situation the innocent child was facing.

"The world would be better without them," the woman spat, her words echoing loud enough for Agnes to hear. "At least the king is doing something to rid us of these parasites! Eradicate them quickly, I say. One less thing to worry about." She retrieved a neatly folded white handkerchief from her pocket and placed it over her nose, taking tiny, shallow breaths.

Her companion stifled a nervous laugh, casting a fearful glance at the apothecary shop across the street. Fear was etched on her features as her eyes darted between the child and the building.

Agnes sighed, knowing why. The silent friend was a witch hiding from the world within the golden gates of privilege. Shame was palpable on her face, guilt eating her alive.

Serves her right, Agnes thought, staring at the retreating figures. *I hope she knows no peace. Turning her back on her people like that!*

To Agnes, the woman's actions were worse than the king's witch hunt. At least the king was honest about who he was. That woman? She was masquerading as a mortal to save her own skin.

She stared at her with disdain, anger bubbling up. Despite her seething rage, Agnes had to admit that she might have done the same if given the chance. She tried to push away the horrible thought, but deep down, she knew it was true—sometimes, saving yourself meant doing things you weren't proud of.

Agnes lifted her head and listened to the solemn ringing of church bells in the distance. Her gaze lingered on the child before she closed her eyes and whispered a prayer to the gods for his safe travel to the Otherworld. It was the only thing she had to offer.

A soft breeze ruffled the boy's hair, and she willed him to take comfort in its caress.

Soon, he would stand on the banks of the River Styx.

Maybe she would meet him again.

On her own journey to the same destination.

Chapter 41- Agnes

December 1590- Edinburgh, Scotland

A gnes shuffled forward, her shoulders hunched, and her gaze fixed on the uneven cobblestones beneath her feet. The sprawling city center loomed before her, alive with the vibrant energy of bustling vendors and wealthy shoppers—a stark contrast to the desolate slums she had just left behind.

The narrow streets were lined with colorful shops, grand playhouses, and ornate churches, each competing for passersby's attention. Agnes took in the sights and sounds of the lively district, preparing herself for what lay ahead at her final destination.

Soon enough, she would cross the final barrier separating her from the castle. There, she would blend into the shadows of countless others who had come before her. Their stories and names faded into obscurity, lost in the majestic fortress's grandiose halls and sweeping gardens. She could feel the weight of history and forgotten legacies pressing down on her as she took each step toward her uncertain future.

There was no point in wishing for a different outcome. Hope, as Agnes learned, was dangerous. It misled individuals into believing that life held endless possibilities and attainable dreams.

But that was rarely the case.

Agnes turned a corner, her breath catching in her throat. Edinburgh Castle loomed before her, its stone borders rising towards the low gray clouds. Her friend, Patrica, had warned her about the castle's secrets - how the king was rumored to have enchanted the windows, using them as extra eyes to monitor the supernatural.

Standing in front of it, Agnes believed her.

She could almost hear the frantic cries for help echoing from within - desperate souls searching for peace.

Or their heads.

This is where she was supposed to convince the king that supernaturals were harmless.

It seemed unlikely.

Gods help her.

The stench of death and despair filled the air as she took a breath to calm herself. Screams reverberated against the buildings, and she watched bewildered as passers-by walked by indifferently.

Did they not hear them? Or had they become accustomed to the sound?

She was about to turn around and run away when the heaviness of an unseen hand pressed against her shoulder, and the warmth of someone's breath tickled her ear.

You're not alone, Nava's soothing voice whispered in her ear as a woman's moans of fear and anguish echoed across the castle grounds.

Was that Geillis? Agnes whipped her head around, searching for her friend. More blood-curdling screams reverberated through the air again like a warning bell.

Stay with me, she pleaded. *I can only do this if I know you are near.*

I will not leave you, Nava assured her. Agnes silently expressed her thanks.

Her relief quickly faded as a dark figure stepped into the courtyard. The king's gaze pierced through the snow, his eyes lighting up as he saw Agnes slowly walking toward him. She stumbled on the slippery cobblestones, her knees barely keeping her upright before she dropped into a deep curtsy.

"You made it!" the king exclaimed, in a joyful tone, as his dark brown eyes lingered on Agnes. "I just sent my men out to ensure you got here safely, and here you are! Just like I hoped. We have a lot to discuss, Agnes Sampson."

"Yes, Your Majesty." Agnes stared at the ground, thick flakes landing on her neck like tiny frozen fingerprints. Her teeth chattered as she struggled to kneel, not daring to move without the king's permission.

He stood towering over her, his eyes full of amusement and curiosity. Suddenly, his attention shifted to his feet, and a frown appeared. With one quick motion, he kicked off the snow that clung to his shoes, sending tiny shards of ice stinging against her skin.

Rude!

Agnes fought to suppress her seething rage at the blatant disrespect. She gritted her teeth and held back a curse, refusing to give the guards the satisfaction of a reaction. The thought of all the better ways the money spent on those terrible shoes could have been used consumed her mind: providing shelter for a dying child or feeding the hungry. It was painful to see such disregard for more meaningful and worthwhile causes.

Anything was preferable to the shoes the king would probably only wear once anyway.

"Get up," the king commanded, waving at the men surrounding him.

Three guards approached, their boots crunching against the ice. They moved in unison as two of them grabbed Agnes' arms and yanked her from the ground. The third stood guard behind her. Agnes met the king's regard, expecting disdain or contempt, but instead, he viewed her with genuine curiosity.

"The guards will show you where to stay. Unfortunately, I have some commitments to attend to. But rest assured, I look forward to talking to you soon." With a wave, he directed the guards to take her away.

Agnes kept her gaze steady, her back straight, and her expression neutral as they dragged her down the winding stone steps into the dungeon's heart. The guard's smirk told her everything. They were excited. One guard licked his lips in anticipation.

Agnes grimaced as he leered at her, and he threw his head back laughing. "I have been looking forward to this for a long time, witch," he spat. Wickedness curled in his voice like smoke as his eyes roamed over her chest. "I can't wait for you to see what I have planned," he vowed.

She froze, unable to breathe.

The guard laughed again. "Welcome home," he said with a sneer.

He stopped before an iron gate and pushed it open with a loud clang. Agnes stumbled inside, realizing she'd been spared from the 'interrogation' rooms, at least for now. The king wanted to see her, and he wouldn't get any answers if she'd been beaten beforehand.

But that didn't mean it wouldn't happen.

Agnes fought to suppress the queasiness in her stomach, wishing she hadn't eaten so much. She breathed a sigh of relief when the guards shut the door to her cell and walked away, their whistling echoing up the stairs.

A nervous sweep of her surroundings revealed the harsh reality: it was a cage.

She had once been a wife, mother, and respected woman in her village, and now she was locked in a cage. Her hands trembled as she gripped the bars in disbelief, her mind racing with unanswered questions and mounting fear. How did it come to this?

Tears streamed down her face as she realized she'd never return home.

Before leaving, Agnes tidied everything up so that nothing was out of place: the fire was dampened, and the surfaces dusted. She placed fresh linens on the bed and ensured the candles were easily located. Her final gesture of love was to arrange a bouquet of dried flowers in her mother's prized vase.

So many happy moments were tied to the house: the day she and her husband moved in, giving birth to their children, hearing their kids' laughter and squeals of delight as they played, birthdays, anniversaries, and holidays—all spent around the same table. Although poor, her life had been rich in love.

She wanted the same for the new owners.

Whoever they would be.

Agnes brushed away her tears and tried to harden her heart against the stinging memories. Wrapping her thick cloak around her body, she looked out the window and watched snowflakes swirl, carried by an icy gust that blew into the cell and left a chill behind. She could feel the cold settling into her bones, and her teeth chattered.

It would be a long winter.

Chapter 42- Chloe

Modern Day- City of the Unspoken

"I thought the Witch of Endor's mother was dead?" I glanced over at Isabelle for confirmation. "Died of some mysterious disease, right?"

Isabelle shrugged. "That's what my aunt told me."

"Isabelle isn't wrong. Her mother is dead, but that doesn't mean she isn't alive," Lilith corrected.

"What the hell does *that* mean?" Eidolon asked, exasperated.

Lilith arched her brows, frowning. "I thought I wouldn't have to explain, given what you have been through recently. But for brevity's sake, her situation is similar to Morrigan's and Aelle's. Dead but still alive."

"Can you give us a *little* more information?" Victor asked. "Like how? Or why?"

"Her mother died of a disease, probably tuberculosis if I had to guess. But the Fates had other plans for her soul. She became one of the eight guardians of the Tree of Life. Arawn couldn't monitor all the passing souls, so with the help of the Fates, he created these guardians to oversee the comings and goings."

"Isn't that what Eidolon does?" Isabelle asked.

Lilith shook her head. "No, Eidolon only guides lost souls to the gates. He can't actually cross. Thousands of people die daily, and another thousand are born. Those are the souls the guardians manage."

"What does this have to do with the Witch of Endor and her mother?" I asked.

Lilith shifted her gaze to me, her eyes shining with frustration. "The Witch of Endor knew what her mother had become. And when she refused to do what Taliesin asked, he threatened her and her family. The Witch of Endor had no choice; she needed to hide her mother from him. And the only way to do it was to erase Endor village from the map."

"Seems extreme." I looked at her in surprise.

"No. It was the right decision," Lilith answered darkly. "She did what she had to do to save her family and protect the Tree of Life."

"And that's when they disappeared?" Eidolon asked.

"Yes and no. Odin and Freya are right. They occasionally popped up in history but never stuck around long enough to be detected. Well, until the 1500's. There was a rumor that one of them fell in love and..." She paused, her gaze lingering on Isabelle and Watson with a question. "You know, I don't know how you met."

"Why do you want to know?" Watson locked eyes with her, his voice laced with silent warning.

"Amuse an old woman."

"I don't understand how the details of my love life will help," Watson growled. Isabelle elbowed him in the side, frowning.

"Don't be impolite, Watson!" she scolded, turning to Lilith with a grin. "It's quite charming, actually. I was at the market when I sensed someone staring at me. When I whirled around, there he stood, dapper in a suit and tie. It was love at first sight for me.

"Before I knew it, he invited me to dinner. Granted, he played hard to get, but I won him over eventually." Her eyes twinkled as she reached out her hand to caress his.

"I could never stay away from you." Watson's lips curved into a smile, but it was unconvincing.

He was nervous.

My key started to hum lightly under my sweatshirt. Something was off about the story, but what?

As I scanned Watson's face, I detected a slight shift in his expression: his mouth tightened, and his brow furrowed as he studied Lilith and Freyja. The tension between them crackled like electricity.

Watson is not telling us something, I whispered down the bond to Eidolon.

I can see, he answered, his eyebrows raised in surprise.

"That is a delightful tale," Lilith said, not dropping Watson's gaze. "I would *love* to hear Watson's version of events, but he is right. We have things to do." She stood up, clapping her hands as she walked towards the library. "I hope everyone is packed! We are heading home!"

I stood at the altar, where Taliesin's book and Lucifer's feather had once resided. Aelle crossed my mind, a complicated figure who had been both a foe and a friend on this journey. It didn't feel right to leave without her. After all, Isabelle and I had made a promise to Max that we wouldn't abandon her.

And I was determined to keep that promise.

I just didn't know how.

As it stood, I wasn't feeling too confident about anything. Diana's warning lingered in my mind as we prepared to head back to Scotland.

Taliesin needs you because you are chosen to find the Books of the Veiled. Those books are what he wants, along with your blood, to open the Tree of Life.

What if the Fates brought me back to the City of the Unspoken, not as a visitor but as a permanent resident of the Otherworld? My fingers trembled with the thought, gripping Geillis's book so tightly that my skin seemed to meld into the soft leather cover.

My eyes flickered upwards, meeting Eidolon's intense gaze as his strong hand enveloped mine. "Nothing will happen," he promised in a firm yet gentle voice, lifting my hand to his lips and reassuringly kissing my knuckles. "I won't let it."

I nodded in agreement, my eyes flickering over to Isabelle, who was staring intently at her husband.

Watson stood with one arm propped against a towering bookshelf, the other hand cradling a small flask to his lips. His golden eyes were rimmed with red, and his clothes hung off of him disheveledly. His tousled hair fell into his face, partially obscuring the distant look in his eyes as he took a long, slow sip. The smell of alcohol wafted around him, mingling with the musty scent of old books.

Isabelle shook her head slightly and then turned to me, a slight, almost imperceptible frown playing on her lips. Inhaling deeply, she seemed to steady herself for what was to come. "Are we ready?"

"Is Moll and Max not coming?" I asked, looking around for my mentor. She wasn't returning to Scotland with us, but I still wanted her here, just in case.

"No, luv. Moll doesn't want her presence to interfere with our travels. But don't worry. It's easier to go back to somewhere you've already been. Think about walking through the lobby of the hotel we stayed in, the scent of white heather and rain, or the cute cafe you and Eidolon visited and how amazing real coffee smells...and we will be back before you know it."

She turned to Eidolon. "Just like last time, I need you to remember what the gates to the Otherworld look like and then find the gate leading us back home. You will be the arrow, and I will be the bow. Now, everyone, gather around Geillis's book and put a hand on it."

The group moved closer, and Watson reached for Isabelle's hand. She gripped it tightly as she glanced up at him in sorrow and resignation.

"We are heading home, my love. Whatever secrets you're holding on to, we can deal with them then," she said with a determined face.

"700 years plus 700 years is never enough," Watson whispered, a pained look on his face.

A collective hush fell over the room as they held onto each other, their fingers intertwined in a desperate grip. We held our breath, hoping against hope that they could find a way forward together. But deep down, I dreaded the possibility of whatever Watson was hiding tearing them apart.

The weight of 700 years plus another 700 years of secrets and lies hung heavily in the air, threatening to shatter everything they had worked so hard for.

Isabelle pulled away first, quickly kissing his cheek before turning to me. "Okay, luv. Close your eyes and do your magick."

"Listen up," I demanded, trying to sound cheerful. "This high-speed roller coaster includes sudden and dramatic acceleration, climbing, tilting, and dropping. Please remain seated with your hands, arms, feet, and legs inside the vehicle at all times. And whatever you do... don't let go."

Isabelle giggled as I placed my key on the book, its blood-soaked cover glittering in the candlelight. The ancient pages called out to me as I leaned in close, inhaling their musty scent saturated with a hint of burnt paper. My fingers caressed the delicate paper, feeling each indentation and imagining the tall trees that once held those fibers captive.

In my mind's eye, I saw Geillis writing, her pen moving awkwardly across the page as she whispered her words into existence.

The longer I held her book, the more alive the story became. The intensity of Geillis's self-control jumped from the pages and filled the room with a determination I could feel coursing through me. My curiosity and sense of duty tugged at my core, urging me forward - a promise I would not let her suffer in silence.

I took a deep breath and pushed through the space between us and into the vision.

Chapter 43- Chloe

Modern day- Peebles, Scotland

The smell of wet grass, pine, and oak trees and the sound of water rushing down the River Tweed greeted me home.

Thank the gods!

The trip had not been easy for me.

The miles between the worlds stretched forever, and Geillis' last days flashed like an old black-and-white silent movie. I felt her terror as she was drugged from her prison cell and the acceptance of her fate rippling across her face. The memory flashed to the moment before her death, surrounded by three women shrouded in dark shadows standing behind her as she took her last breath.

She didn't fear death in the end. She welcomed it.

A part of me was glad she died so she didn't have to live in misery anymore. She'd been reduced to a shell of her former self, plagued by guilt and shame for what she'd done.

Too many times, I wanted to stop mid-journey and reassure her that it wasn't her fault. But if I stopped in the vision, we would have all been lost to that moment in time.

So, I pressed on. Leaving Geillis behind to face her fate alone.

And I cried.

I was still crying when I opened one eye and looked around. We were home. Struggling to support myself on unsteady legs, I winced with pain as I sat up and cracked my neck to loosen the tension. My whole body ached from the impact of the fall. And once again, I landed on a painfully hard rock. I gingerly touched the tender spot on my ass, wincing at the painful throbbing.

Shit! That's going to leave a bruise.

Glancing around me, I was glad everyone had made it back safely. The rest of the group were fast asleep, curled up like cats, clutching the faded book.

"You made it!" A booming voice jarred me out of my thoughts as an oversized god strolled confidently toward me. Two hellhounds flanked either side of him, their glowing red eyes washing over me, ensuring I arrived in one piece. "I was worried you got stuck in the timeline."

"Arawn! Long time no see!" I huffed, standing up stiffly and rolling my shoulders. "How did I guess I would be seeing you?"

"Intuition," he said, strolling up and hugging me. "I'm sorry about your friend," he consoled, looking down with a slight frown.

"Have you seen her?" I asked, hopeful.

"No. But Aelle's in good hands. Don't you worry."

Worry? Obviously, he didn't remember Aelle. I wasn't worried about her. I was worried about whoever trained her to become the next caretaker. Aelle was a lot to handle on a good day and reminded me of a rabid wolf on her bad ones. Hopefully, whoever got the job hadn't quit yet because I wasn't sure how long Max would wait before going to find her.

"What *are* you doing here?" I narrowed my eyes and stepped back. "You only show up when you have bad or life-altering news. So, what is it this time? Is the world ending? Did someone steal Pandora's Jar? Dragons are real and running loose?"

Arawn's laughter echoed among the trees, with matching howls from his hellhounds. "You are always so dramatic. I'm here because you promised me a Scotch pie." He tilted his head to the side, his eyes lingering on my bag, hopeful that I brought one of his favorite treats.

I shook my head and offered an apologetic smile. His expression fell, and he sighed. I couldn't help but giggle until his gaze met mine again. The brightness in his eyes was gone and replaced with seriousness.

"And to remind you not to die," he said, his eyes burning with intensity and concern. "What you have been through so far will be a walk in the park compared to your next challenge. You are about to enter an era of terror for the supernatural. You think you've experienced fear, greed, and lies? That's nothing compared to the evil lurking in the shadows during the 1500s. Families destroyed from within. Friends betrayed friends. Monarchies rose against religions while religious leaders turned their backs on their faith. No one was safe."

"I know Arawn," I said in annoyance. "I do have a background in history. I am well aware of what happened during the European witch hunts."

"Do you really think your books even begin to give you a glimpse of the horror of the time?" His eyes narrowed. "Did your books smell like burning flesh? Could you hear the desperate cries of those left to starve while their king feasted until he couldn't eat another bite, only to throw the scrapes to the pigs? You know nothing, lil' Writer. But you are about to learn."

Laced with cruelty, a laugh escaped my lips. "Do you think you can frighten me?" My voice was cold and vicious, like a viper's bite. I stood tall, undeterred by his power, for I seen darkness beyond anything I wanted to admit. My fingernails dug into my skin as I steeled myself to face the god of the Otherworld. "I'm not scared."

"Not scared? You would be foolish not to be scared. You are about to come face to face with one of the most powerful witches of all time. And maybe even Taliesin. The fact that Morrigan's book showed up in that timeline doesn't give me a warm and fuzzy feeling. I have no idea what the Fates are up to, and it makes me nervous."

"The Fates won't let me fail," I declared half-heartedly.

Right?

I found myself not believing my own words. This piece of the puzzle in this story didn't fit together. Lilith wanted to keep the Books of the Veiled safe from Taliesin rewriting them, so she handed them off to the Fates.

But they turned around and hid them, and now we were on a wild goose chase to track them down.

But why hide them in the first place, only to be found again?

That was a question Lilith couldn't even answer.

What was the point?

And why was I the one who had to find them?

Chapter 44- Chloe

Modern Day- Peebles, Scotland

Perched on a mossy boulder at the edge of the River Tweed, I watched as a silver mist ghosted up from the water's surface, imbuing the world with an ethereal glow. Exhaling slowly, I allowed my thoughts to drift to Arawn's words, letting them pool deep within me.

I was scared. After years of being indifferent to death, it was a difficult pill to swallow.

But Arawn had done an excellent job of reminding me of my mortality.

My ears perked at the sound of shuffling behind me. Picking up a rock, I threw it into the water and waited for Eidolon.

I took a deep breath as he sat down, allowing his scent of cedar and smoke to calm me.

"How long have we been out?" he asked, rubbing his neck and grimacing.

"Not long," I admitted. I grabbed a jagged river rock from the mud and hurled it with all my might, aiming for a boulder on the other side. It made it halfway before sinking. Frustrated, I scoured the ground for another rock, this time finding one that was smooth and flat, suitable for throwing. With a grunt, I hurled the stone into the air, not paying attention to how close it flew past a startled bird.

"Calm down, killer," Eidolon joked as he grasped my hand before I tried again. "Want to tell me what's going on?"

"Arawn showed up," I admitted, refusing to look at him.

"Ahhhh. And what did he have to say this time?"

"Nothing much. He just warned me not to die. Same old, same old," I said dismissively, rubbing my hands against my jeans.

"What else? You wouldn't be this angry if that's all he said."

"I'm not angry," I cut him off with a glare. "I'm fine. Just need a coffee and a nap."

"*Really*? Not angry? You could've fooled me," he laughed, moving behind me and massaging my tense shoulder muscles. "Now, why don't we try again? What did Arawn say that drove you to take down a defenseless bird mid-flight?"

"He told me that I had no idea what I was getting myself into. He made it quite clear that he thought I was incompetent."

"He said you were incompetent?" Eidolon asked in a tightly controlled voice; his eyebrows arched in surprise.

"Well, not exactly," I admitted sheepishly. "But he made me feel useless. He thinks we will run into Taliesin."

"And you're worried?" Eidolon guessed correctly, sliding to sit beside me. He tilted my face towards him, his eyes burning with promise. "I won't let anyone or anything hurt you, even if it's my parents."

And let's add another layer of guilt, buddy, I grimaced. When I dreamt of finding my soul mate, I pictured heated debates over whose family got the Christmas honors and bartering between both sets of parents for birthdays and summer vacation spots.

I was sure that living close enough to them would be a requirement so that holiday visits to both families would be possible.

I even considered the remote chance I wouldn't mesh well with the in-laws.

But never once did I entertain the thought that my father-in-law would want me dead.

"Eidolon..." I started before he cut me off.

"We will cross that road when we get there," he said with resolve, his indigo eyes fixed on the horizon.

I took my glasses off and rubbed the bridge of my nose as I sighed. "Here's the thing that bothers me. Taliesin has been held captive in an ancient oak tree for hundreds of years, and you have his book." I pursed my lips as I considered the implications. "Do *you* think we will run into him?"

"I have his book, not his body. He still exists, just like Lilith does. I imagine we will run into who he was, not who he is now." He turned to study me, his dark gaze piercing like a dagger. "When we find him, you will stay out of it. Run away, hide, and wait for me, no matter what happens. Don't get involved. Do you understand?"

His words were a chilling command, the consequence of disobedience heavy in the air.

"Of course," I lied. I had already lost enough friends by following the rules; I wouldn't let that happen again. When the time came, I wouldn't hesitate. I would give everything up without a second thought as long as he stayed safe.

But Eidolon didn't need to know that.

I was relieved when I heard the rest of the group shuffling around, wanting to get as far away as possible from the conversation. Lilith was already on her feet, brushing dirt from her clothes. As she glanced at me, a tiny hint of a smile was on her lips.

"That was a memorable experience—traveling with someone else for a change. I think I prefer my method—it's less painful." Lilith grimaced, glancing down at her mud-stained shirt. "And less dirty."

I shrugged. "I gave a safety briefing before we left."

Eidolon snickered as Lilith glared at me, running a hand through her hair, working out the tangles.

"I think you left out some key points," she mumbled as she pinned her hair back. She scowled at the forest behind her before glancing back at me. "I have something to do. Tell Esme I'm looking forward to her pot roast when I return."

And then she vanished like a shadow disappearing into the night.

Watson frowned as he stood beside me. "Wondering where she is going?" he asked.

"Does it matter?" I asked, glancing at him from the corner of my eye.

He let out a weary sigh as he shook his head, and a tic started up in his jaw. He had perfected the art of lying, but I knew he was doing it again.

But like all good soldiers, he kept his thoughts to himself, smiling as he reached for Isabelle's bag.

"Shall we go? I need a drink." His confident stride led the way as he headed into town, whistling an old tune.

Chapter 45- Chloe

Modern Day- Peebles, Scotland

"Welcome back!" Esme's friendly voice echoed as we walked towards the hotel we had stayed at before traveling to the Otherworld.

It was a captivating home. Nestled near the center of Peebles, the house was far enough away from the hustle and bustle of the town to be tranquil but close enough to be a part of the village's daily life.

Every corner was lovingly decorated for the holidays. Esme stood at the door with a broad smile framed by a stunning wreath hanging behind her. String lights wrapped around each window, lighting snowflakes made from white construction paper.

On either side of the main entrance, two miniature Christmas trees sparkled brightly, adorned with gleaming red and gold ornaments and tiny twinkling lights.

It still threw me off that we had left on Samhain, and now we were about to celebrate the winter solstice.

I always loved the Christmas season, with its bright lights and general excitement, and I hoped this year would be no different.

Eidolon smiled at me, his indigo eyes softening as he glanced down. Taking my hand in his, he squeezed it gently. My heart swelled with anticipation; this would be our first holiday spent together.

And I hadn't the faintest idea of what to buy him.

Maybe a watch? Or a book?

What *did* you buy a guy you just met, bonded by the Fates, but never been on a date with?

A gift card?

I nervously nibbled on my bottom lip, trying to figure it out. Eidolon smiled mischievously at me before squeezing my hand again.

"You could take me to the coffee shop and buy me a piece of their chocolate cake. One fork," Eidolon whispered, winking at me.

My pulse quickened, and I could feel my cheeks heating up. A smile tugged at the corners of my mouth as I nodded in enthusiastic agreement.

Before I could fully process the moment, Esme engulfed me in a hug. Her grip was sure and firm, radiating warmth. Without warning, she reached for Isabelle's wrist and pulled her into our embrace.

Isabelle stumbled with surprise and laughter, and soon enough, we laughed with happiness as the unspoken promise of friendship filled the air.

"Oh, you poor girls. You look like you have been to hell and back. But of course, you have," she laughed, glancing down at my stained sweatshirt and wind-blown hair. "How was your trip?"

"Eventful," I admitted. "But we are glad to be home."

Esme beamed. "Aye, you are home." The love on her face almost made me cry before she clapped her hands. "Now, let's head up to your bedrooms so you can have a hot bath and relax after your travels. Have you lost some weight? You look thinner," she noted while looking at my frame. "Doesn't matter. I will put some meat back on your bones before you know it."

That sucks, I silently moan. The gods knew that I was weak when it came to good food, and Esme was a fantastic cook. I was going to have to start working out again.

Ughhhh.

"You, my dear, look fabulous as always. How *do* you manage to stay so put together?" Esme asked as her eyes skimmed Isabelle's up and down.

"Years of practice and the right concealer. If you saw me without makeup, you would think otherwise." A short giggle escaped her lips, and I frowned. Isabelle wasn't wearing makeup. But her face still glowed as if she had visited a posh beauty salon. Her long, golden tresses cascaded down her shoulders in immaculate curls like a professional styled them.

"You must give me the brand's name," Esme said as she took our hands and started up the stairs into the hotel. "The boys will handle the luggage while I get you two settled. Same bedrooms as before. Unless there is a different sleeping arrangement I should know about," she raised an eyebrow at me.

I blushed and was sure I looked like a flawless imitation of a fish trying to find my words when Eidolon jumped in.

"One bedroom, please, Esme." Swinging around, I caught the devilish glimmer in his eye, and my knees trembled at his suggestive tone.

Esme clucked her tongue, "Cheeky fellow. But what a looker," she winked at me.

Can this be any more embarrassing? I thought as we climbed the stairs to the second floor, and Esme directed me to my old room.

Yes! Watson answered. *I could tell them about that steamy daydream you had on the plane.*

Shut up, Watson, I hissed, throwing a heated glance over my shoulder at him as he and Eidolon followed with our bags.

I pushed the door open with a huff and stepped inside. My gaze drifted around the well-furnished room, taking in the immense walnut four-poster bed with its azure and sea-foam curtains billowing softly in the light breeze from the open window. A grand cherry wood desk stood against one wall, decorated with ornate gold trimmings. On the opposite side of the room was an inviting armchair and a warm fireplace tucked into the corner. My tension eased as I approached the enormous picture-framed window overlooking the lush Scottish countryside.

"Just as I remembered," I whispered.

Esme walked beside me and nodded. "It's beautiful, isn't it?" I nodded, unable to tear my eyes away from the beauty. Below us, a deer tiptoed out of the small grove of trees and glanced up before turning towards a patch of grass.

"It's perfect. Thank you, Esme. For everything," I whispered.

"My pleasure," she said over her shoulder as she walked away. "I'll finish dinner while you clean up. See you downstairs in an hour?"

I nodded, my gaze fixed on the horizon outside the window. I heard a soft scuffle as Esme left the room and the thump of our bags being thrown on the bed. Eidolon's presence behind me was like a warm cocoon as he pulled me closer to him. "It's good to be back."

"Even if we left some behind?" I asked, spinning around in his arms and looking up at him. "Like your grandmother? And Aelle?"

"We will see them again. But the Otherworld is the safest place for Moll right now. I don't want her running into Taliesin."

"What about you?" I dared to ask. "What will you do if you run into him? He's your dad."

"I don't know Chloe. I wish I did, but I can't focus on that now. I'm more worried about what to do when I see my mother."

"Why?" I asked, confused.

"I've never—I don't know how to introduce someone I love to my family," he said, the words falling out of his mouth like a confession. The dim light cast soft shadows along his skin. The tattoos on his arms and neck danced with anticipation as he met my gaze, a conflicted mix of fear and hope.

An invisible fist squeezed my heart, and my breath caught in my throat.

Love?

Love was such a powerful word. It was a raging fire that refused to be extinguished. It meant you would be willing to do anything for the other person. It would mean linking our lives together and never letting go.

Was I in love with Eidolon?

As much as I didn't want to admit it because love at first sight was something you found in books, I did.

But I hadn't known he felt the same.

My lips trembled, and I was desperate to speak the words that had burned in my heart for so long, but I held them back.

The last time I said those three magickal little words and meant them, a wave of destruction nearly consumed me.

No, I couldn't risk it again. Instead, I remained silent, burying the longing deep within my soul.

I couldn't bring myself to say it back, yet I didn't want my feelings to remain unknown. So, I did the only thing I could think of: I kissed Eidolon, hoping he could feel what my heart wanted to express but couldn't say.

Not until I found a way to save him.

Chapter 46- Nava

December 1590- Nether Keith, Scotland

"I'm bored, I'm cold, and I want to go home," Ysabel complained as she stepped closer to the fireplace.

Nava knew there was no use in arguing with her sister. The frostiness of a Scottish winter chilled them through, pushing down on their optimism like a lead weight. The walls of their tiny cottage seemed to shrink inwards as if they were trying to swallow them up. The ocean winds tore through the home, roaring like ancient beasts. Sheets of rain pounded against the windows, shaking the house's foundation as if calling for vengeance.

Of course, it'd given them time to explore their new home. Nava was pleasantly surprised to find the woman who lived here had left clean sheets on the bed and candles in the cabinet. Going through the small back room, she'd found plenty of jars and mugs of potions, along with an impressive amount of dried herbs and flowers to make more.

Very efficient, Nava thought to herself as she made a mental note of everything.

She didn't expect less. After all, Agnes was her flesh and blood, resulting from a relationship she thought would be fleeting, which evolved into something more.

Cain.

Their paths crossed unexpectedly, and their friendship blossomed gradually, fueled by their mutual passions for gardening and wine. Whenever Nava inquired about his background, Cain would divert the conversation to topics like farming techniques or breeding plans, avoiding any personal details or references to his family. Despite her curiosity, he remained tight-lipped.

It took months for Nava to discover Cain left his village after a bloody battle between him and his brother over a sacrifice, which ended in his sibling's death.

A fight that marked him as a murderer. He was banished. His name struck from his family's history.

The gods selected Cain as a representation of their power. Bearing a mark and exiled, his fate seemed inevitable. Yet he resolved to make something of it. Branded and cast out, his destiny was set in stone. But he refused to accept this fate.

Cain understood that someone had to be first, and he was determined to use his position in history to make the world a better place.

He spent years roaming the world searching for redemption but never found anyone who saw him for who he was and not what he once was.

Nava presented him with a chance to start over. She understood what it was like to be despised for something beyond one's control.

For a time, she had a love known to few. Her husband was kind and strong, understanding her in ways no one else could. His commitment to farming, respect for the ancient gods, and their relationship were unfailing.

They worked together to create a peaceful haven away from society where they wouldn't be subjected to criticism or rumors. With the arrival of their son Jacob, their happiness seemed complete until two years later, when Catherine entered their world.

But the Fates had other plans.

They were celebrating her daughter's sixteenth birthday when Taliesin returned.

Nava was devastated when she discovered Taileson tracked her down. She had put up all of her protections, and it should have been impossible for anyone to locate them. With no time to question how it happened, she traveled to the gates of the Otherworld and begged Arawn to conceal her husband and children within the City of the Unspoken.

Nava kissed them goodbye, desperately clinging to the promise of her return.

Then she ran.

Her husband waited for her. Year after year, he never gave up hope.

Until he realized the truth.

Nava was never coming back.

Not that she didn't want to. Her need to return was an ache that ate away at her, each moment of temptation tearing her soul apart until nothing was left.

But Taliesin would have found them, so she remained in the shadows, watching as her family rebuilt their lives. She watched as the man she loved went slowly insane, leaving in the middle of the night from the City of the Unspoken and never seen again.

Now and again, she would look in on her son, still under Lilith's watchful eye. He matured into an attractive young man, full of strength and vitality, inheriting Cain's green thumb. Jacob spent his days tending to the gardens encircling the Library of the Unread, ensuring his father's favorite flower bloomed—the black rose.

A relic of the past no longer found in the mortal world, the black rose represented the fragility and continuity of life, a constant reminder that beauty and death were forever intertwined.

Her daughter married the man of her dreams, another child of a lost story. They'd grown up in the City of the Unspoken but began a new life together in the mortal world: having kids, building a home, and creating a life far from anything that reminded them of who they were.

Children of the forgotten.

For years, Nava stayed away.

Until now.

This time, Agnes' urgent plea for assistance could not be ignored. Nava's heart ached at the sight of Agnes' despair, knowing she had to tell her there was nothing she could do to save her friends.

But she would protect her soul.

The Fates be damned.

Nava's plan needed to be meticulously executed and required the manipulation of every individual involved. She understood she had a chance at success if she convinced everyone they were simply following Fate's path.

As long as Lilith did her part.

Nava slowly rose from her seat and shuffled across the room to the kitchen counter. She filled a mug with steaming mead, watching the steam curl up in delicate tendrils as she thought of her oldest friend, Lilith.

Nava's mind drifted back to their first encounter. Lilith was a formidable presence, having lived through countless lifetimes and retaining the memories of each one.

An immortal bestowed with incredible abilities and vast knowledge, she commanded both respect and fear. Despite her seemingly human appearance, one could sense the immense power simmering within her.

She could vanquish any good or mortal who dared to challenge her.

But she was also modest, gentle, funny, and occasionally moody.

It was Lilith who showed them how to use their abilities and survive. All she could do now was hope Lilith got her message. A simple statement that was sure to grab her attention.

Nava had her book.

Chapter 47- Nava

December 1590- Nether Keith, Scotland

"Are you even listening to me, Nava?" Ysabel demanded.

Nava snapped back to the present, realizing her sister had been talking to her the whole time.

"Yes, yes. You're cold and bored," Nava answered with a wave of her hand. "Put another peat log on the fire, and I will make you something to drink."

"I don't want something to drink," Ysabel huffed, shuffling to the peat pile. "I want to go home."

"We can't go back, you know that," Nava sighed, her ancient bones protesting as another gush of frigid air blew through the window. "The Fates brought us here for a reason. We just need to figure out why."

"Punishment. They sent us here as punishment," Ysabel grumbled as she layered another cloak around herself. "I told you we shouldn't have gotten involved. You couldn't have saved him."

"I had to try," Nava replied with a frown.

They had this argument before, but Nava refused to back down. Dietrich Flade may not have been a friend of the supernatural, but he tried to stop the senseless murders of innocent men and women. And for that, Nava was willing to try to save his life.

She'd met him by accident one night when she ventured into town for fresh supplies. He'd been at the local bakery talking to some friends. As a judge, he'd been forced to listen to countless witchcraft accusations and was unhappy about the church's involvement in their punishments.

So much so that he defied the church's position and released so-called 'witches' due to lack of evidence.

It was a small win for the supernatural community, but it put him in a precarious situation. Johann von Schönenberg accused him of being a warlock.

Dietrich did his best to evade capture, somehow managing to stay hidden for two weeks with the help of friends.

Unfortunately, he was caught and put on house arrest before being thrown into prison, tortured, and condemned to death by fire.

At least they granted him the mercy of strangulation before.

Nava was by his side at his death, unable to do much for the innocent man other than ensure his death was quick and his transition to the Otherworld smooth.

Arawn met them at the gates, giving her the same warning he always did when she got involved.

Don't tempt the Fates.

Unfortunately, Nava would have to tempt them again, and she was pretty sure it wouldn't escape their attention this time.

"And what good did it do?" Ysabel sneered. "Other than send my poor Wystan off on a wild goose chase, putting his life at risk to save ours."

"He's immortal and can handle himself," Nava replied with a roll of her eyes.

"So can we." Ysabel's voice thundered from her chair as she bellowed, "It didn't have to be this way. You always need to make everything harder, don't you? Chasing shadows and pulling us into danger - yet Taliesin finds us every time." A fire raged along her skin, her eyes blazing, searing with fury.

"Ysabel," Nava started, stepping toward her; her voice was quiet but held an undercurrent of a warning. "You need to calm down."

Ysabel's anger crackled like lightning, and Nava could feel it electrifying her skin. The last time Ysabel flew into such a rage, an entire town was swallowed up by molten lava and sooty ash, leaving nothing but sizzling devastation over a single burnt loaf of bread. The poor village hadn't been discovered until a few years ago.

She trembled at the thought of what might happen this time if Ysabel didn't get herself under control.

"You asked too much from me this time," Ysabel spat, her eyes narrowing at her sister, her fists clenched. "I have followed you faithfully, never questioning your decisions. Look where it left us! Stuck in some strange woman's house, eating her food and sleeping in her bed. We can't even leave because of the blasted storm. How will Wystan find me now?"

Ysabel screamed in agony as she stumbled towards the door, desperate to escape her despair.

She flung it open and rushed outside, the torrential rain cascading around her like a relentless waterfall of sorrow. Dropping to her knees, she released one final cry before collapsing in a heap. The roar of the storm eventually drowned out her silent sobs.

"I can't live without him," she cried. "It feels like my heart is breaking. It hurts."

Nava raced to her sister, sinking into the mud beside her and embracing her tightly. She swayed back and forth as the rain poured around them.

"Shhh, everything's going to be all right. Wystan will find us; you know how efficient vampires are at tracking. They can find a snowman in a snowstorm."

"And if he doesn't? What do I do then?" Ysabel whimpered.

"He'll come. And when he does, he will take you somewhere safe, far from here. I promise." Nava glanced up and dared the gods to contradict her.

She *would* find a way to fix this. One way or another, her sister would have the happily ever after she deserved.

The storm outside poured relentlessly for two more days, rain beating against the windows and fierce wind whipping the trees into submission. Inside, the sisters were locked in a tense stalemate, barely speaking to each other.

Ysabel quickly became lost in her own world, mesmerized by the hypnotic dance of the flames in the fireplace or watching the ice melt against the windowpane, tracing their watery paths down the glass with her finger.

When the storm dissipated, the morning sky shined an icy blue-white, and the sisters emerged from their frost-covered home. They raised their faces to the weak sun as they surveyed the damage done by the windstorm: tree branches gnarled and twisted like bony fingers littered the garden, and patches of thatch were missing from the roof, leaving a jigsaw puzzle of holes.

Without saying a word, they started cleaning up the mess. It was a tedious task, but they welcomed the distraction from their thoughts.

Nava was stacking wood into the lean-to when the earthy smell of whiskey wafted in the breeze. She paused, gazing toward the source of a familiar tune whistling in the distance.

Thank the gods, she smiled, throwing down her load, picking up her skirt, and racing to the front of the house.

Wystan found them.

Chapter 48- Nava

December 1590- Nether Keith, Scotland

"Nava, my dear! It's been ages since I've seen you."

With each step, Wystan's boots squelched against the damp ground, announcing his approach as clearly as a shout. His tousled hair was plastered to his forehead, strands sticking out at odd angles from melted ice. Despite the disarray, a mischievous grin lit up his face, giving him a boyish quality that belied his actual age. His clothes, usually pristine and well-tailored, were now crumpled and caked in mud, evidence of the adventure he had just embarked upon.

"What happened to you?" Nava asked, looking him up and down.

"When the storm hit, I had to find shelter in a grimy cavern near here. A terrible place." He shuddered. "Not at all suitable for an extended stay." He pulled Nava into a tight embrace, his chin resting on her head. His eyes darted around the area, examining the surroundings as he sniffed the air. "Now, come on, tell me where my girl is."

"She's gone for a stroll but should be back shortly." Nava gestured towards the cliffs. "While we wait for her, I can whip up something for you to eat." Nava studied Wystan's disheveled appearance with a critical eye. He looked as if he had been trampled by a cart and dragged through the bushes for miles.

Wystan nodded, a bright smile spreading across his face as they walked down the path. He entertained her with all the latest gossip from their friends and acquaintances back in Trier that they had left behind.

Nava bit her lip, swallowing hard, before asking, "Is anyone left?"

Wystan's brow furrowed in concentration, his eyes taking in every detail of the room as they walked through the front door. The smell of musty books and aged wood filled his nostrils, mingling with the faint scent of herbs and oils from Ysabel's healer's bag. He moved gingerly, favoring one leg as he settled onto a stool, wincing from the throbbing pain of old battlefield wounds.

"It was quite unpleasant," he admitted, rubbing his hands up and down his leg. "Dozens of villages burned down, and hundreds died. Countless others were begging for food or shelter. And the smell of rotting flesh..." He shuddered. "I'm glad you got out when you did."

"And Taliesin? Did you lose him?" Nava asked, setting a mug in front of him before sitting across the table.

"More like he got away from me. I got him to the border, and he suddenly changed course. I followed but lost him in the forest. I assumed he'd returned to Trier, but there was no sign of him when I returned. He just vanished."

"And no one has seen him since?" Nava guessed.

Wystan's shoulders slumped as his gaze fell to the ground. "I'm sorry, Nava," he murmured with a heavy heart. He had tried everything he could think of, but it wasn't enough. The weight of failure sat heavily on his shoulders, and he couldn't meet her eyes.

Nava reached over to touch his hand. "You saved us," she brushed his apology aside. "He was getting close. Too close for comfort. I'm not sure what would have happened if it weren't for you."

"Why is he looking for you and Ysabel?" Wystan had wanted to ask her for weeks and wouldn't leave until he got his answer. "What does he want?"

"It's a long story," Nava replied wearily.

"Well, I suggest you start talking before Ysabel gets home," he warned with a growl. "I need to know what is after my mate."

Nava looked at him for a long moment before nodding.

"Once upon a time, there was a king…"

The door swung open forty minutes later, and Ysabel flew into Wystan's waiting arms. She showered him with kisses while he held her tight, relief written on his face that his mate was safe and they were together again.

"I knew you would come," Ysabel said, her voice breaking as her eyes filled with tears. She reached up, curling her fingers around his neck and drawing him closer. "I had a feeling it would be today, but I didn't want to get my hopes up until I saw a vision of you sitting in our kitchen. What took you so long?"

Wystan smiled down at his petite witch and tucked a lock of her hair behind her ear. "I got here as fast as possible, but the horrid storm delayed me. It has been a long time since I had to hole up in a cave with only my thoughts and rodents to keep me company. I would not recommend it." He laughed, but his eyes darted at Nava with a frown. "I would have been here sooner, but I got sidetracked."

Nava's heart constricted, a vice-like grip squeezing her chest as she prepared for whatever he was about to reveal. She gripped the table so hard that her knuckles turned white, unsure if she could handle more devastating news.

"I was strolling along the outskirts of town, keeping to myself, when a muffled scream caught my attention. As I turned the corner, I narrowly avoided being run over by a wagon surrounded by four guards. Inside was a young girl, her hands tied, her mouth gagged, and her body covered in bruises. The guards seemed to be in a rush. One of them mentioned the king was waiting."

Wystan paused to gather his thoughts, shuttering at the memory. "I will never forget the moment her swollen eyes met mine. She was resigned to her fate. It took everything in me not to try to rescue her." He wrapped an arm around Ysabel's shoulder and pulled her closer, kissing her forehead. "She was a witch."

"Do you know who she was?" Ysabel asked as she pulled him down on the stool and sat beside him.

"No. But those men had the same expression as rabid wolves on a hunt. And they loved every moment. If my suspicions are correct, the Scottish king is trying to eliminate witches." His face twisted into a sneer. "Just like the pope. Have you heard anything?"

"We haven't been to town, but I saw something in a vision," Ysabel's voice quivered, her mouth trembling as she continued, "I think you're right. Taliesin is with him."

"Vision? What vision?" Nava asked, surprised.

Ysabel slid off her stool, eyes brimming with tears as she walked over and put her arms around her sister. "I didn't want to add more pressure on you until I was certain. I know we always agreed not to keep secrets from each other. But I wasn't sure how you would react after everything that happened in Trier. I didn't want you running off and getting into trouble again."

Nava's hand shook as she patted her sister's arm, a conflicted half smile on her face. On the one hand, she appreciated Ysabel's concerns, but on the other, she was struggling. Her visions weren't coming through as clearly as they used to.

And she couldn't cross the gates to the Otherworld.

Her powers were fading, and she didn't know why.

"What is it?" Ysabel asked, seeing Nava's worry. "What's wrong?"

"Nothing," Nava said, detaching herself from the embrace and slowly pushing herself onto her feet. As she stood up, her bones creaked and crackled like dried leaves underneath her skin, causing a sudden pang of worry to course through her as she realized this wasn't an ache she had ever felt. "I'm just tired. I'm going to bed."

She'd aged in the last few days. Just that morning, she'd seen a reflection of herself revealing that her once bronze skin was now ashen. Fine lines lined her forehead and around her mouth. Even her hair was heavy with age - grays now outnumbered the reddish-brown strands. With each step and breath, her joints cracked like dry wood, and her body trembled from the slightest exertion.

She could feel death's looming presence in every fiber of her being, knowing it was almost time for her final goodbye.

At least she knew where she was going.

But it didn't make leaving easier. After a lifetime of watching the world develop, as religions faded and were replaced by new ones, as people grew skeptical of governments and each other, she'd found serenity in the thought that it was almost over. She could finally be with her family again.

And, hopefully, find some peace.

Chapter 49- Agnes

January 1591- Edinburgh Castle

She wouldn't be alone at the end. That was some comfort, at least.

Agnes gingerly rolled over, grimacing when she touched her broken ribs. One of her eyes was swollen shut, the result of the rope used to secure her head slipping down during the interrogation. Her right eye was blurry from where she caught an elbow to the face for not walking fast enough on her bruised feet. She groaned as she thought about the distance to the corner, needing to relieve herself.

Was it worth the effort?

No. Not anymore, as much as Agnes didn't want to admit it.

A wave of gut-churning nausea overcame her as a sewage stench penetrated her every breath. Agnes tried to block out the smell with a handful of rotten hay, but the putrid odor was a suffocating fog. She ran a hand down her arm, her skin crawling with a thousand tiny feet as an army of fleas and cockroaches swarmed over her.

She was thankful the guards shaved off her hair, even though the knife was dull, and took pieces of her scalp with it. If they hadn't, who knew what kind of creature would have taken up residence in it. She winced at the cold winter air biting her bare arms, wishing she still had her fur-lined cloak.

The guards had taken it, along with her clothing, leaving her with only a thin linen undershirt that did little to cover her body. Her fingers and toes showed signs of frostbite, and Agnes knew it was only a matter of days before she lost one or two of them.

If she'd never wished for death before, the prolonged suffering made her reconsider.

Anything would be preferable to this new type of hell.

It was a long and arduous process, but Agnes finally managed to sit up. She pulled her bruised legs close to her chest and rested against the cold stone wall of the cell. The distant screams of others being tortured echoed through the damp chamber, but she didn't flinch. Over time, it had become easier for her to tune out the constant suffering around her to survive.

She stiffened at the glimpse of movement in the shadowy corner of the hallway, fearing it was one of the guards returning to make their rounds.

No one came. But someone was watching.

With one good eye, Agnes looked around her cage, finding a silhouette lingering in the far corner, floating in and out of focus. She tried to concentrate on it, but the pain was too much, and she closed her eyes. Whatever it was, if it wanted to talk, let it. She had no energy to start the conversation. She barely had the stamina to survive.

Agnes just needed to wait until the king called for her. He'd sent word that he would see her in a week.

Seven more days.

Seven more long days.

She was determined to hold onto her sanity and not give in, but the pressure was starting to wear her down. Agnes shifted, trying to ease the tightness in her chest before finally surrendering to sleep.

While she drifted off, the shadow crept towards her, winding its way around her body like fog and settling on top of her injuries. The darkness infiltrated her soul, soothing away her pain while carrying her further into peaceful rest.

When she opened her eyes the next day, the pain had lessened. Running her fingers over her arms and legs, she felt the scabs from cuts that healed. She unfurled her hands and realized that her broken bones had mended, and she could see through both eyes. Even her fingers started taking a flesh tone, and she could wiggle her toes.

Someone had wrapped Agnes in a threadbare blanket. The dried splotches of rust-colored blood staining the material made her cringe, but she draped it around her shoulders for the small amount of shelter it provided from the icy drops of rain beating against the prison. She started shivering from the chill in the air, and soon, she was covered in a thick layer of muck and mud.

What she wouldn't give for a bath and something to eat.

For six days, Agnes was left alone in her dark cell. The guards never paid her attention, focusing on their other 'guests,' only throwing a moldy scrap of bread and tipping a tin of water towards her once a day. They laughed as she scrambled to lick the moisture off the floor, but no one touched her. No more questioning. No more torture. Only the deafening silences of her thoughts.

It was worse than if they had continued the inhumane treatment.

Every morning, Agnes paced the tiny cell like a ritual, counting each step as she shuffled along the rough floor. Five steps from one end to the other and five steps back. Nothing more. Nothing less.

She imagined as she stood under the window that the rain was the salty mist of the ocean and that she was standing on its rocky shoreline, watching the ships sail away for their daily excursions.

Why didn't she ever leave on one? Ride the waves to some distant land, far from the poverty and gloom of the country she'd called home, somewhere warm with sandy beaches, endless fresh water, and exotic foods.

Last summer, while shopping at the market, she stumbled upon a fruit stand run by a vendor who sold exotic fruits from around the world. One particular description of a fruit captivated her mind: it had a rough, gold-green exterior with a hint of sweetness and tartness in its flesh. He called it a pineapple, and she often daydreamed about what it would be like to taste it.

She should have escaped when she had a chance. There had been nothing holding her back after the last of her children left the house and her husband died.

But she stayed. Because that was what women did, they persisted. And hoped someone would bury them when the time came.

There would be no burial for her now. She would be thrown into a pit, a nameless corpse no one would remember.

"You. Let's go. The king wants to see you."

Agnes had been dozing, her head resting against the cold stone wall, and she hadn't heard the guard sneak up. Instinctively, she scuttled backward into the corner and held her breath as he pulled the keys to her cell from his belt.

Had it been seven days already? It couldn't have been.

She'd scratched lines into the cell wall with a piece of rock. Glancing over, she counted the seven stripes and swallowed the bile threatening to spill out of her.

"Let's go, witch," the guard yelled, glaring at her with pure hatred. He stood at the cell gate, a thick wooden club in one hand and a tightly bound bundle of leather straps in the other. Agnes's heart sank as her eyes met the jailer's; she'd seen him use the same strap too many times on the others to know that it caused extreme pain.

As if gagging her would stop her from casting a curse upon the cruel man.

"Don't make me tell you again," he smirked as he dangled the leather from his outstretched hands. "We wouldn't want to make the king wait, now would we? He's got a lot of questions for you."

Agnes turned, facing the wall. "Does it make you feel powerful knowing people are at your mercy when confined and can't protect themselves? Do you feel like a god?" she hissed as he grabbed her arms behind her and tied them together.

Agnes knew she was playing with fire for taunting him, but she was long past the point of caring. Besides, she was gambling on the fact that they'd left her alone for the last week because the king ordered that no 'real' harm should come her way.

From how the guard tensed up, she knew she'd guessed right. Bravely, she smiled over her shoulder at the beast, cocking an eyebrow.

"The king is waiting," she reminded him, her voice steely with authority. She thrust her chin upwards and faced the wall, her slender shoulders regaining strength and determination.

The guard was rougher than usual, securing the clamp around her mouth and dragging her up the stone stairs to the castle, but he didn't say anything to her, which was a small blessing.

Chapter 50- Agnes

January 1591- Edinburgh Castle

"Agnes, you're here! Wonderful!" the king called from his throne, his feet dancing in anticipation.

A shiver ran down Agnes' spine as she struggled to lower herself. "You asked for me, Your Majesty?" Agnes' parched voice barely reached her tongue; the words felt sticky and unnatural. She glanced at his feet, keeping her eyes downcast, curious to see what stylish shoes he would be wearing today.

They didn't disappoint. They were beautiful—shiny black with an intricate thistle pattern flowing from the heel to the considerable tongue. The stitching alone would have taken days for skilled workers, let alone how long the cobbler took. They must have cost a fortune.

How long will he wear these? Agnes thought to herself as she waited for the king's permission to get up. Unfortunately, his attention was diverted as he argued with one of his advisors about the fate of another prisoner.

A man was accusing a local woman of poisoning his sheep flock. Four years ago.

And now he wanted her to answer for her crimes.

"A sign of witchcraft," the advisor declared, his patchy face red with anger. "The witch must be punished, and her family held responsible for paying for the lost flock."

Why not just blame the witches for everything that's gone wrong since the beginning of time?

Agnes tried to hold back her frustration as her legs started shaking. But the king seemed content to ignore her as he discussed the merits of a full interrogation of the woman.

"I recommend, Your Majesty, we move quickly on this one. She doesn't have much more time. If we want to get the names of her accomplices, I suggest we start right away," another advisor suggested, a glean in his eyes as he bounced on the balls of his feet.

"Fine, fine. Do what you think is necessary." The king waved him off and turned his attention back to Agnes. "Get up, Witch."

Agnes pushed herself up from the frigid ground, fighting through the numbness and pain in her left leg. Her hip throbbed with intense agony from sleeping on a rock during the night. But she ignored the discomfort, meeting the king's intense stare with determination in her eyes.

"You look like a witch," he proclaimed, his eyes narrowing as he scanned her up and down, stroking his goatee. "Is it true you can talk to the dead?"

Agnes was surprised by his question but masked her face. "No, Your Majesty," she replied, shaking her head.

"But you know someone who can?" the king pressed, fiddling with his shirt sleeves and glancing at the door behind Agnes. His slight smile sent shivers down her spine, and she fought the urge to turn around and see who entered.

"No, Your Majesty, I know no one alive with the ability."

Agnes stared at the banner behind the king's throne, her shoulders tense and her mouth a tight line. She swallowed hard and forced herself to keep calm, careful not to let any hint of the truth escape.

"She's lying," a voice said from behind her. Agnes was powerless to move as the figure moved to stand before her, his dreadful words cutting through the air like a jagged blade. "She knows more than she lets on."

Agnes glanced at the man watching her, taken aback by his intense, assessing stare. He was unlike any human or witch she had ever seen before. The air surrounding him shimmered with electricity, and a subtle aura radiated from his being. His appearance held a curious balance between otherworldly and tangible as if he had straddled the line between the living and the dead.

"Is that true, witch?" the king asked, leaning back on his throne, frowning.

"No, Your Majesty. I do not know anyone in the city who can talk to the dead," Agnes said, meeting his stare and crossing her fingers.

It wasn't a complete lie. Agnes had no connection to anyone in Edinburgh besides the old apothecary who supplied her with licorice candy and new ink. And he was so old that he could barely lift a teacup, let alone raise the dead.

"Tsk, tsk, lil' Witch. I think you know someone, and you are not saying," the stranger's voice sang. Agnes shivered as his fingers ran across her face. "So much potential. So much untapped energy."

Agnes focused on the king, hoping he would speak up about being touched. But his eyes had grown glossy, and he appeared on the verge of dozing off.

The voice laughed again. "Don't worry about the king. He can't hear us. This conversation is just between me and you, lil' Witch. Why don't we skip the niceties and get to the point? Do you want to live?" he asked.

"Of course, I want to live," Agnes answered, looking at the stranger. "No one wants to die."

"We both know that isn't true." He arched an eyebrow in amusement. "There are plenty of people who would accept Charon's call. But I seek those who cannot." The stranger moved to stand next to the king, looking at him in disgust. His unnatural eyes flew to her, glowing with dark magick.

The stranger moved to stand next to the king, towering over him with an intimidating aura. His eyes, an unsettling shade of silver, glowed with dark magick as he locked gazes with her.

"Show me where they are, and I will make this painful situation disappear. I'll even let you keep your family's grimoire--all you have to do is answer my question. Where are the sisters?"

"I don't know..." Agnes started as the room suddenly trembled. Like the banshees of the night, eerie voices filled the chambers and echoed in her head. Paralyzed with fear, she collapsed to her knees and clamped her hands over her ears to block out the terrorizing sounds.

"DO NOT LIE!" the man yelled before taking a deep breath and kneeling beside her. Gently, he reached out and lifted Agnes's face to his. "Let me help you. Let me help your friends. Tell me where the sisters are, and I swear I will make this all disappear."

"How?" Agnes gasped, her voice shaking with fear and hope as she leaned into the man's warmth.

His velvet touch caressed her soul, erasing all the pain and anguish of the last few weeks. Agnes gaze was transfixed on his mesmerizing green eyes, filled with swirling sparks moving like electric currents through a stormy sky.

"This is not your fault. The sisters dragged you into something beyond your control. Unfortunately, they will have you believe it is fate. But fate is nothing more than a lie. It's just an excuse for why terrible things happen to good people! Give me what I want, and I will end this nightmare."

"And my friends?" Agnes dared to ask.

He glanced down at her, a triumphant smile playing on his lips. "And your friends," he promised.

Chapter 51- Chloe

Modern Day- Peebles, Scotland

"Where should we start?" Eidolon leaned forward, his intense gaze sweeping over the group as we sat around the kitchen table, eagerly digging into Esme's famous chicken potpie. The golden crust crackled under our forks, revealing a steaming mound of tender meat and vegetables in a rich, savory sauce.

I couldn't fathom how she found the time to cook such elaborate meals, but every bite tasted like pure magick and brought back memories of my childhood.

"We need to retrace our steps to the beginning," Isabelle replied thoughtfully, taking a slow sip of her rich red wine. "Agnes and Geillis were dragged away to Edinburgh Castle for questioning, the same fortress where Geillis penned her infamous book. Before we make any further decisions, we should explore the surrounding area and get a sense of its layout."

Watson took a long swig from his flask, the rich amber liquid burning down his throat. His eyes narrowed and became heavy-lidded, fixing on me with a penetrating gaze. I could see the weight of his thoughts in the creases of his brow and the set of his jaw.

"If you want to start from the beginning, we must go to Nether Keith first. That is where the story begins. Agnes had visited a cave nearby before arriving in Edinburgh."

Isabelle slowly turned to stare at him, stunned, her mouth dropping a notch. "How would you know that?"

Watson's face hardened, and he looked away, a pained expression flashing across his features. "I must have heard it somewhere and just remembered," he said, staring down at his empty flask with a frown.

He's not telling us something again, I mentioned down the bond to Eidolon.

I saw, he replied with a frown. *But what?*

I don't know, but it makes me nervous.

"Is Nether Keith your next stop?" Esme asked, her arms laden with homemade apple pie and a steaming pot of freshly brewed coffee. The aroma of the warm, buttery crust and sweet apples filled the room, mingling with the rich scent of coffee. I nearly drooled in excitement.

"Seems so," Isabelle responded with a curt nod, her fork stabbing at the food on her plate with a borderline aggressive intensity. Tension radiated from her every movement as she tried to hide her frustration and anger behind a facade of composure.

Victor's head snapped up in surprise, his gaze darting between me and Eidolon with concern. Eidolon shrugged but kept a watchful eye on Watson.

Isabelle and Watson barely exchanged a word during dinner, their emotions and thoughts spoken through stolen glances. Isabelle leaned back in her chair, sipping at her rich red wine. She stole glances at her husband, his sharp features illuminated by the flickering candlelight as he sat lost in thought. Tension hung heavily between them, their eyes skirting around each other but never quite connecting.

"You'll love it!" Esme continued, not reading the energy of the room. "It's one of my favorite places to visit. My husband and I go up twice a year. One night, we stayed till morning watching the stars cascading from the heavens above. They were so bright I swear they were raining on us. Nine months later, my youngest son was born," she finished with a cheeky wink at me and Eidolon.

"No one is trying to conceive anything, Esme. Just find clues." Eidolon ran a hand through his hair in embarrassment.

"We'll see," Esme laughed as she walked out. "The stars never disappoint."

My eyes followed Esme's retreating figure, my mind racing as I tried to make sense of her words. She couldn't mean what I thought she meant. *Right?*

The last time we were in Scotland, Eidolon mentioned that Moll believed the Fates had brought us together, destined as soulmates. To him, it was a continuation of his family's heritage of Writers and Librarians, chosen by the gods to uphold their ancient legacy.

But a continuation meant babies.

Something that I hadn't thought about.

We control our destiny, Eidolon growled down the bond. *It's our decision when we have children—not the stars. Not the Fates. Us. We will decide when we are ready for kids.*

I couldn't stop staring at him. Had Eidolon already considered having children? The weight of such a huge responsibility was overwhelming. We hadn't even gone on our first date, yet we were already on the road to discussing things like changing diapers and buying car seats.

Shouldn't I at least get dinner before having to consider such weighty matters?

Did I even want to bring a child into the world?

Months ago, my answer would have been an unequivocal yes. But now? I wasn't so sure.

"What do you think, Chloe?" Isabelle's voice sang out.

I glanced up to see everyone looking at me strangely. "I'm sorry, what?"

"I asked if you agreed that we should split up. The boys can go to Nether Keith, as Watson seems knowledgeable about it. As for you and me, we can travel to Edinburgh and try to gather information there." Isabelle's jaw clenched; her voice strangled as she tried to hide her rage.

Knowing Isabelle's emotions could have a physical reaction, I eyed her wearily. Watson stared at her, his hand reaching out to her only to pull back at the last second.

The way Isabelle fidgeted with her hands, tiny sparks flying from her fingers, she and Watson also needed a break from each other.

While I didn't want to separate from Eidolon, I also knew it would be foolish to test our luck. Staying together had the potential to bring about consequences that we were not ready to tackle.

Parting ways was the safest option.

With a decisive nod, I reached for a generous slice of pie. "Sounds like a delicious plan to me," I declared with a grin, savoring the buttery crust and sweet filling melting in my mouth.

Isabelle was determined to be the first in line for a tour of the Royal Mile, so I dragged myself out of bed before sunrise, still groggy and disoriented. The pale light of dawn had barely begun to filter through the windows, casting long shadows across the room. My eyes struggled to adjust to the dim light as I stumbled to get ready, trying my best not to trip over any stray objects on the floor.

It hadn't been a restful night.

Esme's words had lingered in the air like a heavy fog, and neither Eidolon nor I were willing to address the elephant in the room. So, we spent the night tossing and turning, pretending to sleep while fully aware that the other was awake.

Eidolon stayed in bed while I dressed, watching me move around the room with my cell phone flashlight, trying to be quiet.

"You can turn on the light," he said as I hit my toe on the bed for the third time.

I spun around. "You're awake!"

"You are not exactly quiet." He shrugged, the blanket falling to his waist when he sat up and turned on the nightstand lamp next to him. The soft glow highlighted his tattoos, and I had to turn away, my mouth drying at the sight.

"Sorry about that." I sat on the edge of the bed and pulled on my shoes.

"Don't be. I should get up, too. Watson wants to get going after breakfast. How did you sleep?"

I glanced over my shoulder and forced a smile. "Great! And you?"

"Liar," he chuckled as he threw off the covers and got out of bed. His low-hanging sweatpants showcased his perfectly formed abs, and my breath caught. "I'm going to jump into the shower." Eidolon walked over and kissed me on the forehead. "Be careful today. Remember what you promised me? If you run into Taliesin, you run in the other direction and call me immediately."

I glanced up at him, unnerved by his proximity to me.

No baby-making happening today, I reminded myself. Eidolon chuckled.

"You need to control your thoughts, lil' Writer," Eidolon said, winking at me. "Though I do enjoy how imaginative you are. I will see you tonight." He kissed me again and headed to the bathroom.

Gods help me.

I didn't know how much longer I could control myself around him. As I slipped on my sweatshirt, I heard him chuckle.

Ditto.

I smiled as I walked out the door.

Chapter 52- Chloe

Modern Day- Peebles, Scotland

"Coffee! I need coffee," I begged as I walked to the foyer, my coat draped over my arm.

Isabelle stood before the fireplace, staring into nothingness with a frown. Her skinny jeans hugged her hips, and the beige sweater flowed over her curves. She sported an oversized, military green jacket that dwarfed her tiny frame. Her locks of golden hair were braided in a loose style that cascaded down her back, showcasing the elegant gold hoops adorning her ears. A plaid scarf wrapped around her neck added depth to the earthy colors of her outfit.

I was lucky to have found a clean sweatshirt and socks. My hair was pulled up in a messy bun, and I barely remembered to apply foundation to camouflage the dark circles underneath my eyes.

At some point, I would have to get it together and present a more polished version of myself. There was an unwritten expectation for women in their middle-aged years to be skilled at styling their hair and makeup.

Hell, even Dolly Parton looked like she was 37 for the last 40 years.

"There's a coffee shop on the way. It makes the most delicious Pumpkin Spice latte and coffee cake," Isabelle promised as she turned to look at me with sad eyes. We'll head there first."

The sight of my friend, the once strong and proud woman, now broken and insecure, was unsettling. She was nothing like the energetic woman who'd been the first real friend I made in the Raven Society—the one who strode into a room with her head held high, her laughter ringing like bells, and commanding everyone's attention without trying.

I wasn't sure how to help her. I didn't have many close friends and the ones I did have lived too far away to hang out with. Our interactions were limited to social media, where we exchanged likes, memes, and book recommendations. But that was all; our relationship never went beyond that digital screen.

The situation between Isabelle and Watson was beyond my capabilities. Still, I pushed myself to offer some measure of comfort by lightly patting her shoulder, feeling awkward and unsure of what else to do or say.

"Don't worry, luv. I'm fine," Isabelle reassured. "Nothing that won't sort itself out with time. Now, let's find you some coffee, and you can tell me about your night with Eidolon. After what Esme implied, I would have given anything to be a fly on the wall."

My groan elicited a laugh from her as I rubbed the bridge of my nose. I was at a loss for words. Unfortunately, there was nothing to report. But I had agreed to this painfully slow pace, so I had no one to blame but myself.

"I don't need to hear all of the particulars; I just want you to know I claim the role of godmother," she chuckled, taking my silence for agreement.

"We didn't 'practice' if that's what you're implying. We're taking it slow," I admitted, readjusting my bun.

"Interesting." Isabelle shook her head in amazement. "You have better self-control than me. Have you seen Eidolon? He's delicious."

"Isabelle," I moaned, putting on my coat.

"Just saying," Isabelle exclaimed with a spark in her eyes. "Anyhoo, let's get out of here and do some exploring. I've been looking forward to our girls' day out."

I nodded in agreement, glad to move on from the heavy topic of children and Eidolon. We dashed through the pouring rain to reach our awaiting cab, trying our best to avoid getting drenched by the morning downpour. I let out a sigh of relief as we reached the warmth of the car, and I could feel the heater already blasting hot air.

The cold touch of the Otherworld still lingered in my bones, refusing to dissipate even after we returned to Scotland. Even my shadows were complaining.

And you knew it was serious when your imaginary friends were bitching.

I stared out the car window, my mind wandering as the vehicle swayed to the beat of the road. The sky was a monotonous grey, but the fields rolling past us were a lively green, sparkling like jewels in the sunlight. I could envision myself settling down here permanently. A cozy cabin with a porch wrapping around it, a tiny garden bursting with vibrant blooms and luscious vegetables leading to a peaceful backyard.

In my daydream, a clamshell path would lead to a tiny smokehouse painted deep azure, with a tin chimney puffing out gray-blue smoke. Instead of hanging fish from its rafters, I would make it a she-shack, with bookcases lining the walls and a coffee area beneath one of the windows. An enormous desk would sit in the middle of the room, complete with an updated laptop, notebooks, pens, and a Tiffany lamp.

I could get so much writing done.

My book. I hadn't thought about my incomplete manuscript for months. It was sitting on my desk back home, waiting to be finished and sent to the editor.

Did I even have an editor anymore?

Probably not. I was supposed to give her the final draft weeks ago, but I forgot to reach out.

What would I have said anyway?

Hey Lisa. I'm in the Otherworld. AT&T hasn't made it this far, so the internet access sucks. I'll need to extend my deadline a bit.

The truth was that working on anything other than the Book of the Veiled was a distant dream. I promised Moll I would use my abilities to protect history, but in doing so, I gave up my aspirations. Every time I submerged myself in the different timelines and myths, it became increasingly difficult to remember my life before the Raven Society.

When Moll told me what it meant to be a Writer, it sounded so adventurous, but now I wasn't so sure.

Being a Writer was lonely.

Losing myself in my musings, I fixed my gaze on the steady stream of raindrops dancing against the car windows before sliding down in a haphazard pattern. The faint sound of a sob snapped me back to reality.

Isabelle's shoulders trembled as she fought to hold back her tears. Her eyes squeezed shut, and her hands were tightly clasped together. A soft whimper slipped from her lips, a fragile sound amidst the overwhelming chaos of her emotions.

"Isabelle, is everything alright?"

She turned her head to stare out the window, her fingers tapping nervously on the armrest. "I honestly don't know. But I can tell Watson's keeping something from me. We've never had secrets, but his reaction last night was a red flag."

"Maybe he's just worried," I tried to comfort her, putting my hand on hers. "He doesn't want you to get hurt."

"No." Isabelle shook her head. "It's more than that. He knows who the Witch of Endor is," she whispered, a tear running down her cheek.

I stared at my friend, my mouth hanging open in surprise. "What do you mean he knows who the Witch of Endor is?"

"I mean, he knows her name because he met her. And her sister."

"That can't be right," I muttered, taking my glasses off to clean them. "They lived thousands of years ago."

Isabelle glanced at me, raising one eyebrow. As I put my glasses back on, it all clicked.

Watson was a vampire—a very old vampire—which meant he could very well know who the Witch of Endor was.

But why didn't he tell us?

Isabelle shrugged her shoulders, knowing what I was thinking. "Great question," she replied with a frown, dabbing a tear away with a napkin. "It doesn't matter though. Let him keep his secrets; we'll have our own."

A sense of unease crept over me as I observed the steely glint in her eyes. It was a look that meant she had something brewing in that devious mind of hers.

"What do you got in mind?" I asked, noticing the driver looking at us through the rearview mirror. His eyes glinted with a familiar glint like silver spun from the stars and set in deep green pools of enigma. I squinted, trying to recall where I had encountered him before.

Catching me staring, he flashed a knowing smile that sent chills down my spine like I was a fly caught in a spider web. He raised his chin in acknowledgment before turning away and resuming his journey through the countryside.

"We will find the Witch of Endor before the boys do," Isabelle declared with a slight bounce in her seat. My eyes narrowed at her sudden mood change. Sad and angry, Isabelle was terrifying.

But happy Isabelle? Well, she could be downright dangerous.

I hesitated to ask, but curiosity gripped me. "And how do you propose we do that?"

"I will tell you over coffee," she promised, looking at her wedding ring before glancing back out the window. "I have a friend in town who might be able to help us."

Chapter 53- Chloe

Modern Day- Edinburgh, Scotland

A few minutes later, the driver parked next to an alleyway after a near accident between us and a wandering sheep.

"I'll wait here for you," he said, glancing over the front seat as we exited.

"You don't need to do that, luv," Isabelle protested, her hand hovering over the car door.

He shook his head. "I think I do," he replied before turning his attention to his phone.

Isabelle and I exchanged a shrug before she slammed the door shut, the sound echoing down the quiet street. With no obligation to return, we stepped onto the cracked sidewalk, the concrete rough and uneven under our feet.

An unsettling sensation washed over me like a cold wave crashing against my skin. I couldn't shake off the feeling that someone was watching us. My instincts urged me to turn around, and when I did, I locked eyes with the driver, his intense gaze never leaving mine.

Rude!

Isabelle grabbed my arm before I could say anything and tugged me around the corner. The streetlight faded as we strolled into a dim alleyway adorned with flickering gaslights set in intricately carved stone sconces.

Oh shit, I thought as my eyes widened.

It was no ordinary alleyway but a secret passageway, subtle and irresistible. Tall, weathered stone walls extended to the sky and framed the entrance like an ancient castle gate. Inside, small shops lined either side of the cobblestone path, illuminated by narrow streams of the rising sun, creating a wicked pattern of shadows across the road.

"What in the world?" I whispered as I peered through the store window on my left. Its exterior resembled a dark-age castle, with a massive sign looming above the front door that read "The Dollhouse" in red lettering that dripped down the wood like freshly spilled blood.

Every dusty surface was covered with an array of strange and wondrous items. A colossal bird carcass hung from wires on the ceiling, frozen in mid-flight, its beady glass eyes following my movement. Bottles filled with swirling smoke lined shelves around the room, while metal sculptures of all shapes and sizes perched atop pedestals. Everywhere I looked, I found something new and bizarre.

At the back of the room, a towering bookshelf hugged the corner. Its aged ledges were lined with antique porcelain dolls, each dressed in elaborately detailed Victorian garments. Their eyes sparkled like small diamonds in the dim light, their tiny fingers twisted together, frantically reaching for freedom. I shuddered as their desperate gaze begged for help.

That's not strange at all, I thought as I turned wide-eyed and hurried to catch up with Isabelle.

"I never had the nerve to go in," Isabelle shuddered, wrapping her coat around herself. "Too eerie for my taste. They say if you go in, you never come out if you stay too long. Some spell, I think. I only know that another doll is added to their bizarre collection every year."

The temperature dropped a few degrees, sending shivers across my skin and raising goosebumps on my arms. "I believe it," I muttered, unease settling in my stomach. "There's definitely something off about that place."

Isabelle nodded, taking my hand and pulling me down the street. "Come on, we are almost there."

I followed, awe overtaking the feeling of dread. The other stores were much more appealing in comparison—bright lights, pleasant music, and inviting displays filled their windows. A sense of surrealism lingered in the air as if stepping into one of these shops would send you into an alternate reality. Now and then, the storefronts twitch and shimmer as though they weren't quite real.

Or not of this time.

Welcome to Wonderland, my inner voice warned, but the aroma of food and coffee diverted my attention from any uneasiness. There was nothing I couldn't handle as long as an apple fritter and caffeine were involved.

As we headed to the cafe, I glanced into a bakery's window lined with whimsical delights. Center stage, I spotted a groom's cake in the shape of a whisky bottle with 'Under New Management' written on the label. Further along, a tray of classic French fruit tarts was nestled next to sugar cookies with pink frosting and colorful sprinkles.

I wanted to stop, but Isabelle was leaving me behind. I hurried to catch up.

My feet floated across the cobblestone as I walked towards the beautiful bouquets lining the street. I could easily picture my mother reveling in the sweet smell of roses and the colorful array of sunflowers. As I paused to admire them, something else caught my attention: an apothecary store nestled in a secluded corner, its wooden sign swaying in the breeze.

I had never seen an authentic apothecary before, and I hurried over. Peeking through the window, I spied lavender, rosemary, and parsley bouquets hanging from the ceiling. A glass-doored cabinet grabbed my attention; its contents were an array of tiny bottles filled with spices, herbs, and essential oils.

The perfect witches display of ingredients.

My eyes drifted to a table in the middle of the room, stacked with colorful boxes of chocolates, butterscotch discs, and jars of cinnamon-flavored hard candies. I glanced down at the windowsill, and a miniature, framed ink illustration tucked into the corner drew my attention.

It was of a child standing barefoot, his tiny frame shivering and his face contorted with hunger. He begged for scraps from two well-dressed women who had their backs to him. Their long fur cloaks looked out of place against the dirty cityscape.

Leaning down to take a better look, I caught a glimpse of movement from the corner of my eye. Something shifted in the shadows on the other side of the street. However, when I tried to focus on it, I only found an old fire hydrant, a rusty sentinel guarding its post.

Get ahold of yourself, I commanded, returning my attention to the ink drawing.

The boy's eyes seemed to gaze back at me, and I could sense his sadness, loneliness, and longing for something he couldn't quite comprehend. The longer I stared, the more I connected with him.

The more I felt what he felt, the more it felt like we had become interchangeable.

The delicious aroma of freshly baked bread tempted him from the bakery across the street, but he couldn't bring himself to go inside. His hands were numb and frozen from the cold as he stood outside the flower shop. Inside, a warm fire crackled, but no one invited him in. He could hear women's voices calling him names and complaining that he hadn't been 'taken care' of yet.

Despite his young age, the boy understood what they were trying to say. He wasn't wanted. He could see the looks on their faces and hung his head in shame as he left, each step seeming more painful than the last.

My heart broke as I tried calling him to come back. Then everything got dark.

Not again!

I found myself lying in a shallow pit surrounded by countless corpses. A man stood on the edge, looking down with a Bible in one hand and a lit torch in the other. Unexpectedly, another man gently touched the priest's shoulder, whispering something in his ear. The priest nodded, looking at me with pity before throwing the flame.

My heart raced as the blazing inferno scorched me, searing my clothes and igniting my hair. The flames multiplied, ravaging my body as I frantically tried to extinguish them. I scrambled to find a way out, but the beast continued to spread with an insatiable appetite, devouring bodies around me in its wake.

My throat burned as I let out a terrified scream, my eyes darting towards the figure behind the priest. A familiar figure clad in a long, black robe stood still and silent with its hood covering its face, but recognition filled my heart like a dark void.

The man from my dreams.

"Chloe! Chloe! Wake the hell up," Isabelle yelled, followed by a painful slap to my face. The fiery red welt left behind by her hand throbbed on my skin as she searched my face for signs of life.

"What happened?" I gasped, my breathing ragged and unsteady.

Isabelle's slim hand grasped mine, and I allowed her to help me sit up. I frantically glanced around for the hooded figure, but he was nowhere to be found. The tension in my chest loosened a fraction as I exhaled a deep sigh of relief.

"I don't know. One minute, you were fine, and the next thing I knew, you were on the ground screaming like someone was trying to kill you."

"That was insane," I confessed, rubbing my head. "This vision was different. I wasn't watching. I was there. It happened to me. And the boy." I spun around, looking for him. "I hope he survived."

"Who are you talking about?" Isabelle knotted her eyebrows as she tried to make sense of my story.

"The boy in the picture," I said, pointing to the apothecary window. "I saw him. Before the fire."

Her eyes widened in alarm, and my skin crawled under the intensity of her gaze, suddenly needing to throw up.

"Come on, let's get you some food and coffee. It'll make you feel better." Isabelle wrapped her arms around me, embracing me in her calming presence as I breathed in the soothing aroma of honeysuckle and vanilla.

"Okay, but I want a double shot and extra whip," I said, eyeing her. "And you're paying."

Chapter 54- Chloe

Modern Day- Edinburgh, Scotland

The cafe was loud, crowded, and warm. It had an old-world charm, with stone walls and an enormous fireplace in the corner. Edison lights hung from the copper ceiling, illuminating the espresso machine and the extensive assortment of coffee and baked goods along the bar.

I skimmed with interest the walls covered with art from local artists and photographs of the owner hugging customers. Bookshelves lined the back wall, bursting with books that spilled over onto piles on the floor. A team of teenagers sat cross-legged around it, laughing at something one of them had said.

The atmosphere was vibrant and bustling, with conversations bouncing through the room. I breathed in the scent of freshly brewed coffee and marveled at the eclectic mix of people. College students sprawled over wooden tables, a couple engrossed in animated discussion, and a family of five ordering pastries from the counter. As I walked by, I listened to the snippets of conversations, making mental notes for my next book.

A booming female voice called out over all the noise, cutting through the chatter. "Isabelle! Where have you been?"

A petite, round-faced woman bustled between the tables with an air of familiarity and kindness. Her rosy cheeks flushed from her quick movement, like a hummingbird flitting from flower to flower. The soft melody of her voice carried through the bustling crowd as she greeted customers and inquired about their families with genuine interest.

I watched in fascination as she navigated through the sea of people, gracefully avoiding collisions as if she had a sixth sense. Her bright smile never faltered, lighting up her whole face as she stopped before us.

"I haven't seen you in years! Where have you been hiding? And where is that handsome mate of yours?" The woman looked around, expecting to see Watson.

"He's having a boy's day," Isabelle greeted, hugging her. "My dear, you don't look a day over twenty-five. How *do* you do it? I must get your skin care regimen."

The woman chuckled, rolling her eyes. "Says the blonde bombshell."

Her eyes flew over me, taking in my messy hair and stained sweatshirt. She frowned. "Isabelle, your friend looks positively frozen and hungry. It's a good thing you stopped by. I have a fresh batch of rolls in the oven. I'm betting you like your coffee with cream and sugar?" she guessed. I nodded in agreement. "Why don't you find somewhere to sit, and I'll make you a cup? Isabelle, do you want your usual?"

"You know me well." Isabelle chuckled as the woman walked away with a playful wink.

Isabelle gestured towards a table nestled in the corner. It was close enough to bask in the cozy heat yet discreetly tucked away from prying eyes. With a nod of agreement, we maneuvered through the bustling crowd toward our secluded spot. The crackling fire and flickering shadows provided a comforting ambiance as we settled into our seats.

As I looked around the room, my eyes fell upon a boar head mounted above the fireplace, with a piece of mistletoe dangling from one of its tusks. A dove figurine perched next to it, peering over a nest adorned with twinkling lights.

"Who is she?" I asked, trying to take in all the details, wanting to remember everything.

"That's Anne. She's owned this place longer than I can remember." Isabelle turned in her seat, looking for something.

"How did you guys meet?" I asked, following her gaze.

"Watson introduced us," she answered, glancing back, her eyes saddening at the memory. "This is where he took me on our first date after we got married."

"That's nice." I cringed as soon as the words came out. *That's nice.* That's all I could come up with? I was a sorry excuse for a friend.

"Don't fret, luv," Isabelle brushed off my discomfort. "Our disagreement doesn't mean I'm sulking. Returning here reminded me that we didn't always share every detail of our lives. When we first met, there were plenty of secrets between us. But we managed it alright."

Her eyes lit up as she rose from the armchair and approached the fireplace. She ran her fingertips along the cold stone wall until she found a barely noticeable etching with faint white lines. As she traced its curves, a graceful pattern appeared.

"I remember the day he carved this. He said it would be our secret. An act of defiance against those who said we shouldn't be together."

She stood frozen in time, her eyes glazing over with memories of years past. I was about to turn away when Isabelle jolted forward, her hand hovering just above the names carved into the stone surface. Her hands trembled, and her skin paled to a ghostly white.

"What's wrong?" I asked, rushing to her side.

"Someone scratched out Watson's name and wrote something else next to it. I didn't notice it initially, but it's not the same handwriting."

"What does it say?" I leaned in to get a better look, but Isabelle blocked my view.

"W-Y-S-T-A-N," she spelled out slowly.

"Wystan?" That was strange. "Why would someone change Watson's name?"

Isabelle straightened, looking at me, her eyes wide. "I don't know, but I'm about to find out." She peeked over my shoulder, a flash of determination in her eyes.

I turned my head to follow her gaze and spotted Anne heading our way. She was deftly carrying a tray loaded with an assortment of pastries and a colorful fruit platter.

"Here you go, ladies. Fresh out of the oven." Anne placed the tray of freshly baked goods in the center of the table, her smile beaming at us as we eagerly took our seats. She poured me a cup of coffee with just the right amount of cream and sugar, and I danced happily in my seat.

"Anne, can I ask you a question?" Isabelle asked, passing me the plate of pastries. I eyed her nervously as I nibbled an apple fritter and groaned in pleasure. "What do you know about Watson's history?"

Anne's eyes darted to Isabelle, her jaw tightening. "What do you mean?" she asked in a strained voice.

"I want to know about Watson. Before I meet him," Isabelle clarified, delicately sipping her coffee as if she had no care in the world.

"I can't imagine what you think I can tell you that he hasn't," Anne said dismissively, not meeting Isabelle's stare. "He's your mate."

"Anne O'Donnell. I'm not asking," Isabelle spat out, her eyes blazing with uncharacteristic anger and intensity. "Tell me what you know," she repeated, her voice soft but firm.

Anne leaned back in her chair, arms folded across her chest in defiance. "Are you questioning me as a friend or as the high priestess?"

A knot formed in my throat as they stared at each other. The tension was almost tangible. I felt like a bystander, unable to intervene as they silently challenged one another. Clearly, this conversation was about to take a dark and uncomfortable turn.

Isabelle smiled, but her tone contained a warning. "I wanted to take the friendship route, but if it comes down to a power struggle, I won't hesitate," she stated firmly. "So, I will ask you again. What do you know about Watson?"

My eyes widened as I watched their silent battle, my apple fritter forgotten. Anne's shoulders tightened, and her eyes shifted like she was searching for an escape route.

She played with her napkin, folding and unfolding it several times before looking up to meet Isabelle's gaze. I could practically see fear radiating off her - her skin paled, her fists clenched, and her breathing quickened as Isabelle waited for a response.

Oh, she is hiding something, I thought.

"It's a long, sad tale," Anne warned.

I groaned. Of course, it was a long story. But from Isabelle's face, we wouldn't be leaving until she heard all the details.

Reaching for the coffee pot, I poured another cup and settled in.

This was going to take a while.

Chapter 55- Nava

December 1590- Nether Keith, Scotland

"Want to tell me what's wrong?" Wystan asked, walking up behind Nava.

Her feet left the ground, and a jolt of surprise shot through her body. She assumed he would still be inside, keeping Ysabel company.

Not following her to her sanctuary.

Every afternoon, Nava would make her way to the cliffs, leaving Watson and Ysabel alone and giving herself some much-needed time to think. She welcomed the solitary journey, finding solace in the sound of the crashing ocean as it calmed the tumultuous emotions within her. They served as a reminder that memories were like waves - fleeting and temporary, leaving only faint remnants behind.

"You are liable to give an old woman a heart attack sneaking up on me like that," Nava complained with a forced laugh.

The vampire looked at her with amusement and curiosity.

"You're barely older than me," Wystan reminded her. "And seeing as you can't die, I don't think you have anything to worry about."

Nava rolled her eyes, gesturing down the path. "I was headed to the cliffs if you want to join me."

"Lead the way, old friend."

Wystan's gaze was fixed on the ground, following Nava's lead as they made their way through the dense forest. The trees towered above them, their rustling leaves creating a soothing melody that blended with the sound of their footsteps.

As they trudged up the winding path, blades of grass tickled against their bare feet as they maneuvered around the gnarled roots that protruded from the steep slope, like fingers reaching out from the earth to challenge their ascent.

As they approached, the cliff's summit towered over the ocean like a menacing giant, its jagged edge creating an imposing contrast to the lush greenery that enveloped the area. Only those in desperate need sought out this spot, hoping for some sort of escape from their lives.

Either they left feeling rejuvenated or simply vanished, never to be seen again.

Nava's eyes lit up as they finally reached their destination, and she gestured for Wystan to join her on the smooth, flat rock perched high above the Northern Sea.

From their viewpoint, they could see for miles in every direction - the endless blue of the sea meeting the horizon, the distant cliffs and rolling hills, and the sparkling winter sun reflecting off the water like diamonds.

It was Nava's favorite spot, a place where she felt at peace and connected with nature.

Wystan's brow furrowed as he met her gaze, his hand reaching down to scoop up a smooth pebble. "Are you planning on telling me what you're doing?" His voice held a hint of frustration and curiosity, mirroring the tension in his muscles as he prepared to throw the stone.

Confusion creased Nava's brow as she pushed a stray lock of hair out of her face. "I don't know what you mean."

"Don't play dumb, Nava. It's not your style. You smell different," Wystan replied drily. "Old."

Nava's gaze darted quickly to his face before she turned away, her head hanging low in shame. The weight of the unspoken truth hung heavily in the air between them. "How long have you known?"

"A couple of days," he admitted. "I was waiting for you to say something."

"I didn't know what to say." Nava's voice was barely a whisper as she stared out at the vast expanse of the ocean, tossing a smooth stone into its depths. "I had no choice. I had to make the deal."

It was not that she hadn't tried to find a way around it. The king left her no choice.

Find Samuel, and he would let her and Ysabel go.

Little did Nava know, Arawn would have his own ultimatum awaiting her arrival.

There will come a day when the past, present, and future exist simultaneously, and I will need your help guiding someone back to the Otherworld. They may not want to come, and things could become problematic.

"How long do you have?" Wystan whispered, wrapping his arm around her shoulders.

"Not long." Nava leaned in, her voice muffled against his chest as a single tear slipped down her cheek. "I had a feeling when we first arrived," she added, her words tinged with sadness and regret.

"Ysabel doesn't know, does she?"

Nava's gaze sharpened, her eyes narrowing into thin slits as they locked onto his face. "Not yet," she stated firmly, leaving no room for argument.

Wystan arched an eyebrow. "You're going to have to tell her sooner or later."

"I will," Nava sighed. "I wanted to make sure everything was in order first."

She hadn't told anyone about her plan, and she was fully aware of the risks that came with asking the Fates for a favor. But she couldn't just sit back and do nothing. Ysabel deserved better.

And Nava would stop at nothing to help her sister.

Besides, her place wasn't in the mortal world.

Not anymore.

Everyone Nava loved was in the Otherworld, and it was time to reunite with them. Trading her soul for Ysabel's life was worth it.

She only hoped that 700 years plus 700 years would be enough time for them.

Wystan nodded with a sorrowful smile on his face. "Thank you."

Nava waved away his gratitude, but he forced her to look at him, holding her chin between his fingers. "I mean it, Nava. You didn't have to do this."

"She deserves her happily ever after. And so do you," Nava whispered.

"Will she remember?" Wystan asked a few minutes later.

"Not at first. But she will." Nava looked up at him, her eyes pleading. "Be patient when that day comes.

Wystan was lost in thought as he nodded slowly. His forehead creased, and his bottom lip trembled as he struggled to articulate the thoughts swirling in his mind. He opened his mouth but hesitated and closed it without uttering a word.

Nava gave him space to gather his thoughts. She enjoyed the peaceful lull in conversation and was not ready to answer more inquiries.

She known for a while that this day would come, but now that it was here, she was scared. The girl Arawn warned her about was coming.

And death followed in her wake.

Chapter 56- Agnes

27 January 1591- Edinburgh Castle

"Are you sure?" The king raised a skeptical brow as he leaned back in his throne chair. His finger absentmindedly stroked his goatee as he mulled over the surprising declaration.

"Yes, Your Majesty. I interrogated her personally. She is not guilty," Taliesin said, leveling the monarch with a piercing gaze that challenged him to disagree.

The king stared at his advisor, a wave of conflicting emotions passing through him. On the one hand, Geillis had presented some damning evidence against Agnes and her alleged dealings with the devil.

On the other, Taliesin had proven himself to be an efficient and effective interrogator.

If he believed Agnes was not guilty, she must not be.

But someone *had* attempted to harm his wife, the queen. Somebody summoned the gale that nearly sank her ship.

If not Agnes, who?

"Geillis named her as one of the leaders. She gave a detailed account of Agnes' transactions with the devil. She tried to kill my wife!" he reminded Taliesin, pounding his fist against the armrest of his throne.

"An unfortunate incident that Agnes had nothing to do with," Taliesin dismissed with a wave. "I assure you, she had nothing to do with the storm."

"But someone did," the king countered. "My bride almost drowned because of these *witches*, and I want their blood."

"I understand your anger. The individuals responsible will not go unpunished. But, if you execute Agnes, people will doubt you and your claim. She is a well-respected woman in her village and poses no threat. Your Majesty, I urge you to free her from custody and focus on the suspects who have already confessed."

"I'm not sure," the king said slowly. "If we let her go, people will think our intelligence isn't reliable. It'll create a sense of safety among the witches; they'll all assume they're untouchable if one escapes justice. The devil will infiltrate and destroy our kingdom from within."

"Rest assured, the devil realizes he has no dominion over this land. I'm certain he's in his infernal domain, regretting his decisions and whom he chose as followers," Taliesin replied with a chuckle.

"Your Majesty, if I may?"

Taliesin's eyes flashed as he spun on his heel to face the noble who had dared to speak out. The advisor shrank away from him, his hands twitching in fear. He opened his mouth, but no sound came out except a whimper. His gaze darted anxiously towards the king.

"What?" the king asked, annoyed.

"The people may challenge your decision." The advisor swallowed hard as the king leaned forward with a deep frown, and his eyes narrowed. "But if we examine her again, perhaps by you, it will put the rumors to rest. Who can argue against the king's own interrogation?"

"I assure you, my questioning..." Taliesin started, dark shadows forming in his eyes before the king jumped in.

"No one doubts your tactics, Taliesin," the king waved him off. "I will interview her myself, and if she proves her innocence, she will be free to go."

"As you wish," Taliesin said in a tight voice as he bowed his head and backed away from the throne. His strides were deliberately shorter than usual to show his reluctant obedience, and he left the room without looking back.

Rage coursed through Taliesin's veins as he stalked through the silent corridors, heading for the dungeons. He staggered forward, struggling to keep himself upright as his inner demons loomed over him. They were a tangible presence, sapping his strength and courage.

The constant jumps in time were becoming too difficult for him to manage for much longer. His mind and body were torn apart whenever he juggled alternate versions of reality. A deep rumbling reverberated through his bones, causing a fiery ache that seared his muscles and drained him.

Taliesin leaned against the rough stone wall, eyes closed as the chill of the stones seeped through his cloak. Taking deep breaths, he exhaled slowly, imagining all the stress and worries being released with it. Gradually, he became aware of his surroundings, bringing his thoughts back into focus.

Time was running out. Soon, he wouldn't be able to save his sister's soul.

With a weary groan, Taliesin pushed himself off the wall and headed toward the dungeon. The hallway was cloaked in darkness, illuminated only by sparse pools of light emanating from flickering candles nestled within ornate sconces.

Trudging down the dimly lit corridor, his footsteps fell silent against the cold stone floor as if he were nothing more than a mere whisper in the shadows that trailed behind him.

He needed time to prepare Agnes and was determined to uphold his end of the bargain.

He refused to let another king undo all his progress.

He would find the sisters, and Agnes was the crucial piece of the puzzle. She was the reason the girl would come.

And when she did, Taliesin would be ready.

Agnes's shrill and piercing screams tore through the air, bouncing off the chamber's stone walls with a deafening echo.

Taliesin stood frozen in shock as Agnes writhed in pain beneath the king's cruel guards. His stomach clenched, and bile rose in his throat at the sight of her swollen and bloody body, tears streaming down her bruised face.

His knuckles turned white as he clenched them to stop himself from lunging forward to protect her, tasting iron in his mouth from where he had bitten down hard on his lip.

The questioning started pleasantly enough.

Agnes objected to the accusations.

Just as she and Taliesin had rehearsed.

Not that coaching was needed. Agnes hadn't done anything. All she had to do was tell the truth.

And the king believed her at first.

But that damn advisor weaseled his way into the king's chambers, slyly offering devious comments and suggestions that clouded the king and Agnes' minds. The advisor's words twisted reality until the king had no choice but to proceed with the interrogation in a more 'hands-on' approach.

And that's when everything went wrong.

Agnes confessed.

Despite Taliesin's best efforts, he was powerless to stop the unfolding events. He watched as Agnes stood in the center of the room, gazing at the floor as two guards ripped away her gown and examined her.

She trembled and swallowed hard as they located a tiny red mark, branding her a witch. Tears rolled down her cheeks as she revealed she had attended the king's first night with his new bride.

Agnes went so far as to repeat every word from the king's and his bride's conversation that evening, confirming her confession.

Taliesin's mouth fell open as he stared at her, wondering what she was doing.

This was not what they discussed.

Had Taliesin been paying attention, he might have spotted the two silhouettes lurking in the corner of the room. He might have heard the faint sound of a woman's voice prompting Agnes to say something that would ultimately end her life.

But all he could think about was his sister.

Morrigan.

He had failed her, like everyone else in his life.

Vivian.

His daughter Aelle.

His son Eidolon.

Even Diana didn't trust him anymore. She had been fed lies and believed he was trying to destroy the world.

Well, let them all hate him. It didn't matter anyhow. He knew what he had promised the Fates.

"I had no choice," Agnes mumbled, collapsing against her cell wall. She wedged herself as far into the corner as possible, trying to shut out the icy chill that seeped through the cracks of her prison. No matter how hard she tried, she could not escape the sense of hopelessness and fear that swallowed her whole.

"Everyone has a choice," Taliesin shot back through gritted teeth, pacing back and forth. He stopped and spun on his heel to face her, his eyes blazing with anger. "We had a deal."

"Deals are meant to be broken. Especially when faced with no other option." Agnes looked up, wincing in pain. "Can you please stop moving? It hurts my head."

Taliesin's voice was like a searing blade slicing through the air. "A headache will be nothing compared to what awaits! The king has commanded you to go to the abbey and beg for mercy. How could you have been so foolish to confess such crimes?" His face contorted with rage as he spat out every hateful word.

Agnes' confession had gotten darker and more horrific by the second, from her presence in the marriage chambers to having carnal relations with the devil and consuming the flesh of infants. Taliesin couldn't believe what he heard.

"You know, you're not what they said you were," Agnes said, her one good eye focusing on him. "I was expecting something different."

"Who?" Taliesin stepped forward, his eyes narrowing on her. "Who told you about me?"

"The sisters."

"And what did they tell you?" Taliesin sneered, pacing again, his dark cloak fluttering around his calves.

"That you were worse than the devil," Agnes admitted, wishing she hadn't said anything.

"Is that all? I'm hurt." Taliesin grabbed his chest in mock pain.

"It doesn't bother you, does it?" Agnes asked, surprised. She hissed in pain as she shifted her body to get more comfortable.

"No," Taliesin answered as he dropped to a knee, reaching over and placing a hand on her shoulder. "You're in pain."

"It's not pleasant." Agnes looked up with a false smile.

His green eyes flashed with lightning as the pain dissipated from her body. The healing warmth began at the top of her head, healing the cuts and rope burn across her face, resetting the bones in her fingers. The soft comfort followed along the bruises on her legs before reaching her feet, soothing the deep burns left there.

"Thank you." Agnes held up her hand, admiring his work.

Taliesin grunted as he stood up, running his hand through his hair.

"I care. More than you will ever know. But it's easier if everything thinks I am the bad guy—the devil, as you so casually put it." He glanced over his shoulder and frowned at the cell across the hallway. "It's better this way."

"Why?"

"Because I made a deal with the Fates."

"That doesn't explain anything." Agnes shook her head in frustration and slowly stood up, using the wall as an anchor. "Why are you chasing the sisters? What do they have to do with anything?"

"I'm not chasing them!" Taliesin growled, anger dancing across his face as shadows gathered around his legs.

"Yes, you are! Everywhere they go, you show up, and the witches die!" Agnes threw her hands up, yelling back. "But then you turn around and promise to keep me and my friends safe. What happened? Did you have a change of heart and want to atone for your sins?"

"I have no sins to atone for," he sneered. Agnes stepped back from the icy tone. "You have no idea what you are talking about. You only have one side of the story, which can be dangerous."

"Then tell me. What is your side of the story?" Agnes asked gently, fighting the need to comfort the strange man.

Taliesin sighed, running his hand over his face again. "It's a long story."

"They always are."

Taliesin sighed, his shoulders dropping under the weight of his story. "Once upon a time, the gods created a brother and a sister..."

Chapter 57- Chloe

Modern Day- Edinburgh, Scotland

"**A**re you telling me Watson is Wystan?" Isabelle questioned Anne with furrowed brows, her tone heavy with disbelief. "And he was in love with the Witch of Endor's sister?"

Even I had to admit that this was a plot twist I wasn't expecting. A chill ran up my spine as a faint glimmer of energy sparked and flicked around Isabelle's fingers. She was on the verge of losing control, and I was beginning to worry.

I was pretty sure starting a fire inside the coffee shop would be frowned upon.

Anne smiled weakly, taking a sip of the hot tea and peeking over the rim of her cup at Isabelle's display of power. She was nervous, and I couldn't blame her.

"Why didn't anyone tell me?" Isabelle asked. Her face turned a sickly shade of grey, and her expression showed an unmistakable look of panic.

"I can't answer for Watson, but how would we have known you didn't know?" Anne huffed. "You clearly weren't interested in being High Priestess. I don't remember you attending any ceremonies or gatherings, not even for your aunt's celebration of life. We all assumed you had no interest in being a part of the coven or hearing from us."

I frowned and bit into my apple fritter, its glaze leaving an oily sheen of icing on my lips. "That's rude," I mumbled around the mouthful.

Anne's emerald eyes fixed on mine, her gaze narrowing with sharp judgment. "Someone needs to say it," she declared before shifting her focus to Isabelle. "Not one word for the last ten years. Gossip running rampant." She waved her hands in the air, emphasizing her words. "All we knew was that our High Priestess opted for a vampire over her coven."

Isabelle's eyes flashed with indignation as she shot back, "I had no choice. He is my mate."

"Everyone has a choice. You made yours, and we tolerated it. Now, you walk into my place of business and demand answers. If anyone is being 'rude,' as Chloe so elegantly put it, it's you, Isabelle."

"Hey," I protested. "Don't drag me into this."

Anne's face turned a deep, alarming shade of crimson, her chest heaving with anger and her eyes blazing like fiery orbs. I couldn't help but instinctively lean away, pushing away from the table as she fixed me with a fierce glare that could rival the heat of the sun.

"You were a part of this long before you assumed your role as a Writer."

My heart skipped a beat as I paused, my eyes widening in astonishment and alarm at her bold announcement. How did Anne know about my ties with the Raven Society?

And even more concerning, how did she know I was a Writer?

Anne's thin smile turned up at the corners. "Ah, Chloe," she said in a calm yet knowing tone. "We've been aware of your presence for quite some time now. Imagine my astonishment when Isabelle suddenly appeared with you in tow."

Isabelle's eyebrows knitted together as she stared at Anne. "What are you talking about? Who told you about Chloe?"

"Your aunt did before she died," Anne confessed, toying with her bracelets. The delicate charms danced and tinkled as she twisted them between her fingers. "She warned me that she would be coming."

I wearily rubbed my fingers over the bridge of my nose, smudging the lenses of my glasses. Taking them off to clean them with the hem of my sweatshirt, I tried to calm my racing heart.

Somehow, our conversation had shifted from Isabelle and her relationship issues to me, and I felt like I was on the Titanic—doomed and headed for disaster.

Looking back up, I met Anne's gaze. "Why would she warn you about me?"

"You really don't know, do you?" Anne questioned, her eyebrow raised to her hairline and with a hint of confusion in her voice. "You will be responsible for sealing the gates to the Otherworld. You are the end to the supernatural."

"No."

"Yes."

"You're wrong!" I snapped, desperation creeping into my voice. My heart pounded like a frenzied beast as I tried to mentally prepare myself for whatever hell was about to rain down on me. But deep down, I knew no amount of preparation could shield me from the upcoming storm.

Not now.

Not ever.

I was the good one. Chosen to protect the gates to the Otherworld and destined by the Fates to save the supernatural and their stories.

Not destroy them.

The instructions were crystal clear. My mission was to help locate the missing Books of the Veil, deliver them to the Otherworld, and magickally revive all eight portals so the supernatural could access their own realm of eternity.

I didn't know how. But I would figure it out later.

"What does this have to do with Isabelle and Watson?" I asked, trying to piece the puzzle together.

Anne let out a weary breath. "Your destiny is tied to hers," she said mysteriously.

"Who's? Mine?" Isabelle asked, her fingers drumming against the table.

"No. The sisters." Anne looked at me like it was the first time seeing me. Her head tilted as she said, "You look like her."

"Are you planning on sharing who you are talking about? Or is that a secret, too?" Isabelle asked sharply.

Anne eyed her cup of coffee, playing with the handle. "Her name was Ysabel. And before you ask," Anne said, glancing at me. "The Witch of Endor's name was Nava."

"Nava," I rolled the name off my tongue. "Nava and Ysabel."

Finally. I had a name. It made it seem so much more real now. Nava wrote the book that was hidden in my bedroom. Saying her name out loud sparked memories I didn't know I had.

A cave surrounded by eight gates.

Two women standing before a ghost, her body filtering in and out of focus.

A village on fire. Screams from men, women, and children as they ran from men brandishing whips and knives.

A woman sitting on a boulder overlooking the ocean, crying.

A woman standing over a grave, holding a golden hair child on her hip with eyes the color of the sea.

Eyes that looked eerily like Isabelle's.

Chapter 58- Chloe

Modern Day- Edinburgh, Scotland

With a sudden jolt, I pushed my chair back from the table, my thoughts scattering like startled birds. Breathing heavily, I focused on the present and willed myself to shake off the weight of the past.

"You okay, luv?" Isabelle's face was etched with concern as she reached out a hand to touch mine.

"Yeah," I waved her off, slipping my glasses back on. "Just in shock." I paused. "Don't you find it ironic that your names are so similar?"

Isabelle tilted her head in question. "Whose names?"

"Ysabel and Wystan. Isabelle and Watson. It seems suspicious if you ask me. I mean, what are the chances of that happening?"

Anne carefully tilted the teapot, watching the amber liquid flow smoothly into her cup. "Pretty high since they are essentially one and the same," she replied, her voice laced with a sense of cautiousness.

What the hell? My mouth dropped. What was she talking about? Who was the same?

"Where to begin?" Anne mused, gazing out at the bustling cafe as she swirled a spoonful of sugar in her cup. A guest caught her eye, and she gave them a warm smile and waved goodbye as they left.

"At the beginning," Isabelle countered, frowning as she scooted her chair forward to let a family by. "Usually an acceptable place to start, luv."

Anne nodded, casting a meaningful gaze at the other patrons in the coffee house. The atmosphere in the room seemed to shift, and all eyes turned towards our table. They hurried to gather their belongings and vacated the building without saying a word.

As soon as the last couple disappeared through the door, Anne refocused her attention on us.

"I assume you've heard of Taliesin?"

"Of course we have," I huffed. "Demi-god who sacrificed his sister. He stole Morrigan's power and is now trying to bring her back from the dead. And he's using the Book of the Veil to do it."

I didn't mention that Taliesin needed my blood. Or that he was rewriting the supernatural's story. But from the way Anne frowned at me, I had the feeling that my simplified version of the narrative was about to be dissected.

"All wrong." Anne waved her hand like she was erasing a blackboard. "Morrigan was meant to die on that battlefield whether she wanted to or not. It was her fate. But her blood does not stain Taliesin's hands. He inherited her power when she fell, but not to hold on to it forever—to transfer it."

I frowned. Of course, we didn't know the whole story. Did we ever? It seemed like our understanding of reality was only a part of the total picture. We were little more than performers in an elaborate play for which we didn't have the entire script.

"Transfer?" Isabelle asked, leaning forward. "To whom?"

"I have a suspicion, but I can't say for certain," Anne shrugged. "But your aunt was confident Taliesin's power would transfer in this lifetime. She claimed it would lead to bloodshed, broken gates, and the end of the supernatural in the mortal world. When she announced her prediction, it wasn't well received." Her eyes darted between us before settling on me. "The elders believe it's you he's looking for. And they plan to stop it from happening."

"What do you mean 'plan to stop it from happening,'" I asked, hoping she wasn't suggesting what I thought she was.

"They wanted you dead," Anne answered, her eyes darting to the fireplace.

That sucks. But it did explain why Arawn kept telling me, '*Try not to die.*' But it didn't explain how Isabelle and Watson were connected to me. We sat in stunned silence, listening to the soft chimes of the grandfather clock.

"They planned to give the power to Isabelle," I said softly, understanding dawning on me.

Anne nodded.

A gasp escaped Isabelle's lips, and her hand flew up to cover her mouth in shock. Her eyes widened and sparkled with intense emotion—disbelief, horror, or perhaps a mixture of both.

"No!" she exclaimed, her voice trembling with raw emotion.

"Yes," Anne said with a weary sigh. "But your aunt, stubborn as she was, refused to accept it. She confided in me that there were two paths: one where justice prevailed, and life could continue as it always had. The other?" She paused. "That path would destroy the gates and seal off the Otherworld for eternity."

"That's rather unfortunate," I muttered, pouring another cup of coffee. The dark liquid swirled in the mug, reflecting the room's dim light. It was a stark contrast to the previous cup with its dollop of cream and sprinkle of sugar; this one fit the somber mood of our conversation.

"To say the elders weren't thrilled with her prediction is an understatement," Anne continued. "They put it to a vote—behind closed doors, of course. And the next thing we knew, the High Priestess was dead."

"The elders killed my aunt?" Isabelle exclaimed, her hands flickering with energy.

Anne's eyes darted around the room before she leaned forward and whispered, "No one knows for sure, but we all suspect they did. I think they were sending a message."

Sending a message, my ass. The elders were cold-blooded killers, and my hatred for them burned like a raging inferno deep within me.

I loved Isabelle and the fact she was a witch. But I was beginning to question the coven elders' sincerity and actions. Anyone willing to take a life to enforce their rigid beliefs was evil beyond comprehension.

I wanted to hurt them like they hurt Isabelle. I wanted them to feel the same fear and pain that Isabelle's aunt must have felt when they killed her.

I wanted revenge.

The shadows within me stirred, excited at the prospect of doing what I do best. My fingers tingled, and my legs bounced as energy pounded through my body.

I felt alive.

But one glance from Isabelle made me pause. Her gaze reminded me she needed my support, not my anger and vengeance against her coven. I pushed aside the darkness consuming me and did what any good Writer and person should do: I would stay and help my friend.

"What message? I didn't get a message," Isabelle mused, glancing at me like I had the answer.

"I don't know..." I began, and suddenly, everything clicked into place. "They left you a message, didn't they?" I asked in disbelief. "The day you found out your aunt was dead? Didn't you tell me that the elders gave you a letter?"

Isabelle nodded, her eyes glistening with tears as she remembered the day she found out her aunt was murdered. A letter had arrived, but the elders were adamant about not opening it, convinced it held some curse.

But Isabelle did read it.

The message had been clear: she had to choose which side she wanted to be on. If she wanted to stay clear of trouble, she needed to decide if she was with or against them—signed with a single drop of blood.

At the time, I assumed it had something to do with her connection with Watson. As the High Priestess, being in a relationship with another species was frowned upon, especially with a vampire.

But now it seemed it had nothing to do with Watson. But with me.

She had to choose between saving the supernatural or me.

My! My! How the tables have turned!

Chapter 59- Chloe

Modern Day- Edinburgh, Scotland

Anne grabbed our hands into hers, her grip solid and reassuring. "Let's not get too frazzled. It all sounds overwhelming now, but it's not the end of the world. We just need to tackle it one problem at a time."

I folded my arms across my chest and demanded, "Tell me, which problem is not too much to handle? Is it Isabelle's strange connection to Ysabel? Or her aunt's vision of me destroying the gates to the Otherworld?"

"All of them." Anne winked at me.

My blood boiled with fury, and I could feel my face turn red. My hands balled into tight fists, gripping so hard that my knuckles turned white in an attempt to contain the raging emotions inside of me. I bit down on my lip to stop myself from lashing out.

Time was moved impossibly slow as I struggled to regain control of my anger, forcing myself to take deep breaths and count slowly until it finally subsided.

Isabelle needed me, and I needed to stay focused.

"And where do you suggest we start?" Isabelle interjected, her eyes blazing with determination as she rolled up her sleeves. Her long locks were swept up into a high ponytail, giving her the look of a fierce warrior ready to plunge into battle.

"At the end, of course." Anne's calloused hands moved swiftly across the table, wiping off the food crumbs with practiced efficiency. I snatched up the last piece of apple fritter before she threw it away.

"At the end? What the hell does that mean?" I called after her as she headed toward the kitchen.

"You'll see." She vanished behind the weathered red saloon doors at the end of the room, and I turned to face Isabelle.

"Are you okay?" I asked with concern. She seemed to have aged significantly in just a few hours; fatigue etched into every line of her face. Her usually vibrant eyes appeared sunken and surrounded by dark circles. The wrinkles around her mouth, which were once barely noticeable, now stood out boldly.

"I'm okay. Considering," she replied, fidgeting with her bracelets. Her eyes scanned the room before resting on the fireplace. "I didn't anticipate all this when I said we were going on an adventure."

The flickering light from the fire highlighted Watson's name, which had been scratched out and replaced by his former identity.

Wystan.

"It's been a strange day. But nothing we can't handle." I ran my fingers along the rim of the table, not sure what to say to make her feel better.

Or myself.

Isabelle's warm, gentle hands covered mine, and for a moment, the world stilled. "Just because the Fates dictate one path doesn't mean it's the end all, be all. We have the choice to follow or create our own path. It's up to us. Don't let my aunt's vision or what Anne says stop you from being who you are."

"What about you and Watson? Doesn't it bother you that he was in love with Ysabel? Or that she is you? Or you are her?" I asked, confused about how the whole reincarnation thing worked.

"Does it bother me? Sure, a little." Isabelle shrugged. "I wish Watson had told me the truth, but it doesn't change anything. I married him, knowing I would never know about parts of his life. But it doesn't change who he is or the love I have for him."

"700 years plus 700 years wouldn't be enough," I whispered. The first time I heard Watson say the phrase, I thought it was cute and enduring. But now I realized he meant something else.

Watson meant he would always find Isabelle.

Or Ysabel.

Honestly, it didn't matter. That kind of love was unimaginable and indescribable. It was the kind of love you read about or watched on a Hallmark Channel Christmas movie.

It was pure magick.

"Yes," Isabelle said, her eyes searching mine. "And when you find that kind of love, you never let go."

I hesitated, uncertain of what Isabelle was implying; before I could ask, Anne strolled over. She wore a long black cloak with delicate silver embroidery along the edges, and her thick dark hair pulled back into a tight bun at the nape of her neck.

She slung a large leather bag over her shoulder, smiling. "You ready, ladies?"

My eyes narrowed as I glanced at her. On the one hand, she was eager to help and had knowledge that could prove invaluable. But on the other, I couldn't help but wonder if she had ulterior motives. If there was something in this for her.

"Let the adventures begin," Isabelle replied, standing up and glancing at me sternly. The same look a mother gave their child when they acted up in the grocery store. Reluctantly, I followed Isabelle's lead, gathering my coat from the wall hook.

"Where are we going?" I mouthed, slipping my arms through my rain jacket as Isabelle wrapped her scarf around her neck.

"I'm not sure, but I trust Anne. She was my aunt's best friend. Obviously, she trusted her enough to tell her about her vision," she declared confidently.

"We'll see," I muttered as we followed Anne toward the front door and stepped out into the cold winter air.

The pale light of the morning sun scarcely penetrated the narrow alleyway, leaving me shivering in its dimness as the cold dug deep into my bones like icy tendrils. I cursed myself for leaving my gloves at home as I jammed my numb fingers into my pockets.

When we got back to the hotel, I was going to take a hot bath and not come out until I was warm again. The relentless chilliness was beginning to affect my mood.

"Don't worry. We aren't going far." Anne gave me a reassuring glance as she locked the door and flipped the coffeehouse sign to 'Closed.' "We'll take the shortcut."

"What shortcut?" Isabelle asked, confused.

Anne swept past us, pulling the hood of her cloak over her hair. "You'll see."

Helpful!

We followed her down the street, passing by the Apothecary again. I peeked through the window, searching for the boy's portrait, finding nothing except a thin film of dust on the ledge where the frame used to sit.

The only proof of his existence missing.

Stopping, my vision blurred as I stared at the empty spot. I'd shared the child's memories and felt his anguish firsthand, and now the only proof of his life was gone? I couldn't help but wonder what had become of him. Did he die that night? Or did he survive and build a life for himself? I kept searching the ledge, hoping for a clue, but there was nothing.

Disappointment flooded me as I realized I didn't know his name. Names. They held so much power and importance. Everyone in the world was complex and multidimensional; they possess the capability to be nurturing caregivers or agents of destruction. Prosperous businesspeople or failing figures of authority. Champions of humanity or catalysts for its downfall.

I wanted to believe people were masters of their destinies.

But was your life worth anything if no one remembered your name?

Would the success of individuals like Rockefeller and Carnegie still be revered if their names were not remembered? Or was it their renowned names that kept them in our collective memory?

I had no idea. The Witch of Endor had been important to history, but she became a myth without a name.

Just like the boy in the drawing. Someone had taken their time to capture that final moment in his life, but they hadn't stopped to ask what name his mother had given him.

Which meant he didn't exist.

A single drop of icy water splashed across the bridge of my nose, and I pulled the hood of my sweatshirt over my head. Of course, it had to start raining when the world was in a downward spiral.

"I will remember you," I whispered to the empty shelf. With one final look, I forced myself to turn away and follow Anne and Isabelle back onto the main street.

The taxi driver waited for us at the head of the alley, his engine running and headlights illuminating our path. I offered a half-hearted wave, feeling guilty for forgetting him. Even through the midst and the constant swish of the wipers, his bright green eyes cut right through me. They bore into my soul with an intense yet undecipherable gaze.

Anne looked over her shoulder, her eyebrows arched in surprise. "Friend of yours?"

"Friend? No. Just a very dedicated taxi driver. I think Esme told him to stay with us."

"Interesting." She looked suspiciously at the driver. "Let's hope he knows what he's doing," she muttered under her breath as she marched towards an alleyway.

Chapter 60- Chloe

Modern Day- Edinburgh, Scotland

"Do you think you could give us a clue as to where you're taking us?" I called out, hurrying to catch up as Anne rounded the corner.

I stopped in my tracks, pushing the hood of my sweatshirt back. It was nothing like the alley we'd come from. Both sides were lined with random stores of blackened stone and soot-covered bricks lighted by flickering gaslights set in carved stone scones. The windows were dark, covered with old rags and a layer of dust that made it impossible to see through.

As we walked further down, the feeling of despair grew stronger, suffocating me with its heavy weight. The air was thick with the stench of rot and decay. Isabelle pulled her scarf tighter around her nose and mouth, her eyes darting around the area. Anne's grip tightened on my arm as one of the stones gave way beneath my foot, catching me before I fell.

"Don't let it fool you; this place was once full of life." Anne pointed to an old wooden sign, creaking as it swayed in the breeze. The faded gold lettering read, 'Last Chance Book Store.' "When you have time, I highly recommend stopping in. The selection of books is amazing. It has first editions and original manuscripts you can't find elsewhere. But, be warned." She winked. "The new owner can be a bit feisty."

I took a step closer, brushing away a layer of grim with my sleeve, instantly captivated by the meticulous organization of ancient texts and scrolls. Books so old their spines had worn away were safely tucked away in glass display cases. Further back, I could make out shelves of aged wood, with books of various sizes, journals, and parchments tucked away between them.

I was reminded of the Library of the Unspoken and couldn't shake the feeling that Aelle would have run through the front door if she had been here. It was the kind of place she would love to explore.

A pang of sadness and guilt settled in my chest, but I forced it away. Aelle made her own choice, and I had to deal with it.

"We will find a way to bring her here," Isabelle whispered as she linked arms with me and stared through the window as well. "And watch Aelle terrorize the poor owner with her constant questions and demanding attitude. It'll be fun," she chuckled. I smiled in response.

"Come on, you two, we're almost there," Anne said from behind us, heading further into the alley.

We picked our way along the icy pavement, skirting around rain puddles and avoiding cracks forming in the road, all while stealing glances at the ghostly abandoned storefronts.

An old tailor's shop stood ramshackle, with moth-eaten linens piled against one wall. The butcher's window held a grisly display: a framed pig's skull. In the middle of the otherwise empty street, an overturned cart filled with desiccated fruits was next to another with a selection of mussel shells and fish bones.

Anne stopped at the end of the road, standing in front of stairs that led down into a dark abyss. She grabbed a lantern hanging from a hook on the side of the entrance, its glass stained with soot and cobwebs, fumbling in her pocket for a lighter to ignite it. Its orange flame quivered, throwing long shadows down the long, narrow path.

Rolling her shoulders, she headed down, and I watched in horror as she disappeared.

"You want us to go down there?" I yelled in disbelief. "No way in hell!"

Anne's head popped out of the entrance, laughing at me. "Scared lil' Writer?"

"No," I replied haughtily. "But my mother always said not to go down dark underground stairs with strangers."

"Good advice. But I'm afraid you will have no choice if you want to find what you are looking for."

Isabelle eyed the entrance with a frown. "Anne, *where* are you taking us?"

"To the dungeons, of course," Anne shrugged. "This is the quickest way. And we don't have to deal with tourists."

"Of course," I muttered. "And *why* are we going to the dungeons?"

"Because it was the last time the Witch of Endor was seen alive."

"The Witch of Endor was here? In these dungeons? Alive?" I asked, taking a step forward, excitement running through my body.

"She was," a man's voice said from behind me, and I froze. Slowly turning on my heels, I faced the newcomer, and my heart dropped.

You got to be kidding me!

Chapter 61- Chloe

Modern Day- Edinburgh, Scotland

"Ah, Chloe. A pleasure as always!" Arawn greeted, shaking the water off his cloak from the rain.

No matter how many times I ran into the god of the Otherworld, I was always struck by his towering height and the way he seemed to radiate energy. Standing next to him felt like standing next to a charging storm, electrifying and exhilarating all at once.

"What do you think you're doing here?" I scanned the area, trying to figure out where his hellhounds were hiding. I doubted they were welcome in the mortal realm, but knowing the god, they had to be nearby.

"I came to see you, of course," he laughed at me.

"Of course," I said, forcing a tight-lipped smile as I brushed away the droplets of rain he had thrown on me. "But that doesn't explain why..."

"And who is this?" Anne called from the dungeon entrance, her voice dripping with delight. She stepped around me and grasped Isabelle's arm, batting her eyelashes at the speed of a hummingbird's wings mid-flight.

I groaned, my eyes rolling in exasperation. This was a distraction I didn't need right now. We were so close to finding the Witch of Endor and Morrigan's missing book. And now I had to deal with an arrogant god and a witch smitten by lust.

Gods help me!

Arawn's eyes sparkled as he looked down at Anne. He cocked his head and winked. "Are you going to introduce me lil' Writer?"

Anne's face reddened in response to his velvety voice, ensnared by its low and throaty resonance. I fought the urge to roll my eyes again.

"Seriously?" I stared in disbelief at Arawn. He returned my gaze with a nod. "Anne," I said with a sigh, "this is Arawn—the God of the Otherworld and a pain in my ass."

"So dramatic, lil' Writer." Arawn grinned, his eyes twinkling with amusement as he winked at Anne.

"Did I lie?" I asked, shrugging my shoulders. Glancing around the area, I asked, "Where's Hestor?"

I hadn't seen my favorite hellhound in weeks, and even though we hadn't spent much time together, the beast held a special place in my heart.

"I left her home. Mortals tend to get skittish when I bring hellhounds to this realm." Arawn explained, running a hand through his hair and surveying the dungeon entrance with interest.

"Speaking of realms, what are you doing here, luv?" Isabelle extracted her arm from Anne's grasp and glided to Arawn, planting a delicate kiss on his cheek. A red hue of embarrassment crept across Arawn's face.

I couldn't help but laugh at the sight—Isabelle was the only woman in the world who could make Arawn speechless.

"I heard a rumor that you two were about to step into an ambush, so I came to lend my blade," he said in a low baritone voice. His billowing black cloak swept the ground as he spun around with majestic flair, revealing two sparkling long swords sheathed in leather scabbards on either side of his hips.

"Who told you that?" My mouth dropped as my eyebrows shot up in surprise. We'd just arrived back in Scotland, and I hadn't even had time to unpack yet. Until a few moments ago, I didn't know where Anne was taking us. So, why would anyone tell Arawn we were in trouble? And when?

"It doesn't matter," Arawn waved me off. "Anne, darling, I assume you are our guide into the unknown?"

Anne blushed again, nodding in agreement as she struggled to stand upright under his intense gaze. "Yes..." she stammered, pointing to the entrance.

Arawn clapped his hands together, rubbing them eagerly. "Great! Then let's go!" he exclaimed, his voice filled with excitement. He gave me a sharp glance that hinted at disapproval. "Chloe promised me a Scottish pie and has yet to deliver. I'm hoping she'll follow through once we get this nasty business done and over with."

He brushed past me, and I reacted as any self-respecting woman would when a man provoked her.

I stuck my tongue out at his retreating frame.

"My coffee shop is known for its Scottish pies! I would be thrilled if you could try them. Free of charge, of course!" Anne offered.

"Really?" Arawn's expression changed to genuine surprise and joy, his lips stretching into a wide smile. He closed the distance between them, wrapping his arm around her shoulders and pulling her closer. "I think you are my favorite witch."

He flashed her a crooked smile, showcasing his dimples. A giggle escaped Anne's lips, causing his eyes to light up. Leaning forward, he tilted his head, beckoning, "Now, tell me about yourself."

I rolled my eyes at Anne's reaction as they walked away, leaving Isabelle and me to follow.

Isabelle shuddered as raindrops pelted her coat, tightening her scarf around her bun to keep her hair dry. "Is he always like this?" She motioned towards Arawn. "Such a flirt?"

I tugged my glasses off, grumbling under my breath as I tried to wipe the lenses dry with my sweatshirt. "He's never been like that with me," I replied, squinting to see better. "Should I be offended?"

Isabelle was right; Arawn looked at Anne like she lit up the world with her smile, teasing her mercilessly as she swatted his arm in mock anger.

Every time he spoke to me, it was only to remind me not to die because it would cause him an inconvenience. And he never flirted or teased me with pretty words.

Rude!

Hearing my thoughts, Isabelle threw her head back in amusement and laughed. "I wouldn't worry about it; Arawn knows about Eidolon. And between you and me, I'm pretty sure Eidolon can take him."

My mouth curled into a delighted grin as I imagined Eidolon's chiseled chest glistening with sweat, his muscles bulging as he fought for my honor. I had always been attracted to his raw physical strength, and the way he moved with such grace and power was breathtaking. So, the thought of him defending me filled me with a desire I couldn't ignore.

My mind wandering, I failed to notice Anne and Arawn standing with crossed arms like sentinels in front of the dungeon entrance. The light from the streetlamps gave their faces an eerie, ghostly glow as they stared into the darkness of the staircase beyond.

Anne turned to face us with a warning: "Stay close. It's easy to lose your bearings down there," she said. Her voice echoed off the stone walls, and her gaze became rigid and authoritative. "Remember, far more dangerous creatures inhabit this place than you can imagine. If you encounter one of the trapped souls, don't stop—keep moving and don't engage."

"She's not wrong. The souls trapped in this physical realm are profoundly different from those from the Otherworld," Arawn agreed, his eyes scanning the area, darting from one corner to another, looking for something or someone lurking in the shadows. "They are entrapped in a loop of perpetual misery, reliving the worst day of their lives over and over. Stuck within the confines of their memories, unable to escape the grasp of their twisted recollections.

As Arawn and Anne descended the stairs, Isabelle tightened her grip on my hand.

"Can't you help them?" she asked Arawn.

"Yes and no. I can offer to guide them to the Otherworld, but more often than not, they refuse. They have lost all hope for something better than what they live in now."

Arawn grabbed another torch, its dried-out husk of an old branch ready to burst into flame. With a flick, he lit it and threw it down the stairs. I watched it tumbled, sparks flying until it vanished into the darkness below. Isabelle's eyes widened in shock as she looked back and forth between the now-extinguished flames and me.

"For those who accept your offer, do things get better for them?" she asked.

"I can't say they do." Arawn's words hung in the air as we followed the torch Anne held in front of her down the stairs, the flickering flame casting shadows on the damp stone walls surrounding us.

Well, this should be fun, I thought grimly.

Chapter 62- Chloe

Modern Day- Edinburgh, Scotland

As we descended into the dark depths of the dungeon, cobwebs clung to our faces and hair, sticky strands clinging like desperate fingers. The air was thick with a putrid stench of decay and excrement, growing stronger with each step. Our feet squelched through piles of slimy muck, making our footing in the treacherous environment difficult.

Once we reached the ground floor, we paused to let our eyes adjust to the muted lighting. A gasp escaped us as a long corridor emerged. To each side stood cells that were almost indiscernible in the darkness. The metal bars were a dreary shade of orange-brown with rust streaks cascading down and clinging to the floor.

We trudged silently through the murky depths, the only sounds accompanying us being droplets of water echoing throughout the hallway and the crunch of animal bones under our feet. We passed by decrepit wooden beams, fragments peeking out from beneath centuries-old dirt so decayed they resembled brittle twigs, barely clinging to their existence.

Distress and despair washed over me as I walked down the dark, musty hallway. The air grew thick with the acrid scent of burnt wood and the sharp sting of smoke, leading me further towards the source. Each pulse of pain from those who had suffered unimaginable torture beckoned me closer, like a siren's call summoning me to its origin.

The lost souls were trying to tell me something.

They wanted me to see where they died.

I yanked my hand from Isabelle's grip and stormed past Arawn and Anne, my heart racing and my face flushed with anger. My feet thudded on the hard-packed floor as I flew towards the open door on the left. When I arrived, my breath hitched, and my eyes widened in shock at the scene before me.

In the center of the room stood an imposing wooden table, its surface worn and weathered from years of use. In the back corner, a smaller table held a chaotic collection of sharp knives, pliers, tongs, and other menacing tools. My gaze traveled the length of the walls, showcasing an array of cruel and twisted torture devices, each more gruesome than the next.

I fought back the bile, unable to put into words what I was seeing. What kind of monster would delight in inflicting this level of misery and brutality on his people?

What type of broken, demented, and heartless creature takes pleasure in others' suffering?

"Fear is a powerful weapon," Arawn's voice was laced with venom as he placed his arm around my shoulder. "Used in grotesque ways to achieve the most inhumane goals."

"What kind of depraved goal could warrant such an atrocity?" I demanded, my fists clenched in rage.

"Take your pick. Executioners ripping vampires open to discover their secrets of immortality. Strapping witches to tables to uncover the source of their magick and harness it for the monarch's own means. Tormenting shapeshifters until they were forced into their animal forms and used mercilessly by madmen who dreamed of creating unstoppable armies."

"That's not what the books say," I complained.

But as I glanced around, the reality of his comment resonated in my core. I'd always known that history was written by those who held power, never to be challenged or contested; their words became the law and absolute truth.

But I'd never seen it displayed so proudly.

This was a slap in the face, and my trust in humanity faltered.

"I tried to tell you," Arawn reminded me softly.

"I know," I whispered, wiping a tear with the sleeve of my jacket, not looking at him.

My heart pounding, I edged closer to the long wooden table in the middle of the room. Its rough planks were covered with scratches and carvings, and four iron clamps waited at each corner like clawed beasts ready to grasp their prey.

I closed my eyes, picturing a man strapped to it. He was naked, his body trembling from anxiety and pain as a single tear ran out of his blackened eyes and down his swollen cheeks.

I saw the executioner out of the corner of my eye, slowly approaching. He held a long and rusted knife in his hand, the blade's handle clenched in his fist. The man on the table squirmed as the frigid metal hovered over his fingers before plunging with surprising speed, its sharp edges slicing through his flesh effortlessly.

Piercing screams filled the room, echoing off the stone walls. Blood dripped from the man's wounds, staining the floor below. He writhed against the tight restraints that bound his limbs, beads of sweat trickling down his neck. He gritted his teeth in determination to stay conscious despite the steadily growing puddle of blood beneath him.

How much blood could someone lose before they died?

A lot, judging by the amount that crept toward my boots.

The man shifted his head in my direction and opened his eyes. The moment I locked eyes with him, a chill ran through me. I knew who he was.

"Find her," he whispered before shutting his eyes tight again.

Astonished, my mouth dropped in shock. I couldn't understand why or how Taliesin was there. "Who?" I asked nervously.

"Agnes," he drew in a labored breath, opening one eye to look at me again. "She must be found. For Morrigan's sake." He fell silent, but his plea lingered in the air like a desperate whisper for a desperate hope.

My legs gave way beneath me, and I hit the ground with a loud crash. Agnes? Why would I need to find Agnes for Morrigan?

And why was he being tortured?

Taliesin. Morrigan. Agnes. The Witch of Endor. How were they connected?

The answer was almost within reach, but it slipped through my fingers every time I reached for it. Fatigue, stress, and the vision had depleted my remaining energy. No matter how hard I tried, I couldn't understand it all.

I need a nap, I thought as I closed my eyes.

"Chloe!"

I woke up to Isabelle shouting, shaking me furiously. Fear and worry twisted her face as she leaned close, her eyes searching mine. "What happened?"

"Taliesin," I whispered, closing my eyes again.

"Taliesin?" Arawn asked, kneeling beside me. "Did you see him?"

"He was here," I said shakily, pointing to the table. "He said we needed to find Agnes."

Isabelle's bright blue eyes searched my face. Her fingertips brushed my temples, pushing away a strand of hair that had fallen from the messy bun on my head. "Did he say why?" she asked.

"To save Morrigan."

Chapter 63- Agnes

27 January 1591- Edinburgh Castle

"So, what do we do now?" Agnes asked, looking at the man before her with new eyes.

All the stories and rumors about Taliesin were wrong.

Nava and Ysabel were wrong about him.

But he didn't want them to know. That surprised Agnes the most. Why didn't he want them to know what he was doing?

"It won't change anything," Taliesin said sharply. "I made the deal. I knew what the consequences were, and I still agreed."

"But Nava, Ysabel, Lilith. They all believe that you are hellbent on destroying the supernatural. In their eyes, you're practically the devil himself. Why would you let them think such horrible things about you?" Agnes asked, her voice gentle and concerned.

Taliesin shrugged nonchalantly. "Why not?" he asked. "After all, the rest of the world has already formed negative opinions about them, so why should I be any different?"

"You're not making sense," Agnes stomped in frustration.

"I don't have to." He raised an eyebrow at her. "It's my story to tell. Right now, all I have to do is save you."

"Remind me again. Why?"

"Because if you die, Morrigan will too." Taliesin turned to face the cell across from Agnes, eyeing the woman sitting in it.

She was writing in the book he had discreetly left for her a few days ago. His brow furrowed as he noticed blood streaming from the cut on her arm, mingling with the dark residue of coal she was using to write.

Despite her condition, Geillis would survive for a while longer. But at what price?

Would her soul find peace? Taliesin wasn't sure, but he would try to help her.

"Because she lives in me?" Agnes asked, trying to understand how Morrigan could somehow live in her.

With a slow nod, Taliesin spun on his heel to fully face her. A smirk stretched across his lips as he spoke. "You, Nava, and another," he said. "The Fates chose the three women who could bear her immense power. But only in death."

As he spoke, he pulled a small leather-bound book from his pocket and opened it to reveal intricate illustrations of the three Fates and their chosen vessels.

Three women who looked like her.

"Morrigan can't survive without access to her power. She will soon fade into nothing if the source of her energy doesn't exist in the Otherworld. All her efforts to create a safe environment for the supernatural will be in vain."

"Who has her power now?" Agnes asked, needing the truth.

"I do. But I was never meant to carry it. It will kill me."

"And what is her power source?"

"Her book," Taliesin confirmed.

"Oh." Agnes nodded in understanding. "It makes sense now."

Taliesin arched an eyebrow in amusement. "You see where my frustration lies? My sister will die again if I can't find her book and send it to the Otherworld with her power. The only way to do that was to get the past, present, and future together in one place at one time. I needed the three to take the book for me."

"And we have to die to journey to the Otherworld," Agnes concluded. "That's why you tried to save Nava. You needed her to live until the timelines intersected."

Taliesin nodded, his expression grim. "I'm afraid I've come across a slight predicament," he stated, running his finger over the intricate designs etched into the book's cover. With great care, he opened it and passed it to her. "There are others who want my sister's power and will go to no ends to take it from me. I must transfer it soon before it falls into the wrong hands."

Agnes leaned in closer, eyes scanning the pages filled with words and images. As she turned the page, a picture of a woman standing amidst roaring flames caught her attention. Despite the chaos around her, the woman appeared serene. Two figures stood behind her, cloaked in dark robes and holding books in their hands. They gazed at the sky solemnly, as if deep in prayer."

As the light flickered in the cell, a dark figure emerged from the corner of the page. Her piercing gaze fixed on the others, filled with intense hatred. She clutched a leather-bound book, its cover embossed with an intricate oak tree design.

"Turn the page." Taliesin's commanding voice broke the tense silence. Agnes hesitated, her hands shaking, afraid of what revelations or horrors it might hold.

The disheveled woman in the corner now stood before the roaring fire. She held the book precariously close to the dancing flames. Her anguished expression betrayed her inner turmoil.

"What is she doing?" Agnes asked.

"Burning Morrigan's book."

"Why?" Agnes glanced up at Taliesin in shock.

"I don't know," he admitted. "All I know is that if the book is destroyed, everything Morrigan did will be in vain. It will be the end of the supernatural. The Otherworld gates will be destroyed. The Tree of Life will die. Life as we know it will be no more."

"Who is she?" Agnes pointed to the figure.

"Her name is Chloe." Taliesin's gaze flickered with concern as he turned to look at the women in the opposite cell. His mind raced, hoping the book he had given her would be enough. He clenched his fists, feeling the weight of responsibility on his shoulders.

It had to be enough.

"Why not just tell her?" Agnes asked, her words laced with urgency. "And Nava. If everyone knew the truth," she paused, gently touching Taliesin's arm. His eyes flickered to her in surprise. She swallowed, needing to believe there was a way to change her future. "I'm sure everyone would do what's right."

Taliesin shook his head. "I can't. The Fates won't allow it. Luck was on my side when I found a loophole to talk to you. Nava and Chloe? They need to decide for themselves. I think Nava will be amenable to my plan. It helps her get to where she wants to be. But Chloe? I'm not sure. Her decision will affect everything and everyone."

They stood side by side, their eyes fixed on the drawing strewn with possibilities. Agnes chewed her lip anxiously, flipping through the rest of the pages, hoping for an answer. But they were blank. Her disappointment hung heavy between them as she closed the book.

"Do you think you can stop her from destroying the book?"

"Me?" Taliesin laughed grimly. "No. But my son might be able to."

The guards came for Agnes that night.

They never saw the man standing in the shadows watching.

Chapter 64- Chloe

Modern Day- Edinburgh, Scotland

"What do you mean we need to find Agnes?" Arawn asked as he pulled me back to my feet, dusting the dirt off my coat. "Did you have another weird Writer vision?"

"They are not weird," I mumbled, glaring at him from the corner of my eyes. "They are a concept of reality—the truth behind the inconsistencies in history."

"Well, what truth did you learn?" he asked, rolling his eyes.

Frustration knotted in my stomach, and I let out a sharp sigh. My fingers tangled in my hair before pulling it back into a messy ponytail. With a quick swipe of my sleeve, I cleaned my glasses and perched them on the bridge of my nose, scowling.

"I don't know. The information provided was severely lacking," I scoffed, my tone dripping with annoyance. "Something about finding Agnes."

"She's dead," Anne stated, giving me a strange look. "Her ashes were thrown into the wind. Along with the other executed witches."

"Well, that's not necessarily true," Arawn said sheepishly. "We know she died, but she never entered the Otherworld."

"What?" Isabelle exclaimed, turning to face Arawn in shock.

He shrugged, looking annoyed. "I told you that not all souls travel to the Otherworld. Some of them are stuck in this realm. If they don't have someone to help them cross over..."

"Can't you locate her?" I asked, gripping his forearm, desperation tinging my voice. "Help her cross over?"

"It doesn't work that way, lil' Writer. She would have to reveal herself to me."

"What good is it to have the god of the Otherworld with us if he can't even find the dead?" My words were laced with venom, and Arawn's posture stiffened as he stood tall, towering over me with a dangerous gleam in his eyes.

"Don't try my patience, lil' Writer. I warned you once before not to believe everything you read." A shadow covered Arawn's entire body, casting him in a cloak of darkness. His eyes, gleaming with otherworldly power, pierced through the veil and glinted in the dim light. His radiating energy was palpable, pulsing and crackling with raw intensity.

"Do not question my abilities, mortal, for I have lived far longer than you can imagine and hold power beyond your comprehension."

My heart raced as I stepped back, my mind finally registering what Arawn truly was - a god. How could I have been so foolish to think that my tiny bit of ability gave me the right to question him? My pride and sense of self-importance crumbled as I realized the magnitude of his true form.

Part of me wanted to cower and beg for forgiveness, while the other wanted to know why he couldn't find Agnes.

But I wasn't willing to fight that battle right now. So, instead, I bowed my head and apologized because Arawn was a god. And my friend.

Arawn enveloped me in a comforting hug, his strong arms wrapped around me like a shield. His deep voice rumbled in my ear, "Don't let your anger consume you, lil' Writer. We need a clear head for what's to come." As he pulled away, I could see the weight of sadness in his eyes. He gently cupped my chin, forcing me to meet his gaze. "Do you understand the gravity of this situation?"

I nodded slowly, my brow furrowed in confusion by his sudden change in tone. Arawn was more than a little concerned, and I didn't know why. But a wave of relief washed over me, and I was grateful everything between us seemed to be back on equal footing.

"Chloe! Where are you?" A familiar voice echoed down from the stairwell, his footsteps getting louder as he descended.

Isabelle's eyebrows shot up in surprise as she glanced at me. Eidolon was supposed to be with Watson and Victor, scouring Nether Keith for clues.

Not in Edinburgh.

Something must have gone wrong.

"Plot twist," Arawn laughed as I rushed out of the room.

"Over here." My voice reverberated down the long hallway as I hurried towards him.

Eidolon emerged from the shadows of the staircase, his disheveled appearance catching my attention. Strands of cobwebs clung to his hair, and his jeans were covered in grime. He paused and blinked several times, allowing his eyes to adapt to the dim light.

When our eyes met, a smile spread across his face as he enveloped me in a warm hug. I closed my eyes and breathed in his familiar scent as I nestled into the space between his neck and shoulder.

"You're okay," he muttered against the top of my head, his arms tightening.

"I'm fine," I peeked up at him, confused. "How the hell did you find us down here?"

"I followed the bond." He nodded over his shoulder towards Watson and Victor. "We had a change of plans."

Victor's eyebrows shot up in surprise as his eyes darted around the unexpected location. His lips formed a slight "O" as he curiously took in the surroundings. Watson, however, had a fierce scowl on his face, his jaw clenched tightly, and his nostrils flared in anger.

"Chloe," he greeted, his lip curling in disgust as he scanned the dark dungeon with its grimy walls and rusty bars. He gazed down at the scattered bones on the floor, shaking his head. "I see not much has changed over the years."

"What are you doing here, Watson?" Isabelle approached him with a graceful stride, stopping before him and pressing a soft kiss to his cheek. His eyes softened, and a slight frown danced across his face as he looked her up and down, ensuring she was still in one piece.

"Something told me you weren't going on the tour." Watson's voice cracked with barely contained intensity as his eyes flickered between Isabelle and the surrounding cells. His jaw tightened in determination as he locked eyes with her. "Before you stumbled into a dangerous situation, I needed to ensure you heard the whole story."

"Watson. I know," Isabelle said, gently taking his hand and tracing the creases and calluses on his palm with her fingertips.

As soon as Isabelle said the words, Watson's mouth opened in shock. His eyes grew wide with disbelief, and his entire body went rigid, struggling to comprehend the weight of her statement. "How?"

"I told her." With an air of confidence, Anne strode towards us, her long cloak billowing behind her.

Arawn trailed after, a smirk plastered on his face as he scanned the group curiously. Eidolon nodded, acknowledging their arrival. He pulled me closer to his side, protectively wrapping his arm around my waist.

"She needed to know Watson, and obviously, you weren't going to tell her," Anne finished, her voice firm and unwavering as she widened her stance, prepared to battle the vampire.

Watson squirmed under her piercing stare, and I couldn't help but snicker. It was a rare sight to see Watson at a loss for words.

"It wasn't your story to tell," he grumbled.

"No, it was yours," Isabelle reminded him sharply. "And you chose not to share. On the other hand, Anne *was* willing when I found your name crossed out on the fireplace and substituted with someone else's."

"What fireplace?" Watson's eyes darted toward her in confusion

"*Our* fireplace." Isabelle's hand shot out, landing squarely on his chest as she pushed him back with surprising force. Her fingers dug into his flesh, leaving a slight indentation as she held her ground, her eyes daring him to move closer.

The tension between them crackled like electricity, and I could feel the heat radiating off of her body. It wasn't the gentle touch of a lover but the determined push of someone who meant business.

"The one that you carved our names into after we got married. Your name was replaced by someone else's."

Watson paled. "To what?"

"Wystan."

"Watson's name was substituted with his name?" Arawn asked, running a hand through his hair. "That's the huge secret? You mortals crack me up."

"Not Watson. W-Y-S-T-A-N." Isabelle's long hair whipped behind her as she turned to face him, the end slapping Watson across the cheek. He winced, rubbing the offended area with a frown.

"So? Same person. Different spelling." Arawn shrugged his broad shoulders, grinning at Watson. "I prefer the old way. More dignified."

"You knew?" Isabelle asked, her eyes narrowing.

"Of course I did. In case you've forgotten. I'm a god." Arawn huffed, insulted. "There's not much that I don't know."

"And no one thought to tell me?" Isabelle asked, glancing at me.

I held up my hands in defense. "It was news to me."

"Let's calm down," Eidolon jumped in, releasing me from his hold and stepping in front of Isabelle and Arawn, glancing at her with concern. "And maybe someone could tell me what the hell is going on? A few minutes ago, Chloe was projecting a lot of emotion, and Isabelle is ready to throttle her husband."

Tension hung like a noose as I anxiously shifted my gaze between the group. Anne's piercing stare bore into Watson, demanding an explanation. But he remained silent, his hand shaking as he ran it through his hair.

The anticipation was suffocating, each passing second feeling like an eternity of uncertainty and dread.

"I don't think this is an appropriate time," Victor's voice cut through the air like a knife, interrupting the uneasy quiet. He pointed down the hall with a trembling finger, his eyes widening as he whispered, "We have company."

My heart raced as I heard footsteps coming closer, their sound bouncing off the stone walls and sending shivers down my spine. I whirled around to face the direction Victor was pointing to. A woman stood in the hallway, seemingly materializing out of thin air. Her modern attire contrasted with her ethereal presence. Her eyes sparkled with an otherworldly light, and her skin had a golden glow similar to the sun's rays.

"Hello," she greeted, watching Isabelle with interest before she glanced at Watson with a smile. "It's been a long time."

Watson swallowed, drawing Isabelle under his arm. "That it has. How have you been?"

The woman chuckled, her grin widening as she stepped closer to us. "Busy." She nodded to Arawn before looking at me with a scowl. "There you are. I've been waiting to meet you."

"Good to see you, my friend. May I introduce..." Arawn started before she cut him off with a pointed stare.

"I know who she is. You're the one that told me about her, remember." Her regard turned to Eidolon, and her frown deepened. "You must be the shadow man."

Eidolon arched an eyebrow at her. "Never been called that before. And you are..."

"Nava. Better known as the Witch of Endor." Her piercing gaze cut through me like a hot knife, leaving me frozen in place with the key around my neck burning with a warning. "You have been looking for me, Chloe?" she asked, her eyebrow raised.

"Yes," I stammered. "I found your book."

"No, I left my book for you," Nava corrected. Her gaze fell on a cell, and she stepped closer, wrapping her hands around the bars. "I assume that you found the other one?"

"It was in the Library of the Unread," Isabelle offered. "I found it the other day."

"That's good," Nava's words hung heavy in the cold, damp air of the dungeon. "Now, I happened to overhear the conversation between Isabelle and Watson. And while I agree with Anne," she looked pointedly at Watson. "I think this discussion would be more suited for a warmer location. There are too many voices here for my liking. I can't hear myself think." She surveyed the dreary surroundings with a disapproving expression.

"We can go back to my coffee shop," Anne offered, looking at Nava like she was standing before royalty.

"No," Nava said with a wave of her hand. "I have somewhere else in mind."

Abruptly, the world plunged into darkness, and I was weightless, drifting through the endless expanse of time and space. It was a dizzying sensation as if I had become detached from the mortal realm and merged with the vastness of time.

I hoped it didn't hurt when I landed this time.

Chapter 65- Chloe

The corner of past, present, and future

It was an elusive limbo, a realm that existed beyond the constraints of science and religion, where myths and legends roamed free and untamed. Peacefully, I drifted into my new reality, watching history play out before me.

This is amazing, I thought as I hovered above the Eiffel Tower, still in its early stages of construction. I marveled at the iconic structure's sheer height and grandeur. From my vantage point, I could see the bustling workers scurrying along the scaffolding, their voices and clanging tools drowned out by the gentle hum of the city below. My curiosity piqued; I longed to descend and hear their conversation.

As I floated down, excitement surged at the thought of the book I could write. A first-hand experience that no one had ever had before.

Except for the nameless people who built it. I would remember them and give them back their life.

But reality fought back, and I was violently thrust into its harsh grasp. The impact was brutal, and I was consumed by a wave of misery and overwhelming emotions: despair and terror. Like an inferno, stress engulfed me, suffocating me with its unyielding hold.

I hit the ground with a jolt, the blow sending a sharp rock digging into my backside. As I gasped for air, my eyes landed on a roaring bonfire that mirrored the burning pain in my body. The smoke stung my eyes, and the heat seared my skin, pushing me backward. Trapped and surrounded by flames, there was no way out.

Just like in my nightmares.

Without warning, a hand appeared out of nowhere, yanking me onto my feet. They guided me to a nearby tree, where I gratefully sank against its sturdy trunk, struggling to catch my breath. Rubbing the tears from my burning eyes, I surveyed the scene, taking note of the ancient oak tree that provided me with much-needed support.

Its trunk was twisted and gnarled, with thick roots dug deep into the ground. The leaves were vibrant green, shimmering in winter sunlight.

But what struck me the most were the intricate carvings covering every inch of its bark - symbols and figures depicting stories from ancient mythology.

It was the most beautiful thing I had ever seen.

"You're lucky I found you," a female commented, her voice low and husky. She sat down next to me, wiping soot off her forehead with the sleeves of her shirt.

"I don't know about you, but I am not a huge fan of fire. A few more minutes, you would have been on a very different side of the tree."

"How did I get here?" I choked out, cleaning off my glasses and putting them back on, wincing when I realized they were lopsided.

Damn it! I just got these! I thought, mentally counting the days until the insurance company would cover a new pair.

"You fell. From somewhere up there." The woman pointed to the sky. "I was standing atop the hill, watching the various realities unfold, when I saw you slip and tumble toward the fire. It didn't seem like you were slowing down, so I jumped into this reality to catch you."

"What do you mean, *watching the various realities unfold*?" I asked, leaning forward and peeling off my jacket as unexpected warmth spread through my chest and arms. After weeks of freezing, the sudden surge of heat felt like a hot flash.

"That's what you're worried about?" The woman laughed. "Not where your friends are or why you landed face-first in a burning pyre?"

"I've traveled enough not to question," I mumbled, exhausted. "It's easier to accept the unacceptable."

"Good point," she acknowledged, picking a daisy and twirling it in her fingers.

We sat side by side, staring into the fire's glowing embers as charred pine scent filled the air. The occasional sound of a log shifting and sparks flying broke the stillness around us. I leaned my head against the rough bark, inhaling deeply and exhaling slowly as I tried to clear my mind.

"By the way, I'm Agnes," the woman said with a smile, still looking at the pyre. "I assume Nava will join us shortly."

I turned to face the woman before me, my eyes widening in shock. "You're Agnes?"

"The one and only," she laughed, picking the leaves off the flower stem.

"I'm guessing," I point to the pyre, "this is your reality?"

"Yes," she said sadly, looking at the scene before her. "A day I'd like to forget. I've been waiting a long time for you, Chloe."

"How long?" I asked, not wanting to know but needing to.

The thought of her being trapped in the never-ending cycle of reliving her death sent shivers down my spine. How could she bear it? How many days, months, and years had she endured the torment?

"Over four hundred years, give or take a few days," Agnes chuckled. "One tends to lose the concept of time when just 'hanging out,'" she air-quoted.

"Why were you waiting for me?" I stumbled over my words, my mind still reeling from the fact I was sitting next to Agnes Sampson. She didn't look like a witch.

Moll looked like a witch.

Isabelle moved like a witch.

But Agnes? She looked like me: middle-aged, reddish brown hair, hazel eyes, and a crooked nose.

"It will all be explained," she sighed. "I need you to do me a favor, lil' Writer. I need you to listen to the tale you're about to hear." Her eyes bore into mine with an intensity that made my mouth dry. "I mean, really listen to the story."

"Of course," I promised. Wasn't that what I was trained to do? Listen.

"Good," she said, pointing to two figures walking towards us. "Because things are about to get interesting."

I shifted to see where she pointed. My heart dropped.

Ah, shit.

"Chloe, what a pleasant surprise."

"Taliesin," I greeted with a sneer. "What are you doing here?"

"Came to see you, of course," he said with a bright smile, his eyes dancing with lightning.

"Well, you saw me." I turned my attention back to Agnes with a frown. "Can you send me home now?"

"You said you would listen, Chloe," she reminded me with a pointed stare.

I gestured towards Taliesin. "Well, that was before I realized you wanted me to hear his tale. But trust me, I already know it, and it doesn't have a happy ending."

Taliesin chuckled, and I spun around to face him. My shadows quivered at my fingertips as my anger grew. "I have nothing to say to you.

I know who you are and what you want from me. And you won't get a drop of my blood."

"Woo now, who said anything about blood?" Taliesin asked, throwing his hands up in surrender. "I have a simple request. Hear me out, and I will let you decide what to do next. No tricks, no lies. Just the truth."

Nava walked up from behind him, frowning. "Have you told her yet?"

"I was about to," Taliesin glanced over at her, pushing his glasses up his nose.

I was shocked by what I saw. Nava, who I believed despised Taliesin, was now standing beside him as if they were long-time friends.

"What in the world is happening here?" I yelled, giving Nava a fierce glare.

Nava's voice flowed like honey as she spoke, her eyes shifting to the tree behind me with a wistful sigh. "Chloe, my dear, please try to calm yourself and listen. I have a story…"

I raised my hand to stop her. "Nope. No stories. Just give me the cliff notes."

"Fair enough," Agnes agreed. "It's only fair that you know the facts so you can make an informed decision." Her words hung in the air as she eyed Nava and Taliesin." Who wants to do the honors?"

Nava waved her hand towards Taliesin. "He should. It's his plan, after all."

"What plan?" I asked, exasperated.

Taliesin took a breath, "When Morrigan's powers transferred to me, it was not meant to be a permanent solution. A body can't hold that much energy. I have been lucky to survive this long. But the situation has changed, and her power must be transferred. Soon."

"I know. You'll give it to Isabelle. Anne already told us."

Taliesin's head shook vigorously, denying the possibility.

"That was never part of the plan," he said. He glanced at the tree, his expression hardening with determination. "I will return it to its rightful place."

"How?" My voice trembled as I asked the question, fear gripping my heart.

Had they brought me to this place only to sacrifice me, to summon Morrigan with my blood?

Taliesin's gaze drifted between Agnes, Nava, and me. "You three embody the essence of the past, present, and future. A healer, a writer, and a necromancer. The sum of who Morrigan was. For years now, I have maintained the balance as long as I stayed in the oak tree. But, like I said, our combined power is too much for one person to hold. I will die if I don't transfer it back to her."

"How do you plan on doing that?" I asked, glancing at Nava and Agnes. I was taken aback to see that both of them were holding their breaths, staring at me with such concentration that I couldn't help but look away.

"I will transfer the power to you three. The last descendants of her line. You will return the power to the Otherworld to safeguard Avalon and the Tree of Life."

Chapter 66- Chloe

The corner of past, present, and future

The world fell into a deafening silence, stripped of all movement and leaving only haunting emptiness. I heard Taliesin's unspoken words in the void—a request that tore at my soul like jagged claws.

Eidolon wasn't the one bound for the Otherworld.

It was me.

How could I have been so blind?

The weight of all the lies, mistruths, and misdirections crushed down on me like an avalanche. Every step I've taken has been building up to this pivotal moment, ordained by the cruel hands of Fate.

And I walked right into their trap.

Taliesin never tried to bring his sister back.

Moll didn't need me to replace her.

I wasn't supposed to be the Writer, but Aelle was, which is why she never returned to the Library of the Unread.

Because they knew I would have to go back eventually.

My eyes narrowed as I asked, "What about the Books of the Veiled? Why did we have to find them? Or was that a lie?"

I seethed with anger, feeling the shadows within me swell and surge, offering a sense of calm amidst the chaos. I needed their twisted embrace to contain my rising fury.

"A consequence of the god's game of deceit, I'm afraid," Taliesin answered, eyeing me cautiously. "And the deity's inability to see past their noses. Maybe if I'd explained my reasons for seeking out Morrigan to Lilith, she would have been willing to lend a hand. But in the heat of the moment, my anger clouded my judgment.

"Had I not taken her mate as retribution, she would never have sought Vivian's assistance in seeking revenge against me. Diana and I may not have been exiled to the tree. Eidolon could have had a family, and Moll wouldn't have spent her final years searching for her daughter."

He regarded me sadly. "One wrong decision, and now I face a lifetime of repercussions that I'm struggling to rectify."

"Why did everyone lie to me?" I asked, feeling the blood trickle down my hand as my nails dug into my skin from clenching my fist tightly.

"No one lied to you, Chloe." Nava moved to stand in front of me, lifting my chin to meet her gaze. "You heard their truths. But when you step back and see the bigger picture, cracks appear. Your ability to detect these inconsistencies makes you such a skilled Writer."

"But I'm not the Writer, am I?" I asked, wrapping my shadows around me. "I'm a pawn in your game. And now I have a decision to make. Help you fix your mistake." I glanced at Taliesin with a sneer. "Or choose my own path and walk away."

"Like I said, the choice is yours," Taliesin bowed in agreement. "I just ask that you think it through before making a rash decision that could affect the world."

"No offense, Taliesin. But you are not the one to lecture me on making rash decisions. You're the reason we are in this mess."

I glanced at Agnes, her expression filled with distress and worry.

But I didn't care.

"Send me back. I need to talk to Eidolon."

"As you wish."

"What happens now?" Agnes asked Taliesin, running her hands up her arms to ward off the cold chill that settled around them.

"We will wait," he answered, pinching the bridge of his nose. "And hope Chloe makes the right decision.

"And if she doesn't?" Agnes turned to look at the old oak tree, its bark turning an alarming shade of gray since Chloe returned to her timeline.

"Arawn cautioned us that she may not cooperate willingly. If she resists, we must use whatever means necessary to bring her with us," Nava replied, her eyes narrowing at the tree.

Agnes looked doubtful. "Is there anything she can do to stop this from happening?"

She had been watching Chloe for years and knew the woman was resourceful and cunning. If there were a way to save the Otherworld without sacrificing herself, Chloe would find it.

"Only one," Taliesin admitted. "She finds Morrigan and Lilith's story before we do.

Chapter 67- The Fates

Somewhere hidden in time

The Fates watched as Chloe walked away from Taliesin, Nava, and Agnes.

"Do you think she'll go find Morrigan and Lilith's books?" Clotho frowned as the vision faded. Reluctantly, she returned to her spinning wheel.

With so many lives to oversee, she was always working. Everyone had a beginning, and she was the only one who could create it.

Lachesis glanced at her sister with a proud smile. "She certainly is. And I bet she finds them."

At least, Lachesis hoped Chloe did. She had enjoyed the unpredictable paths that Chloe's life had taken throughout the years, and it would be a tragedy for her to be confined to the Library of the Unread forever.

Chloe's life would fade into obscurity, just like the stories she was tasked with protecting—something Lachesis didn't want to happen.

"She's going to end up like Medusa if she's not careful," Atropos huffed from her chair. "Sooner or later, the gods won't care for her streak of independence. They will force her to become something she doesn't want to be."

"Can we do anything to help?" Clotho looked up from the new thread she was making.

"More than we are already doing?" Lachesis asked in surprise. "I've already lengthened her thread. If we do anymore, the gods will notice."

"Doesn't seem fair to me," Clotho mumbled, returning to her work.

"Life is never fair," Atropos repeated her favorite saying. "So why should Chloe expect anything to be different for her? It would be easier for everyone if she simply embraced her new role."

Atropos glanced at the freshly sharpened scissors in her hands, the light from the fire reflecting off their polished blades.

A note smoldered in her pocket, tempting her to retrieve it.

But she didn't dare—not in front of her sisters.

It was from Arawn, and it contained the list of names that would be occupying her time tomorrow.

Not that she normally minded. Snipping threads was her job.

Atropos's dilemma was figuring out how to break the news that Chloe's name was written on it.

Afterword

'The conclusion of a story is never the ending.' -Book of the Veiled Instructions

Witch Trials.

No matter where you are, the phrase will conjure up horrific images of helpless individuals standing before a bloodthirsty mob. They were condemned to death based on hearsay and corrupt trials. Their screams still echo through the streets where they were mercilessly executed, their lives snuffed out by those in power's twisted desires.

The Witch Trials mentioned in my books revolve around my exploration of the witch craze that occurred in the 1500s. It was a bleak time in history when religion, science, and progress all converged at a tumultuous intersection. Early on in my research, I stumbled across the mention of the Witch of Endor, and my curiosity peaked. If religious texts denounce the existence of the supernatural, why was there a mention of witches?

Or one witch in particular.

The Witch of Endor.

Her story, buried deep in the Old Testament, was barely a blip on the radar of greater tales. Yet, every time I read that brief mention, I was filled with conflicting emotions. Was she just an insignificant character, or did her story hold untold layers and complexities? What secrets and truths were glossed over by only a few lines?

She was cast aside; her presence was deemed insignificant and easily forgotten by history's victors.

They didn't even remember her name.

Please be warned; the name I came up with for the Witch of Endor was my own invention.

A female name of Hebrew origin that means *Beauty*.

The name seems fitting for a woman who played a crucial role in altering history. Yet, she has been forgotten by time and buried under historical records' inconsistencies.

And then there was Agnes Sampson. A victim of the infamous witch hunts, sentenced to death by the same man responsible for one of the most widely used Bible versions - the King James Bible. Her name is forever etched in history as a sacrifice, unjustly persecuted and brutally executed in the name of religion.

My introduction to Agnes was through the Outlander series, penned by the renowned Diana Gabaldon. Gabaldon focused on Geillis Duncan, who plays a role in this book, but Agnes sparked my curiosity.

Agnes Sampson (b.unknown- executed 28 January 1591) was a healer and alleged witch from Scotland. She resided in Nether Keith, part of the Barony of Keith in East Lothian, Scotland. Known for her healing abilities, she also served as a midwife for her local community. Referred to as the Wise Wife of Keith, Sampson gained notoriety for her unfortunate involvement in the North Berwick Witch trials during the late 1500s.

Acknowledgements

'To remember the people in your life is live with more love.' -Book of the Veiled Instructions

To my best friend. The person who taught me to ride a motorcycle, bought me way too many books, and supported me in this next great adventure. Thank you for trying to be quiet in the morning, listening to me when I complained about formatting and promoting, and for always sharing my posts.

To my children. I am in constant awe of your fearlessness, humor, and ability to think outside of the box.

To my family- thank you for supporting me when I turned off my phone and forgot to text back.

A big thanks goes to the History Channel, PBS, and YouTube. I honestly wouldn't know where to begin my research without your informative content. You are my source of entertainment while writing and my non-judgmental companion during the editing process. Most importantly, you are my stress relief. I have already compiled a list of episodes for future programming when you eventually run out of material.

To the crew at Woods Coffee. You're amazing. The coffee is always hot, perfectly brewed, and served with a real smile. Between you and me- I prefer you over Starbucks.

To Jelly Roll. Thank you for putting into words what it's like to struggle with inner beasts. Your songs have gotten me through more dark times than I can count.

And finally, because I forget about this person all the time- to me.

I have experienced moments of tranquility while resting atop a tanker truck in the heart of the Iraqi desert. I have laughed amidst a snowstorm in Afghanistan. I have wandered through the bustling Christmas markets of Germany and fought my way out of heavy snow in Northern New York.

I have been attacked by Georgia's giant insects and chased down by wild boars. I have conquered the treacherous roads of Alaska and marveled at the beauty of the Northern Lights in -32-degree temperatures.

Every new address, every new experience, every new phone number has led me to this moment in time.

A moment that I have found peace in the fact that I am not perfect. I drink too much coffee. I have more sweatshirts than socks. I prefer moody music, candlelight, and good books over parties. I rather ride my motorcycle than go shopping. I will spend too much money on new books and good food.

I am okay with my crazy and my shadows. It is a part of me.

And I'm okay with saying that I want my name to be remembered.

About the Author

R.L. Geer-Robbins is an avid coffee drinker, reader, historian, veteran, and author. She can usually be found riding her Harley Davidson alongside her better half, drafting her next book, or watching the History Channel.

During her career of 20+ years in the U.S. Army, she had the opportunity to travel to places that had only been a tiny dot on a map. During these adventures, she discovered the power of myths, folk tales, and oral histories, which led her to pursue higher education in history and preservation.

Writing has become her way to reconnect and rediscover stories and truths lost to the pages of history.

Newsletter: https://rlgeerrobbins.com/about-me/newsletter/

Facebook: https://www.facebook.com/RoseLGeerRobbins

Instagram: https://www.instagram.com/rlgeerrobbinsauthor/

Also By R.L. Geer-Robbins

The Writer and The Librarian

Three things I was sure of:
First, I was not a Hero.
Second, magic still existed.
And third, I was willing to walk through the Gates of Hell for my
friends.

For years, Chloe has hidden from the shadows of her past, trying to escape its haunting. That is all about to change when she discovers a note taped to her front door inviting her to join The Raven Society.

Thousands of years ago, the Raven Society was created to protect, maintain, and preserve history deemed too dangerous for society. Their priceless secret? The Book of the Veiled. Its discovery could open Pandora's box of consequences, for whoever holds it can rewrite history and change the course of the future.

And it has been stolen.

The Raven Society's search for the book must survive the Gates of the Otherworld, betrayals, deception, and deadly motivations. But, in the end, they will realize that myths and fables aren't just bedtime stories but stories of forgotten lives that have been driven into the shadows.

How far into the darkness would you be willing to travel to discover the truth?

Also By R.L. Geer-Robbins

The Myth and The Monster

I am the mother of all the supernatural. Your fantasies of dark witches wielding power, vampires shimmering with unholy energy, shapeshifters morphing into dangerous beasts, and warriors ready for war all come alive through me. I am the creator of nightmares and dreams.

Unleash your imagination and feast your eyes on a world of pure magic.

In 537 A.D., a fierce struggle took place that would decide the world's future. The victor wields the ability to alter the future of humanity.

Rising from the ashes, The Raven Society was formed to guard and maintain the purity of history.

Their mission? To find the inconsistencies in history and protect the ones whose stories have been forgotten.

Rising from the ruins, three women, whose lives have spanned the ages, are united by an invisible thread woven by the Fates. Their mission? To safeguard a weapon feared by the gods themselves.

In order to find the missing Books of the Veiled, they will have to build new bonds, confront their demons, and unearth a new reality.

Failure is not an option. Their lives depend on it.

Made in the USA
Middletown, DE
10 September 2024

60101335R00220